SHAW 17

The Annual of Bernard Shaw Studies
Volume Seventeen

Fred D. Crawford   John R. Pfeiffer
General Editor   *Bibliographer*

Editorial Board: Charles A. Berst, University of California at Los Angeles; John A. Bertolini, Middlebury College; R. F. Dietrich, University of South Florida; Bernard F. Dukore, Virginia Tech; Leon H. Hugo, University of South Africa; Frederick P. W. McDowell, University of Iowa; Michael J. Mendelsohn, University of Tampa; Margot Peters, University of Wisconsin, Whitewater; Sally Peters, Wesleyan University; Ann Saddlemyer, Graduate Centre for Study of Drama, University of Toronto; Alfred Turco, Jr., Wesleyan University; Stanley Weintraub, Penn State University; Jonathan L. Wisenthal, University of British Columbia.

SHAW AND
SCIENCE FICTION

Edited by
Milton T. Wolf

The Pennsylvania State University Press
University Park, Pennsylvania

Quotations from published Bernard Shaw writings are utilized in this volume with the permission of the Estate of Bernard Shaw. Shaw's hitherto unpublished writings © 1997 The Trustees of the British Museum, The Governors and Guardians of the National Gallery of Ireland, and the Royal Academy of Dramatic Art.

ISBN 0-271-01681-7   ISSN 0741-5842

It is the policy of The Pennsylvania State University Press to use acid-free paper for the first printing of all clothbound books. Publications on uncoated stock satisfy the minimum requirements of American National Standard for Information Sciences—Permanence of Paper for Printed Library Materials. ANSI Z39.48—1992.

Note to contributors and subscribers. *SHAW*'s perspective is Bernard Shaw and his milieu—its personalities, works, relevance to his age and ours. As "his life, work, and friends"—the subtitle to a biography of G.B.S.—indicates, it is impossible to study the life, thought, and work of a major literary figure in a vacuum. Issues and people, economics, politics, religion, theater and literature and journalism—the entirety of the two half-centuries the life of G.B.S. spanned was his assumed province. *SHAW*, published annually, welcomes articles that either explicitly or implicitly add to or alter our understanding of Shaw and his milieu. Address all manuscript contributions (in 3 copies) to Fred D. Crawford, General Editor, *SHAW*, Penn State Press, Suite C, 820 North University Drive, University Park, PA 16802. Subscription correspondence should be addressed to *SHAW*, Penn State University Press, Suite C, 820 North University Drive, University Park, PA 16802. Unsolicited manuscripts are welcomed but will be returned only if return postage is provided. In matters of style *SHAW* recommends the *MLA Style Sheet* and advises referring to recent volumes of the *SHAW*.

CONTENTS

NOTICES

Request for Manuscripts: *SHAW* 19

SHAW 19, guest-edited by Gale K. Larson, will have as its theme "Shaw and History." The volume will include articles on various aspects of Shaw's concept of history (treated by J. L. Wisenthal in his 1988 publication *Shaw's Sense of History*) with special emphasis on the Shavianizing of history in the plays and other works by Shaw. Of particular interest are the uses that Shaw has made of history in delineating character while dramatizing historical events, often expressed as challenges to other artists/historians (one and the same for Shaw) with whose interpretation of people and events of history Shaw took issue. Articles that focus on specific historical/literary sources used throughout his writings and the manner in which they affected his own works will also be acceptable for *SHAW* 19.

Contributors should submit manuscripts in three copies by December 1997 to Fred D. Crawford, *SHAW* Editor, Penn State Press, Suite C, 820 North University Drive, University Park, PA 16802. Contributors should follow the *MLA Style Sheet* format (referring to recent *SHAW* volumes is advisable) and include postage for return of material.

36th Annual Season, Shaw Festival
Niagara-on-the-Lake

The 1997 playbill of the Shaw Festival (Artistic Director Christopher Newton) will include two plays by Shaw, *Mrs Warren's Profession* and *"In Good King Charles's Golden Days"*, as well as *The Chocolate Soldier* (the Oskar Straus musical based on *Arms and the Man*) and, as part of the Bell Canada Reading Series, *Why She Would Not*. Other productions include *Will Any Gentleman?* by Vernon Sylvaine, *Hobson's Choice* by Harold Brighouse, *The Seagull* by Anton Chekhov, *The Playboy of the Western World* by J. M. Synge, *The Children's Hour* by Lillian Hellman, *The Secret*

Life by Harley Granville Barker, *The Two Mrs. Carrolls* by Martin Vale, *The Conjuror Part II* by David Ben and Patrick Watson, and *Sorry, Wrong Number* by Lucille Fletcher. In addition to Shaw's *Why She Would Not*, the Bell Canada Reading series will include *Still Stands the House* by Gwen Pharis Ringwood, *The Titanic* by E. J. Pratt, and *The Intruder* by Maurice Maeterlinck.

For further information, write to Shaw Festival, Box 774, Niagara-on-the-Lake, Ontario, Canada L0S 1J0 or call 1-800-511-SHAW (7429) or, locally, (905) 468-2172.

Sixteenth Annual Milwaukee Shaw Festival
21 February–8 March 1998

The 1998 Milwaukee Shaw Festival (Artistic Director, Montgomery Davis) will feature performances of Shaw's *Too True to Be Good* and Samuel Beckett's *Waiting for Godot.*

For ticket information either call (414) 276-8842 or (414) 291-7800 (box office), or write to Milwaukee Chamber Theatre, Broadway Theatre Centre, 158 N. Broadway, Milwaukee, WI 53202.

Milton T. Wolf

FOREWORD: SHAW AND SCIENCE FICTION

To Fred, who pushed it up the hill;
To Ray, who kept it there.

This special issue of *SHAW* devoted to Shaw and Science Fiction gathers essays that show both the close relationship that Shaw had with the emerging genre of science fiction and Shaw's continuing influence on the still-developing genre today. A similar examination of Shaw's relationship to science fiction was published in the *Shaw Review* 16:2 (May 1973). The twenty-four intervening years have seen the status of science fiction rise out of its ghettoized, low-brow heritage to assume a much more important role in the unfolding history of literature and culture. What American jazz has become to world music, science fiction is becoming to world literature (see Ray Bradbury's "G.B.S.: Refurbishing the Tin Woodman: Science Fiction with a Heart, a Brain, and the Nerve!").

No less an authoritative voice of the literary establishment than the *Columbia Literary History of the United States* (1988), under the section "The Fictions of the Present," describes science fiction as "arguably the most significant body of work in contemporary fiction," citing it "as a major literary genre" and one of the "most significant new directions in recent American fiction."

According to Frederic Jameson, a much-admired authority in the contest for scholarly verification and intellectual propriety, although science fiction "can be either expanded and dignified by the addition of

all the classical satiric and Utopian literature from Lucian on or re-
stricted and degraded to the pulp-and-adventure tradition; [it can also
be seen] as a historically new and original form which offers analogies
with the emergence of the historical novel in the early nineteenth
century."[1]

While this elevation to official acceptance is largely based on the
impossibility of denying the convergence of themes and style inherent
in postmodernism and "cyberpunk" science fiction (SF), the early history
of SF, which was almost coterminous with Shaw's formative years, has
been counterpointing mainstream literature from its inception. That SF
developed at about the same time as modern science should come as no
surprise, for it followed the rise of science like a cub reporter on the
trail of a big story.

Strongly influenced by the scientific romance, the utopian novel, the
imaginary voyage, Faustian adventures, and the future-war story (see
Ben P. Indick's "Shaw's Science Fiction on the Boards"), SF began as a
commercial vehicle for explaining the wonders of science to a new
mass audience, largely generated by the highly successful Victorian
educational system. These newly literate lower classes felt a strong
sympathy with a future that would be different from the present and
past, and they formed a new market for the aborning SF genre. The
famous two cultures of C. P. Snow, the literary one of the upper classes
and the scientific one of lower- and middle-class origins, began making
its first appearance. In relationship to SF, Shaw took the high road and
H. G. Wells the low.

The less-than-classically-educated readers of the lower classes supported a number of new popular magazines, like *The Strand* (1891), that
began making their appearance toward the end of the nineteenth
century. *Pearson's* entered the lists, serializing *The War of the Worlds* in
1897, and later the *Pall Mall* printed *The War in the Air*. These publications both satisfied and created an appetite for fantastic fiction and for
SF, which were, in many respects, joined at the hip (and still are). As
Arthur C. Clarke once put it, fantasy deals with things that can not
happen, and we wish they would; science fiction with things that could
happen, and we hope they do not.

These popular magazines were responsible for creating a mass market
for stories that made people aware of the technological changes that
were taking place around them, about new modes of living, about
the increasingly accelerated differences between generations and their
ability (or inability) to accept the newfangled inventions that were
permeating the social landscape. This new attitude is clearly caught by
Shaw in *Man and Superman* in the person of the chauffeur/auto mechanic
who knows that a different future is not only going to happen but also

going to be very different from what the conservative upper classes think.

Shaw, iconoclast that he was, knew early on that the current literary conventions had to be surmounted (compare Shaw's contemporary Witkacy, the Polish dramatist, and his similar dilemma in Elwira M. Grossman's "Witkacy and Shaw's Stage Statues") if any truly imaginative ideas were to permeate the stock-in-trade of the cultural aristocracy. His familiarity with the utopian tradition (see J. L. Wisenthal's "Shaw's Utopias" and Shaw's lecture "Utopias," never before published) has been well researched, but few have seen the important relationship that it has to SF, Shaw, and the human need for change.

As the twentieth century has well documented, controlling elites contribute to the arts so long as they are well-behaved in that they stick to aesthetics, polishing the veneer of culture and sipping the sweet life as opposed to revealing the underbelly of the economic beast. Shaw came to realize that economics, more than art, moves the human pieces on the political board—that thought is an evolutionary process, not a revolutionary one.

Shaw saw that the utopian genre had been gradually, but thoroughly, discredited by the politicians and capitalists of his time. In fact, they could easily destroy new economic plans or social reforms, such as those proposed by the Fabians, by labeling them "utopian drivel" fabricated by dreamers who did not understand the politically established reality of scientific determinism (with its convenient justification of "survival of the fittest"). But Shaw found other literary devices, borrowed from different genres, to expose the reigning "reality" of English culture, Horseback Hall, and its class hegemony. Shaw helped construct the literary path that a technological culture must travel if it is to see itself more clearly (see Jeffrey M. Wallmann's "Evolutionary Machinery: Foreshadowings of Science Fiction in Bernard Shaw's Dramas").

Shaw's forays into the speculative and fantastic, as ways of symbolizing reality, were always a part of his literary bent. In 1879 his short story "The St. James Hall Mystery" featured an apparition of Mozart. In another story "The Miraculous Revenge," written in 1885, a graveyard moves from one side of a river to the other, and two years later, in "Don Giovanni Explains," Shaw introduced the ghost of Don Juan, which he later expanded in *Man and Superman*.

Shaw's use of time travel by setting his scenarios into the future and the past, often employing dream states (see Rodelle Weintraub's "Bernard Shaw's Fantasy Island: *Simpleton of the Unexpected Isles*"), can be observed as early as 1889 in the story "A.D. 3,000: The True Report of a County Council Candidate's Dream" (reprinted in *SHAW* 6, pp. 158–64), which portrays the cultural shock ("future shock") of a late-nineteenth-century political abecedarian transported to a futuristic utopian London. "Aerial Footfall" (1905) revolves around the reception of a charwoman and a bishop into the next world. Other uses of the fantastic include a talking plaster bust of Shakespeare in "A Dressing Room Secret" (1910), a disembodied child conversing with Kaiser Wilhelm II during a military engagement in "The Emperor and the Little Girl" (1916), and, in *The Adventures of the Black Girl in Her Search for God,* visits with such luminaries as the God of Noah, the God of Job, Ecclesiastes, Micah, Jesus, Mohammed, Voltaire, and that latter-day prophet G.B.S.

Shaw was essentially a scientist of ideas. Like the twentieth-century evolutionist Richard Dawkins, he would have embraced the concept of "memes," those self-replicating ideas that influence the evolutionary future by leaping, virus-like, from brain to brain. Shaw's numerous futuristic dramas and essays mark him not only as a person of his times but ahead of them as well. His prescience enabled him to see almost as far as thought could reach. His visionary speculations about human destiny align him with many other writers of the time, and later, who forged a new genre of literature that ultimately took the name in 1929 of "science fiction."

Appearing initially in lock step with the onset of the Industrial Revolution, SF, a marriage of scientific fact and human imagination, reflected the advances that were giving a new dimension to concepts of time and space and a new power to technological tools and machines. The scientist, mad or sane, was the new Prometheus, the creator of a brave new world, a radical future in which knowledge and mechanical power were joined. Technology would, for good or ill, take us where no one had gone before.

SF, then, is a literature of anticipatory processes, suggesting a spectrum of future worlds and, by this creative act, reminding society how transient contemporary culture is. As the Industrial Revolution gathered momentum and turned sweet Albion, to quote Blake, into "those dark Satanic mills," is it really coincidence that a new writing came forth to transcend the old dispensation? For the first time, society possessed tools of such extreme power that foresight in their use became imperative if disaster and social upheaval were to be contained.

Shaw, more than many of his contemporaries, understood that society's future goals would be selected from the array of images, metaphors, and ideas created by its collective imagination and that a poverty of images would severely limit its choices. As Isaac Asimov, one of the great popularizers of science who believed in the humanizing and democratizing effects of scientific literacy, repeatedly said, "Science is too important to be left to the scientists." And so thought Shaw.

Not constrained by the necessity of waiting for excellent theories to be proven, SF can extrapolate from what is known and pursue possible outcomes, suggesting what may, in fact, occur. And this is certainly what Shaw did. He speculated about what mankind might do and what mankind might become. His familiarity with the science of his day was intimate. Whether his speculations are true or false is immaterial. As Poul Anderson has remarked, ". . . I do not mean that absolute scientific accuracy is a sine qua non of good imaginative literature. For one thing, the scientific picture is always changing. We can still enjoy C. S. Lewis's *Out of the Silent Planet* for instance, in spite of what our space probes have since told us about Mars. Much of the cosmology in Olaf Stapledon's *The Star Maker* is now obsolete, but his magnificent cosmic vision has lost nothing thereby. Yet I do invite you to note how solidly timbered these works are."[2]

And I would invite you to do the same with Shaw, a master builder of ideas. His influence on SF has been significant because his ideas are significant. Arthur C. Clarke (see Elizabeth Anne Hull's "On His Shoulders: Shaw's Influence on Clarke's *Childhood's End*"), Ray Bradbury (see John R. Pfeiffer's "Ray Bradbury's Bernard Shaw"), Aldous Huxley, Kurt Vonnegut, Gore Vidal, Colin Wilson, Joanna Russ, and Robert A. Heinlein (see George Slusser's "Last Men and First Women: The Dynamics of Life Extension in Shaw and Heinlein") have all referenced Shaw. Heinlein, for example, unhesitatingly borrowed from Shaw for his 1941 book *Methuselah's Children*. Supermen with super powers are a staple of SF (see John Barnes's "Tropics of a Desirable Oxymoron: The Radical Superman in *Back to Methuselah*").

That Shaw, in turn, utilized SF conventions has been well established. J. O. Bailey was one of the first to show that Shaw's "plays made use of imaginative contrivances and plot devices characteristic of science fiction."[3] One such SF prop that Shaw made significant early use of on stage was the newfangled invention, such as the typewriter and the automobile. And his writings include the futuristic contraption as well: the moving sidewalk, videophones, flying machines, and robots (see Julie A. Sparks's article "Shaw for the Utopians, Čapek for the Antiutopians"). Shaw was quite aware of the effect that science and technology were having on civilization and was compelled to remark upon its far-reaching implications. It is this extrapolation concerning the effects of science, especially genetics, on the future that associates Shaw inextricably with the twentieth-century literary movement now known as SF.

For Shaw, if the future was to avoid Orwell's "boot stamping on a human face—forever," then art would have to appeal to human transcendence, to that which evoked the will into action for the well-being of humanity. Without transcendent goals, mankind merely re-

peated the mistakes inherent in its baser nature, even as its material
well-being gradually improved (see Susan Stone-Blackburn's "Science
and Spirituality in *Back to Methuselah* and *Last And First Men*").

Shaw railed at and cajoled those who posited that there was no future,
but at the same time he imbued his futuristic plays with much political
satire and many utopian projections solidly based on contemporary
events. His aim was to "lay down a line of political conditions for the
future."[4] Like his fellow Fabian H. G. Wells, Shaw utilized the techniques
of speculative fiction to sugar-coat the philosophical and socialistic pill.
And like H. G. Wells, whom many consider to be the "father of science
fiction," Shaw, while contentious about scientific materialism, understood that, in many ways, scientists attempt to formulate principles that
enhance our abilities to predict consequences, in effect the future. And
the future was a time about which Shaw cared greatly.

Even during Shaw's ascent to fame, the guardians of high culture did
their utmost to seal off any contamination by popular, mass-cultural
advocates, such as Shaw's irascible friend, H. G. Wells. History, however,
often confounds the best-laid plans of self-imposed arbiters of taste and
resurrects cultural endeavors that languished or were stifled at the time.
Thus, H. G. Wells is now seen as having contributed rather substantially
to the overall literary and cultural forum and as having influenced
Shaw's playwriting (see R. F. Dietrich's "War of the World-Betterers,"
reviewing the Shaw/Wells correspondence).

Wells's biological pessimism, however, found ample riposte in Shaw's
Lamarckian optimism, a much-needed anodyne for a humanity with a
future. In essence, both Shaw and the developing field of SF understood
that science had to be monitored, that the power of the individual to will
the future, to ameliorate human destiny, to transcend the body by
whatever means, was as essential to human destiny as breathing. Both
knew that adapting to change was more important than the stagnation
of utopian perfection, that the unexpected was necessary to existence,
and that human intervention would become the dominant mechanism
of evolution.

The atrocities of the First World War, many of them aided and abetted
by scientific know-how, cast a pessimistic pall over Western society. In
Back to Methuselah, Shaw's quintessential science fiction work, he attempted to counter the prevailing *Weltschmerz* (contrast Karel Čapek's
seemingly different response in Sparks's article) by exploring the new
powers of life inherent in Creative Evolution. It was a relief to him to
escape the present and to forage in the future, to suggest a philosophical
basis from which thinking persons could ratchet themselves up the
evolutionary cliff and rebuild a more lifegiving civilization.

Shaw knew that the future is contained in the present, but he also knew that the present is also a passing phase of history, that crisis and the toppling of governments is sometimes the price for significant and vital change. He "dreamed of a renewal of faith that would measure conduct by the longest conceivable perspective, and of an imaginative rather than academic lens through which to regard our history. He wanted to go as far as thought, and much farther than facts, could reach. After all, historical truth was a matter of interpretation. Therefore an instinctively trained eye was needed to recognize the tiny shoots and buds sent out by the Life Force—for example, the natural tendency for people in the twentieth century to live longer."[5] Shaw foresaw that the human "biology barrier" could be, if not overcome, at least pushed back.

It is ironic, perhaps, that SF would come to fruition in fin de siècle England but ultimately make its name in the United States more than thirty years later. But England was trapped in its social and literary traditions, fearful of fantasy and comfortable in its fictive Newtonian cosmos—a victim of its own class stratifications. And for Shaw it was the perfection of society, particularly English society, that first motivated his writings. After World War I, however, when Shaw was coming to intellectual terms with such concepts as Einstein's theory of relativity and Planck's quantum theory, Shaw quickly realized that a mutable humanity, related to lower life forms, was inexorably moving toward a destiny that was unknown—perhaps even unknowable. It is at this point that Shaw becomes a bona-fide science fiction writer.

His later plays reveal a multi-layered view of a disintegrating society and have a prophetic quality that speaks to contemporary events as if time within his plays has been waiting for the reader to catch up. His surreal political fantasies are surprisingly prophetic anticipations of the future and extrapolations from the known to the unknown, an SF technique *par excellence*.

For Shaw, ideas were the essence of history, not mere facts. For history to come alive, facts had to be imaginatively interpreted. Shaw believed that "The evidence of history might teach us to be pessimists, but the human spirit demands optimism. Since our roots lie in the past and our hopes reach towards the future, it followed that by changing our concepts of the past we could ordain our future."[6] (See Tom Shippey's "Skeptical Speculation and *Back To Methuselah*.") Echoing this thought, Frederik Pohl once remarked, "There's no such thing as the future: What there is instead is an almost infinite range of possible futures."[7]

Shaw at an early stage utilized what SF writers refer to as futuristic gadgets and themes, and he returned to such literary devices throughout his career to carry forward his drama of ideas and to outline "possible futures." While *Man and Superman* and *Pygmalion* employ SF conventions, with *Back to Methuselah* Shaw embarks upon futuristic writing that puts him into the SF mainstream. Lilith's words at the end of *Back to Methuselah* have echoes in all the major SF writers and could easily serve as a creed for the genre: "Of Life only is there no end; and though of its million starry mansions many are empty and many still unbuilt, and though its vast domain is as yet unbearably desert, my seed shall one day fill it and master its matter to its uttermost confines. And for what may be beyond, the eyesight of Lilith is too short. It is enough that there is a beyond."[8]

This beyond constitutes the essential bailiwick of SF. Shaw understood that "mind over matter" is the impetus that draws humanity forward, that ideas, "memes," are the "life blood" and purpose of being. The theatrical stage, unfortunately, proved to be an inadequate vehicle for his later wide-ranging ideas. The imagination, alone, can provide sufficient backdrop for his vision (see Peter Gahan's *"Back To Methuselah: An Exercise of Imagination"*). Imagination is often a more important door of perception than knowledge. As Shaw's friend Einstein once remarked, "Yet it is equally clear that knowledge of what *is* does not open the door directly to what *should be*. One can have the clearest and most complete knowledge of what *is,* and yet not be able to deduct from that what should be the *goal* of our human aspirations."[9]

For it is the imagination that allows us to simulate life, to try out things mentally, to make our mistakes in the renewable reality of thought. Shaw would be amused that we are increasingly amplifying brainpower electronically as during his day we amplified musclepower mechanically. The biological barriers of the human being are constantly under reconstruction as we move ahead with what has always been the tool-makers' ultimate experiment, even if we have not always recognized it: man-made evolution. And he would agree with Einstein that "Science without religion is lame, religion without science is blind."[10]

It may be that our technological enhancements to the mind and body make our relationship to our forebears analogous to their relationship to the apes, and we may yet live lives of pure thought. It is certainly scientifically feasible—and very good science fiction.

Notes

1. Frederic Jameson, *Postmodernism, or, The Cultural Logic of Late Capitalism* (Durham: Duke University Press, 1991), p. 283.
2. Poul Anderson, "Nature: Laws and Surprises," in *Mindscapes*, ed. George E. Slusser and Eric S. Rabkin (Carbondale: Southern Illinois University Press, 1989), p. 8.

3. J. O. Bailey, "Shaw's Life Force and Science Fiction," *Shaw Review* 16:2 (May 1973): 48.

4. Michael Holroyd, *Bernard Shaw, 1918–1950: The Lure of Fantasy* (New York: Random House, 1988), p. 480.

5. Ibid., p. 37.

6. Ibid., pp. 412–13.

7. Frederik Pohl, "Monolude: The Imaginative Future," in *Imaginative Futures*, ed. Milton T. Wolf and Daryl F. Mallett (San Bernardino: Borgo Press, 1994), p. 9.

8. Bernard Shaw, *Back to Methuselah*, in *Complete Plays with Prefaces* (New York: Dodd, Mead, 1963), 2:262.

9. Albert Einstein, *Ideas and Opinions*, ed. Carl Seelig (New York: Bonanza Books, 1954), p. 42.

10. Albert Einstein, "Remarks to the Essays Appearing in This Collective Volume," *Albert Einstein: Philosopher-Scientist*, ed. Paul Arthur Schilpp (Evanston, Ill.: Library of Living Philosophers, 1949), p. 678n.

Ray Bradbury

G.B.S.: REFURBISHING THE TIN WOODMAN: SCIENCE FICTION WITH A HEART, A BRAIN, AND THE NERVE!

In the spring of 1954 when I had just finished writing the screenplay of *Moby Dick* for John Huston, my London publisher received a letter from Lord Bertrand Russell, commenting favorably on my latest novel *Fahrenheit* 451.

Lord Russell was inclined to let me visit for a short time some evening soon. I leaped at the chance.

On the train traveling to meet him I panicked.

My God, I thought, what do I say to the greatest living philosopher of our time? I, a Lilliputian running about in his shadow?

At the last moment a fragment of opening conversation inspired me. Ringing the doorbell, I was admitted by a most friendly Lord Russell and seated for tea with Lady Russell.

With great trepidation I blurted out, "Lord Russell, some years ago I predicted to my friends that if you ever wrote short stories, they would inevitably be science fiction. When your first book of stories appeared last year, that's *exactly* what they were!"

"Indeed," Lord Russell smiled. "In these times, there is nothing *else* to write about."

And we were off on a conversational gallop.

The same would apply today. I dare to imagine that if Bernard

Shaw were alive, and aiming his beard, he would fire off rounds of science fiction.

For isn't it obvious at last: Those that do not live in the future will be trapped and die in the past?

Just as those who do not recall history are doomed to relive it, the above truth is a truth redoubled. For consider, what topic do we talk about every hour of every minute of every day?

The future

There is nothing else to discuss!

What will you be doing an hour from now?

That's the future.

What about tomorrow morning?

That's the future.

Next week, next month?

The future.

Next year, twenty years from now?

The same.

We are always blueprinting our immediate minutes, our seasons, and our years of ripeness and decay.

How is it then that quasi-intellectuals, intellectuals, and other haute-philosophers find science fiction contemptible? Or if they think of it at all, *ignore* it?

Much of science fiction of course has lapsed in a tangle of robot legs.

Too many imaginative writers have not seen the human forest for the mechanical talking trees. They have busied themselves computerizing rockets and rarely questioned any ramshackle philosophy of what in hell to do with them.

Re-reading *Back to Methuselah* and its copious notes, I wish that Shaw had survived a few more years to see a remarkable musical film, the finest of all time, *Singing in the Rain*. How so? Would the Old Man have held still in the cinema dark to watch some flimsy excuse for a technologically creative life? I dare to think so. The film, by its title, might seem to portray a dancing optimist, with or without umbrella, doused but unaware because he is in love with life. But that is hardly the philosophical point of the musical.

Philosophical point?

Indeed. For the film dreams up a future dead-on in the mid-Twenties when the silent flicker would suddenly clear its throat and croak a song. Not only that but sit up and *speak*. It is, in sum, a fiction about science becoming technology and technology implanting a voicebox in the throats of black and white mannequins on screen.

Singing in the Rain is, that I know of, the only science-fiction musical film ever made. Delete the music and you still have plot: The invention of sound and its shattering consequence, or, how do you construct a philosophy, simple, skeletal, workable, to bridge the gap between silence, unemployment, then re-employment with vocals?

This problem occurs, does it not, every time a new invention looms and threatens? The computer was supposed to throw millions out of work, right? Wrong. It has quickly re-employed those jobless in brighter offices, higher towers, better homes. Television would fire countless radio thousands, yes? No. It hired them back to run a thousand TV stations as against a few hundred radio outlets.

All of this would have been grist for Shaw's brain, intellectual gum for him to chew in the matinee twilight.

I dare say you could have flashed the first half hour of *Singing in the Rain* on screen, shut it off, and then turned to Shaw and said, "What happens *next*? What will sound do to the actors, the studios, the world?"

"Dear Lord! Stand aside!" Shaw would have cried. "No, don't show me the rest. I'll finish the scenes, the dialogue, the whole glorious gallivant in the lobby. Where's my pen?"

Knowing Shaw, a few hours later he would have predicted, blue-printed, and constructed the flesh, blood, and actions of Gene Kelly and chorus, in continuing rains.

Later, seated back in the movie loges, screenplay freshly done under his curiously twitching fingers as the rest of *Rain* poured down, he would have hooted with delight. "See? I *knew* it. That, that, and *that! All* of it! Bravo for Androcles and the MGM lion. Bravo for me!"

I would then hand over one of Yeats's finest poems, "Sailing to Byzantium."

In the last lines of that poem I found the answer to life, world history, science and invention, science fiction and Shaw.

A pretty big serving. Let's digest it. One bite at a time.

First, the quote: "Of what is past, or passing, or to come."

The entire history of beast man, man beast, and man from the cold cave to the hot Egyptian sands to the even colder shores of the Moon, and all that lies between. Some banquet, eh? But Shaw would sit down to it gladly. Why? Because the entirety of our past, everything to do with mankind has been science fiction.

Not much science, of course, and one helluva lot of fiction. But nevertheless, the art of imagining this afternoon, this midnight, tomorrow at dawn.

Impossible? Incredible? Come view another author.

H. G. Wells's stirring film *Things to Come* ran a lot of young men like myself out of the theater in a state of Becoming. In the years since, *I* have become *me*. I was sixteen at the time and needed someone to stir my blood. Wells did just that by sensing in the human animal the

Becoming Factor, that need that other animals do not sense. They exist unknowing, but we inherit that extra gene: we *know* that we know. And in that knowledge, both terrifying and exalting, we panic to evolve, do fast footwork before the fangs seize, the blood runs, and we no longer exist. In that fusion we are less Darwin's and more Lamarck's. It was Lamarck, after all, who said that the giraffe dreams for a longer neck, thus influencing his genes to Become the long-necked beast stretched up after the high fruits, flowers, or leaves. Darwinians disagreed. It was the fit who survived by their fitness, not through dreaming long necks to align genetics and create a proper spinal cord.

Nevertheless it is tempting to theorize that since we humans are cognizant of our cognizance we have begun to teach our genes and chromosomes behavior. We dream a long neck, build it, and reach up to the Moon, then Mars, then the Universe. Carl Sagan protests that this is merely survival of the fittest carried to the nth degree. We are the end product of failures upon failure surrounding a final product, surviving man. His dreams and accomplishments are not Lamarckian, no matter how much it seems they resemble technological giraffes with extensible necks that reach from Canaveral to Copernicus Crater. Echoing both views, I have on occasion put together a gaggle of bright companions and entrained them for Land's End or the Cosmos. Riding along with his portmanteau brain packed with notions, fancies, and concepts, Shaw would be introduced to Nikos Kazantzakis.

For it was Kazantzakis not long after Shaw who published his amazing *The Saviors of God*. His shout, similar to Shaw's Life Force perorations, was head-on: "God cries out to be saved. We are his Saviors."

In other words, why grow a forest and chop a tree if there are no witnesses to the simply miraculous. The old cliché: if a tree falls unseen, *does* it fall, *does* it exist? The Universe, the Cosmos, the lightyear immensities existed without Eyes for as many billion lightyears as can be counted without foundering. We have been summoned, Kazantzakis says, and Shaw pronounced early on, to discover the impossible, the inexplicable, the cycles of rampant life here and on worlds so far distant we shall never know them. Notwithstanding we dream them in our fictions and go a-traveling *up*. We are the Beginners. We are beholden. Tens of millions were born and died before us. They are a sweet burden which we must carry into Space. Our destiny was born on the day the primitive eye was invented in the merest animal specule and began to see, examine, and one day realize that stuff in the sky, that mystery of stars.

In our new and spectacular age, we witness the growth of Space Travel at Canaveral, lift-off our desires from gantries 300 feet tall, proper strait-jackets for King Kong, gun carriages to be fired against Time,

Distance, and Ignorance. Shaw would have vacationed here to tonic up his spirits. Imagine him striding the Florida sands, interviewing astronauts but hearing himself as they replied.

At almost the same instant of our lunar landings, electronic brains fell among us to melt down from huge houses, rooms, then cubicles and closets to lap and wrist size. Kasparov won out over a computerized chessplayer, thus scoring a victory for mankind? Bosh. Sniveling bosh. Shaw would have been the first to write a curtain raiser in which the computer is convicted of fraud, for as we all know it was not a single machine that faced Kasparov, but the intellectual guts of three dozen men who peed their brightness into the nerve endings of the Dumb Player. The computer only *looks* like a machine. It is the neuron endings, gastric juices, lifeblood, sweat, and ganglion fire that hide within, masking its stuffs with wires, fused by ten thousand instant welds.

I have never wondered at such. Visiting Apple Computer or any other electronic gizmo works, when the tour guide said, "Isn't that wonderful?" I cried, "No!" Shocked, they asked me what I meant. "I mean," said I, "*it* is not wonderful. *You* are wonderful. You dreamed it. You blueprinted it. You built it. You infused it with process, with dream, with electronic imagination. It does not know it exists. You exist. You are the god I worship. A computer cannot best Kasparov. A legion of flesh-and-blood brains hid in a computer might. All hail Kasparov, all hail Apple battalions."

Man is, after all, the Ghost in the contrivance. The lift under the wing of our aircraft is not miraculous, it is man who lifts the airplane by discovering the invisible presence of "lift." Man makes visible all the unseen and contrives to make it palpable. With the X-ray and the microscope Mankind blew the cover on death's-head skeletons closeted in living flesh. Bacterial annihilators were then reined in and destroyed for the first time in the history of our Earth.

All of these inventions would have been Life Force invigorators for Shaw. With the laptop computer as Moses' tablet, Shaw would have hyperventilated the modern stage, strutting his soul and outwitting Wells and all of us.

To Wells, whose last book was the sad *Mind at the End of Its Tether*, he would have cried, "Sit, Herbert George, be still! Your tether laps the world, encircles Saturn, to unravel beyond Centauri. There *is* no end but only an eternal Beginning. My behavior, as example, guarantees it. Melancholy entombs itself. Pessimism is a self-fulfilling prophecy. Let Canaveral be a New Year's Eve Fourth of July. Let all the rusted gantries jump alive with liquid oxygen-hydrogen fire. Let each gantry be a Christmas Tree, decorated with life aloft to Anywhere But Here. Dear Herbert George, *Hamlet* may very well start with tombs and ghosts, proceed with skulls and graves, end with suicides and murder. *I* write me a *new* text, H.G., not from tomb to tomb, death to death, but launch pad to launch pad, rockets shouting fire, men shouting a joyful rage against Unknowingness. Come, H.G., shed that despair, Canaveral is the kindergarten of Time, Evolution, and Immortality. Don't spoil it. Don this silly helmet, blow this horn. Run, leaving your footprints to be blown away with the firewind as the Last Rocket targets the great Cosmic wall."

Shaw, as I have said, alive today, would dare to instruct gravity, admonish Congress, reprimand the do-nothings and the know-every-things-who-profess-nothing, then nest himself in a missile to be fired up and outrace all lightyear spacecraft shouting along the way: If I am not the Holy Ghost, *who* is? To which we, following, would respond: If you're not God, along the way you'll do.

Speaking thus, of Shaw and Science Fiction, we must then bring up with thunderous tympani and a battalion of brass, Hector Berlioz, whose *Symphonie Fantastique* might as well have been Symphony Future Incredible. For it was Berlioz who was not only a fine short story writer, but a great autobiographer, who made a rare headlong dash into the future with his *Euphonia, The Musical City*, which appears in his amazing *Evenings with the Orchestra*. In this story he imagined a town in 2344 whose inhabitants, everyone, played or sang or acted music or experimented with acoustics and sound.

Well, then, what of this? I propose that we eject Shaw from his grave to collide in mid-air with a similarly projectiled Berlioz over the Florida Space Life Preserve to root them by the nearest abandoned gantry, there to relight that great tree with celebratory notes and festive fires. There Berlioz would compose the architecture of his Euphonia and conduct it on the fiery turf at sunset on the night of Going Away, a symphony of Departure and Arrival, to depart the gravities of Earth, to accept the centrifuges of the planets so that they might whirl us on out to the final Arrival: Centauri, where the immortality of Man, as promised, predicted, and outlined by G.B.S., the Mountebank, will achieve its procreation and assurance. If the soul's heart and blood of *Methuselah* does not circumnavigate this, I will discard my intuition to be dry-cleaned.

The imagination of man is the promise of our flesh and blood delivered to far worlds. Not just by fitness or experimentation, but by wild desire, incredible need, fantastic dream. Not by unfit accidents, but by waking intuition, blueprint, construction, and culmination.

Berlioz and Shaw conjoined could let Shaw write treatise, lyric, and prologue, then double in cymbal and lunar drum, and on occasion elbow Berlioz off the podium to pound the orchestra into submission, then leap off to sit as audience and caper his pen to criticize composer, choirs, as well as the Man with the Gunshot Beard lurking with his brass. From there, Shaw might vault to the nearest planetarium to advise Cosmos and God, the Whole Dominion, on all planetary arousals and diminishments.

So on the vast stage of Cosmic History that stage whisper overheard will rise from the prompter's nest where G.B.S., stashed, could choreograph Moses with an empty tablet, Christ poised to vanish from the tomb as a great illusion, and the Big Bang theory shown as pip-squeak pop-gun non-event.

Can this be done? With careful planning now we can fuse Shaw and Berlioz on the Florida dunes just beyond 2001. They are, after all, the Founders of Awe. The young cubs Spielberg, Lucas, and Kubrick are merely Promoters. They did not engender the Universe. Shaw swam over the whole damned spread to seed the cosmic eggs.

With his Methuselah brain out-living his body he was an entire committee which created not that infamous camel but a Lamarckian giraffe.

Whose neck, look there, will never stop growing!

Ben P. Indick

SHAW'S SCIENCE FICTION
ON THE BOARDS

" 'As Far As Thought Can Reach,' The Latest Scientification Novel by Bernard Shaw!" is the banner headline on the cover of Hugo Gernsback's 1926 *Amazing Stories*, with a gloriously gaudy cover by Frank R. Paul, illustrating newborn boys and girls, already in their teens, hatching from eggs. The corner newsstand is crowded with eager fans, quarters in hand, all recalling the excitement of the master of science fiction's earlier novels.

This scene is, of course, whimsy, and, indeed, in writing such a speculative epic as *Back To Methuselah*, science fiction *per se* was scarcely the primary intention of the great playwright. It was, nevertheless, part of his achievement. Few commentators, however, have chosen to consider it as such. Discussing the play in *Journey To Heartbreak*, Stanley Weintraub does not go beyond the word "futuristic" as description and sees the play as Shaw's answer to the gloom of his own *Heartbreak House*, an attempt to escape sheer pessimism.[1] Arnold Silver calls it a "huge and misanthropic work which sneers at love and youth and at the very method of procreating the human species."[2] Alfred Turco, Jr., finds in the stirring concluding speech of Lilith "a thinly disguised acknowledgment of . . . defeat."[3] Readers or viewers see the play on their own terms, but, without distortion, it may as easily and legitimately be considered science fiction, a term none of these writers uses. If Shaw's writing never did appear in science fiction magazines, he did know the genre, before it even had its name, and he used it here and elsewhere in his plays.

Born in 1856, Shaw antedated the full flowering of science fiction, but by the time he was an adult, it had become a thriving literary form in England. Modern science fiction in England can be said to have begun with Mary Wollstonecraft Shelley's *Frankenstein* (1821), although conceived by her as a Gothic tale. Its popularity spread with the tales of the American Edgar Allan Poe (1809–49) and the novels of the Frenchman Jules Verne (1828–1905), which were quickly translated into English. In 1871, Edward Bulwer-Lytton (1803–73) published his utopian novel, *The Coming Race,* which is reported to have been "a favorite book of [Shaw's] boyhood."[4] On its heels, in 1872, Samuel Butler (1835–1902) published a utopian satire, *Erewhon.* Half a century later, each would exercise some influence on *Back to Methuselah.*

Monthly magazines emerged in England in response to the popular desire for romantic fiction in this genre and abounded in the fin de siècle and Edwardian periods. Science fiction stories, often tales of interplanetary adventure and popular astronomy, as well as monsters, lost races, and unknown lands, copiously and well illustrated, were staples in such magazines as the *Strand Magazine, Windsor Magazine, Pearson's Magazine, Cassell's Magazine,* and more. Their authors included such popular writers of the day as C. J. Cutcliffe Hyne, M. P. Shiel, and George Griffith, the latter the most popular science fiction writer of his day, as well as H. G. Wells, who quickly supplanted Griffith with a flow of brilliant novels and stories.[5]

Science fiction on stage had appeared as early as 1821 in the first of a series of unlicensed adaptations of Mary Shelley's novel *Frankenstein* (1818), capitalizing briefly on its fame. They were melodramatic and sensationalistic.[6] Fantasy as such has long been a theatrical staple, but science fiction *per se* has not. Shaw's *Back to Methuselah* and almost simultaneously Karel Čapek's play *R. U. R.* (1920) were not consciously beginning a new stage movement, although both playwrights could scarcely have been unaware of the more revolutionary aspects of their plays. The core of each, however, was concern for the human condition, not pseudo-science. Čapek wrote fantastic satires, but no other true science fiction plays; Shaw incorporated elements in a number of plays, but in no full play for another quarter century. There have been plays by other writers, but there are specific problems inherent in science fiction theater, and all have faced the problems that Shaw and Čapek did.

Most immediate is that audiences have expected fantastic elements and stage wizardry to predominate in such plays, whether a play about long-lived people of a remotely distant future and the inherent marvels such a scene might offer, or a play about robots, a new word and a new concept for its time. It is not unusual for the playwright or producer to surrender to the temptation of a crowd-pleasing spectacle in this new genre. The problem for a serious writer is that the stage effects will usually predominate over human concerns and at the expense of characterization.

Another problem is the philosophical content that is frequently the intent of science fiction novelists, whether Aldous Huxley in his dystopian novel *Brave New World* (1932) or Dan Simmons in his metaphysical space journey novel *Hyperion* (1989). It may outweigh the reality of the characters themselves, leaving an allegory enacted by puppets. Shaw wished to show what a longer life-span might do for humans and carried evolution to an undreamed-of conclusion. Čapek's robots became real only when they were pseudo-human beings. An audience might expect to see non-human futuristic representations in the one case, wind-up dolls in the other. Any production of either of these plays may accommodate the desire of the audience for spectacle, but not at the cost of characterization. Most subsequent theatrical science fiction has not attempted to do more than dazzle the eye and offer trite philosophies. Shaw and Čapek have yet to discover true successors in equally successful employment of the genre both for itself and for deeper purposes.

Shaw's stage use of modern mechanical devices prefigured fantastic conceptions: a typewriter in *Candida* (1894), Professor Henry Higgins's obsessive vocal study equipment in *Pygmalion* (1913), a dentist's office in *You Never Can Tell* (1906), and even an automobile, starting and driving off, in *Man and Superman* (1902). Audiences are still happily surprised by the appearance of an automobile on stage.

Going beyond mundane fact, the widely read Shaw could hardly have been unaware of the science-influenced fantastic stories already very popular, although in his published letters he refers to only a few titles by H. G. Wells, his friend and sometime Fabian Society rival. In a letter to Robert Loraine, wounded in World War I, Shaw wrote (c. 10 August 1918), "It seems to me that when it comes to aerial combat, the more of you that is artificial the better. Wells' Martian [referring to *The War of the Worlds*], a brain in a machine, is the ideal. You could carry spare limbs and replace damaged ones whilst you were volplaning."[7] To James B. Fagan, a playwright and manager, he described an actor who played his Captain Shotover in *Heartbreak House* too slowly (20 October 1921): "he was like a drowning man, or rather like a man sitting on Wells's Time Machine, and aging ten years every minute."[8] In his "Epistle Dedicatory to Arthur Bingham Walkley," appearing in print with *Man and Superman*, he describes creating a character as a "contemporary embryo of Mr. H. G. Wells's anticipation of the efficient engineering class which will, he hopes, finally sweep the jabberers out of the way of civilization."[9]

Major Barbara (1905) is an ostensibly realistic play that prefigures the paradoxes of George Orwell's *1984* in the rationalizations of the munitions-maker about charity, but it also has a touch of prophetic science fiction when his son Stephen tells his mother of his father's inventions: "The Undershaft torpedo! The Undershaft quick firers! The Undershaft ten inch! The Undershaft disappearing rampart gun! The Undershaft submarine! and now the Undershaft aerial battleship!" (1: 345). There is, quite possibly, a debt here, and perhaps a gibe, at the military science fiction of H. G. Wells in *The War of the Worlds* (1898) and *The Land Ironclads* (1903).

The Doctor's Dilemma (1906) was a bold incursion by Shaw into medical pseudo-science. He posited the existence of a "nuciform sac" in the body, a repository for decaying matter, which may ⊘r may not exist. Always eager to condemn vaccination, Shaw had a field day of serious humor at the expense of the doctors. In response to a pompous physician's discovery of an antibody that coats invasive bacteria and makes them susceptible to destruction by phagocytes, Shaw writes, "the phagocytes wont eat the microbes unless the microbes are nicely buttered for them," and the danger of inoculation is that the "butter factory [must be] on the up-grade" (1: 93). Inoculation was dangerous, he wrote in his 1911 Preface, because general practitioners refused to learn cautious technique. Shaw suggests testing the antibody level at specific intervals to determine the safest time for injection, a venture into practical predictive scientific technique.

Press Cuttings (1907) is set in a very near future inasmuch as its thrust is topical, during "The Women's War in 1909." It is a slight one-act vaudeville farce, scattershot in its nature, with many puns, some on politicians now obscure, bumbling generals and privates, slapstick, and a *reductio ad absurdum* in a battle between Women Suffragettes and Women Anti-Suffragettes. Aside from a line that "in these days of aeroplanes and Zeppelin airships [the moon] will be reached at no very distant date" (6: 304), the science-fictional significance of the sketch is that it indicates Shaw's acquaintance with a science fiction sub-genre already popular in Britain for several decades, the Imaginary War or Invasion of England theme.

This form had been appearing in both popular magazines and novels since the first and perhaps most influential example, *The Battle of Dorking* by Sir George Tomkyns Chesney (1871), of war by an unidentified foreign power, in all likelihood Germany, and the subsequent destruction of Britain. It led to comparable novels, including *The Great War of 189–: A Forecast* by Rear-Admiral Philip Colomb and others (1891), James Eastwick's *New Centurion: A Tale of Automatic War* (1895), Fred Jane's *Blake of the "Rattlesnake"; or the Man Who Saved England: A Story of Torpedo Warfare in 189–* (1895), and Erskine Childers's *Riddle of the Sands* (1903). Surely influential on Shaw, a novel he could scarcely have missed, would have been the enormously popular *The War of the Worlds* (1898) by his fellow Fabian H. G. Wells, with its annihilative attack on London and England by Martian invaders.[10]

In the Preface to his pessimistic *Heartbreak House*, Shaw wrote that the cultured class of pre-war Europe, the "Heartbreak people," were "full of the Anticipations of Mr. H. G. Wells . . . helpless and ineffective in public affairs" (1: 452). Captain Shotover has a store of dynamite, and with it hopes to "discover a ray mightier than any X-ray: a mind ray that will explode the ammunition in the belt of my adversary before he can point his gun at me" (1: 527). His science fictional experiment cannot succeed, for, at the end, his stock of dynamite is lost in a mysterious bombing incident from the sky.

If Shaw had toyed with scientific extrapolation before, with the gimmicks, toys, and themes readers of his age associated with what would later be called science fiction, it all paled before the huge new play he commenced work on in 1918. It was *Back To Methuselah*, and it would occupy him between 1918 and 1920. Here he would engage fully his beliefs about Darwinism and evolution, subjects always of concern to him. Now he would write a multi-part fantasy about substantially lengthening the span of life and then would suggest the ultimate destiny of mankind. Past the age of seventy, Shaw faced a daunting task, a play such as none before him had attempted. Perhaps Shaw's despondency during the horrendous years of World War I led him to consider the need for biological alterations that would enable human beings to live meaningful lives. In the 1921 Preface to the play he discusses what he defined as "creative evolution" and "voluntary longevity." Of the former he argues that the process of evolutionary change might be manipulated by will, a theory adapted from the writings of the French philosopher Henri Bergson. Of the latter, influenced by the works of the German biologist August Weismann, he argues that death is not inevitable but simply an expedient to prevent overcrowding of the world, and longevity, it follows, is a matter of will. *Methuselah* would dramatize these theorems.

Ever theatrically astute, however, he adds, "To make the suggestion more entertaining than it would be to most people in the form of a biological treatise, I have written *Back to Methuselah* as a contribution to the modern Bible" (2: xix). It was a terminology not new to him. As early as *Man and Superman*, in "A Foreword to the Popular Edition" (22 March 1911), he wrote that its third act, *Don Juan in Hell*, was a "careful attempt to write a new Book of Genesis for the Bible of the Evolutionists" (3: 748). He continues in the Preface that "all that is necessary to make [man] extend his present span is that tremendous catastrophes such as the late war shall convince him of the necessity of at least outliving his taste for golf and cigars if the race is to be saved. This is not fantastic speculation: it is deductive biology" (2: xix). Clearly, Shaw was aware of the extraordinary nature of his ideas; his defense merely buttresses it.

Creative Evolution is "the genuinely scientific religion for which all wise men are now anxiously looking" (2: xix). He began with the fabled beginning of all things, Evolution and Longevity included, with Adam and Eve in the Garden of Eden. In this unexpected atmosphere of fantasy he discusses and applies his scientific themes. It required more than a single play of normal length could encompass; Shaw allowed himself the luxury of a multi-play cycle. Subsequent parts developed into a broadly imaginative series of episodes stretched across far reaches of time, from his own into the future. The fantasy, science, comedy, and tragedy proceed in the enormous epic at a length that does justice to its namesake (who is a symbol, not a character).

The germ may have been in the work of Samuel Butler, whom Shaw knew and about whose writing he was enthusiastic, in particular Butler's utopian (as well as dystopian) anti-Darwinian satire, *Erewhon* (1872), revised as *Erewhon Revisited* (1901). When Shaw wrote his own story of Evolution, he had to face a serious problem. As he wrote later in his "Postscript After Twentyfive Years" (1945), "I threw over all economic considerations, and faced the apparent impossibility of a performance during my lifetime" (2: xcvi). Was this "impossibility" due to its inordinate length, or was it a question of stageworthiness? In his 1921 Preface, Shaw had uncharacteristically feared "my sands are running out" (2: lxxxix). Yet *Saint Joan* and many provocative plays and writings lay ahead in the final third of his lengthy life, including *Farfetched Fables,* a consecutive group of sketches written in his ninety-third year, a recapitulation but also a reconsideration of *Back to Methuselah.*

Shaw considered his vast play as his *Ring,* after Wagner's model, and, indeed, it is a collective cycle of five individual plays with a common theme. The plays consist of one three-act play, one two-act, and three one-acts. Even the lengthiest is not as long as Shaw's average play. Their purpose allows for no subplot. They are filled with discovery and amusing asides, but are unconcerned with the essence of most dramatic characterization in which actions of the characters are dictated by but are often in apparent opposition to underlying motives. They are plays of dialectic, and the characters speak their minds for the most part very directly. In comparison, Eliza, in *Pygmalion,* is not simply an illiterate girl being taught to speak. She grows and reacts in unexpected ways, dictated by her own needs as a woman. Her character emerges from this. Few characters in the five-play cycle have this opportunity.

They are nevertheless clearly drawn, as would be expected of an author who can always turn a stereotype or caricature into a breathing individual with a telling line or quip. There is character conflict, but most often shallow, simply for thematic explication of the creative evolution of the human race. Adam and Eve, in Part 1, are petulant children who must grow up, and there is banter and even disagreement, but no real conflict. Only in Part 4 is conflict important, where it leads to perhaps the most emotional scene in the entire epic, when the Elderly Gentleman realizes he is an anachronism in this strange new world and can no longer live. By underplaying human conflict and by exchanging his characters for new ones in each play, in a strong sense Shaw deprived his audiences of the element that makes for a strong play, identification through empathy. An exception might be the Elderly Gentleman, who represents humanity as we know it; he is, however, one element in one play. Even Wagner's *Ring of the Nibelung*, with its four distinct operas and separate plots, was essentially the story of a single hero who could be followed from even before his origins to his death. Is Shaw's vast vision enough to unify unique and loosely connected parts, or is it the vanity of a single-minded, thesis-ridden author?

The five component plays are consecutive but individual, are linked intellectually only, and are not continuous. The second and third parts are perhaps the most readily acceptable because the attitudes of the characters in both are recognizable to the contemporary sensibilities of an audience. Indeed, in the third play, the characters, like the author, appear happily bemused, as would be the audience, by the plethora of science fiction devices and gadgets. In addition, these two parts are still relatively close in time, and two of the characters, although dressed quite differently in the third play, are familiar from the second. As a minor tie, an individual in Part 2 mentions the Garden of Eden, which was the setting for Part 1. A young woman in Part 4 resembles another in Part 2. The names Burge and Lubin, distorted over time, connect Parts 2, 3, and 4. Otherwise, until a brief reprise of characters from Part 1 at the climax of the final play, some ten hours later, there is no reappearance of characters or even situations. The single connecting thread is the concept of an extended life-span and its ultimate effect upon the human imagination.

Part 1, *In the Beginning*, is a two-act play. Shaw, with characteristic hubris, subtitles his work "A Metabiological Pentateuch," appropriating the term from the Five Books of Moses, whose first book, *Genesis*, opens with the words "In the beginning." He offers his own version of Eden. Lilith has divided herself to produce Adam and Eve. Adam bemoans the monotony of eternal life and Eve agrees, hoping that one day they shall find what else there may be. Shaw had anticipated her argument as early as 1909–10 when he wrote *Misalliance*. An older man, Tarleton, says about death, "You think death's natural. Well, it isn't. . . . There wasnt any death to start with. You go look in any ditch outside and you'll find swimming about there as fresh as paint some of the identical little cells that Adam christened in the Garden of Eden. But if big things like us didnt die, we'd crowd one another off the face of the globe. And so death was introduced by Natural Selection. You get it out of your head, my lad, that I'm going to die because I'm wearing out or decaying. There's no such thing as decay to a vital man. I shall clear out; but I shant decay" (4: 127).

The dialogue and surprise of Shaw's treatment of the biblical story has its peaks and valleys, amusing although discursive, the manner, twitting the Scriptural account, curiously reminiscent of Mark Twain's *Extracts From Adam's Diary* (1904) and *Eve's Diary Translated from the Original MS* (1906). As in Shaw, Twain's Eve is the more intellectually curious while Adam is placidly accepting. Twain's Adam is more senti- mental. Having lost Eden, at Eve's death, Adam says, "Wheresoever she was, there was Eden." Twain also anticipates Shaw's preoccupation with longevity and death in *The Tragedy of Pudd'nhead Wilson* (1894) in the epigraph of Chapter 3: "Whoever has lived long enough to find out what life is, knows how deep a debt of gratitude we owe to Adam, the first great benefactor of our race. He brought death into the world."

In the Beginning satisfies Shaw's intentions about using the Bible as an opening stage for his argument. However, Adam, Eve, and company, in fig-leaves or snakeskin, while delivering his ideas, are more entertaining as human characters with human foibles than as soap-box lecturers. It is puzzling since the discussions of Adam and Eve about a suitable lifespan are in favor of diminishing, not lengthening it, whereas the subsequent parts are involved with the opposite. Although its fantasy is finally sobering, no audience will accept this play with purely fabulist characters as biological science. At best it can only seem like an imaginative overture to the more realistic parts, where even the science fiction bears the ring of truth and possibility, however fantastic. Nevertheless, as a preamble, it allows Shaw to begin at the beginning of a presumed human history, and, at the climax of the cycle, the biblical characters return to round off the entire epic in a grand poetic manner.

Shaw had to be aware of the generalities of this first play when he had startling specifics to bring up. In Part 2, *The Gospel of the Brothers Barnabas*, he opens abruptly within his characteristic present timespan and proposes that three hundred years is a better life-span than seventy to ninety. It is an amusing and thoughtful one-act play, with a very slight bridge to the first in Savvy's comment that she suspects that she is Eve reincarnated (2: 75). Shaw does not offer a specific technique to achieve longevity other than a conscious decision to do so, which is, after all, the essence of his voluntary longevity, but he does anticipate many science fiction stories about the political problems involved. Lubin, an elderly politician based on Asquith, states, "it would be in the last degree upsetting and even dangerous to enable everyone to live longer than usual," and Burge, a more glad-handing politician based on Lloyd George, agrees. Thinking the secret of longevity is a substance, he warns that it would be "stuff that everyone would clamor for. . . . There would be blue murder. It's out of the question. We must keep the actual secret to ourselves" (2: 83).

Shaw recognized the difficulties of reconciling characters and situations common to his theater with the fantastic theme he wished to elaborate. He had intended a second act in Part 2, "A Glimpse of the Domesticity of Franklyn Barnabas," but in a foreword, Shaw admits that it tended to "confuse my biological drama with a domestic comedy" (2: cix). It has a caricature of G. K. Chesterton in the guise of Immenso Champernoon, maliciously funny, and also contains a flippant scene with Savvy as a charming flirt. A reader could wish that Shaw had made something of it in other circumstances. However, the atmosphere of creative evolutionary fantasy previously established is here dissipated in endless conversation, and Shaw quit with the characters still talking. "How this conversation ended," he noted in an afterword, "I cannot tell; for I never followed up the adventure of Immenso Champernoon with Mrs Etteen, and dont believe it came to anything" (2: cliii).

For the third part, *The Thing Happens,* a one-act, Shaw reveals his acquaintance with the mechanics of science fiction propounded in early prophetic stories. He simply rollicks in a stage-set full of delightfully imaginative science fictional atmosphere, his tongue wickedly in his cheek when discussing politics and race in the year A.D. 2170. The parlor of the President of the British Islands is accoutered with push-buttons, pointers, a giant telephone-television screen, and futuristic clothing. Wealth has been redistributed. An American has invented a method of breathing under water.

After fascinating his audience with the technological razzle-dazzle display, he returns to his theme of longevity, extrapolating the possibilities for joy and sadness inherent in it. An archbishop states that he has already lived the length of several ordinary lifetimes, nearly three hundred years. He is not alone. The parlormaid by that time has done likewise.

H. G. Wells, who was with his wife a close friend of the Shaws, was not amused by Shaw's new evolutionary theory. Shaw, he wrote, "has restored the inheritance of acquired characters by proclamation. He seems to be suggesting at times that man can do anything by merely willing it."[11] The meticulous Wells had, after all, spent many pages in the opening sequence of his science fiction novel *The Time Machine* (1895) establishing a rationale for time traveling within a "fourth dimension" that he postulated. Nearly thirty years later Wells still felt compelled to justify his fantasy. In his novel *Men Like Gods* (1922) Wells takes pains to have scientists of a future utopian world explain to Mr. Barnstaple and his vacationing friends how they stumbled into this world thanks to an accidental juncture of spatial dimensions. Wells may also not have appreciated Shaw's mischievous if complimentary reference to him by name in the play. The Archbishop compares his own solitary longevity to the solitude of the would-be leader in a story, "The Country of the Blind" by "that twentieth-century classic, Wells," and concludes "By the way, he lent me five pounds once which I never repaid; and it still troubles my conscience" (2: 115).

Part 4, *Tragedy of an Elderly Gentleman*, is a three-act play, obviously indebted to Swift, set in A.D. 3000. After the bright and imaginative humor of Part 3, an audience might have expected an epic dimension for such a leap into the future. Instead, Shaw turns inward, examining the maturity possible in a person with extended life. It is, in terms of science fiction, a remarkable leap into the more mature style that would succeed the phase of merely introducing technological marvels. The new world now consists of both long-lived and short-lived people. One of the latter is an elderly man who has been made up to resemble Shaw. He converses with a woman attendant in a sequence of double-entendres, non sequiturs, and weak puns, not without humor but sometimes slowed to a crawl by self-indulgent lengthy harangues on Shaw's favorite themes. A long-lived woman is literal and humorless, and her world seems flat and dull. An audience may justifiably be confused as Shaw, figuratively on stage before it, appears to be mocking the future he has espoused through three plays. Actually, it is daring writing and establishes new parameters of science fiction. Shaw is demonstrating the effect, and the pain, of the evolutionary leap, and instead of simply stating it, he allows his audience to experience it directly. The Elderly Gentleman agonizingly realizes that to the long-lived attendants, his kind are but children. An oracle takes pity on him. She looks at him, and he falls dead. "Poor shortlived thing!" she says. "What else could I do for you?" (2: 202).

Shaw had earlier in the play noted that the long-lived had learned to utilize a powerful electromagnetic force inherent to any body, and it is this force that the oracle mercifully applies to the unhappy old man. Shaw borrowed the notion from Bulwer-Lytton's futuristic *The Coming Race*, where it was called *vril* and the people *vril-ya*. It is part of the science fiction with which Shaw creates a future reality, which also includes a portable tuning-fork-like telephone carried by the woman on her belt, a cellular phone three quarters of a century before its time. Shaw also employs an appropriately eerie set, placed impressively in a gallery overhanging an abyss, with interesting lighting effects and music, filled with alien awe. More than any of the other parts, the tragedy of the Elderly Gentleman is that of *immaturity.*

A light, even affectionate tie to Savvy, his flippant young woman earlier in the cycle, is present in this fourth play since she could double for Zoo, a young-looking woman who describes herself as a "flapper." Shaw escapes the anachronism of the term by having Zoo define it as an "archaic word which we still use to describe a female who is no longer a girl and is not yet quite adult" (2: 150).

In a poetic, often elegaic, and highly original finale in one act, Part 5 is set in A.D. 31,920, *As Far as Thought Can Reach.* Without question, H. G. Wells's *Time Machine* was an inspiration for the sweeping, if relatively modest, reaches of time that Shaw achieved. Wells's Time Traveller ultimately went more than thirty million years into a bleak, dying, vacant future. The young Wells, however, was pessimistic, whereas Shaw was still, past seventy, an optimist.

The landscape of this final play is classic, and the beautiful classical names for once belie Shaw's peculiar ideas of comic nomenclature. His imagination is boundless and the reader is swept along by the flow although his demands upon his audience were uncompromising. Newborns are hatched from large eggs, emerging already in their late teens. They indulge in aimless dancing, singing, and love-making until the age of four. This is their period of growth, condensing fifty of our own years. They then lose interest in childish pursuits, becoming "Ancients." They will live a thousand years or more, die only by accident, and seek a greater meaning to life. After a diversion about Art, the characters gradually fade away into the darkness and Adam and Eve reappear, stating what they have created and have represented, and they then disappear. This reconciles the fantasy and the science fiction, and their brief reprise lends unity to the sprawling work. It remains for Lilith to reappear and to state that Life will continue to go forward. It will be in a new phase, of redemption from the flesh, "vortex freed from matter," but retaining "the greatest of gifts: curiosity." She concludes magnificently, and nowhere, in science fiction at least, is her speech excelled: "Of Life only is there no end; and though of its million starry mansions many are empty and many still unbuilt, and though its vast domain is as yet unbearably desert, my seed shall one day fill it and master its matter to its uttermost confines. And for what may be beyond, the eyesight of Lilith is too short. It is enough that there is a beyond" (2: 262). She vanishes, and at last the audience may release its collective breath. Whatever else commentators have found beneath her words, Shaw has expressed incomparably a philosophy inherent in science fiction at its most imaginative.

Nor did his farsighted philosophy ever leave him. He was quoted when he was near death by Judy Musters: "I believe in life everlasting; but not for the individual."[12]

Lilith's words are echoed in the conclusion to H. G. Wells's film script for *Things to Come*: Man "must go on—conquest beyond conquest. This little planet and its winds and ways, and all the laws of mind and matter that restrain him. Then the planets about him, and at last out across immensity to the stars. And when he has conquered all the deeps of space and all the mysteries of time—still he will be beginning."[13] The solemn Wells must have known the speech of Lilith and recalled her words in his own stirring oratory, linking the indubitable master of science fiction with the roguish Irish dramatist.

The play has had a problematic critical history, either ignored in short encyclopedia biographies, such as *The Columbia Encyclopedia* (Third Edition, 1963), or, as in *Chambers's Biographical Dictionary* (1962), described as "a not altogether successful excursion from the Garden of Eden to 'As Far As Thought Can Reach.'" T. S. Eliot was wholly unenthusiastic about the cycle, believing that Shaw, "master of a lucid and witty dialogue prose hardly equalled since Congreve, and of a certain power of observation" was "squandering these gifts in the service of worn-out, home-made theories, as in the lamentable 'Methuselah.'"[14]

Its box-office history is important both for Shaw and for the genre of science fiction theater. Shaw was convinced that it was his masterpiece, despite his fears expressed in 1921 that it would be a financial failure. He was, fortunately, not entirely correct about this. Lawrence Langner of the subscription-based Theatre Guild in New York City had already staged some Shaw in revivals, and among its world premieres was *Methuselah*. Shaw good-naturedly labeled Langner a "lunatic," but the Guild premiered it on 27 February 1922, with Parts 1 and 2 in a three-hour evening, 8:10 to 11:15, which was early for that time of 8:40 curtains, and the next three parts over a nearly four-hour evening, from 7:30 to 11:25. The two halves were not done consecutively, according to the program, but as a week of each. It was not merely an endurance test but a financial challenge for audience and producer alike, and the program contained a two-page note on the difficulties inherent in doing the play. The Guild played twenty-five complete cycles over nine weeks, doubling its subscribers and garnering good critical response, but losing $20,000. They were not unhappy and felt that they might even have made money with a larger theater. In an anthology of Theatre Guild productions, Langner proudly noted that the play had been considered by Shaw himself "almost impossible of production."[15]

Shaw's pessimistic expectations were happily confounded when other producers mounted productions. One, Barry Jackson, a wealthy man mad about theater, had founded a small theater in Birmingham, England. Having already produced nine of Shaw's plays, he took on *Methuselah* as his tenth. Shaw, ever conscious of box-office receipts, wrote in the Postscript, "When I asked him what he had lost by the *Methuselah* adventure, he said with every appearance of satisfaction: 'Only 2500 pounds.' Later on, when he repeated it in London and I repeated my question, he answered exultantly 'I have not lost: I have made twenty pounds.'" Shaw comments, "Clearly then, *Back to Methuselah* was not a commercial job" (2: xcvii). Prior to this, Shaw states too modestly, "I wrote such shameless potboilers as *Pygmalion, Fanny's First Play,* and *You Never Can Tell,* to oblige theatre managers or aspiring players" (2: xcvi), but he was proud of his oversized offspring. When the 1925 Nobel Prize for Literature was awarded him in 1926 (probably, he quipped, in gratitude for his having published nothing that year), it specified no particular play. It recognized him "for his work, which is marked by both idealism and humanity, its stimulating satire, often being infused with a singular poetic beauty."[16] However, *Back To Methuselah* was likely a major factor, together with *Saint Joan* (1923), in the choice, coming not long after the productions of each. He concludes in the Postscript that being "the manifesto of the mysterious force in creative evolution . . . made [Goethe's] *Faust* a world classic. If it does not do the same for this attempt of mine, throw the book into the fire, for *Back To Methuselah* is a world classic or it is nothing" (2: cvi).

Some of the photographs of older productions have an indubitable charm. Especially ingenuous are scenes from the final part, illustrating teen-agers awakening in their cracked egg-shells, a stageful of near-Botticelli Venuses. Critics, however, complained about Shaw's asexuality, whether in a naïve Adam and Eve in skins or in a parthenogenetic far future and, indeed, the ultimate disappearance of humans into disembodied thought. Shaw was first but hardly alone in this. In 1930 Olaf Stapledon's novelistic history of mankind yet to come, *Last and First Men,* moved in that direction, and Arthur C. Clarke's *Childhood's End* (1953) postulated the same. As co-scenarist, Clarke hinted at it in the climactic scene of Stanley Kubrick's brilliant film, *2001: A Space Odyssey* (1968).

The Library of the Performing Arts at Lincoln Center, New York, has programs and critical reviews for at least six other productions, including the Old Vic in London in 1969 and Niagara-on-the-Lake in the same year. An interesting effort to obviate the cycle's formidable length was a severely cut version by actor Arnold Moss in 1957, with the permission of the Shaw Estate. Although it represented all five plays, it eliminated many characters, including one of the Barnabas brothers, and cut the playing time for all five parts to two and one half hours! It starred Tyrone Power, Faye Emerson, and Arthur Treacher, all major names, and reached the Shubert Theatre on Broadway, where its run was even more limited than intended, with poor reviews.

A Shaw play can still sell tickets, but the financial and artistic logistics of the *Methuselah* cycle are formidable. In our own time, there have been marathon plays, including the Royal Shakespeare Company's brilliant two-evening adaptation of Dickens's novel *Nicholas Nickleby* in a limited engagement, the only financial success; Alan Ayckbourn's three-play *The Norman Conquests,* the three plays offering different views of the same situation; and Robert Schenkken's two-play *The Kentucky Cycle.* Shaw's is the most difficult of any, unconcerned with melodrama, family humor, or historical drama. Not devoid of humor or even pathos, it is above all a play of ideas, highly idiosyncratic in the Shavian manner. Its use of fantasy and science fiction challenges an audience unlike any other drama.

Nevertheless, for all its faults, its digressions, didactics, paternalistic lecturing, and a dubious scientific base, as well as for its glorious imagination, daring, humor, and dramatic brilliance, the play is indeed, as Shaw firmly stated, a classic, in concept and in execution. The boards of Broadway are burdened with trivia. The time is at hand for a brave producer, an imaginative director, a creative designer, and an adventurous cast to reawaken the slumbering giant for a new generation of theater-goers.

Science fiction would continue to appear in Shaw's theater. *The Apple Cart,* written in 1929, is ostensibly the future world of 1962. A king rules without the aid of his aristocracy or cultivated bourgeoisie, neither being interested. Breakages, Ltd., is a huge industrial corporation dedicated to obsolescence and short-lived manufactured products to insure a fully active labor force. It buys up useful new ideas to preserve this imperfect condition. It is clearly Shaw's analogy to capitalism. The American ambassador declares that the Declaration of Independence has been canceled and that America has "decided to rejoin the British Empire" (4: 296). France is "too busy governing in Africa," Shaw adds, appearing to anticipate an engineering marvel still seventy years away, "to fuss about what is happening at the ends of your little Channel tube" (4: 298). Actually, he is reflecting a popular theme of science fiction novels written half a century earlier, when the construction of such a tunnel, using steam locomotives for traveling, was propounded.[17]

In 1931, in *Too True to Be Good,* Shaw still fears ultimate destruction. Prescient of the horrors of World War II and its saturation aerial bombardments, Shaw wrote, "London and Paris and Berlin and Rome and the rest of them will be burned with fire from heaven all right in the next war" (4: 691).

In *Geneva* (1938), subtitled "A Fancied Page of History," Shaw prophesies, incorrectly, as has often been the fate of science fiction authors, that "Japan has declared war on Russia and is therefore in military alliance with Britain. And the result of that is that Australia, New Zealand and Canada have repudiated the war and formed an anti-Japanese alliance with the United States under the title of the New British Federation" (5: 673–74). An impotent League of Nations court invites the world's dictators to attend, including "Signor Bombardone" (representing Mussolini), "Battler" (Hitler), and "General Flanco" (Franco). Still Socialist, Shaw did not involve Stalin, nor did he comprehend the monster that Hitler represented, so Mussolini is his chief spokesman. Shaw's judge castigates *all* world leaders, including the British representative, "Sir Orpheus Midlander", who is credited for assisting in the victory of General Flanco by his non-intervention policy. The judge has no actual power, but in holding the leaders accountable, Shaw anticipates the war criminal trials of Nuremberg.

"In Good King Charles's Golden Days" (1939) is garrulous even for Shaw, with a king, a pretender, churchmen, a parade of mistresses, politics, and an understandably fogged and fatuous Isaac Newton all within its first act, heavily dependent upon actors with style. However, before the first curtain, Newton arouses himself and the audience with a vision of grand scope beyond the purview of his own time: "There may be stars beyond our vision bigger than the whole solar system. When I have perfected my telescope it will give you your choice of a hundred heavens" (6: 71–72). Machine-mad Hugo Gernsback, in the most didactic of his *Amazing Stories* science fiction, could not have topped that. Shaw does not attempt to. Newton does not even appear in the brief and coy second act.

In 1946 Shaw, at ninety-one, demonstrated a positive interest in space science, actual and speculative, by becoming a member of the British Interplanetary Society (B.I.S.). Arthur C. Clarke, already a recognized science fiction author, scientist, and chairman of the Society, had referred briefly to Shaw in a paper that he delivered, titled "The Challenge of the Spaceship." It was printed in the *Journal* of the Society. Clarke reminisced some years later about the sequel. "There seem very few subjects in which Shaw was not interested, and fewer still on which he was not prepared to express his opinion. Nevertheless, it may surprise most people to learn that towards the end of his life the ubiquitous playwright concerned himself with such advanced ideas as space-travel and supersonic flight. . . . [Soon after the Journal appeared] I came across the magnificent speech with which Lilith closes the play *Back to*

Methuselah. This, I thought, showed a considerable sympathy with the ideals of astronautics, so I sent Shaw a copy of the British Interplanetary Society's *Journal* containing my lecture—not in the least expecting a reply."[18]

Shaw not only responded, but became a life member. "Many thanks for the very interesting lecture to the B.I.S.," Shaw wrote. "How does one become a member, or at least subscribe to the Journal?" He then speculated on what had caused the recent crash of an experimental jet plane and its young pilot, a friend and neighbor of Shaw's. He reasoned that the aircraft had "reached the speed at which the air resistance balanced the engine power and brought it to a standstill. Then he accelerated, and found out what happens when an irresistible force encounters an immovable obstacle." Clarke gently corrected Shaw's reasoning and suggested the fault was likely a structural defect. Shaw defended his argument, but concluded, "However, this may be my ignorant crudity; so do not bother to reply."[19]

Despite this "polite brush-off,"[20] Clarke was impelled to correct Shaw's pseudo-science with facts. They included a comparison of the ill-fated plane with the German V–2, which attained speeds of 3,000 m.p.h. and reached England with very little air resistance even at heights the plane could not attain. This time he received no response. Shaw, however, continued to be a member of the B.I.S. until his death three years later, the oldest member that it had ever had. Clarke concluded, "Yet whatever one may think of the old man's aeronautical confusion, it is hard not to admire his efforts to keep abreast of the times. How many of us will do as well at the age of 91?"[21]

Shaw continued to ignore his advanced age, a believer in and achiever of the Gospel of the Brothers Barnabas. In 1948–49, the atomic bomb on his mind, Shaw, a year before his death, mused again about the future of mankind in a group of six short plays he entitled *Farfetched Fables.* They are brief and ironic sketches, indicating a loss of hope for the dream of *Back to Methuselah.* They are too short for impact, but are humorous and thought-provoking, making a diverting and sobering evening of theater.

Shaw remained fully aware of science, and his imagination was still active. In the First Fable, Shaw foresaw the possibility of a device similar to the later neutron bomb: "Somebody will discover a poison gas lighter than air! It may kill the inhabitants of a city; but it will leave the city standing and in working order" (6: 493). The second criticized political leaders for using terrible weapons, safely enough for them far off in someone else's land. The Third Fable is set in a Huxleyian world, with Mediocrities and Anybodies. In the Fourth Fable, Shaw waggishly solves the food problem as some people manage to subsist on air and water:

"People can now, freed of food requirements, concentrate on the arts" (6: 506). In the Fifth Fable, sex is finally freed of the body altogether, and ecstasy is associated with the discoveries of the mind. Indeed, it would be useful to do away with the body altogether and simply be mind, pursuing knowledge. In the Sixth Fable, however, in a classroom of the future, students are confronted by Raphael, a youth clothed in feathers, who explains that he had been disembodied before his sudden appearance in the class. Such an evolutionary development was part of the climax of *Back to Methuselah;* Shaw is emphasizing the ability to control evolution. Raphael explains, "Evolution can go backwards as well as forwards. If the body can become a vortex, a vortex can become a body" (6: 520). He urges the class to study and then leaves. The students, however, refuse to listen to their teacher's affirmation of study: "We can never want to know too much," she implores them (6: 521). Shaw, however, no longer has faith. A march is heard, and they tramp out like robots.

The Milwaukee Shaw Festival staged the Fables in November 1992. A subsequent symposium revealed mixed opinions among its participants, from descriptions of the whole as "rotten little skits" to "pure Shaw that shines through the life of the mind, undimmed by those ninety-two-plus years."[22] To an indulgent devotee of both Shaw and science fiction, delightedly discovering both in these "Farfetched Fables," the brilliant nonagenarian had lost none of his imagination. Written solely for his own amusement, they are sometimes wise, sometimes heavy-handed, brooding over the message of *Back to Methuselah* and a lifetime of trying to make audiences listen. He is disillusioned, yet has not forgotten how to laugh and how to make others laugh.

Fanciful Postscript

The Elderly Gentleman puts away his notebook and tugs a whisker. The *Fables* are only a "few crumbs dropped from the literary loaves" of his lifetime's work. It might have been different, his work might perhaps have reached more people, if he had not stopped with his youthful attempts at science fiction stories. His work as a critic had been intelligent, and despite his late start, his plays were vividly alive. But, he muses, curling that errant whisker, all that time spent on novels no one wished to read, and all those letters, so many, many, to those actresses, beautiful as they were, might have been used, he thinks ruefully, on what old Wells called scientific romances, and he could still have had time for his plays. Well, just a few letters, to Ellen, and Stella, and yes, Charlotte. Competitors? Wells? Hah! Against his own rapier wit! As for the others, that unreadable nineteenth-century man of wild adventure and plodding prose, George Griffith, and his Olga Romanov, they would have paled like watery borsht beside his own flashing-eyed heroines as much at home among Griffith's planets as in a salon. Mad M.P. Shiel's penny-dreadful yellow peril, ludicrous next to his brilliant Confucius from *Methuselah*. The pathetic gimcrackery of journeymen scriveners in *Blackwood's Magazine*, paltry next to himself, he, the innovator of television, cellular telephones, and psychic weaponry on stage right before an audience's disbelieving eyes! If the Barnabas Brothers could help him gain a second century, perhaps—but, no. Yet it has not been bad. Lilith, Adam, Eve, that little flapper Savvy, all from his fantasy, and that other cast in his life, real, bless them all, the beautiful matrons, the flower girls, the gallant soldiers, that blackguard cowboy, and the God-besotted saints and Devil-inspired sinners! All!

Notes

1. Stanley Weintraub, *Journey to Heartbreak: The Crucible Years of Bernard Shaw 1914–18* (New York: Weybright & Talley, 1971), pp. 293–98.

2. Arnold Silver, *Bernard Shaw: The Darker Side* (Stanford: Stanford University Press, 1982), pp. 261–65.

3. Alfred Turco, Jr., *Shaw's Moral Vision*, (Ithaca, N.Y., and London: Cornell University Press, 1976), p. 267.

4. Michael Holroyd, *Bernard Shaw, 1918–1950: The Lure of Fantasy* (New York: Random House, 1991), p. 50.

5. Of the many anthologies of period British science fiction, I would recommend *Science Fiction by Gaslight*, ed. Sam Moskowitz (Cleveland and New York: World Publishing, 1968) for both the choice and its excellent introduction, and *Science Fiction by the Rivals of H. G. Wells*, ed. A. Kingsley Russell (Secaucus, N.J.: Castle Books, 1979).

6. See Ralph Willingham, *Science Fiction and the Theatre* (Westport, Conn.: Greenwood Press, 1994), for a good overview of history and problems, with an annotated list of plays and operas.

7. Bernard Shaw, *Collected Letters 1911–1925*, ed. Dan H. Laurence (New York: Viking, 1985), p. 560.

8. Ibid., p. 739.

9. Bernard Shaw, *Complete Plays with Prefaces* (New York: Dodd, Mead, 1963), 3: 506–7. Subsequent references to this edition will appear parenthetically in the text.

10. Other Future War titles may be found in *Science Fiction: The Early Years*, ed. Everett F. Bleiler (Kent, Ohio: Kent State University Press, 1990); *The Encyclopedia of Science Fiction*, Second Edition, ed. John Clute and Peter Nicholls (New York: St. Martin's Press, 1993); and I. F. Clarke, *Voices Prophesying War* (New York and Oxford: Oxford University Press, 1992).

11. H. G. Wells, *The Way the World is Going* (New York: Doubleday, Doran, 1929), pp. 296–302.

12. Bernard Shaw, *Collected Letters 1926–1950,* ed. Dan H. Laurence (New York: Viking, 1988), p. 883.

13. H. G. Wells, *Things to Come* [screenplay] (London: Cresset Press, 1935).

14. T. S. Eliot, "The Idealism of Julian Benda," *New Republic* (12 December 1928), p. 107.

15. *The Theatre Guild Anthology,* Introduction by Board of Directors of The Theater Guild (New York: Random House, 1936), p. xi.

16. Tyler Wasson, ed., *Nobel Prize Winners* (New York: H. W. Wilson, 1987).

17. I. F. Clarke, *Voices Prophesying War,* p. 227. Futuristic channel tunnel titles include Grip (Pseud.), *How John Bull Lost London; or, The Capture of the Channel Tunnel* (1882), and A. F., *The Seizure of the Channel Tunnel* (1882), which also involve future war.

18. Arthur C. Clarke, "Shaw and the Sound Barrier," *Virginia Quarterly Review,* 36:1 (Winter 1960): 189–90.

19. Ibid., pp. 190–93.

20. Ibid., p. 193.

21. Ibid., p. 194.

22. "From Symposium: *Farfetched Fables,*" *SHAW* 14, ed. Bernard F. Dukore (University Park: Penn State University Press, 1994), pp. 83–92.

Elwira M. Grossman

WITKACY AND SHAW'S
STAGE STATUES

The names of Bernard Shaw and Stanisław Ignacy Witkiewicz (known also as "Witkacy") are never juxtaposed since they are considered playwrights who not only have little in common, but also represent contradictory views on philosophical and artistic issues. Although broadly true, this opinion should not be taken at face value. In fact, Shaw's and Witkacy's drama, albeit from radically different cultures, can be perceived as complementary, especially in their uses of fantasy.

Many of the strategies typical of speculative fiction are exploited by both dramatists. In Shaw's as well as in Witkacy's plays can be found dreamlike conventions, non-realistic mixtures of comic and tragic elements, unexpected twists in plot, the blending of standard dramatic modes with parodied genres, the rejection of traditional psychology in dramatizing behavior, and the creation of fantastic characters, including petrified bodies and theatricalized statues.

Shaw freely applies these devices in plays he collected as "tomfooleries": *The Glimpse of Reality, The Music Cure, Passion, Poison, and Petrifaction,* and other short plays. He also uses them in portions of some of his full-length plays, such as *Man and Superman, Back to Methuselah, Too True to Be Good,* and later self-described "extravaganzas." While he admits to his attempts to break with realistic conventions while employing many of their strategies, Witkacy openly advocates a theater of sophisticated fantasy and produces plays that illustrate his theory of "Pure Form." Both playwrights' ideas coincide more in practice than in theory.

Even in theory, however, there is some meeting of minds. While

Witkacy stresses the necessity of creating theater that can make the audience "experience the mystery and strangeness of existence," Shaw contends that he is not only interested in the conflict of ideas, but also sees the theater as a place for transcendent experience, observing in the preface to his 1907 collection of dramatic reviews that he considered the theater the successor to the church as a venue for experiencing metaphysical feelings, and, as well, "a factory of thought, a prompter of conscience, an elucidator of social conduct, an armory against despair and dullness, and temple of the Ascent of Man."[1] Witkacy ascribed magical and ritual functions to the theater as well and saw it as an antidote to the absurdity of human life that, unlike other arts, was still alive with potential to make men wonder at the universe and themselves. In his essay "On a New Type of Play" (1920), Witkacy argues, "What is essential is only that the meaning of the play should not necessarily be limited by its realistic or fantastic content, as far as the totality of the work is concerned, but simply that the realistic element should exist for the sake of the purely formal goals—that is, for the sake of the synthesis of all the elements of the theater: sound, decor, movement on the stage, dialogue, in sum, performance through time, as an uninterrupted whole—so transformed, when viewed realistically, that the performance seems utter nonsense."[2]

In the same essay, Witkacy explains that "artistic freedom" for the playwright can be equivalent to "nonsensicality" in painting, as long as it is "adequately justified and . . . valid for the new dimension of thought and feeling into which such [a] play transports the spectator."[3] This is his "Theater of Pure Form" and is akin to the parodies of the realistic tradition that one finds in many of Shaw's plays.

Witkiewicz (1885–1939) remains largely unknown in English despite translations and criticism, much of both by Daniel Gerould, who has also written on Shaw. Like Shaw, Witkacy was very versatile and was also a painter, novelist, philosopher, and critic. His numerous trips to Italy, Germany, and France, as well as to Australia—the latter (1914) with Bronisław Malinowski, whom Shaw also admired—influenced his life and thought. During World War I he served as an officer in the Russian army, witnessing, from Petersburg, the decay of the empire and the revolution. Returning to Poland in 1918, he began his first mature works of drama and criticism, and between 1918 and 1925 he completed the major plays and sketches by which he is known although he kept writing and painting until his death. At the outbreak of World War II he fled Warsaw to the east, away from the attacking Nazis. When on 18 September 1939 he learned of the Russian invasion of Poland in concert with the Germans, he committed suicide in the village of Jeziory (now part of Ukraine).

Witkacy's philosophical and aesthetic views, considered advanced in his time, anticipated postmodernism and deconstructionism. In parallel in the West, Shaw's experimental practice, as in his "tomfooleries," anticipated Absurdism.[4] The drama of both playwrights created a theater in which farcical and grotesque vision displaces the orderly universe, where laws of causality and logic are violated in thought-provoking yet amusing ways. Hence it is not surprising that their theatrical imaginations sometimes led them to similar and often fantastic dramatic solutions, one example of which is *Don Juan in Hell*, the independent third act of *Man and Superman* (1903), and *The Cuttlefish* (1922).

In both plays a statue is introduced as a character. In Witkacy's comedy it is Alice d'Or, the main female character, classified by many Polish critics as the femme fatale of the play,[5] although she is clearly described in the stage directions as a "living" statue rather than an actual woman. The description of Alice, who is dressed in "a tight-fitting sheath resembling alligator skin," indicates that her appearance is supposed to draw the audience's attention to the animalistic, carnal part of her personality, but, being a statue, she can only represent the idea of the femme fatale; she cannot actually be one. In Gerould's words, Alice is now "a monument of fossilized desire."[6] As a statue, she cannot enter into any physical relationship with Paul Rockoffer, an artist and philosopher, the main character in the play; she can only stimulate him mentally or intellectually from a distance, unlike any flesh-and-blood archetype of the femme fatale. Consequently, Rockoffer is tormented by her ideas, thoughts, and judgmental statements about his own behavior, not by her sex appeal.

The idea of introducing a statue as a character brings to the Polish reader's mind a drama by Stanisław Wyspiański (1869–1907) who was also a painter, designer, and theater visionary. Inspired by the Greco-Latin world as well as Polish romantic drama, Wyspiański developed his own unique style, overcoming many provincial traits dominating Polish art at that time. In his 1903 historical play *The November Night* [Noc listopadowa] monuments and statues of Greek gods and goddesses come to life, while in *Acropolis* [Akropolis] (1904), historical figures come down from the canvases and mythological deities perform their roles like other dramatis personae.[7] Witkacy himself admired Wyspiański and considered him a precursor of Pure Form theater.[8] However, it is in Shaw's and Witkacy's plays that characters close to living persons onstage are statues who interact with, and converse with, flesh-and-blood figures.

In *Don Juan in Hell*, Doña Ana's father is presented as "*a living statue of white marble, designed to represent a majestic old man.*"[9] For the English reader, a living statue as an active character is usually associated with

Shaw's play, derived, of course, from two sources: Tirso de Molina's drama and Lorenzo da Ponte's libretto. The similarities between Shaw's and Witkacy's statues are not only revealed in the way they function in the plays—largely their intellectual and mental influence on others—but also in the subject matter they discuss. For example, the conversation between the Statue and Rockoffer in *The Cuttlefish* clearly resembles Don Juan's situation:[10]

> STATUE: Think how many women you could still have, how many nameless mornings, softly gliding through the mysteries of noontime, then finally how many evenings you could spend in strange conversations with women marveling at your downfall.
> ROCKOFFER: Don't talk to me about that. Don't rip open the innermost core of strangeness. All that is closed—forever closed, because of boredom: galloping, raging boredom. (627)

As the idea of having many more women does not excite Rockoffer, the idea of sensual love no longer fascinates Don Juan. They both find themselves in a similar existential situation and reveal their self-awareness in the following lines:

> ROCKOFFER: . . . I've wasted my life. Two wives, working like a madman—who knows why—after all, my ideas are not officially recognized, and the remains of my paintings were destroyed yesterday, by order of the head of the Council for the Production of Handmade Crap. I'm all alone. (626)

> DON JUAN: I am really very sorry to be a social failure. (258)

In addition, both characters appear to be overwhelmed by a boredom, ironically caused by love, the same force that motivated their active lives in the past. Don Juan exclaims,

> DON JUAN: [*impatiently*] Oh, I beg you not to begin talking about love. Here they talk of nothing else but love: its beauty, its holiness, its spirituality, its devil knows what!—excuse me; but it does so bore me. They dont know what theyre talking about: I do. They think they have achieved the perfection of love because they have no bodies. Sheer imaginative debauchery! Faugh! (253)

Boredom as an indispensable element of love and life is warned of by Rockoffer when he describes to his fiancée, Ella, their inevitable future together:

ROCKOFFER: Love? Shall I tell you what love is? In the morning I'll wake you with a kiss. After the morning bath, we'll drink coffee. Then I'll go paint, and you'll read books, which I'll suggest for you. Then dinner. After dinner, we'll go for a walk. Then work again. Tea, supper, a little serious discussion, and finally you'll fall asleep, not too fatigued by sensual pleasures, to conserve strength for the next day.
ELLA: And so, on and on, without end?
ROCKOFFER: You mean: to the very end. . . . (630)

Thus love, whether discussed in its earthly or spiritual terms, is always associated in its final stage with endless boredom, and consequently is dismissed by both playwrights as the main motivating force in human life. Discarding love, Rockoffer and Don Juan turn to the world of ideas, namely philosophy, where they begin their search for truth and more inner strength. Don Juan becomes an Apollonian character praising the intellect and Life Force, while Rockoffer concentrates on creating a new reality (not art!): "Together, we'll create pure nonsense in life, not in Art" (637). He feels compelled to carry out his mission on this planet, which is to rule the Kingdom of Hyrcania as Paul Hyrcan V. As Gerould points out, "the Hyrcanian world view is the most powerful of all temptations, for it offers the power to transform life."[11] Hyrcania, having its equivalent in history (it was a province of the ancient Persian Empire located on the Caspian Sea),[12] is the artificial kingdom created by Hyrcan IV, Rockoffer's friend from his youth.

The philosophical idea of Hyrcania—as defined in the monologues of Hyrcan IV—is inspired by Nietzsche's concept of the Superman, but its artistic prototype can be found in *Enrico IV* by Luigi Pirandello. Julius II from *The Cuttlefish* is a resurrected Renaissance Pope, and his character is based on Giuliano della Rovera (1445–1513), who was elected Pope in 1503. Being a patron of the arts, he commissioned Michelangelo to paint the ceiling of the Sistine Chapel.[13] Julius II points out the importance of Nietzsche's inspiration:

JULIUS II: But, sire, as I see it, Your Royal Highness is a follower of Nietzsche, at least in social questions. Nietzsche himself recognized Art as the most important stimulus for personal power. (632)

Although Hyrcan IV denies this influence, his vision clearly resembles Nietzsche's ideas and as such becomes the main target of Witkacy's socio-political criticism. Like Shaw, Witkacy realizes that twentieth-century society is in a desperate search for a new direction for its development, but unlike Shaw, Witkacy does not accept the idea of the

Superman as the ultimate solution. Witkacy raises and then ultimately dismisses Nietzsche in the argument between Hyrcan IV and the protagonist. Rockoffer speculates on possible improvement through examining the basic political mechanisms of Hyrcania and abolishing those principles that interfere with his own version of a new world. According to Rockoffer, the concept of the Superman cannot result in anything better than "an ordinary theatrical hoax, a regime in the old style, a disgrace, 'bezobrazia' a la maniere russe, or simply dictatorship" (634). As the argument between the characters progresses, it becomes increasingly more obvious that Witkacy deals with specific historical and political circumstances of his own country. Yet, Gerould extends this allusion widely, arguing that "*The Cuttlefish* has remained perennially fresh and contemporary, equally applicable to conditions under Hitler, Stalin, or any oppressive regime of whatever ideology, country or historical period."[14] Still, it is probable that Witkacy conceals his catastrophic vision concerning the future of Poland behind the mask of Nietzsche's philosophy and Hyrcan's imaginary kingdom. Using quasi-Aesopian language, Witkacy predicts the communist regime and dictatorship, and he warns the reader against their specific political consequences for Poland. When Hyrcan IV announces that in his kingdom, religion has come to an end and he believes only in himself, but is ready "to believe in anything if he ever needs to," Julius II concludes, "Without religion there are no countries in the old sense of the word. There can only be an anthill" (632). Hyrcan IV corrects the Pope:

> HYRCAN IV: No, no—not an organized anthill, only the great herd of straggling cattle, over which I and my friends hold power. (632)

To this response, Rockoffer and Julius II add their own opinions:

> ROCKOFFER: Bandit. You are actually a petty robber baron, not an important ruler. You're only great given the extremely low level of civilization in your country. Nowadays, Nietzsche's superman can't be anything more than a small-time thug. And those who would have been rulers in the past are the artists of our own times. Breeding the superman is the biggest joke I've ever heard of. (633)

> JULIUS II: Your Hyrcania, Sire, strikes me as a kind of sanatorium for people sick of society. The way you describe it, of course. Actually it's the lowest kind of whorehouse for the playboys in life. ... (634)

In 1922, one cannot ask for a better description of the upcoming totalitarian ideology followed by the Stalinist regime in both Russia and Poland.

Witkacy's double intention is missing in the dramatic vision of Shaw, who discusses the Nietzschean concept through his characters in more abstract and general terms than does Witkacy. Realizing this essential difference between the two playwrights, it comes as no surprise that Shaw presents a significantly more favorable reading of Nietzsche than Witkacy. This is how the Devil explains to the Statue who "that German Polish madman" is:

> THE DEVIL. Well, he came here first, before he recovered his wits. I had some hopes of him; but he was a confirmed Life Force worshipper. It was he who raked up the Superman, who is as old as Prometheus; and the 20th century will run after this newest of the old crazes when it gets tired of the world, the flesh, and your humble servant. . . .
> THE STATUE. Good. [*Reflectively*]: All the same, the Superman is a fine conception. There is something statuesque about it. (293)

Thus, the same philosophical idea that serves for Shaw as a point of arrival and a possible answer to what direction contemporary society should choose for its development, becomes only a point of departure for a quasi-political discussion initiated in Witkacy's play.

These two visions of future worlds share a similar hierarchy of values in which the highest priority is given to philosophy. Don Juan, in the following monologues, shows the advantages of using one's brain in a thoughtful existence, analyzes the current state of fashionable philosophical ideas on earth, and concludes that the Superman (who has not been created yet!) might save the species from the dissolution of earlier forms of life:

> DON JUAN. . . . I said with the foolish philosopher, "I think; therefore I am." It was Woman who taught me to say "I am; therefore I think." And also "I would think more; therefore I must be more." (276)

> DON JUAN. . . . The great central purpose of breeding the race: ay, breeding it to heights now deemed superhuman: that purpose which is now hidden in a mephitic cloud of love and romance and prudery and fastidiousness, will break through into clear sunlight as a purpose no longer to be confused with the gratification of personal fancies. . . (281–82)

DON JUAN. . . . my brain is the organ by which Nature strives to understand itself. . . . The philosopher is Nature's pilot. And there you have our difference: to be in Hell is to drift: to be in Heaven is to steer. (290)

Like Don Juan, Rockoffer wishes to be in charge of his future life. In order to protect the universe from unexpected events that cannot be controlled, Rockoffer demands to be given the whole world and plans to create "something diabolical" (636). This is how he presents his vision:

ROCKOFFER: . . . I'll create a really cosy little nook in the Infinity of the world. Art, philosophy, love, science, society—one huge mishmash. And not like groveling worms, but like whales spouting with sheer delight, we'll swim in it all up to our ears. The world is not a rotten cheese. Existence is always beautiful if you can only grasp the uniqueness of everything in the universe. Down with the relativity of truth! . . . Long live finiteness and limitations. God isn't tragic; He doesn't become—He is. Only we are tragic, we, limited Beings. (636)

Consequently, both protagonists become Apollonian and finally eliminate the unpredictable artistic parts of their personalities. Don Juan calls the reality of art a "Palace of Lies" and reserves no room for it in a world ruled by the Superman. Rockoffer realizes that "as an artist I have been pretending up to now, and all my art is a hoax, a deliberate, carefully planned hoax" (628). On the surface, Rockoffer struggles to maintain a high status for art in Hyrcania, but it appears to be more wishful thinking on his part than a serious plan. Julius II, who is going to join Rockoffer, calls the existence of art into question: "I wonder if I'll be able to create a new artistic center in this infernal Hyrkania" (637). Thus, both characters leave the former places of their existence with the deep conviction that they will be successful if they remain faithful to their own principles. As the motto of Witkacy's play indicates, "Don't give in even to yourself" (626). The innermost struggle of Rockoffer and Don Juan ends in hope and the belief that progress is possible, and this belief constitutes another important similarity between their world views.

Witkacy's concealment of his political message in the dialogues— which on the surface deal exclusively with Art and an artist—becomes quite obvious in the monologue of Julius II. The resurrected Pope explains to Rockoffer how his art is the "sole Truth" and as such can become a comment on the nature of reality regardless of the artist's intention and awareness:

JULIUS II: *(With his finger pointing toward the ceiling)* Up there, where I come from, they know about it better than you do, you miserable speck of dust. But after all, an artist's worth comes from either rebellion or success. What would Michelangelo have been if it weren't for me or other patrons of the arts (may God punish them for it). A few madmen eager for new poisons raise up the man who concocts them to the apex of humanity, and then a crowd of non-entities adore him, gaping at the agony and ecstasy of the ones who've been poisoned. Isn't the fact that the Council of the Production of Handmade Crap burned your works a proof of your greatness? (628)

Julius II undermines Paul's assumption that all art is a lie and establishes a visible link, in the form of Truth, between the artistic and political aspects of reality.

This introductory discussion on the nature of art between Julius II and Paul Rockoffer continues when the artistic/theatrical nature of Hyrcania is revealed to the crowd present. The question of what is false and what is true about the legendary Hyrcania and its ruler puzzles not only the characters but also the reader. The way this concept is depicted by Witkacy makes the reader wonder about the deceptive nature of reality in general. This is how the Emperor Hyrcan IV is described in the stage directions: *"Tall, thin. Vandyke beard, large mustache. A bit snub-nosed. Large eyebrows and longish hair. Purple cloak and helmet with a red plume. A sword in his hand. Under his cloak a golden garment. (What he has on under that will be revealed later on)"* (626). At first, his appearance bears an obvious resemblance to some kind of an historical king rather than a twentieth-century dictator or an embodiment of Nietzsche's idea of the Superman. On the news that Hyrcan IV has arrived, Rockoffer exclaims, "You know he was a classmate of mine at school. He was always dreaming about an artificial kingdom in the old style" (630). Everybody listens in suspense to his "powerful, commanding footsteps" before the King enters the stage and the actual discussion of Hyrcania begins. Rockoffer questions Hyrcania's real nature from the very beginning: "Isn't your Kingdom only a badly disguised form of insanity, my friend?" (631). To this, however, Hyrcan IV responds in a truly Pirandellian fashion:

HYRCAN IV: . . . Our life is Truth.
ROCKOFFER: So it's a question of Truth. Is Truth also an integral part of the Hyrcanian worldview?
HYRCAN IV: Of course. But if all humanity wears a mask, the problem of truth will disappear all by itself. I and my two friends,

Count de Plignac and Rupprecht von Blasen, are creating just such a mask. Society masked and we alone who know everything. (633)

As the real mechanisms of Hyrcania are slowly yet consistently revealed, its similarities to the dramatic world of Pirandello's *Enrico IV* become really astonishing, especially since *Enrico IV* was performed in Cracow and in Warsaw in 1925. It is highly unlikely that Witkacy had access to the text earlier.[15] The false theatricality of this kingdom is also ridiculed by Ella's mother:

> MOTHER: I've read about that Hyrcania of yours in the newspapers. It's the theatre critics who write about it. Not one decent politician even wants to hear it mentioned. It's an ordinary theatrical hoax, that Hyrcania of yours. A depraved and degenerate band of madmen and drunkards took it into their heads to simulate a regime in the old style! You ought to be ashamed, Mister! (635)

The monologue comments on the real nature of Hyrcania, and at the same time it brings the visions of Pirandello and Witkacy into close correspondence. Through this and other monologues, it becomes quite obvious that the image of Hyrcania carries a serious message regarding the political future of Poland. Rockoffer clearly predicts that the popular trend of socialism can develop into a dangerous form of dictatorship with no room for artistic creativity or individual human values. Rockoffer's questions about what a regular work day looks like in Hyrcania and what really occupies its rulers are answered directly:

> HYRCAN IV: Power—we get drunk on power in all its forms from morning till night. And then we feast in an absolutely devastatingly glorious fashion, discussing everything from the unattainable heights of our reign.
> ROCKOFFER: A reign over a heap of idiots incapable of organizing themselves. An ordinary military dictatorship. Under favorable conditions a really radical state socialism can do the same thing. (633)

Although Hyrcan IV radically disagrees with Paul, he encourages him to leave for Hyrcania immediately so that he can experience this curious phenomenon in person. He tries to persuade Rockoffer that Hyrcania is a reality that is the "incarnation of Hyrcanian desires" (631) and the place where he—as a ruler—creates supermen: "Two, or three—that's enough. The rest is a pulpy mass—cheese for worms" (631). However, this vision does not appeal to Rockoffer, who finally admits,

But isn't there something of a comedy in it all? You know what's chiefly discouraged me? Your costume.

HYRCAN IV: But that's nothing. I thought you were more impressed by scenery and that's why I dressed up this way. (633)

Beneath his fancy costume, Hyrcan wears a well-tailored, normal cutaway, and his hidden clothes confirm the serious political message that Witkacy conceals under theatrical props. Thus, an imaginary Hyrcania with its King becomes far more real than appearances suggest. A strange mixture of past and future, philosophy and art, truth and trickery becomes a vehicle to convey a more profound thought.

The way Witkacy reveals the political mechanisms of Hyrcania offers the reader a far more insightful analysis of what the practical consequences of the concept of Superman can be than Shaw's more positive reading of the same idea. Again, one should keep in mind that Shaw promotes the ideas of Nietzsche in abstract philosophical terms without using them as a vehicle for a concealed political message. However, the very same device of using an imaginary figure to elaborate on the future image of the world is applied by Shaw in *Back to Methuselah* (1918–20) in the second act of Part 4. The Emperor of Turania, who claims that his name is Napoleon, but who may be a madman, appears in mysterious circumstances and has many traits similar to features of Enrico IV and Hyrcan IV. As happens in Witkacy's vision, the character is a mixture of an historical and a literary figure who plays an important role in suggesting the image of a future world. His identity is also called into question by other characters who are not easily misled by his props:

ZOO: *(to Napoleon, severely)* What are you doing here by yourself? You have no business to go about here alone. What was that noise just now? What is that in your hand? *Napoleon glares at her in speechless fury; pockets the pistol; and produces a whistle.*[16]

Unlike Witkacy, Shaw has no artistic intention of concealing the anti-war or anti-dictatorial message that the Napoleon figure personifies, but Shaw's dramatic solution for conveying certain political concepts clearly indicates that both playwrights thought along similar lines.

One may wonder today why the common link between Witkacy and Shaw has not been noticed and discussed before. The habitual way of looking at the writings of these two influential playwrights may answer this question. Critics seem to avoid examining Witkacy's plays in ways other than he himself demanded. Witkacy's critical view of Shaw and Pirandello later became accepted by many Eastern European and Western critics. This is how Witkiewicz concludes his thoughts on modern drama in his essay "On Pure Form" (1921):

> Realism is presently going through a crisis due to complete exhaustion, and it shows up in the theatre as a feverish search for new subjects. Typical manifestations of this process—and they are manifestations of decadence in the full force of its expression—are Bernard Shaw, Pirandello, and to a certain degree, Evreinov. . . . I do not see in these authors—in spite of all the recognition awarded the first two—the beginning of a new creativity, only the final, powerful twitch of a long process of dying. The curiosities in both Shaw and Pirandello, whether strictly naturalistically or symbolically justified, have a strong aftertaste of decadence, of futility, of hopeless impasse.[17]

Witkacy's opinion of Shaw, based on what he saw as Shaw's old-fashioned dramaturgy, does not prevent his own thoughts and concepts from being influenced by the vision of making the conflict of ideas a core element of drama.

Although Shaw's theoretical arguments are less prominent and his solutions are less drastic than Witkacy's, Shaw's theatrical impact has been strong. His views on "theatrical shock treatment" confirm this. As Stanley Weintraub observes, "Shaw believed that indifference in audience or playwright was a major sin, and that the playwright's clear duty was to shock audiences out of that state whenever necessary—and, in fact, more than necessary."[18] To support his statement, Weintraub quotes Shaw: "The plain working truth is that it is not only good for people to be shocked occasionally, but absolutely necessary to the progress of society that they should be shocked pretty often" (348). Witkacy parallels this proposal in his "New Forms in Painting" (1919) when he argues, "For people nowadays, the forms of the Art of the past are too placid, they do not excite their deadened nerves to the point of vibration. They need something which will rapidly and powerfully shock their blasé nervous system and act as a stimulating shower after long hours of stupefying mechanical work."[19] Sharing that conviction, Witkacy and Shaw devoted much of their art to putting the extraordinary onstage, creating plays and designing a theater intended to change the face of the world.

Notes

1. Bernard Shaw, "The Author's Apology," in *The Drama Observed*, ed. Bernard F. Dukore (University Park: Penn State University Press, 1993), p. 1134.

2. S. I. Witkiewicz, "On a New Type of Play," *Four Decades of Polish Essays*, ed. Jan Kott, trans. C. S. Durer and Daniel C. Gerould (Evanston: Northwestern University Press, 1990), pp. 99–100.

3. Ibid., p. 100.

4. Paul Silverstein, "Barnes, Booths, and Shaw," *Shaw Review* 12:3 (1969): 111–16.

5. (1) Jan Błoński, introduction, *Wybór Dramatów* by S. I. Witkiewicz (Wrocław: Ossolineum, 1974), pp. iii–cxi; (2) Jerzy Ziomek, "Personalne dossier dramatów Witkacego," *Studia o Stanisławie Ignacym Witkiewiczu*, Michał Głowiński and Janusz Sławiński, eds. (Wrocław-Warszawa: Ossolineum, 1972), pp. 83–105; (3) Adam Ważyk, "O Witkiewiczu," *Dialog* (1965, no. 8), pp. 70–75; (4) Jan Kłossowicz, "Teoria i dramaturgia Witkacego," *Dialog* (1959, no. 12), pp. 81–93; (5) Michał Masłowski, "Bohaterowie dramatów Witkacego," *Dialog* (1967, no. 12), pp. 84–98.

6. Daniel Gerould, *Witkacy as an Imaginative Writer* (Seattle and London: University of Washington Press, 1981), p. 190.

7. Czesław Miłosz, *The History of Polish Literature* (Berkeley: University of California Press, 1983), pp. 351–58.

8. Gerould, *Witkacy*, p. 333–34.

9. Bernard Shaw, "Don Juan in Hell," *The Portable Bernard Shaw*, ed. Stanley Weintraub (New York: Viking, 1977), p. 254. Subsequent references to this edition appear parenthetically in the text.

10. *The Cuttlefish*, trans. Daniel C. and Eleanor S. Gerould, *A Treasury of the Theatre*, ed. J. Gassner and B. Dukore (New York: Simon and Schuster, 1970). Subsequent references to this edition appear parenthetically in the text.

11. Gerould, p. 193.

12. *The Cuttlefish*, p. 626.

13. Ibid., p. 626.

14. Gerould, p. 186.

15. Alicja Forysiak-Strazzanti, *Teatr Pirandella w Polsce* (Poznań: Wydawnictwo Naukowe UAM, 1993), p. 76.

16. Bernard Shaw, *Back to Methuselah* (New York: Penguin, 1962), p. 239.

17. Witkacy, "On Pure Form," *Aesthetics in Twentieth-Century Poland*, ed. and trans. Jean G. Harrell and Alina Wierzbianska (Lewisburg: Bucknell University Press, 1973), p. 55.

18. Stanley Weintraub, "The Avant-Garde Shaw," *Bernard Shaw's Plays*, ed. Warren S. Smith (New York, London: W. W. Norton, 1970), p. 348.

19. Gerould, p. 208.

J. L. Wisenthal

SHAW'S UTOPIAS

I

It is an unfortunate circumstance that this prodigious subject should have been left, in our arrangements, to unaided private enterprise. Most of our previous researches have been heavily subsidised by the State, which provides many of our members with a genteel competence and an endowed leisure highly favorable to historical research and unhastened digestion of its fruits. On me, who have neither competence nor leisure, has fallen the heaviest burden.

The date is 25 May 1887, the place Hampstead Library in London. The speaker is Bernard Shaw, art and music critic, book reviewer, and well-known public speaker and member of the Fabian Society. He is beginning a lecture on "Utopias" to his fellow-members of the Hampstead Historic Club,[1] a lecture that is now being published for the first time (below, pages 65–80).

Shaw tells his audience that when he accepted the job of talking about utopias he thought the only ones to be dealt with were Thomas More's *Utopia* and Samuel Butler's *Erewhon*, "and I carefully abstained from discovering any fresh ones. But neither my friends nor my own aroused memory refrained from constant suggestion; and diligently as I have sought oblivion, I cannot pretend that I am not bound to deal also with . . ."—and here he reels off a long list of utopian works, from Aristophanes to Edward Bulwer-Lytton's 1871 novel *The Coming Race* and "the prospectus of the Society of the New Life," the precursor of the Fabian Society. "In order to obtain a thorough knowledge of the institutions suggested in these works, it is necessary to read them all carefully through; and I strongly recommend that course to those of you who may be sufficiently interested. I hope to do so myself in the course of time: meanwhile, having within the last few days sampled a few of the most accessible of them, I propose to read the few hasty notes that have occurred to me during the process."[2]

Most of the subsequent lecture is devoted to summaries and discussion of four utopias: More's *Utopia* (1516), Tomasso Campanella's *City of the Sun* (*La Città del Sole,* written in 1602), Francis Bacon's *New Atlantis* (1627), and Michel de Montaigne's essay "Of the Cannibals" ("Des Cannibales," 1580). Characteristically, Shaw draws attention to economic issues and to contemporary late-nineteenth-century analogies. The utopia that he judges most favorably is that of Thomas More. "The first effect of reading More's work," Shaw's discussion of it begins, "is to remove all surprise at the fact that he was eventually beheaded by Henry VIII. The second is a melancholy reflection on how much of what modern socialists call the new gospel is an old gospel which has not gained so much in the way of intelligent exposition as might have been expected. More had much of the modern socialist in him." Then, after a fairly extended account of More's *Utopia,* Shaw turns to Campanella's *City of the Sun.* "On the whole," this section of the lecture concludes, "Campanella shews himself far less able to digest his mass of 16th century learning than More. More wrote like a realist, a man of the world, and a statesman: Campanella like a romancer, a priest and a faddist." The judgment at the end of the section on Bacon's *New Atlantis* is even more hostile: "On the whole, it is pretty evident that Bacon had not in him the moral starch that stiffened Campanella on the rack and More at the stake. The New Atlantis confirms his reputation as a venal timeserver." The discussion of Montaigne's "Of the Cannibals" includes the judgment that "Montaigne does not . . . improve on More. He is shrewd, audacious, and amusing; but he shirks the labor problem, and has neither More's broad grasp nor Campanella's earnestness." Shaw then quotes Gonzalo's utopian speech in Act II of *The Tempest,* which Shakespeare derived from "Of the Cannibals"; mentions James Harrington's *Oceana,* which he dismisses as "indescribable and indiscutable"; and concludes with a brief dismissive paragraph on Swift's *Gulliver's Travels.*

II

For about fifteen years after this 1887 lecture Shaw's interest in utopias seems to have receded, so that the lecture provides an anticipatory glimpse of his engagement with issues that became important to him in the twentieth century. As a dramatist, Shaw began the new century with three plays that explore, in varying ways, relationships between our present world and Heaven: *Man and Superman, John Bull's Other Island,* and *Major Barbara.* Heaven, Shaw told his listeners in 1887, was his own first version of utopia. "The Utopia with which I first became acquainted is the heaven of the Evangelicals, a region so extremely repugnant to my constitution that I lost faith in its reality with a distinct sense of relief." Shaw said he felt that he "was not good enough for it, or that it was not bad enough for me; and I feel much the same with respect to the Utopias of More, Bacon & Campanella." This may seem to contradict the positive Heaven of *Man and Superman,* but in that play it is not really Heaven that is the traditional utopia.

In the 1887 lecture Shaw excluded Hell from consideration as "out of our historical scope; and so I dismiss it, and with it all obligation to deal with the Inferno, Purgatorio & Paradiso of Dante, though these, too, are in their way Utopias." The suggestion here that Dante's *Inferno* is in its way a utopia points toward *Man and Superman,* for in the dream sequence of Act III it is Hell rather than Heaven that is closest to traditional ideas of utopia. *Man and Superman*'s conception of a hedonist, bodiless utopia as Hell is incipient in the 1887 lecture, especially in the lecture's argument that Heaven "is outside the domain of economics, since where there is neither death nor digestion, nor marriage nor birth, nor expenditure, nor recuperation, there can of course be neither wealth nor production, nor distribution; and so, no economics." Compare this with Don Juan's contrast between Hell and Earth, where "hunger and cold and thirst, age and decay and disease, death above all" make men and women slaves of reality. But in Hell all is different. "There are no social questions here, no political questions, no religious questions, best of all, perhaps, no sanitary questions" (2:650). These two passages, written fifteen years apart, seem to me strikingly similar—even Juan's prose rhythms are partly anticipated in the 1887 lecture. And in the 1902[3] Hell, as in the 1887 Heaven, we have a state of being that is drained of life's challenging, invigorating realities. Shaw the lecturer noted that More's Utopians were "in the main Epicureans and Hedonists," and Shaw the dramatist has characters describe Hell as "a place where you have nothing to do but amuse yourself," and as "the home of the unreal and of the seekers for happiness" (2: 642–43, 650). The inadequacy of utopias, which is suggested in the lecture, is fully explored in the play, where Utopia is Hell.

There is another crucial element of *Man and Superman* that is anticipated in the "Utopias" lecture. In Campanella's *City of the Sun,* Shaw told his listeners, "the race is bred by selection on scientific principles, without regard to the inclinations of the parties concerned." Campanella's account of the Solarians' breeding habits is much like Don Juan's prediction that "[t]he great central purpose of breeding the race . . . will break through into clear sunlight as a purpose no longer to be confused with the gratification of personal fancies" (2:674), and like Tanner's eugenic proposals in his Revolutionist's Handbook. The relevant passage from Campanella, in the Victorian translation that Shaw used, runs as follows:

> Moreover, the race is managed for the good of the commonwealth and not of private individuals, and the magistrates must be obeyed. They deny what we hold—viz., that it is natural to man to recognize his offspring and to educate them, and to use his wife and house and children as his own. For they say that children are bred for the preservation of the species and not for individual pleasure, as St. Thomas also asserts. Therefore the breeding of children has reference to the commonwealth and not to individuals, except in so far as they are constituents of the commonwealth.[4]

In his lecture, when Shaw quotes the sentence denying that it is natural to man to recognize his offspring, he adds triumphantly "Here Campanella distinctly anticipates *me*," and he then quotes with great approval Campanella's views on the education of children. Campanella distinctly anticipates the 1887 Shaw, and also the later author of *Man and Superman*.

In *Man and Superman*, Tanner dreams of Heaven—or dreams of himself as Don Juan speculating about Heaven. Dreams of Heaven are also of central importance in Shaw's next play, *John Bull's Other Island*. The serious utopian in this work is Peter Keegan, the unfrocked priest for whom contemporary Ireland is Hell. Like Shakespeare's Gonzalo, he dreams of "this isle" as "th' commonwealth" in which distinctions disappear and oppositions are resolved. "In my dreams," he proclaims, Heaven

> is a country where the State is the Church and the Church the people: three in one and one in three. It is a commonwealth in which work is play and play is life: three in one and one in three. It is a temple in which the priest is the worshipper and the worshipper the worshipped: three in one and one in three. It is a godhead in which all life is human and all humanity divine: three in one and one in three. It is, in short, the dream of a madman.

This is one dream of Heaven in *John Bull's Other Island*. It comes in response to a very different one: the childish, conventional notion expressed by the Philistine English businessman Tom Broadbent: "Once, when I was a small kid, I dreamt I was in heaven. . . . It was a sort of pale blue satin place, with all the pious old ladies in our congregation sitting as if they were at a service; and there was some awful person in the study at the other side of the hall. I didnt enjoy it, you know" (2:1021). Here is almost exactly the dream of Heaven that Shaw presented as his own in the 1887 lecture:

> In Bunyan's famous dream, [Heaven] was a street of gold between rows of shining ones who had entered into the joys of their Lord. In a dream which occurred to myself at an early age, it presented itself as a small square apartment with walls of pearl coloured satin. A low, bent shelf, upholstered in the same material, went round the room, and on this shelf were seated many pious persons whom I had seen in church. They wore white chemises and wings, and I had no doubt that they felt at home there and were in no danger. I, also sitting on the shelf with my ankles dangling and in my ordinary damaged garb, was filled with fears, because I knew that I should presently be brought up for judgment by the recording angel before some awful person in the next room; and I had good private reasons for anticipating that my career would not be found up to the mark. I cannot help thinking it odd that on the only occasion on which I ever dreamt myself in heaven, I was glad when I woke.

In Shaw's own dream and in Broadbent's there are the same satin, the same pious people from church, and "some awful person" (the phase remains identical) in a nearby room. In both cases, too, the dreamer does not find the oneiric experience of Heaven an enjoyable one. It is notable in the two speeches from *John Bull's Other Island* that each version of utopia concludes with a sentence that undercuts what has gone before; Broadbent did not enjoy his dream, and Keegan dismisses his as the dream of a madman.

Broadbent, however, has another kind of utopia on his mind in *John Bull's Other Island*. He raises it in his Act I encounter with the stage Irishman Tim Haffigan.

BROADBENT. Have you ever heard of Garden City?
TIM [*doubtfully*] D'ye mane Heavn?
BROADBENT. Heaven! No: it's near Hitchin. If you can spare half an hour I'll go into it with you.

TIM. I tell you hwat. Gimme a prospectus. Lemmy take it home
and reflect on it.
BROADBENT. Youre quite right: I will. [*He gives him a copy of
Ebenezer Howard's book, and several pamphlets*]. You understand that
the map of the city—the circular construction—is only a suggestion. (2:899)

Then in the final act Broadbent declares that he will establish such a
utopia in Ireland: "I shall bring money here: I shall raise wages: I shall
found public institutions: a library, a Polytechnic (undenominational, of
course), a gymnasium, a cricket club, perhaps an art school. I shall make
a Garden city of Rosscullen." This utopian dream, too, is undermined
in the play, when Keegan scornfully rejects it as a clean and orderly
place of torment. (2:1015)[5]

In *Major Barbara*, Broadbent's Garden City utopia is actually represented on the stage, in the second part of Act III. *"Perivale St Andrews lies
between two Middlesex hills, half climbing the northern one. It is an almost
smokeless town of white walls, roofs of narrow green slates or red tiles, tall trees,
domes, campaniles, and slender chimney shafts, beautifully situated and beautiful
in itself"* (3:157). This "spotlessly clean and beautiful hillside town" (as
Undershaft calls it [3:154]) seems to be very much in the tradition of
utopian fiction, and one is reminded of previous utopias by the fact that
travelers from our world (i.e., the West End world of the audience) are
astonished by the amenities of this ideal community, and have an
audience with the Ruler of the place.[6] But this utopia, like the Hell of
Man and Superman, will not do. Not only is it a munitions factory,
producing weapons of death and destruction, but it satisfies the needs
of the body only and leaves the soul undeveloped. In 1887, Shaw drew
attention to a somewhat similar limitation in More's Utopia, where "The
people are happy, healthy, well-to-do, and wise; but as they are happy
whether they like it or not, one cannot help feeling, with Mark Tapley
[in Dickens's *Martin Chuzzlewit*], that there is no credit in being jolly
under the circumstances, and that life in Utopia, after all, must have
been rather flat." It is not enough to be happy, healthy, and well-to-do,
and Perivale St. Andrews proves to be the mere basis for Barbara's
utopian dreams, rather than the ideal society that the descriptive stage
direction quoted above might suggest.

One of the characteristics of Campanella's utopians that Shaw mentions in the 1887 lecture is that "Their average lifetime is a hundred
years." The actual passage that Shaw read in *The City of the Sun* goes a
bit further: "The length of their lives is generally one hundred years,
but often they reach two hundred."[7] Here is another link between this
early lecture and the utopias of Shaw's plays. In 1944 Shaw recalled

that "I contributed my Utopia in a batch of plays entitled Back To Methuselah,"[8] and the central characteristic of this utopia is the extension of the human life-span. *Back to Methuselah* derives from a variety of previous utopian works, including Plato's *Republic*, Swift's *Gulliver's Travels*, and Mozart's *Die Zauberflöte* (Sarastro's idealized realm in Act II). The most direct borrowing is from Bulwer-Lytton's novel *The Coming Race*, which Shaw mentioned but did not discuss in his lecture. Shaw talks about this borrowing in *Everybody's Political What's What?* and says that he adapted Bulwer-Lytton's powerful substance Vril in creating the Awe "as a means by which my Coming Race kept the Yahoos in subjection."[9] The fourth part of *Back to Methuselah, Tragedy of an Elderly Gentleman*, draws on *The Coming Race* in many ways, including the name of the traveler's guide (Zee in Bulwer-Lytton, Zoo in Shaw), the idea that the utopians will destroy ordinary existing humanity, and even the Long-Livers' way of talking about the primitive past: "'Pardon me,' answered Aph-Lin: 'in what we call the Wrangling or Philosophical Period of History, which was at its height about seven thousand years ago, there was a very distinguished naturalist. . . .'"[10] Bulwer-Lytton's utopians, the Vril-ya, also enjoy a greater longevity than we do. The narrator reports that "the average duration of life amongst them . . . very considerably exceeded the term allotted to us on the upper earth. What seventy years are to us, one hundred years are to them."[11]

The utopias in the last two parts of *Back to Methuselah—Tragedy of an Elderly Gentleman* and *As Far as Thought Can Reach*—are not failures, but nor are they sufficient. They are undoubtedly superior to our primitive way of living (or that is the assumption that Shaw's pentateuch makes), but this does not mean that they are ideal societies made up of perfected human beings. For in *Back to Methuselah* there can be no ideal world, in that "As there is no limit to power and knowledge there can be no end" (*The Gospel of the Brothers Barnabas*, 5:423).

The attempted utopia in *The Simpleton of the Unexpected Isles*, on the other hand, is more distinctly and explicitly a failure. "Twenty years ago," Sir Charles Farwaters explains in Act I, "my wife and I, with Mr and Mrs Hyering, joined this eastern gentleman and his colleague in a eugenic experiment. Its object was to try out the result of a biological blend of the flesh and spirit of the west with the flesh and spirit of the east. We formed a family of six parents." The results of this utopian experiment, this group marriage of the two English couples and the Eastern priest and priestess Pra and Prola, have been disappointing: only four children, and these are without any moral conscience (6:794–96). Prola has taught the children "a game called the heavenly parliament in which all of them told tales and added them to the general stock until a fairyland was built up, with laws and religious rituals, and finally

a great institution which they called the Superfamily." But this utopian
fiction comes to nothing. "Our dream of founding a millennial world
culture," Pra concedes some years later in the next act, "has ended in a
single little household with four children, wonderful and beautiful, but
sterile. . . . The coming race will not be like them. . . . [W]e two have
made a precious mess of our job of producing the coming race by a
mixture of east and west" (6:798, 807, 838). The suggestion in *The
Simpleton of the Unexpected Isles* is that all utopian experiments are bound
to fail, because they try to impose a mechanical regularity on the
unexpectedness of life. Prola refuses to despair over the failure of the
eugenic experiment:

> Well, a dead hobby horse is not the end of the world. Remember:
> we are in the Unexpected Isles; and in the Unexpected Isles all
> plans fail. So much the better: plans are only jigsaw puzzles: one
> gets tired of them long before one can piece them together.
> There are still a million lives beyond all the Utopias and the
> Millenniums and the rest of the jigsaw puzzles: I am a woman
> and I know it. Let men despair and become cynics and pessi-
> mists because in the Unexpected Isles all their little plans fail:
> women will never let go their hold on life. We are not here to
> fulfil prophecies and fit ourselves into puzzles, but to wrestle
> with life as it comes. And it never comes as we expect it to come.
> . . . We shall plan commonwealths when our empires have
> brought us to the brink of destruction; but our plans will still
> lead us to the Unexpected Isles.

And Pra sees that he "must continue to strive for more knowledge and
more power," that change and unexpectedness are the glorious realities
of life (6:839–40). This continuing pursuit of knowledge and power is
also the central subject of Shaw's last utopia, *Farfetched Fables*, written in
his nineties. Each of the six fables dramatizes a stage in life's development, and the implication is that no stage will ever represent a final
consummation.

My emphasis on the inadequacy or incompleteness of Shaw's utopias
might provoke a reference to his enthusiastic endorsement of Stalin's
U.S.S.R. It is true that accounts of Shaw's 1931 visit to the U.S.S.R. read
like works of utopian fiction: the amazed visitor from the inferior
outside world discovers the quality of life in utopia, and marvels at the
social arrangements—and there is even the interview with the Ruler.
Shaw's comment in a newspaper report on his return to England brings
to mind Gulliver's feelings on his return home from the country of the
Houyhnhnms, for example, or Bulwer-Lytton's narrator's attitudes after

returning from the land of the Vril-ya, or the narrator of William Morris's *News from Nowhere* upon awakening from his dream: "It is torture," Shaw declared, "to get back again after being in Soviet land. After you have seen Bolshevism on the spot there can be no doubt but that capitalism is doomed."[12] Shaw was of course not totally uncritical of the U.S.S.R., but his desire to *épater le bourgeois* and also his longing as a political thinker for a utopia that is some-place rather than no-place did frequently lead him to treat the Soviet Union in utopian terms. This is Shaw as a political commentator, however, and my point is that as a *dramatist* he resists the construction of utopias. I think it reveals a good deal about Shaw as a dramatist that all through the period when his mind was so much on the Soviet experiment he included so little on this subject in his plays.[13] There is the Soviet Commissar in *Geneva*, but no dramatic representation of Stalin (as there are of Mussolini, Franco, and Hitler), and not much attention to the U.S.S.R. in this political extravaganza about the 1930s. in *Too True to Be Good* Private Meek tells his Colonel that everyone is asking for a visa for Beotia: "The Union of Federated Sensible Societies, sir. The U.F.S.S. Everybody wants to go there now, sir." But no one in the play does go there, and the Colonel concludes that "there is nothing for it but to return to our own country" (6:523–24). Beotia also appears in the one-act "Revolutionary Romance-let" that Shaw wrote a month after Lenin's Bolshevik revolution. *Anna-janska, the Bolshevik Empress* is set in a fictional U.S.S.R. (or emergent U.S.S.R.), but while Beotia, according to one of several conflicting military orders, "wishes to establish the Kingdom of Heaven on Earth throughout the universe" (5:245), the country in the play is the scene of civil war rather than utopian achievements. *The Millionairess*, written three years after Shaw's visit to the U.S.S.R., includes an alternative ending for use in Russia and in countries with communist sympathies. In this scene Epifania rhapsodizes about emigrating to Russia, but like Barbara Undershaft she plans to move to utopia in order to improve it: "Russia needs managing women like me. . . . I swear that before I have been twenty years in Russia every Russian baby shall weigh five pounds heavier and every Russian man and woman live ten years longer." And as in *Too True to Be Good*, it turns out that none of the characters will go to the U.S.S.R.; the Doctor persuades Epifania to stay at home and "make the British Empire a Soviet republic" (6:968).

III

In the Preface that Shaw wrote in 1930 for the deleted part of *Back to Methuselah*, "A Glimpse of the Domesticity of Franklyn Barnabas," he speaks of the whole range of political conduct "which lies between the plague-stricken city's policy of 'Let us eat and drink; for tomorrow we die' and the long-sighted and profound policies of the earthly paradises of More, Morris, Wells, and all the other Utopians" (5:632). In the plays themselves, however, the treatment of earthly paradises is not as positive as this. In the context of Shaw's plays, a more representative judgment might be that of the English clergyman in *The Simpleton of the Unexpected Isles:* "Damn and blast all these tropical paradises" (6:801). This, after all, is the view implied in the use of the word "Hell" to designate the utopian paradise in *Man and Superman,* and we have seen that in Shaw's plays (with the possible, partial exception of the very late *Farfetched Fables*) utopias are always undercut in one way or another. The main reason for this, I think, is that a thorough utopia, a fully realized ideal society of the sort described by More, Campanella, Bulwer-Lytton, Morris, et al. leaves no room for the unexpected and for change. The anti-utopian world-view of Shaw's plays is encapsulated in another speech from *The Simpleton,* by the Angel who arrives in Act II to signify the arrival of the Day of Judgment. When it comes time for him to leave, he explains that he needs a parapet to take off from: "Like the albatross, I cannot rise from the ground without great difficulty. An angel is far from being the perfect organism you imagine. There is always something better" (6:826). In *Back to Methuselah,* the Ancients in *As Far as Thought Can Reach* are far from being the perfect organisms that a reader of utopias might imagine. There is always something better, and we never know exactly what it is. A utopia means fulfillment, and Shaw wrote to Ellen Terry in 1896 that he dreaded success. "To have succeeded is to have finished one's business on earth. . . . I like a state of continual *becoming,* with a goal in front and not behind."[14] Twenty-five years later, in the great concluding speech of *Back to Methuselah,* Lilith expresses this attitude as a warning to humankind: "I say, let them dread, of all things, stagnation" (5:630). Thus the utopian who believes that the ideal society has been realized is violating the essentially changeful nature of life. Utopias represent a state of stagnation.

In leaving no room for the unexpected and for change, utopias leave no room for drama. In the serene state of Vril-ya society in Bulwer-Lytton's novel *The Coming Race,* there is no literature, and when the narrator expresses surprise at this lack, his host explains: "Do you not perceive that a literature such as you mean would be wholly incompatible with that perfection of social or political felicity at which you do us the honour to think we have arrived?"[15] Utopian drama would be non-existent, or it would be no good—the kind of mindless, unchallenging drama that Shaw railed against as a theater critic in the 1890s. "Here," Don Juan exclaims about Hell in *Man and Superman,* "there is nothing but love and beauty. Ugh! it is like sitting for all eternity at the first act of a fashionable play, before the complications begin" (2:682). For Prola in *The Simpleton of the Unexpected Isles,* utopias are a kind of jigsaw puzzle, and for Shaw the well-made play is just a jigsaw puzzle. A utopia is a well-made society, the political equivalent of the stagnant dramatic form of Scribe and Sardou. Thus Shaw's plays, in their very form, reject the concept of utopia and embrace the spontaneous and unexpected. There is in Shaw's work a deep rejection of utopian finality, and this suspicion of utopias—along with a lively interest in the subject—is an attitude that one can trace right back to the Hampstead Library on 25 May 1887.

Notes

1. Bernard Shaw, *The Diaries 1885–1897,* ed. Stanley Weintraub (University Park and London: Penn State University Press, 1986), 1: 272. The twenty-page holograph manuscript of the lecture is in the Houghton Library at Harvard University (MS Eng 1046.6), by whose permission it is published here. I am indebted to Dan H. Laurence for making me aware of the lecture and arranging for me to borrow a photocopy from the Dan H. Laurence Collection at the University of Guelph Library, to whom I am also grateful for the loan.

2. This rhetorical jest of parading an impressive list of authorities and then implicitly acknowledging that one has not read them oneself is to be found twelve years later in Shaw's Programme Note for *Caesar and Cleopatra (Collected Plays with Their Prefaces,* ed. Dan H. Laurence [London: Max Reinhardt, 1970–74], 2:306). All my references to Shaw's plays are from this edition.

3. The writing of *Man and Superman* was completed in June 1902 (2: 491).

4. Tomasso Campanella, *The City of the Sun,* in *Ideal Commonwealths,* intro. Henry Morley (London: George Routledge and Sons, 1885), pp. 235–36. Cf. an earlier passage in Campanella's book, in which we are told that Love, one of the rulers of the utopian society, "is foremost in attending to the charge of the race. He sees that men and women are so joined together, that they bring forth the best offspring. Indeed, they laugh at us who exhibit a studious care for our breed of horses and dogs, but neglect the breeding of human beings" (p. 224). Shaw did not have access to all that Campanella had to say about selective breeding, for the 1885 translation he used omits several pages of detail about the Solarians' eugenic arrangements for selective breeding; see *La Città del Sole: Dialogo Poetico,* trans. and ed. Daniel J. Donno (Berkeley: University of California Press, 1981), pp. 20, 53–59. Another of the utopias that Shaw discusses in his lecture, Bacon's *New Atlantis,* practices the eugenic breeding of animals; see *The Works of Francis Bacon,* Vol. 3, ed. James Spedding et al. (London: Longmans, 1870), p. 159.

5. In More's *Utopia,* incidentally, the main city, Amaurote, could be considered a Garden City; see "Of the Cities and Namely of Amaurote" in the Second Book.

6. Compare the Hell Scene in *Man and Superman,* where there is also the traveler from our world (Doña Ana), and the interview with the Ruler who explains the superiority of his utopian society.

7. *Ideal Commonwealths*, p. 250. The original text goes further still: "Vivono almeno cento anni, al più centosettanta o ducento al rarissimo"—"They live at least a hundred years, most of them reaching a hundred and seventy and a rare few reaching two hundred years" (*La Città del Sole*, ed. Donno, pp. 88–89).

8. *Everybody's Political What's What?* (London: Constable, 1944), p. 286.

9. Ibid., p. 287.

10. Edward Bulwer-Lytton, *The Coming Race* (1871; London: George Routledge and Sons, 1874), p. 121 (Chapter 16). For a discussion of connections between *The Coming Race* and *Back to Methuselah*, see B. G. Knepper, "Shaw's Debt to *The Coming Race*," *Journal of Modern Literature* 1 (1970–71): 339–53. Knepper notes that in April 1887 Shaw "delivered a lecture on fiction in which he praised Lytton's book in glowing terms" (p. 340). Comments on the relevance of *The Coming Race* to *Back to Methuselah*, and investigation of other utopian elements in Shaw's plays, are to be found in two articles in a special number of the *Shaw Review* on "G.B.S. and Science-Fiction" (vol. 16, May 1973): J.O. Bailey, "Shaw's Life Force and Science Fiction" (pp. 48–58), and Susan Ablon Cole, "The Evolutionary Fantasy: Shaw and Utopian Fiction" (pp. 89–97).

11. *The Coming Race*, p. 129 (Chapter 17); see also pp. 226–27 (Chapter 26).

12. Quoted (from the *Observer*) in T. F. Evans, "Myopia or Utopia: Shaw in Russia," *SHAW* 5 (1985): 125–45 (the quotation is on p. 138). One can read Evans's whole account of the 1931 visit to the U.S.S.R. in the light of utopian fiction.

13. "Some may have hoped," says T. F. Evans, "that, whatever the effect of the Russian experience on the politician and the economist, there might have been some profitable consequences for the dramatist. It was not to be" (p. 140).

14. *Collected Letters 1874–1897*, ed. Dan H. Laurence (New York: Dodd, Mead, 1965), p. 645. "And never stagnate," Shaw advised Ellen Terry a few months later. "Life is a constant becoming: all stages lead to the beginning of others" (p. 722).

15. *The Coming Race*, p. 133 (Chapter 17).

Bernard Shaw

UTOPIAS

[PROVENANCE: Unsigned holograph manuscript, written and extensively revised in ink on 21 leaves foliated 325 to 345, dated at the end of the text "Read to the Hampstead Historical Club. 25ᵗʰ May 1887." The Houghton Library, Harvard University (shelf mark MS Eng 1046.6). © 1997 The Trustees of the British Museum, The Governors and Guardians of the National Gallery of Ireland, and The Royal Academy of Dramatic Art. Published by permission of the Shaw Estate and by permission of the Houghton Library, Harvard University.

NOTE ON THE TEXT: Spelling and punctuation follow Shaw's usage throughout except for silent correction of obvious omissions (such as a missing period at the end of a sentence or an omitted quotation mark) and for placing commas and periods within closing quotation marks.

I am grateful to Dan H. Laurence, John Wardrop, Stanley Weintraub, and J. L. Wisenthal for their sharp-eyed scrutiny of doubtful readings and their invaluable suggestions.—F.D.C.]

It is an unfortunate circumstance that this prodigious subject should have been left, in our arrangements, to unaided private enterprise. Most of our previous researches have been heavily subsidised by the State, which provides many of our members with a genteel competence and an endowed leisure highly favorable to historical research and unhastened digestion of its fruits. On me, who have neither competence nor leisure, has fallen the heaviest burden.[1] When I accepted it I thought that the only Utopias to be dealt with were Sir Thomas More's and "Erewhon"; and I carefully abstained from discovering any fresh ones. But neither my friends nor my own aroused memory refrained from constant suggestion; and diligently as I have sought oblivion, I cannot pretend that I am not bound to deal also with the fantastic cloud nations of Aristophanes, Rabelais, Montaigne's Cannibals, Gonzalo's Utopia in Shakspere's Tempest, Bacon's New Atlantis, Sir Philip Sidney's "Arcadia," Campanella's City of the Sun, James Harrington's "Oceana," Gulliver's Travels, Goethe's Wilhelm Meister and the second part of Faust, Morelly's "Basiliade," Babeuf's "Society of Equals," Fourier's Phalanstères, Cabet's "Voyage to Icaria," Marla's Universal Co-operation, Peacock's "Crotchet Castle," Lord Lytton's "Coming Race" and the prospectus of the Society of the New Life.[2] In order to obtain a thorough knowledge of the institutions suggested in these works, it is necessary to read them all carefully through; and I strongly recommend that course to those of you who may be sufficiently interested. I hope to do so myself in the course of time: meanwhile, having within the last few days sampled a few of the most accessible of them, I propose to read the few hasty notes that have occurred to me during the process.

The Utopia with which I first became acquainted is the heaven of the Evangelicals, a region so extremely repugnant to my constitution that I lost faith in its reality with a distinct sense of relief. I felt that I was not good enough for it, or that it was not bad enough for me; and I feel much the same with respect to the Utopias of More, Bacon & Campanella. I believe my position is a representative one; and that it may be taken as a rule that when a man builds himself a fanciful best of all possible worlds[3] in which to fly from the miseries of the real one, he invariably does what all amateur architects do—makes it quite unfit for himself to live in. There are in the Bible certain descriptions of heaven which run into considerable detail; but it may be doubted whether heaven is not to each individual a conception only partly prompted by the scripture, the rest being spontaneously imagined. In Bunyan's famous dream, it was a street of gold between rows of shining ones who had entered into the joys of their Lord.[4] In a dream which occurred to myself at an early age, it presented itself as a small square apartment with walls of pearl coloured satin. A low, bent* shelf, upholstered in the same material, went round the room, and on this shelf were seated many pious persons whom I had seen in church. They wore white chemises and wings, and I had no doubt that they felt at home there and were in no danger. I, also sitting on the shelf with my ankles dangling and in my ordinary damaged garb, was filled with fears, because I knew that I should presently be brought up for judgment by the recording angel before some awful person in the next room; and I had good private reasons for anticipating that my career would not be found up to the mark. I cannot help thinking it odd that on the only occasion on which

---

*Shaw uses "bent" in its connotation of "curved."

I ever dreamt myself in heaven, I was glad when I woke. I also dreamt
once that I was in hell; but I remember nothing about that except that
two of my uncles were there and that it did not hurt. In my waking
hours I thought of heaven as a part of the sky where the people were
dressed in white, had golden harps, did not eat or drink or learn lessons,
and were wholly preoccupied in being intensely good. All this is childish
and personal; but it is, I believe, typical. If I am right, then heaven is
outside the domain of economics, since where there is neither death nor
digestion, nor marriage nor birth, nor expenditure, nor recuperation,
there can of course be neither wealth nor production, nor distribution;
and so, no economics. There is increase of population by immigration,
it is true; but the immigrants are stomachless, the space at their disposal
unlimited, and the rate of increase extremely slow. Even in the Paynim
heaven, where wine and women were part of a paradise to which warrior
heroes would have frankly declined to go without them, these were
phantom luxuries, involving no labor. Heaven, in fact, is always a place
where labour and decay are eliminated from the conditions of existence;
and hence the only people who can really fix their conception of Heaven
without foreseeing infinite emptiness and boredom, have been those
mystics who, like Porph[y]ry & Plotinus,[5] aspired to an endless ecstasy of
contemplation. Heaven, in the light of modern science, thus assumes a
hypnotic interest, which is apart from the purposes of this paper. Hell is
equally out of our historical scope; and so I dismiss it, and with it all
obligation to deal with the Inferno, Purgatorio & Paradiso of Dante,
though these, too, are in their way Utopias.

I omit Aristophanes, as we left him behind when we skipped from
Plato to early Christianity. Finding that Sir Thomas More lived before
Bacon[6]—a fact of which I was previously unaware, having always sup-
posed that Bacon invented gunpowder, which was certainly known to
More—I take his Utopia to begin with.

The first effect of reading More's work is to remove all surprise at the
fact that he was eventually beheaded by Henry VIII. The second is a
melancholy reflection on how much of what modern socialists call the
new gospel is an old gospel which has not gained so much in the way of
intelligent exposition as might have been expected. More had much of
the modern socialist in him. Nowhere does this appear more strikingly
than in the passages where, after a weighty and generous denunciation
of the barbarity of indiscriminate capital punishment, he proceeds to
explain that in his ideal commonwealth, every infraction of his regulations shall be punished by death, whilst the bourgeois capital code shall
be entirely annulled. He gives two reasons for with[h]olding the death
penalty from slight offences. The first—that God has forbidden us to
kill—is practically no reason at all. The second is valid and scientific,

and was afterwards put forward by Beccaria.[7] It is, that men will commit
murder in order to escape capture if they have already incurred the
worst that can be done to them. As well be hung for a sheep as a lamb.
More's method of dealing with criminals is to set them to compulsory
useful labor, with certain prospects of social rehabilitation dependent on
good conduct. Of the modern claims of private enterprise to be pro-
tected against the competition of industries organized in prisons or
elsewhere by the state, he knew nothing.

   More's fiction, like most of its kind, is presented in the form of a
traveller's tale. Raphael Hythloday, who describes Utopia, is plain and
direct throughout in holding it up as a practicable model of wise
government and rational institutions. The book has nothing of the
ferocious sarcasm and pessimism of Swift: Master Hythloday only once
indulges in a brief passage of banter too mild to be called satire; and his
pessimism is limited to courts, which he regards as morally rotten
beyond all help from good counsel, and to kings, whom he describes as
"corrupted from their childhood with false notions." I shall skip the
mass of geographical and other detail by which More gives verisimilitude
to his fable, and go on to the institutions of the island of Utopia, which
have led Raphael Hythloday to the opinion expressed in these words.
"To speak plainly my real sentiments, I must freely own that as long as
there is any property, and while money is the standard of all other
things, I cannot think that a nation can be governed either justly or
happily: not justly, because the best things will fall to the share of the
worst men; not happily, because all things will be divided among a few
[and even these are not in all respects happy],* the rest being left to be
absolutely miserable." Here the clause "while money is the standard of
all other things" does not necessarily imply a mercantilist error as to the
function of money: it may only mean "whilst income is the measure of
respectability." In Utopia the inhabitants are taught to despise the
precious metals, which they possess in great abundance, but use only for
bribing foreigners. In Campanella's City of the Sun the citizens do the
same. As the gold and silver are obtained in exchange for exported
surplus produce, great stores of it accumulate; for it does not occur to
the Utopians to shorten the working day and so cut off the surplus
produce which brings the despised metal in. However, since the treasure
has a use in war and diplomacy, its accumulation is not exactly senseless.
It is not used in internal trade, because there is no exchange. Property
does not exist: communism is the order of society. But it is the communism of the Platonian republic; for there are slaves; and though More

---

*The brackets are Shaw's. Throughout the manuscript, Shaw does not distinguish between
square brackets and curved parentheses.

tells us that prisoners of war and criminals are made slaves, it is not clear
that he did not assume a natural slave caste as well. By them he meets
the great individualist challenge, "Who is to do the dirty work?" Answer,
of course: the slaves. The social regulations are of the Comtist kind. The
people are happy, healthy, well-to-do, and wise; but as they are happy
whether they like it or not, one cannot help feeling, with Mark Tapley,[8]
that there is no credit in being jolly under the circumstances, and that
life in Utopia, after all, must have been rather flat. To be rich because
you want nothing, and poor because you have nothing, is delicious from
a vagabond point of view. Still, one can hardly feel like a vagabond when
state regulated down to the number of times one must wash one's shirt.
[In Campanella's City of the Sun, by the bye, it was once a month.]*
The only other point of view which commands the conception is the
monastic one; and that is really the one in More's mind. Community of
goods, compulsory labor, and wise laws are his simple receipt for Utopia
making; but they are no solution for the social problem in modern life.
I therefore omit the tempting passages in which More so eloquently
anticipates the quarrel of modern socialism with individualistic society.

Utopia is like Gower St or Denbigh St, Pimlico, inasmuch as "the
buildings are so uniform that a whole side of a street looks like one
house." The rent arising from advantage of site is settled by a decennial
jubilee at which the inhabitants change houses by lot. The social unit is
the family, within which the parental head has absolute power. Thirty
families form a constituency, which elects every year a Syphogrant.
Every ten Syphogrants annually elect a Tranibor. The head of the State
is a Prince, elected by the whole body of Syphogrants from four
candidates nominated by the four divisions of the city. The voting is
secret; everybody takes oath to vote for the best man; and the Prince
rules for life unless "removed upon suspicion of some design to enslave
the people." The removal procedure is not described. Talking politics is
a capital offence; for "it is death for any to meet and consult concerning
the state, unless it be either in their ordinary council, or in the assembly
of the whole body of the people." In council nothing is debated until
the day after it is mooted, lest honorable members should express
rash opinions, and stick to them afterwards from "a perverse and
preposterous sort of shame" of being inconsistent. There are public
lectures every morning before daybreak; but attendance is not compulsory except upon literary men.

The people—both sexes alike—work six hours a day, 3 before dinner
and 3 after; and they sleep 8 hours. During the rest of the time they do
what they like: "yet," says the narrative, "they are not to abuse that

*The brackets are Shaw's.

interval to luxury and idleness." Each person chooses his own occupation, usually his father's, which he learns at home; but if he prefers
another, he is shifted to some family which pursues that other. All wear
clothes of the same sort; and the fashion never changes: the only
distinctions being between men and women and between married and
single. A suit of clothes lasts seven years. Conversation, lectures, music,
and reading are the common pastimes. The numbers of families and of
members of families are limited between maxima & minima. The surplus population emigrates and colonizes. If the natives of the colonized
parts object, the Utopians kill them on the ground that "every man has
by the law of Nature a right to such a waste portion of the earth as is
necessary for his subsistence," thus foreshadowing our own Imperial
policy. All other departments of butchery are treated as dirty work and
left to the slaves. If a man wishes to travel within the precinct of his own
city, he can do so provided he obtains his father's permission and his
wife's consent. For longer journeys, he requires a state passport, which,
however, is easily granted. They never make war except on the highest
moral grounds; but when they do, they go at it with a vengeance, using
their accumulations of gold to bribe savages to fight for them, and to
demoralize the enemy by corrupting the generals; offering premiums
for desertion, and huge rewards for the assassination of the hostile
prince. They do not plunder or annex, but content themselves with
teaching their neighbours the expediency of leaving them alone. About
moral philosophy they dispute much as other people do; but they are in
the main Epicureans and Hedonists, deriving egoism from altruism in
this fashion. "A life of pleasure," they say, "is either a real evil, and in
that case we ought not to assist others in their pursuit of it, but on the
contrary to keep them from it all we can, as from that which is most
hurtful and deadly; or if it is a good thing, so that we not only may, but
ought to help others to it, why then ought not a man to begin with
himself?" Obviously for the same reason that a wise physician never
attempts to heal himself as he heals other people; but the Utopians, who
successfully cultivate bodily health as a positive happiness, know little
about physicians. They believe in miracles and the efficacy of prayer,
but draw the line at "auguries, and the other vain and superstitious ways
of divination"; for at these they laugh. To incurable invalids they point
out that life is a burden, and that an overdose of opium is an accident
that might happen to anybody. They then retire, leaving opium about.
If the incurable is found dead in the morning they bury him with honor.
If a capable citizen commits suicide, they throw his body into a ditch.
They are unacquainted with vaccination. Monogamy prevails; the marriage age is 18 for women, 22 for men; and the couples take extreme
precautions against being deceived in their choice. Divorce can be

obtained on the score of adultery or insufferable perverseness; but the
petitioner alone has the right to marry again: the respondents being
"made infamous." Husbands have power to chastise their wives, and
parents their children. There are religious sects who contemn learning
and devote themselves to perpetual hard work. Some of these are
vegetarians and ascetics into the bargain, and are regarded as the holier,
though the others are accounted the wiser, of the two sects. They aim at
perfect freedom of religious opinion, and jealously maintain it, with
such trifling exception as may be gathered from the following. "Utopus
therefore left men wholly to their liberty, that they might be free to
believe as they should see cause; only he made a solemn and severe law
against such as should so far degenerate from the dignity of human
nature as to think that our souls died with our bodies, or that the world
was governed by chance, without a wise overruling Providence; for they
all formerly believed that there was a state of rewards and punishments
to the good and bad after this life; and they now look upon those that
think otherwise as scarce fit to be counted men, since they degrade so
noble a being as the soul, and reckon it no better than a beast's: thus
they are far from looking on such men as fit for human society, or to be
citizens of a well-ordered commonwealth; since a man of such principles
must, as oft as he dares do it, despise all their laws and customs; for
there is no doubt to be made that a man who is afraid of nothing but
the law, and apprehends nothing after death, will not scruple to break
through all the laws of his country, either by fraud or force, when by
this means he may satisfy his appetites. They never raise any that hold
these maxims, either to honours or offices, but despise them as men of
base and sordid minds: yet they do not punish them, because they lay
this down as a maxim that a man cannot make himself believe anything
he pleases; nor do they drive any to dissemble their thoughts by
threatenings, so that men are not tempted to lie or disguise their
opinions, which, being a sort of fraud, is abhorred by the Utopians." We
are also told of a Utopian who was converted to Christianity and took to
preaching it in the manner of the Salvation Army. "He was condemned
to banishment, not for having disparaged their religion, but for his
inflaming the people to sedition; for this is one of their most ancient
laws, that no man ought to be punished for his religion." In the same way
when we in modern London wish to suppress Socialism, we condemn the
speakers, not for their opinions, but for obstructing the thoroughfare.
When it is added that the priests in Utopia have power to excommuni-
cate, and that excommunicated persons are punished by the secular arm
for impiety, it will be seen that in Utopia as elsewhere, conformity was
an implied condition of toleration.

Campanella's City of the Sun, as described by a Genoese sea captain to a Grand Master of the Knights Hospitallers, derives an allegorical flavor from the names of its magistrates, Love, Wisdom, Metaphysic; and of the doctors, Astrologus, Cosmographus, Arithmeticus and the like. It is artlessly introduced by the Genoese mariner as follows. —"In the course of my journeying I came to Taprobane, and was compelled to go ashore at a place where, through fear of the inhabitants, I remained in a wood. When I stepped out of this I found myself on a large plain immediately under the equator." "And what befell you there?" says the Grand Master. "I came upon a large crowd of men and armed women, many of whom did not understand our language," answers the captain; "and they conducted me forthwith to the City of the Sun." The Hospitaller's next speech, "Tell me after what plan the city is built and how it is governed," is not good dialogue; but it is the captain's cue for a plunge into description without further preliminary. Much that follows is either fantastic or borrowed from More. There is no private property; and the solution of the consequent difficulties is again the characteristic Utopian one of communism, compulsory labor, and wise laws. There is community of wives among the magistrates; but the race is bred by selection on scientific principles, without regard to the inclinations of the parties concerned. The chief ruler, a widely accomplished philosopher, is called the Hoh, and is not eligible for election until he is 35. The people rallied the Genoese captain on the European superstition by which a man was esteemed learned when he was deep in grammar, logic, and Aristotle. "For such knowledge as this of yours," they said, "much servile labor & memory work is required, so that a man is rendered unskilful; since he has contemplated nothing but the words of books; and has given his mind with useless result to the consideration of the dead signs of things: . . . . .* He who knows only one science, does not really know either that or the others; and he who is suited for only one science and has gathered his knowledge from books, is unlearned and unskilled." They go on to explain that the Hoh is "prompt and expert in every branch of knowledge." This is rendered possible by a Pestallozzian[9] system of education, by which the boys acquire knowledge very easily. Women are not allowed to manufacture arms; but they are allowed to paint pictures if fit to do so, and music is left to them and to the boys, though they "have not the practice of the horn & drum." If they paint or wear high heels they are killed.† The people wear "white undergarments, to which adheres a covering, which is at once coat and legging, without wrinkles"—evidently what is now called a "combination." Rain water is filtered through pipes full of sand. Children are weaned at two years old, and then taken from

*The ellipsis is Shaw's.
†This sentence is John Wardrop's transcription of Shaw's shorthand insert.

their parents and given into the charge of masters or mistresses; for the people deny "that it is natural to man to recognize his offspring and to educate them, and to use his wife & house & children as his own." Here Campanella distinctly anticipates *me*. "Since," he most excellently adds, "individuals for the most part bring forth children wrongly and educate them wrongly, ...* the Sun Citizens commit the education of the children, who as it were are the element of the republic, to the care of magistrates; for the safety of the community is not that of a few." For transport purposes use is made of "waggons fitted with sails which are borne along by the wind even when it is contrary, by the marvellous contrivance of wheels within wheels." The Genoese captain is no more loyal than Raphael Hythloday; for he says of the king of the Sun City, the people "do not regard him with loathing as we do." Humanity to animals led them to vegetarianism until they reflected that a vegetable too has life and is sensitive in its degree, whereupon, slaying being unavoidable, they slew cows & sheep. Their average lifetime is a hundred years; and they suffer a little from consumption "because," says the text, "they cannot perspire at the breast." The criminal courts are presided over by the head artificers of the trades; and the punishments are exile, flogging, blame, deprivation of the common table, and exclusion from the church and from the company of women. There are also retaliatory punishments for personal injury, a Jewish feature† which appears again in the practice of executing capital punishment by stoning by the whole people. There is human sacrifice; but the victim is not killed: he is only placed on a shelf, and hung up, nearly fasting, for twenty or thirty days in the dome of the temple, after which he is let down and allowed to presume considerably upon the incident during the rest of his life. They cremate their dead, and practice auricular confession, astrology, and other matters, a list of which would be tedious and insignificant. On the whole, Campanella shews‡ himself far less able to digest his mass of 16th century learning than More. More wrote like a realist, a man of the world, and a statesman: Campanella like a romancer, a priest and a faddist. Their main points of agreement are upon the evils of property, the wisdom of state disparagement of the precious metals, and the need of reform in education and in the treatment of criminals.

In the New Atlantis of Bacon, we have the inevitable seaman describing an Australian continent with a Christian city in which the institutions are of the most advanced order the author could conceive. That they

---

*The ellipsis is Shaw's.
†Shaw originally wrote "feature," substituted "terror," and then restored "feature."
‡Shaw originally wrote "Campanella is a worse romancer and shews" and then crossed out "is a worse romancer and" in pencil.

are too advanced for the author himself in this case may be inferred
from the fact that the seaman's first experience in the New Atlantis is
the failure of his attempt to bribe the public officials. The customs of
the place differ from those of Utopia and the City of the Sun in many
details. Instead of a plain uniform dress for all, there is much bravery of
apparel and pomp of office; and there is an external glow and colour in
the picture presented to the imagination which would make it superficially more attractive than Utopia if it were not also much less realistic.
Splendid ceremonies are described; and the history of the place includes
an account of the miraculous revelation of Christianity to the inhabitants
by the appearance at sea of a great pillar of light, with a resplendent
cross, both of which, when the inhabitants have clustered about in their
boats, break up into a firmament of stars, and discover a floating ark
with a copy of the Bible inside. All this affects the reader like a regatta
with a display of fireworks, and greatly enlivens the narrative. The
people of the New Atlantis, like the Utopians, derive their institutions
from a wise king of olden time with, says the book, "a large heart,
inscrutable for good, and wholly bent to make his people and kingdom
happy." King Salomona had King Utopus's belief in the importance of
making his country absolutely independent of foreign trade by the
comprehensiveness of its industries. He also agreed with him in being
chary of admitting strangers or attracting them by allowing the fame of
his kingdom to spread abroad. But instead of merely excluding aliens
in the Chinese fashion, to which contemptuous allusion is made, he
simply forbade his subjects to travel, and though he did not prevent
shipwrecked refugees from returning to their own country, it was found
in practice that they were only too glad to stay—except a few who either
did not know when they were well off or had extraordinarily pressing
concerns at home. The reports spread by these were—not altogether
without reason—received with more or less indulgence as harmless
exercises of the imagination. No case is mentioned, by the bye, of a
refugee desiring to return in order to rejoin his family. Every 12 years a
mission of wise men is sent out to the old world to collect news and to
keep their countrymen abreast of the general march of progress. "Thus,
you see," says one of them, "we maintain a trade, not for gold, silver, or
jewels, nor for silks, nor for spices, nor for any other commodity of
matter; but only for God's first creature, which was Light: to have light,
I say, of the growth of all parts of the world." The central social organ is
a vast physical laboratory, in which a bureaucracy of scientists revel in
an unlimited state endowment of research. No explanation is given of
the means taken to prevent the sinecurist from getting the better of the
scientist in these gentlemen. Outside the laboratories, observatories,

model farms and so on, the social arrangements are conventionally respectable. The executive is an enlightened Bumbledom[10]; the inhabitants, like the village blacksmith, "go on Sunday to the church"[11]; the fact that the Jews are patriotic is the high water mark of toleration; and not a word is said against property, nor is there a hint at More's bold assertion that one creed is as good as another provided it recognize the worshipfulness of one god and the immortality of the soul. On the whole, it is pretty evident that Bacon had not in him the moral starch that stiffened Campanella on the rack and More at the stake. The New Atlantis confirms his reputation as a venal timeserver.

Montaigne's Essay on the Cannibals has a sturdier ring. In it we have our Sinbad of the Renascence recommended to us as "a rough hewen, simple fellow"; for, remarks the author, as translated by John Florio, "subtile people may indeed mark more curiously and observe things more exactly; but they amplify and glose them; and, the better to persuade, and to make their interpretations of more validity, they cannot choose but somewhat alter the story." Montaigne admits that his Cannibals are barbarous and savage if it be true that everything that is not French is necessarily barbarous & savage; but he very distinctly conveys that in his opinion the boot is on the other leg. He roundly questions the benefit of civilization, and asserts that[,] with much less art than Plato prescribed for maintaining his republic, it would be possible to establish a nation "that hath no kind of traffic, no knowledge of letters, no intelligence of numbers, no name of magistrate nor of politic superiority; no use of service, of riches or of poverty; no contracts, no successions, no partitions, no occupation but idle; no respect of kindred but common, no apparel but natural, no manuring of lands, no use of wine, corn, or metal; and the very words that import lying, falsehood, treason, dissimulations, covetousness, envy, detraction, and pardon, never heard of amongst them." "How dissonant," says Montaigne, "would he find his imaginary commonwealth from this perfection?"

The Cannibals enjoy "this perfection." The following passage[,] referring to their warlike customs, explains their name. "After they have long time used and entreated their prisoners of war well and with all commodity they can devise, he that is Master of them, summoning a great assembly of his acquaintance, tieth a cord to one of the prisoner's arms, by the end whereof he holds him fast, with some distance from him for fear he might attack him, and giveth the other arm, bound in like manner, to the dearest friend he hath, and both in the presence of all the assembly kill him with swords: which done, they roast and then eat him in common, and send some slices of him to such of their friends as are absent. It is not, as some imagine, to nourish themselves with it

[as anciently the Scythians wont to do],* but to represent an extreme
and inexpiable revenge." However, the prisoner can always ransom
himself by a simple confession that he is subdued; and no man is
considered vanquished until he makes such a confession, which, however, he very seldom stoops to do. "I have a song made by a prisoner,"
says the author, "wherein is this clause. 'Let them boldly come altogether
and flock in multitudes to feed on him; for with him they shall feed
upon their fathers and grandfathers that have heretofore served his
body for food and nourishment. These muscles,' saith he, 'this flesh,
and these veins, are your own: fond men as you are, know you not that
the substance of your forefathers[']† limbs is yet tied unto ours? Taste
them well, for in them you shall find the relish of your own flesh.'
An invention," adds the translation quaintly, "that hath no show of
barbarism." The Cannibals cultivate courage as distinct from prowess.
They opine that "it is a prank of skill and knowledge to be cunning in
the art of fencing, and which may happen unto a base and worthless
man. The reputation and worth of a man consisteth in his heart and
will: therein consists true honor." They have Prophets who prognosticate
of things to come, and are hewn in a thousand pieces when their
prophecies do not come off. As to the exhortations of these prophets,
we are told that "all their moral discipline containeth but these two
articles: first, an undismayed resolution to war, then an inviolable affection to their wives." These exhortations do not produce much effect;
for we presently learn that "their men have many wives, and by how
much more they are reputed valiant so much the greater is their
number. The manner and beauty of their marriages is wondrous strange
and remarkable. For, the same jealousy our wives have to keep us from
the love and affection of other women, the same have theirs to procure
it. Being more careful for their husband[']s honor and content than of
anything else, they endeavour and apply all their industry to have as
many rivals as possibly they can, forasmuch as it is a testimony of their
husband's virtue. Our women would count it a wonder; but it is not so:
it is virtue properly matrimonial, but of the highest kind." The Cannibals live on fish and flesh, plain boiled or broiled, without sauces. They
live two or 300 in a house. They use a very hard wood for their swords,
gridirons, and other hardware. They rise with the sun, and breakfast is
the only meal they take. They spend the whole day dancing or hunting,
whilst the women warm their drink for them. They shave cleanly with
wooden razors, and believe their souls to be eternal. Communism is

*When quoting Montaigne, Shaw uses square brackets where Florio's translation has
curved parentheses.
†Shaw transcribed this accurately from Florio, who omitted the apostrophe.

founded, not on compulsory labor, but on the spontaneous fruitfulness of the soil. There is no claim to property or inheritance except "that," says the text, "which Nature doth plainly impart unto all creatures, even as she brings them into the world." This strikes me as rather a large exception. They fight only for honor and the maintenance of right— never for plunder or conquest. "They wear," we are told, "no kind of breeches nor hosen." In their opinion of European society they echo Raphael Hythloday. "Three of that nation," says Montaigne, "ignorant how dear the knowledge of our corruptions will one day cost their repose, security, and happiness, and how their ruin shall proceed from this commerce, which I imagine is already well advanced [miserable as they are to have suffered themselves to be so cosened by a desire of new fangled novelties, and to have quit the calmness of their climate to come and see ours]* were at Rouen in the time of our late King Charles IX, who talked with them a great while. They were shewed our fashions, our pomp, and the form of a fair city: afterward some demanded their advice, and would needs know of them what things of note and admirable they had observed among us. They answered three things, the last of which I have forgotten and am very sorry for it: the other two I yet remember. They said, 'First, they found it very strange that so many tall men with long beards, strong and well armed, as it were, about the King's person [it is very likely they meant the Switzers of his guard]† would submit themselves to obey a beardless child, and that we did not rather choose one amongst them to command the rest.' Secondly [they have a manner of phrase whereby they call men but a moiety one of another]‡ 'They had perceived there were men amongst us full gorged with all sorts of commodities, and others which, hunger-starved and bare with need and poverty, begged at their gates; and found it strange these moi[e]ties§ so needy could endure such an injustice, and that they took not the others by the throat, or set fire on their houses.'" This is almost a paraphrase of More, whose death and Montaigne's birth were almost simultaneous.[12] Montaigne does not however improve on More. He is shrewd, audacious, and amusing; but he shirks the labor problem, and has neither More's broad grasp nor Campanella's earnestness. He is also more bitter, and his phrase "The very words that import lying, falsehood &c, were never heard of among them," anticipates Swift's Utopia of horses, who have "no word in their language to express lying or falsehood." The whole description was used by Shakespere in the

---

*Shaw has square brackets where Florio has curved parentheses.
†Shaw has brackets where Florio has curved parentheses.
‡Shaw has brackets where Florio has curved parentheses.
§Florio has "moyties" here and "moytie" above.

Tempest, in the first scene of the second act, where Gonzalo sketches a Utopia. He says

> "Had I plantation of this isle, my lord,
> And were the King of it, what would I do?
> I' the commonwealth I would by contraries
> Execute all things; for no kind of traffic
> Would I admit: no name of magistrate.
> Letters should not be known: riches, poverty,
> And use of service, none: contract, succession,
> Bourn, bound of land, tilth, vineyard, none:
> No use of metal, corn, or wine, or oil:
> No occupation, all men idle, all!
> And women too, but innocent and pure:
> No sovereignty [Yet he would be King of it: the latter end of his
>   commonwealth forgets the beginning.]*
> All things in common Nature should produce
> Without sweat or endeavour: treason, felony,
> Sword, pike, knife, gun, or need of any engine
> Would I not have; but Nature should bring forth
> Of its own kind; all foison, all abundance
> To feed my innocent people.
> I would with such perfection govern, sir,
> To excel the golden age."

This is of course not Shakespere's Utopia but Gonzalo's; and Shakspere takes care to draw attention to the fact that the item "no sovereignty" is not consistent with Gonzalo's postulated kingship. He also puts into the mouth of the two rascally courtiers the familiar comment that such a community would be nothing but a horde of idle scum and dregs of humanity. The effect of the episode in the play is melancholy enough.

James Harrington's "Oceana" is indescribable and indiscutable.[13] Any commonwealth desperately in want of a constitution, a ritual, and a procedure, will find it worth studying. It reminded me at the first glance of Leviticus and Exodus, of an act of parliament, of an old fashioned fifty folio marriage settlement; and I had not time to take a second. I leave it to whichever of us shall deal with the empirical sceptical philosophy—with Hobbes, Locke, Hume, and the Encyclopædists.

*The brackets are Shaw's. Throughout Gonzalo's speech, Shaw omits many interjections by the "rascally courtiers" Antonio and Sebastian, but he pointedly includes these two here. See *The Tempest* II.i.143–68.

Of Swift I need say very little. He added nothing to More's view except despair of human nature. In his Utopia, horses are the rational creatures, and men and women the brutes. Individualism without sufficient pressure of population to make it hurtful, and slavery, with plain living and high thinking among the horses, are the solution of the social problem. There is not a trace of the communism of More, Campanella, and Montaigne.

Read to the Hampstead Historical Club.[14]
25th May 1887.

Notes

1. Various members, such as Webb, were civil servants who could do their research for papers on the job, where they had resources and a salary and were largely left alone. Shaw, a free-lance art and book critic, lacked such advantages.

2. J. L. Wisenthal identifies the most significant of these titles (see pages 53–54 and pages 63–64, notes 4, 7, and 10). Including the prospectus for the Society of the New Life among utopias is a private joke. In December 1883, Dr. Burns-Gibson presented his "Plan for a Fellowship of the New Life" to a group interested in forming an association to advance the cause of socialism. The majority, finding this proposal too visionary and perfectionist, altered it to form a more realistic basis for the Fabian Society. The minority, undeterred, followed the original prospectus to found the Fellowship of the New Life, which continued until 1898. See Margaret Cole, *The Story of Fabian Socialism* (Stanford: Stanford University Press, 1961), pp. 4–6.

3. Shaw alludes to Voltaire's *Candide* (1759).

4. John Bunyan frequently referred to celestial beings as "shining ones" in his "famous dream," *The Pilgrim's Progress from This World to That Which Is to Come: Delivered under the Similitude of a Dream* (1678). In "The Best Books for Children," Shaw described *Pilgrim's Progress* as "the first book I remember" (*SHAW* 9: 25–26).

5. Porphyry (233–c. 301), was the student and biographer of the Neoplatonist philosopher Plotinus (c. 204–c. 270). According to William Rose Benét, *The Reader's Encylcopedia*, 2nd edition (New York: Crowell, 1965), Plotinus "persuaded his friend the Emperor Gallienus to build a city for philosophers, to be governed according to the laws of Plato. . . . Porphyry . . . relates that [Plotinus] refused to eat meat, and that he attained the state of mystical union with God four times while Porphyry knew him."

6. Sir Thomas More (1478–1535); Francis Bacon (1561–1626).

7. Cesare Bonesana Beccaria (1738–94), author of *Tratto dei Delitti e delle Pene* (*Essay on Crimes and Punishments,* 1764). According to *The 1995 Grolier Multimedia Encyclopedia* (CD-ROM, Grolier Electronic Publishing, 1995), "The 19th-century English reformer Jeremy Bentham took up Beccaria's ideas, and they influenced the penal laws of a number of European countries."

8. Mark Tapley, in Chapter 5 of Dickens's *Martin Chuzzlewit,* says that "Any man may be in good spirits and good temper when he's well dressed. There an't much credit in that."

9. Shaw added the extra *l* to "Pestalozzian." Johann Heinrich Pestalozzi (1746–1827) was the Swiss educational reformer who, according to *The 1995 Grolier Multimedia Encyclopedia,* "attacked conventional education as excessively verbal, intellectual, and inorganic. He believed that a child's innate faculties should be developed in accordance with nature. His teaching principles involved an emphasis on accurate observation of concrete objects, moving from the familiar to the new, and the creation of a loving and emotionally secure environment. These ideas, revolutionary in his day, subsequently had a great influence on the development of progressive pedagogy in Europe and the United States."

10. According to the *OED,* "Fussy official pomposity and stupidity," from Bumble, the beadle in Dickens's *Oliver Twist* (1837–39).

11. The fifth stanza of "The Village Blacksmith" (1840) by Henry Wadsworth Longfellow begins, "He goes on Sunday to the church. . . ."

12. That is, Montaigne's birth in 1533 was "almost simultaneous" with More's death in 1535.

13. In *The Commonwealth of Oceania* (1656), James Harrington (1611–77), according to *The 1995 Grolier Multimedia Encyclopedia,* "argued that a strong middle class is necessary to a stable polity. His notions of limited, balanced government prefigured those of some of the U.S. founding fathers, notably Thomas Jefferson."

14. See Bernard Shaw, *The Diaries: 1885–1897,* ed. Stanley Weintraub (University Park and London: Penn State University Press, 1986), 1:60, 91, 136, 274, 309, 530. Mrs. Anne Burrows Gilchrist (1828–85) had "opened her Hampstead home to various radical groups for meetings, among them in 1885 the Marx Reading Circle which Shaw attended." Shaw, Webb, and others used the Marx Reading Circle as a forum for debating Fabian policy. In his entry for 16 June, Shaw noted "Last meeting and supper of Karl Marx readers," and in 1886 he recorded that "The Hampstead Marx Circle became the Hampstead Historical Club." Mrs. Gilchrist had died in November 1885, but her daughter, Grace Gilchrist, continued the tradition of hospitality. Sometimes the group met at the Hampstead Library, where Shaw read his "Utopias" paper. His last diary reference to the "Hampstead Historical" is in his entry for 10 August 1889.

Jeffrey M. Wallmann

EVOLUTIONARY MACHINERY: FORESHADOWINGS OF SCIENCE FICTION IN BERNARD SHAW'S DRAMAS

Bernard Shaw comes close to the fantastic incidents that abound in utopian and dystopian science fiction, particularly in his dramas around World War I, in which setting and characterization become openly symbolic and even allegorical. In more general terms, that Shavian malcontentedness, that deep dissatisfaction with self and society, together with the adventure in it, has assisted in making science fiction a field rich in irritants, rich in dangerous enemies, rich in speculative concepts. As such, he has been an influence on a generation of magazines and fanzines, television and films, and on the passing of science fiction into a new generation of malcontents.

It is in this breakup of things, of things that surely need breaking up, that Shaw's views are especially pertinent in terms of science fiction. After all, technology is fundamental to modern science fiction. Technology frequently provides the *raison d'être* as well as background of a story, as in the "hard" science fiction descended from adventure yarns by Jules Verne or H. G. Wells, involving fantastic machines like atomic submarines, spaceships, and time-travel contraptions. In other stories, like the "soft" science fiction descended from gothic tales by Poe or Mary Shelley, technology is often not a literal great machine, but a figurative or metaphorical device subordinated to social commentary—such as in the portrayal and criticism of mechanistic clockwork worlds. In a third sense, technology is extrapolated by science fiction to explore the increasing mechanization of life itself, with computers that think, androids that feel, and cyborgs in which flesh and machine are intimately and inextricably combined.

Such science-fictional ways of viewing how man and machine are intertwined were adumbrated by Shaw's vision of the relationships between human nature and the shape of society, now and in the future. He intended to "prove" hypotheses that, like utopian and dystopian writing, demand that we think critically about the fate of mankind if left to the devices of contemporaneous machines in all their guises. Over his lengthy career, his speculative theories evolved (and in his latter years, perhaps devolved), but his overall concepts, however valid, foreshadowed science fiction themes about machines in terms of socioeconomic power, political ideology, and scientific and technological progress.

For example, Shaw assaulted the machinery of the British establishment by giving narrative shape to the Marxist condemnation of capitalism. In his first play, *Widowers' Houses*, a young couple's marriage is depicted as an acquiescence to conform to an exploitive social system, and the endings of two other early plays, *Arms and the Man* and *Candida*, resolve problems arising in relationships from external economic and social corruption. Not only did Shaw oppose Victorian codes of conduct and duty, he also disparaged Victorian mechanism and technology, censuring science for not having "lived up to the hopes we formed of it in the 1860's."[1] In *Arms and the Man*, for example, Shaw argues that war is a crippling (and capitalist) system of technology coupled with false honor. As Captain Bluntschli asks rhetorically, "Is it professional to throw a regiment of cavalry on a battery of machine guns, with the dead certainty that if the guns go off not a horse or a man will ever get within fifty yards of the fire?"[2] It is a theme to which Shaw often turns, as again more than two decades later in *Back to Methuselah:* "The statesmen of Europe were incapable of governing Europe. What they needed was a couple of hundred years training and experience: what they had actually had was a few years at the bar or in a counting-house or on the grouse moors and golf courses. And now we are waiting, with monster cannons trained on every city and seaport, and huge aeroplanes ready to spring into the air and drop bombs every one of which will obliterate a whole street, and poison gases that will strike a multitude dead with a breath, until one of you gentlemen rises in his helplessness to tell us, who are as helpless as himself, that we are at war again."[3]

Shaw's dramas, then, can be perceived as post-technological manifestations of post-technological despair—a position that took science fiction another forty years to reach. Granted, a number of largely mediocre post- and even pre–World War I dystopian books were published, and during the 1920s and 1930s a few classic dystopian novels like Zamiatin's *We* (1924) and Aldous Huxley's *Brave New World* (1932) appeared, but virtually all were marketed as mainstream and bought as mainstream, and were in line with the existentialist themes prevalent in much of mainstream fiction then. However, modern science fiction was taking quite the opposite tack. Pioneered by Hugo Gernsback, publisher of the first real science fiction magazine, *Amazing Stories,* the attitude of science fiction was basically positivist and technocrat, with writers churning out action-adventuristic "space operas" and readers dreaming of unusual futuristic things like moon rockets and flying cities. And some science fiction explored, albeit superficially, relationships between technological developments and story characters who (ab)used them.

Such plots often involved improving assorted social problems, and utopian worlds were cast as organized on rational lines, free of superstition and religious dogma. Aside from appealing to socialists like Shaw, the notion of scientifically planned social orders paralleled the visions behind the major political innovations of the time, including Leninism, Fascism, National Socialism, and even the New Deal. Moreover, industrial machines were beginning to replace people in the work force, a trend toward robotics that would accelerate along with Rosie the Riveter during World War II and that many laborers feared as threatening their livelihoods. During the 1940s there were many stories in which machines or robots are positive and sympathetic characters—Lester Del Ray's "Helen O'Loy," for example, or the robotic and the *Foundation* series by Isaac Asimov. Yet this also was the era in which dystopian science fiction began to emerge, with writers forecasting alternative sociopolitical structures whose failures were somehow linked to their uses of science and technology. James Blish's *Cities in Flight* series, for instance, portrays the rise and fall of the entire galaxy as an inevitable cycle in which machine technology is merely a symptom, not the disease; and in Nat Schachner's *Space Lawyer* (1953, but based on his 1940s *Astounding* stories) the total loss of cheap energy causes an old tycoon to declare that men who did not have to work any more would "lose all incentive, get bored, stop thinking and striving, and degenerate into pigs. Young man, within a hundred years they'd be slinking through cities they wouldn't know the use of, and staring helplessly at machines they don't know how to handle."

There were plenty of other stories about robots running amok or computers taking over the world, but because there was a war on and man has always excelled at creating technology for killing, the themes of mass destruction were exceptionally popular—and depressing. In C. L. Moore's dark serial "Judgement Night" (*Astounding,* August & September 1943), a galactic empire as vast as Asimov's self-destructs in civil war. At story's end, an alien envoy condemns humanity: "You and your people have gone too far already along the road all humans go. Every nation digs its own grave, and we are weary of mankind." Right after the war, a spate of atomic doom stories were published, such as Chandler Davis's "The Nightmare" (*Astounding,* April & May 1946), Theodore Sturgeon's "Thunder and Roses" (*Astounding,* November 1947), and Judith Merrill's first story, "That Only a Mother" (*Astounding,* June 1948).

At the same time, horrific alternatives to nuclear destruction were posed by other hell-on-earth stories. Sinister and tragic results of Scientific Enlightenment cause the return of the Dark Ages in Robert Abernathy's "Hostage of Tomorrow" (*Planet Stories,* Spring 1949). In "Brother's Day Out" by William P. Roessner (*Galaxy,* July 1977), a culture declines into barbarism while monks diligently transcribe what knowledge still exists. Perhaps the most ambitious and provocative story along these lines is Walter M. Miller's classic *A Canticle for Leibowitz* (1959), which deals with an eternally recurring cycle of growth and destruction, in this case technology-based growth that strikes the scientific materialism of Gernsback and Wells a punishing blow.

So, by the 1960s, there were two streams in modern science fiction: utopian (the machines will work) and dystopian (no, they won't), and Shaw's plays mostly foreshadow the latter, which since the 1950s has been the more significant of the two. Moreover, another Shavian vision was developing in science fiction: dystopian stories that were less anti-scientific than they were anti-scientistic, criticizing the replacement of an humanist ethos with a technological ethos extolling instrumentalism. For example, in Kurt Vonnegut's *Player Piano* (1954), technology is the immediate problem but human nature is the underlying trouble, with people too inadequate to operate the machines that administer the society. Similarly, in A. E. Van Vogt's "Co-operate—Or Else!" (*Astounding,* April 1942), an alien "ezwal" says, "Human beings have created what they call civilization, which is actually merely a material barrier between themselves and their environment, so vast and unwieldy that keeping it going occupies the entire existence of the race." How similar that sounds to *Back to Methuselah:* "Your task was beyond human capacity. What with our huge armaments, our terrible engines of destruction, our systems of coercion manned by an irresistible police, you were called on to control powers so gigantic that one shudders at the thought of their being entrusted even to an infinitely experienced and benevolent God, much less to mortal men whose whole life does not last a hundred years" (16:69).

An oft-used parallel theme was—and still is—the perversion of science and technology, no matter what their utopian potential, by being put at the service of existing mechanisms of control. A good example is Philip K. Dick's novel *The Man Who Japed* (1956), in which technological advances are justified for utopian reasons, but are employed to enforce a rigid moral code, resulting in massive institutional intrusion on privacy and freedom by a puritanical society devoid of utopian spirit. This echoes Shaw's argument in *The Sanity of Art* that laws are moral hindrances preventing us from thinking or acting on our own. The elite in *Major Barbara* keep power through violence: "the ballot paper that really governs us is the paper that has a bullet wrapped in it."[4] In *Misalliance*, civilization is corrupted by "the constant attempts made by the wills of individuals and classes to thwart the wills and enslave the powers of other individuals and classes."[5]

To varying degrees, then, running through these plays and others—e.g., the destruction portrayed in *Heartbreak House,* hell in *Man and Superman,* and love in *Candida*—is the protoscientific theme of the new technical man detached from conscience and consideration, in contrast to the pre-technological era before the turn of the century. In this respect, Shaw foreshadows dystopian writers like Kuttner, Van Vogt, and Leiber, with their visions of technology gone rampant and wild, and another bunch including Sheckley, Pohl, Tenn, Damon Knight, and Sturgeon, whose more humanistic visions stemmed from the intuition that conventional technology myths would not work at all.

Shaw's assessment of mankind grew increasingly somber and dystopian with the advent of World War I, and perhaps his most pivotal drama of this period is *Man and Superman* with its elements of what had been and what was to come. In the play's "Revolutionist's Handbook" preface, for instance, Shaw, writing as "Tanner," makes clear that he no longer believes that "Man as he exists is capable of net progress. . . . Whilst Man remains what he is, there can be no progress beyond the point already attained and fallen headlong from at every attempt at civilization; and since even that point is but a pinnacle to which a few people cling in giddy terror above an abyss of squalor, mere progress should no longer charm us."[6] Neither does Shaw/Tanner continue to hold that Fabian Socialism or even revolution, violent or nonviolent, can improve the human condition, declaring that "we are to recognize that both . . . Fabian methods . . . and those of the dynamitard and the assassin . . . are fundamentally futile" (3:711). Rather, "The only fundamental and possible Socialism is the socialization of the selective breeding of Man; in other terms, of human evolution. . . . Our only hope, then, is in evolution. We must replace the man by the superman" (3:724, 723).

To Shaw, evolution was not due to Darwinian "accident," but to the Butler-Lamarckian "striving of the individual" in adapting to the environment, success being passed on through the inheritance of "unconscious memory" or habit—all part of a grand design working itself out consciously in the evolution of life. This Shaw called the Life Force, and the striving is what differentiates Heaven from Hell in the Dream scene. Hell is a hedonist's mirage, where the Devil presides over such illusions as romanticism, heroism, religious ecstasy, and sexual passions. To those like Tanner who seek reality, however, an eternity of pleasure is indeed a hell of boredom, so "Don Juan is going to Heaven . . . because it is for those who will work and strive, who will face and become the masters of reality."[7] Actually, Don Juan is driven to go, compelled by the Life Force to struggle to produce a Superman: "I tell you that as long as I can conceive something better than myself I cannot be easy unless I am striving to bring it into existence or clearing the way for it" (3:461).

Later in the scene, in an exchange that anticipates Shaw's more satiric and cynical dramas of the following decade, Don Juan tells the Devil, "To be in hell is to drift; to be in heaven is to steer" (3:646). The Life Force itself requires a pilot, having been blundering along the evolutionary path by a process of trial and error. The needed pilot is the man of genius who has been "selected by Nature to carry on the work of building up an intellectual consciousness of her own instinctive purpose" (3:498). Man, in other words, is the brains of the operation. Guided by man's intelligence and willpower, the Life Force will "replace [man] by a more highly evolved animal," an altogether different creature who will live above and beyond man's socioeconomic machinery with "its quackeries, political, scientific, educational, religious, or artistic" (3:721, 723).

The Shavian vision that the sole salvation of *homo sapiens* is to create *homo superior* began flooding science fiction during the 1930s. That willpower is the key to pursuing Creative Evolution, in fact, not only cropped up in the November 1934 *Astounding* story "Twilight" and the 16 October 1935 story "Night" (both by John Campbell writing as "Don A. Stuart"), but also was spelled out in a 1971 interview with Campbell, who by then had become the famous editor of *Astounding* and *Unknown*. When the interviewer asked, "What keeps human societies going?" Campbell replied, "Competition . . . the ethics of evolution is 'try.'" Asked whether he thought the future was bright, Campbell agreed, his optimism reinforced by "three billion years of experience." He then asked the interviewer "how long has the life-force in you been going on?" The interviewer figured twenty-three years, his age. "No," Campbell said. "Three billion years."[8]

This Butler-Lamarckian concept of evolution manifested itself in some peculiar derivations. Shaw prophesied in *Back to Methuselah* that future children could have "a lot of extra heads and arms and legs"

(16:219), and in *Man and Superman* that the Life Force would create "a special brain—a philosopher's brain" (3:646)—although it should be noted that the science fiction cliché of atrophied bodies and hypertrophied brains, spawning spindly-limbed gnomes with humongous heads, is more the offspring of H. G. Wells from his *War of the Worlds*. Rather, typical of yarns employing the Butler-Lamarckian evolution is an early yarn by David Keller, "The Revolt of the Pedestrians" (*Amazing,* February 1928), in which over-reliance on automobiles is predicted to cause legs to atrophy, to which technology will respond with individualized "autocars." Other mutation stories predicate that the mutation is a genetic improvement which, as Shaw fervently desires in *Man and Superman,* "replace(s) man by the superman" (3:723). In the majority of these stories the mutation takes the form of telepathy, which, in accord with Shavian dystopian irony, almost always backfires on the mutants. Robert Wells's "Mindhunt" (*Galaxy,* April 1972) tells of a duel between two genius telepaths whose powers effectively cancel each other out, resulting in one of them dying in a spaceship crash and the other unable to get the victim out of his mind. In the earlier "The Piper's Son" by Henry Kuttner (writing as "Lewis Padgett" in *Astounding,* February 1945), the community of mind-reading mutants, called "Baldies" by nontelepathic humans, in traditional Shavian fashion can not make up its collective mind: should they wear wigs and join the majority as best they can, or should they go bareheaded and proclaim themselves a biologically superior species? A proponent of the latter declares near the end, "We are the Future! The Baldies! God made us to rule lesser men!" Clearly, quite a bit of modern science fiction echoes Shaw's message that without the human race evolving from its present status to something different, mankind will never reach the stars unaided.

Another form of transformation becomes evident in two plays that followed *Man and Superman, Major Barbara* and *Pygmalion.* According to the Shavian theory of Life Force, that different creature called the superman can never be attained as a by-product of other considerations, but must be deliberately willed into existence, and unfortunately mankind appeared to be in no hurry to evolve itself into extinction. Until and unless humans *en masse* reject the pleasantries of hell and strive for the asceticism of heaven, individual humans of goodwill must cope with their plight of mere mortaldom, unable to attain heaven and unwilling to settle for an earthly hell where man "produces by chemical and machinery all the slaughter of plague, pestilence, and famine . . . There is nothing in man's industrial machinery but his greed and sloth" (so saith the Devil in *Man and Superman,* 3:619).

The Devil could well have been referring to Undershaft, the ethically bankrupt munitions manufacturer in *Major Barbara.* "I moralized and starved until one day I swore that I would be a full-fed man at all costs—that nothing should stop me except a bullet, neither reason nor morals nor the lives of other men" (6:339). Similarly, *Pygmalion*'s Henry Higgins is disguised as a gentleman behind a facade of class position and education, a false prophet promising Eliza salvation while delivering entrapment. As Silver points out, "One of the chief forms of evil in modern times, Shaw intimates, appears in the guise of a would-be benefactor. . . . [T]he manners and distinctions of that social world Eliza wants to enter, constitute even with their imperfections whatever civilization is available, and Higgins in his savagery is its enemy."[9] Eliza, although tempted, ultimately refuses to succumb. "Oh, when I think of myself crawling under your feet and being trampled on and called names, when all the time I had only to lift up my finger to be just as good as you, I could kick myself. . . . I'm not afraid of you and can do without you."[10] Nor does Barbara capitulate to Undershaft and accept his philosophy. On the other hand, neither young woman can return to her previous way of life as if nothing had changed. "You know I cant go back to the gutter," Eliza admits to Higgins (p. 422). And in the finale of *Major Barbara*, Barbara not only asserts her independence from Undershaft, but from her prior existence as a naïve member of the often hypocritical Salvation Army. "Turning our backs on Bodger and Undershaft is turning our backs on life," she tells Cusins, who says, "I thought you were determined to turn your back on the wicked side of life." To which Barbara replies, "There is no wicked side; life is all one" (6:348).

Therein lie their transformations. Eliza and Barbara are neither the saints they initially believe themselves to be nor the devil's disciples that Higgins and Undershaft want them to become. Choosing one or the other side of this black-white dichotomy is simply inadequate for dealing with the world as it is. Rather, both young women learn through their experiences that, as Cusins says, "you cannot have power for good without having power for evil too" (6:346), and that as humans they must come to terms with being both—a combination of soul and flesh, of spirit and materialism, which somehow must be balanced and integrated into one personage.

This issue has become increasing important in science fiction, although because science fiction emphasizes technology, the theme is handled less through stories of biological evolution than through stories of creative—or demonic—fusion of engineering with medicine. The term most associated with this field is "cyborg," referring to those fitted with internal homeostatic mechanisms like pacemakers or artificial joints. An early cyborg story is Lester Del Ray's "Reincarnate" (*Astounding*, April 1940), in which an injured man transplanted into a robot body uses magnets for muscles, gyroscopes for balance, and television lenses for vision. Frequently the creation of cybernetic organisms is used metaphorically for modern alienation and dehumanization. In C. L. Moore's "No Woman Born" (*Astounding*, December 1944), a "dead" actress and dancer continues her career with her brain encased in a graceful robot body, only to find at the end that she is speaking with "the distant taint of metal already in her voice." The machine elements that allow her to live also separate her from the humans among whom she wishes to live. Another story that makes the same point in a more optimistic way is Anne McCaffrey's novelette "The Ship Who Sang" (*Galaxy*, October 1966). Helva—another crippled Cinderella—prefers to be wired into a spaceship as its "brain" to work with human partners called "brawns," explaining, "As this ship, I have more physical power, more physical freedom, than you will ever know." More numerous, however, are dystopian cyborg stories. Philip K. Dick's *Do Androids Dream of Electric Sheep?* (1968, made into the film *Bladerunner* 1982) involves a cop's hunt for androids or replicants—machines virtually indistinguishable from humans. John Varley's story "The Phantom of Kansas" (*Galaxy*, February 1976) tells of a woman who is murdered over and over, but who keeps coming back over and over because her personality is on storage in a memory cube. In discussing the dilemmas and consternations involved in trying to reconcile the dichotomies of human and inhuman, surely such cyborg stories are the deep, distant descendants of Shaw's foreshadowing dramas.

Do Androids and "Phantom" also project forward, for they describe what effects on personality and society may happen from the technology of identity—e.g., sex change, cloning, transfer of memory, state procedure, even new kinds of illicit love. It is this exploration into the cultural problems and variations resulting from technology that has spurred the recent subgenre labelled "cyberpunk," which emphasizes technology's impact on gratifying human desire and parallels the Shavian desire to evolve a higher human capacity. Cyberpunk characters not only can replace mutilated limbs and diseased pancreas, but also can jack into custom cyberspace decks where they project their disembodied consciousnesses into landscapes akin to virtual reality. Their world, like our own, rests on an all-encompassing but hidden electronic world of connections and data that can be investigated and exploited by those with the ability to enter it. Indeed, William Gibson, Bruce Sterling, Lewis Shiner, and other writers of cyberpunk fashion gritty societies where all that computer jockey stuff of the underworld becomes the overground, not dissimilar to Shaw's hell in *Man and Superman*. In their stories there is no utopia, either in reality or in cyberspace. Still, cyberpunk authors also are following Shaw by adding notes of evolutionary optimism to their novels: the possibility that humans might create or assist in the creation of new beings who can achieve what human beings cannot achieve. As Don Juan declares in *Man and Superman,* the law of his life "is the working within me of Life's incessant aspiration to higher organization, wider, deeper, intenser self-consciousness, and clearer self-understanding" (3:637).

Clearly, then, certain themes in Shavian works like *Man and Superman, Major Barbara,* and *Pygmalion* can be seen to adumbrate key characteristics that are found in a wide range of cyborg science fiction stories: the simultaneous desire to offer entertainment and explanation in the context of the narrative; a tenuous synthesis of utopian and dystopian viewpoints, indicating that one can kind of live in and outside of the technology; and a concluding attitude that may be pessimistic concerning the future of humanity but optimistic concerning the future of intelligent life.

This double message—of despair for humanity; hope for a successor—recurs as a strong undercurrent in *Heartbreak House* and emerges again with scarcely contained pessimism in *Back to Methuselah.*

Written during World War I, *Heartbreak House* reflects Shaw's anger at the chaos and violence brought on by the war, as well as his alarm at the perceived disintegration of British society. The aimless drifting alluded to earlier in *Man and Superman* takes on deeper significance in the final scene, when Shotover chastizes Mazzini for believing in "the theory of an overruling Providence," snapping, "Every drunken skipper trusts to Providence. But one of the ways of Providence with drunken skippers is to run them on the rocks."[11] A few lines later, just prior to the arrival of the bombs, Hector asks "what may my business as an Englishman be, pray?" To which Shotover retorts, "Navigation. Learn it and live; or leave it and be damned" (p. 574). There is more than a little irony in Shotover's advice, for although he is piloting his ship of Heartbreak House for the evolutionary advanced "seventh degree of concentration," his fondness for rum is veering "the drunken skipper's ship on the rocks, [with] the splintering of her rotten timbers, the tearing of her rusty places, the drowning of the crew like rats in a trap" (p. 573). Clearly, in his anger and alarm, Shaw is raising a clarion call for the enlightened elite to stop insulating themselves from the tragic realities of the public world, and to take back by force if necessary the reins of power and authority. His message in *Major Barbara* and *Pygmalion* that humans might transform, might adapt, is now supplanted by an anxious demand to reform and be damned quick about it. Time had run out for "a society drifting as opposed to one which has learned the virtue of setting a deliberate course by fixed stars. To navigate is to plan. Laissez-faire, though always delightful for a few, in a crisis is disastrous for all.

There is no alternative to a planned society, that is the burden of the Shaw debate."[12]

Navigation proves downright impossible in *Back to Methuselah*, for in a context of fiercely negative and destructive feeling, Shaw has come to conclude that the art of navigation is beyond man's ability to master. The human race is not merely ignorant; it is congenitally too stupid to save itself. Still, if destruction is the result of a failure of human intelligence, and if human intelligence needs time to develop and mature, then the Shavian solution is to increase the span of human life. Increasing the life-span occurs through Creative Evolution, of course, the result of artificial as well as natural selection of man's unending progressive adaptation to the conditions of existence. "We're going to scatter the West through the stars," Senator Wagoner predicts in Blish's *They Shall Have Stars* (1957), "scatter it with immortal people carrying immortal ideas!"

Extending life-spans to the point of immortality is a very old theme dating back to Taoist, Zoroastrian, and Mesopotamian myths, among others: "For this corruptible must put on incorruption, and this mortal must put on immortality" (I Cor. 15:53). The Shavian distinction lies in what he envisions that this longevity ultimately will produce. Until this point, Shaw's inexorable Life Force was directed toward creating supermen who were biologically superior humans or at least partial humans in nature, but in *Back to Methuselah*, his Life Force leads neither to human procreation nor to supermen who have any human character-istics. After all, if mankind will not help the Life Force to fulfill its purpose, then it will destroy mankind and invent a more appreciative species through the saving power, if this be salvation, of intelligence— mind conquering matter. "The day will come when there will be no people, only thought," the She-Ancient states, and the He-Ancient responds, "And that will be life eternal" (16:253).

Shaw could no longer conceive of his superman evolving from human idealism through human science. Instead the path as well as the goal was pure intelligence, lacking human frailties or sensibilities. As Ed-mund Wilson notes, "The superior beings of *Back to Methuselah* are people who live forever; but . . . [w]hen they achieved it, what the Life Force had in store for them is the mastery of abstruse branches of knowledge and the extra-uterine development of embryos. Beyond this, there is still to be attained the liberation of the spirit from the flesh, existence as a 'whirlpool in pure force.' "[13] An earth laid waste by wars; humanity extinct, no longer the recipient of such Shavian balms as Creative Evolution, Fabian Socialism, or feminine wisdom and vitality. The play confronts bleakness and savagery and the shattering of illu-sions with creatures of unemotional objectivity who grind facts into data, who operate little differently from machines with artificial intelligence. Live bodies "are only machines after all, it must be possible to construct them mechanically" (p. 228). Indeed it is, resulting in a Male Figure and Female Figure who are "mere automaton[s] . . . merely responding to a stimulus" (16:237).

Man is machine. "A cold and pagan grandeur; but there is Mr. Shaw's philosophy."[14] It is in science fiction, as in *Back to Methuselah*, a condition often to be desired. In Damon Knight's bitter "Masks" (*Playboy*, 1968), the psyche of the totally amputated protagonist is placed in what he calls "a tailor's dummy." Protesting, he demands to be installed in a cleanly functioning, all-metal body, and he soon comes to regard all other forms of organisms as repellent. Even more Shavian is Arthur C. Clarke's "Meeting with Medusa" (*Playboy*, 1972), in which a cyborg who must wear a total prosthesis gradually loses his humanness and comes to believe that he is a transitional being between man and the machine that will inevitably rule the universe.

The unemotionally logical functioning of machines has been a prime source of mayhem in science fiction as well. Generally, machines are faced by human characters in one of three ways. First, by surprise. In Tom Godwin's "The Cold Equations" (*Astounding*, August 1954), a naïve stowaway aboard a rocketship must to her shock face the fact that she has to be jettisoned, to die in space, because her extra weight would consume too much fuel for the ship to reach port. A dying man lies in a cave on the moon in Walter Miller's "I Made You" (*Astounding*, March 1954), trapped by a mobile autocyber fire-control unit whose damaged receptors prevent it from telling friend from foe. The man had programmed the unit, which explains why, just before the unit blows him apart, he whimpers, "I made you, don't you understand? I'm human, I made you. . . ." His shock is not different from Pygmalion's in *Back to Methuselah*, who is startled when his Female Figure unexpectedly "picks up a stone and is about to throw it." In the resultant tussle, she bites his hand. He staggers back, crying out. "A general shriek of horror echoes his exclamation. He turns deadly pale . . . [then] falls dead" (16:238–39).

The second reaction is dread. The He-Ancient in *Back to Methuselah* warns of man as machine: "When you have achieved this as Pygmalion did; when the marble masterpiece is dethroned by the automaton and the homo by the homunculus; when the body and the brain, the reasonable soul and human flesh subsisting, as Ecrasia says, stand before you unmasked as mere machinery, and your impulses are shewn to be nothing but reflexes, you are filled with horror and loathing" (16:248). In science fiction, Asimov's robots are restrained by his famed Three Laws of Robotics from harming humans, but many more stories present anthropomorphic machinery designed without restrictions or geared purposely for violence. Particularly if the machines are strangers, humans are bound to be leery of trusting their programming and capabilities. Gort, the giant robot in *The Day the Earth Stood Still* (1951), is so powerful that "there's no limit to what he could do. He could destroy the earth." Undoubtedly the most scarifying machines are Fred Saberhagen's Berserkers, which are "an armada of robot spaceships and supporting devices [whose] fundamental programming was the destruction of all life, wherever and whenever they could find it" ("Inhuman Error," *The Ultimate Enemy*, 1979).

Man's nonlogical thought and his emotions are two of his strongest allies in the war against the Berserkers, strategies that the Shaw of *Back to Methuselah* might not have approved. Berserker or Robbie the Robot, however, machines have no mercy, no imagination, and are immune to argument, so it is not unreasonable for humans to respond with dread— the dread voiced by Shaw in *Heartbreak House*, of fear and alarm and a call to action. Indeed, if the logic of the machine pursued to its conclusion results at worst in human extinction or at best in hideous stasis, then humans must resort to drastic preventative measures. We cannot return to some lost Eden where no machines intrude, no matter how we might wish. As Zoo in *Back to Methuselah* reminds the Elderly Gentleman, "How often must I tell you that we are made wise not by the recollections of our past, but by the responsibilities of our future" (16:164). Similarly, in *Player Piano,* Vonnegut demonstrates that utopia (or any good society) can no more come about without technology than technology can manufacture one. We have only the choice of either smashing the machines before they take us too far—

—or of capitulating, which is the third reaction. The Elderly Gentleman often collapses in defeat, crying such lines as "I can bear this no longer" and "I shall drown myself" (16:141, 145). This is Shavian drollery, of course, but in science fiction capitulation is a response that includes the extent to which humans may be controlled by machines and machinelike systems, and the extent to which humans themselves are or may become machines. An early and well-known example of machines forming the next stage in human evolution is Clifford Simak's *City* (1952), where a human family leaves its responsibilities to the robot butler, Jenkins, to such a point that the humans disappear from earth and even lose human form. Other notable practitioners include the Alfred Bester of *The Demolished Man* (serialized 1952), the Silverberg of *Dying Inside* (1972), and Vonnegut, whose novel *The Sirens of Titan* (1959) bespeaks the mechanization of humans, the characters seeming to accept that humanity is basically unimportant. Closely linked is cyberpunk fiction, in which biological barriers are overcome and the issue of humanism is irrelevant. An ineluctable cultural malaise tends to disable cyberpunk characters, allowing insight to remain but making action impossible. Michael Swanwick's *In the Drift* (1986) exemplifies the dystopian post-holocaust milieu in which the crippled society shows no capacity for regeneration, only further disintegration, eventually to be replaced by a machine civilization. Or, as Cain says near the end of *Back to Methuselah*, "There is no place for me on earth any longer" (16:260).

Such are the prophecies foreshadowed by the Shaw of *Back to Methuselah*. Moreover, his seventy-five-year-old message is as current as tomorrow's headlines, for rapid technological progress in electronic, biomedical, genetic engineering has put us in an era of participant evolution. Children clutch plastic computers that flash not pictures but "graphics." Youths concentrate on video games, bodies moving in rhythm to complex feedback mechanisms. Adults lock into the Internet and World Wide Web in looped circuits of eyes, fingers, and CTR screens. Our flesh and bone become exhausted, defeated by the hard- and soft-ware of obdurate machines. Who controls what, or what controls whom, or is the meshing of human and machine indistinguishable? We may need to change our definition of "human." If this is what we are to become—Shavian beings without emotional tone—then perhaps machines represent in symbolic form Shaw's next stage in human evolution. In which case, we should take heed of his dystopic, if not dyspeptic, cautionary dramas and futuristic visions, and accept a measure of chaos in preference to the sterility and regimentality of logic.

Shaw's vision of man in relation to scientific materialism, although changing over time, has become part of the modern science fiction idiom, subtly infusing its themes and language with his images and concepts. As long as science fiction is engaged with developments in science and technology, the foreshadowings in Shaw's dramas are still relevant to serious speculation, his writing still inspirational for satire and irony. It is due time, after almost eighty years of modern science fiction, that Shaw be acknowledged for his contribution to enriching and broadening and preparing science fiction for whatever awaits it in the next millennium.

Notes

1. Samuel Hynes, *The Edwardian Turn of Mind* (Princeton: Princeton University Press, 1968), p. 132.
2. Bernard Shaw, *Arms and the Man*, in *Nine Plays by Bernard Shaw* (New York: Dodd, Mead, 1963, p. 136.

3. Bernard Shaw, *Back to Methuselah*, in *The Collected Works of Bernard Shaw*, Ayot St. Lawrence Edition (New York: Wm. H. Wise, 1930), 16:72. Subsequent quotations of *Back to Methuselah* are to this edition and are cited parenthetically in the text.

4. Bernard Shaw, *Major Barbara*, in *The Collected Works of Bernard Shaw*, Ayot St. Lawrence Edition (New York: Wm. H. Wise, 1930), 6:324. Subsequent quotations of *Major Barbara* are from this edition and are cited parenthetically in the text.

5. Bernard Shaw, *Misalliance*, in *Complete Plays with Prefaces* (New York: Dodd, Mead, 1963), 4:167.

6. Bernard Shaw, *Man and Superman*, in *Complete Plays with Prefaces* (New York: Dodd, Mead, 1963), 3:713–14. Subsequent quotations of *Man and Superman* are from this edition and are cited parenthetically in the text.

7. Louis Kronenberger, "Shaw," *The Thread of Laughter: Chapters on English Stage Comedy from Johnson to Maugham* (New York: Alfred A. Knopf, 1952), p. 228.

8. Albert I. Berger, "The Magic That Works: John W. Campbell and the American Response to Technology," *Journal of Popular Culture* 5 (Spring 1972): 867–943.

9. Arnold Silver, *Bernard Shaw: The Darker Side* (Stanford: Stanford University Press, 1982), p. 221.

10. Bernard Shaw, *Pygmalion*, in *The Portable Bernard Shaw*, ed. Stanley Weintraub (New York: Viking, 1977), p. 423. Subsequent quotations of *Pygmalion* are from this edition and are cited parenthetically in the text.

11. Bernard Shaw, *Heartbreak House*, in *The Portable Bernard Shaw*, ed. Stanley Weintraub (New York: Viking, 1977), p. 573. Subsequent quotations of *Heartbreak House* are from this edition and are cited parenthetically in the text.

12. Gore Vidal, "Bernard Shaw's 'Heartbreak House,'" *Homage to Daniel Shays: Collected Essays 1952–1972* (New York: Random House, 1972), p. 66.

13. Edmund Wilson, "Bernard Shaw at Eighty," *Eight Essays* (New York: Oxford University Press, 1954), p. 188.

14. J. C. Squire, "A Metabiological Pentateuch," *Books Reviewed* (New York: George H. Doran, 1922), p. 128.

Rodelle Weintraub

BERNARD SHAW'S FANTASY ISLAND: *SIMPLETON OF THE UNEXPECTED ISLES*

A playwright as prolific and intuitively knowledgeable as Bernard Shaw could be expected to have written fantasy dream plays as well as literary dream plays such as the *Don Juan in Hell* interlude in *Man and Superman* and the Epilogue to *Saint Joan*. Whether or not he knew Freud's dream theories, Shaw was certainly aware of the workings of dreams even before Freud published his interpretation of dreams.[1] In 1911 Shaw had written to Gilbert Murray, "I am not very appreciative of the psychiatrists; but there may be something in their theory that repressed instincts, though subconscious, play a considerable part in our lives . . . and . . . the suppression apparently vanishes in sleep. . . ."[2] Indeed perhaps eight of the fifty-odd plays[3] in Shaw's canon can be considered to be—on one level—Freudian-type dream plays. *The Simpleton of the Unexpected Isles* (1934), Shaw's forty-third play, may be the last of these dream plays.

It is now generally accepted, whether or not one be a Freudian, that dream functions as a problem-solving mechanism. To Freud the dream begins with some unfinished business eliciting conflicts from all periods of life.[4] The dream unites the conflicts and presents them in a condensed but ambiguous manner without regard to logical niceties. The conflicts can then be settled along the lines of a wish fulfilled.[5] The underlying fantasy reflects upon and illuminates the manifest surface of the play in much the same way as the latent dream represents the thoughts and feelings of the manifest dream.[6] In the play, as in a dream, we see the story as it unfolds—consciously or otherwise. We also understand the sub-text that illuminates the story and that aids us in comprehending what the story means. To Freud the manifest dream is "composed of various fragments . . . held together by a binding medium, so that the designs that appear on it do not belong to the original [meaning] . . ."[7] It is, therefore, important that the latent content of the dream, or the dream play, not be judged solely by its manifest content, even when it tells a well organized story. "It must be seen as containing a hidden meaning which needs to be unscrambled to find its original meaning."[8] The stories in the manifest dream and the latent dream, or in the manifest play and the plays's underlying fantasy, however, need not be totally separate. Each contains the same ideas expressed in different forms, and the feelings in the manifest dream or play may be undistorted and accurately represent the feelings of the latent dream.[9] The resolution of one character's problem in the manifest play is not totally unrelated to the solving of the dreamer's problem in the dream play. It may even be a means to the solution of that problem. As the episodes in the manifest play help unravel the conflicts hidden in the latent play, the dreamer's frustrations and feelings are paralleled in each.

Shaw subtitled *The Simpleton* "A Vision of Judgment" and described it as a "fable." Others have called it myth, legend, iconography, and a vision.[10] He described the children resulting from the eugenic experiment as "four lovely phantasms," a *phantasm* being an "illusion; . . . an appearance that has no reality; . . . a dream."[11] As the rest of the play becomes a development of the Prologue, in which "what happens in Acts I and II is highly fantastic, . . . [and] what happens in the Prologue is not so much fantastic in itself as fantastically presented,"[12] the structure of the play might be the representation of a dream. In the play's chaotic, non-linear structure, past events are reflected in a distorting mirror in the succeeding acts, suggesting not only an air of fantasy but a dream in which events "go in contraries."[13]

When the play opened, the critics were baffled, and no wonder. What could they make of such absurd goings-on? The play, written immediately after Shaw had visited Jain temples in India, takes place on a tropical island that is part of the British Empire and is located somewhere in the Pacific. The Prologue opens in the Emigration Office, where Hugo Hyering, an unkempt and somewhat inebriated Emigration Officer, and Wilks, his clerk, are confronted by a rather determined Young Woman who wishes to settle on the island. The Emigration Officer, apparently public-school educated and convinced that he should not be condemned to suffer the "horrors" on this forsaken outpost of empire, has put an automatic pistol in his desk in order to murder the clerk before killing himself. The Young Woman, one of Shaw's "born Bosses," spends her life "making up other people's minds for them." Her motto is "Let life come to you." Like the heroine in *Saint Joan,* the Young Woman has something about her that others cannot resist. She has no papers, passport, or reason for being there and is in excess of the Immigration quota. Ordered sent back to England, she has remained. Once she has been admitted to the office, she berates the Emigration Officer for drinking and the clerk for not dusting. Getting her permit, she also gets the "gentleman" to take her on a tour of the island. Wilks knows life has passed him by rather than come to him. He dusts and tidies the office and uses the Emigration Officer's pistol to blow out his own brains—the fifth suicide that month.

The second scene of the Prologue is set atop a cliff overlooking the sea. The young man tells the Young Woman that he hates the climate, the boredom, his inability to have a woman. His salary is too small to support a white woman, and the colored women reject him as ignorant and because he smells bad. The Young Woman agrees that he is disgusting, for he reeks of indigestion, sweaty clothes, and alcohol. He announces that he is going to jump off the cliff and kill himself but is prevented from doing so by the sudden appearance of Pra, a beautifully dressed brown-skinned priest, as comfortable with himself as the young man is discontented. At first Pra tries to dissuade the young man from committing suicide at the cliff of life, offering to direct him to the cliff of death. The young man insists that he will kill himself wherever he pleases but finds that he is unable to leap off the cliff. The priest *"shoots his foot against the E.O.'s posterior and sends him over the cliff."* But he has not been sent to his apparent death. Caught in nets below, he is cleansed, body and soul. In Scene 3 he joins the Young Woman, the priest, and an amber-colored native priestess in their garden. The Young Woman is confused by a priestess who eats no meat, is married, and offers to share the young man with the Young Woman. A rather stuffy English lady tourist distributing tracts joins them. To enlighten her, Pra takes her into the Cave, where everyone but the lady tourist understands that, in this cave, enlightenment is achieved through sexual intercourse. When her husband appears, Prola, the priestess, takes him into the cave. The Emigration Officer hurls the Young Woman over the cliff so that she, too, can be cleansed.

Act II, which Shaw called the play, takes place twenty years later. Hugo Hyering, C.B., the erstwhile Emigration Officer, is now the political secretary of the Isles. The Young Woman is now his wife. The English tourist is now Lady Farwaters and her husband is now Sir Charles, Governor of the Unexpected Isles. The six characters from the garden have formed an unconventional group marriage and are the parents of four children. The two girls and two boys are "magically beautiful" but completely without any conscience or Bunyanesque work ethic. An English clergyman, Iddy, who had been kidnapped by pirates, has been cast ashore. Iddy's father was a scientist who experimented with feeding his son a high nitrogen diet. The human result of this other eugenic experiment is "weakminded."[14] Believing the languid children to be statues, he kisses one of the girls. They come to life and demand that if he loves one, he must love the other because Maya is Vashti and Vashti is Maya. The act ends with Iddy embracing both girls and going off with them into the darkness.

The last act takes place a few years later. The eugenic experiment has failed. The beautiful children are physically as well as morally sterile. Maya and Vashti detest Iddy and want to kill him. Warships from various colonies in the Empire are massed in the harbor, some threatening to attack if Iddy's polygamous marriage is not dissolved, some threatening to attack if it is dissolved. At noon they disappear.

Kanchin and Janga, the sons, bring in the next day's newspaper. The world is in chaos. England is threatening to withdraw from the Empire. Ireland will not allow England to commit such an act of treason. South Africa has given the English ten days to leave all of Africa. The four children want to kill and kill and kill. What seems to be a large bird appears, and gunfire is heard as islanders attempt to shoot it from the sky. The bird is an Angel announcing Judgment Day, when all useless persons will vanish, country by country, beginning in England.

Judgment Day, explains the angel, "is not the end of the world, but the end of its childhood and the beginning of its responsible maturity." Maya, Vashti, Kanchin, and Janga vanish, and their parents cannot even remember that the children had existed. Iddy leaves to return to England to do his work there. The Farwaters pair and Mr. Hyering return to their work, confident that they will not disappear. Mrs. Hyering, the supremely confident Young Woman of the Prologue, is unsure of her worth. Prola reminds her to "Let life come to you" and enigmatically bids her "Goodbye." As the play ends, Pra and Prola, alone on stage, look forward to the life to come.

The playwright seemed to attack all conventions—religious, moral, and social—while calling for the destruction of much of society, only to replace it with an allegedly better world still much like the one that had been destroyed. Yet the play is no tragedy, for its ending contains optimism and hope. Its shapelessness, its absurdities, its moving from despair to hope, suggest that what we are seeing is a dream.

A dream needs a dreamer. That dreamer needs a problem, and that problem should find a solution. Who is our dreamer? In the earlier plays, the identity of the dreamer is obvious. Raina in *Arms and the Man* retires to her bed; the feverish Invalid in *Too True to Be Good* is asleep in her bed. (It is her microbe that speaks to the audience.) Ellie Dunn in *Heartbreak House* falls asleep just after her arrival while waiting for her tea, and Johnny Tarleton in *Misalliance* is in a heat-induced daydream. But in *Simpleton* there is no one who seems to be asleep, dozing, or even daydreaming. There is, however, a rather inebriated young man, bored, socially and professionally frustrated, contemplating suicide. Educated on "dead languages and histories that are lies," he is certain to have read *Faust* and *The Tempest* as well as *Candide, Pilgrim's Progress, The Aeneid,* and the *New Testament,* echoes of all of which can be found in this play. Shaw, in his dream plays, includes language that provides the reader or viewer with clues to the dream-like subtext. In the second scene of the Prologue, the Emigration Officer exclaims when Pra appears, "Is he real; or is it the drink?" When the play opens, might the E. O. be seated at his desk in a drunken stupor rather than sitting at his desk, apparently writing?

Before the play opened, the Emigration Officer had already confronted the Young Woman and denied her an entry permit. Although sexually starved, he has thereby rejected the only potential partner he might have. He hates his job and his clerk. In the dreamlike events that follow, he gets rid of his hated clerk, gets the girl, and rises to a position of prominence, complete with a C.B. When the useless people disappear, he is found to be deserving.

A dreamer, a problem, a solution.

What other clues have we that this might be a dream? In a dream, characters "split, double, multiply, vanish, solidify, blur, clarify."[15] "Within the allegory of the play they (Pra and Prola) represent the Young Woman and the Officer on another level of being."[16] Prola tells us that Pra "has many names." In Pra, the wise, serene, self-confident priest, attractive both to white women and to women of color, we see the reverse of the repressed, unkempt, self-hating white man. In Mr. Farwaters, later Sir Charles the Governor, we see the successful colonial officer that Hyering can barely aspire to be. Somehow all three men are father to the four children, and all three are among those who survive the Day of Judgment.

The Young Woman, Mrs. Farwaters, and Prola seem to be different aspects of the same person. All three are the mothers of the four children. The confident Young Woman becomes the wife of a middle-level colonial officer. Mrs. Farwaters begins as such a woman and rises to become wife of the Governor. In Prola, the priestess, we can see the Young Woman in maturity. Sexually confident, intelligent, serene. While the Young Woman is eager to let life come, Prola knows that life is within

her. The play ends with Prola pronouncing the Young Woman's earlier
words, "Let life come to you. . . . Let it come."

Split images that mirror but distort each other, the Simpleton Iddy
and the four children of the Unexpected Isles are sterile products of
failed eugenic experiments. Iddy, a walking super-ego, all conscience,
morality, and guilt, has neither beauty nor intelligence. Maya, Vashti,
Janga, and Kanchin are art and beauty but have no conscience. Iddy
learns the value of work. The four children never do. Maya and Vashti
insist that they are one, Vashti Maya, Maya Vashti. All vanish from the
Islands before the play ends. The four children disappear as one, and
Iddy returns to England.

Aspects of one's past may appear in a dream, although inverted
or distorted from the reality. In Phosphor Hammingtop—Iddy the
Simpleton—we can see an absurd Prospero of *The Tempest.* Even Iddy's
name, "Phosphor," echoes and distorts "Prospero." Exiled to a faraway
island, surrounded by fantastical characters until he can return to his
homeland, Prospero is content with his books and with his magical
powers. The weakminded Phosphor knows little more than "my little
treasure of words spoken by my Lord Jesus." What books he might have
read he has not retained. Prospero returns to rule Milan. Iddy, wanting
little more than a village, a cottage, a garden, and a church, returns to
the England that the young Emigration Officer longs for.

Christian dogma is inverted when Maya and Vashti proclaim to Iddy
that "We are the way. We are the life," but what they offer is seduction,
not salvation.

Symbols and language are also indicators of the dream. The loaded
pistol that the young man is unable to use seems almost too obvious a
symbol for his sexual frustrations. Water, "particularly immersion in it,
always refers to pregnancy and birth."[17] Both the young man and the
Young Woman are reborn after their immersion in the sea, having fallen
off a cliff. Falling through an unknown is a common feature in a dream.
Caves suggest body cavities, especially female genitalia. Both the English
gentleman and woman are reborn in the caves through sexual intercourse with Prola and Pra. A rather extraordinary exchange, full of
contradictory sexual symbols, takes place when Iddy discovers that the
"statues" are real. Vashti claims that she can see his aura, Maya his halo,
both symbols of female genitalia. The brothers warn Iddy, on the other
hand, "They will break thy spear. They will pierce thy shield" as if he
and they were hermaphroditic. The sun and flames, as are all things
with far-reaching associations with heat, are phallic symbols. But it is the
female Maya-Vashti who chant, "Dare you tread the plains of heaven
with us? . . . We are waves of life in a sea of bliss. . . . We are the life. . . .
I am the light. . . . I am the fire. Feel how it glows."

Ships, vessels that can cleave the water, can symbolize both female and male genitalia. The ships in the harbor, which disappear as suddenly as they appear, have massed to protest, or support, the unconventional (by British standards) marriage of the clergyman and the two girls. Taking a trip, especially westward, and disappearing may be symbolic variants of death. During World War I "going west" (i.e., toward sunset) was a euphemism for dying. The Young Woman does not want to go west to England. She is quite insistent that she wants life to come to her. Iddy, after the disappearance of Maya and Vashti, leaves the Unexpected Isles to go west to England (and Prospero returned to Milan even though "Every third thought will be my grave"[18]).

At several points in the play, Shaw reminds us that what we are seeing just might be a dream. Vashti calls out, "I will return in dreams." Iddy says, "I can take anything if you will only tell it to me in a gentle hushabyebaby sort of way." Hyering tells Iddy, "Try to sleep a little . . ." and Iddy responds, "Sleep. I will not sleep. . . . I wont relax." Janga says the Pope "calls on all Christendom to celebrate the passing away of the last vain dream of earthly empire. . . ." Pra says to Prola, "Helen was a dream. You are not a dream" and refers to "Our dream of founding a millennial world culture; the dream which united Prola and Pra as you first knew them. . . ."

Their dream, the Unexpected Isles, is a failed utopia, and "no true Utopia has any reference to reality, but is merely an image of what the mind considers desirable."[19] But just as there is a optimistic note there is a prophetic warning, for "occasionally, the symbol may stand for itself."[20] Pra tells us, "There is no Country of the Unexpected. The Unexpected Isles are the whole world."

The symbols of death abound in *Simpleton*. Written in 1934, it decries the destruction of World War I, the angel reminding the audience, "If you want a great noise, you have your cannons. If you want a fervent heat to burn your earth you have your high explosives. If you want vials of wrath to rain down on you, they are ready in your arsenals, full of poison gases. Some years ago you had them all in full play, burning up the earth and spreading death, famine, and pestilence." Pra, predicting the destruction that was to begin only five years later, says, "We shall plan commonwealths when our empires have brought us to the brink of destruction; . . . We shall make wars because only under the strain of war are we capable of changing the world; but the changes our wars make will never be the changes we intended to make. . . ." In the world, as in the Unexpected Isles, there is nothing permanent. The empire that England threatened to leave, would instead leave England. The colonies that massed their ships in the beginning of Act II would disappear, as did the ships, to become sovereign nations. Pra and Prola may urge us to work for the best and to hail the life to come, but the young gentleman's wish-fulfillment dream in the play would in reality become a nightmare.

To make sense of Shaw's design we must recognize that the play is a fuller, alternative version of the content of the first scene. Examining the fantastical series of events that occur as a dream shows us a young man reaching beyond his immediate frustrations to become a useful being. Whether in the manifest play or the dream play, he rejects suicide, letting life, not death, come to him.[21]

Notes

1. See Rodelle Weintraub, "Johnny's Dream," *SHAW* 7 (1987): 175–77, for a fuller discussion of the pre-Freudism in Shaw's early dream plays.

2. Bernard Shaw, *Collected Letters 1911–1925*, ed. Dan H. Laurence (New York: Viking, 1985), pp. 18. In Bernard Shaw, *Collected Letters 1926–1950*, ed. Dan H. Laurence (New York: Viking, 1988), p. 391, Laurence states, "It is doubtful if Shaw had more than a second-hand acquaintance with the works of Sigmund Freud (1856–1939), though he made frequent reference to him in the later correspondence." *Collected Letters 1926–1950* includes five letters in which Shaw mentions Freud or Freudianism. There are no references to Freud in the earlier three volumes of the *Collected Letters*.

3. I exclude play fragments.

4. Before Freud wrote his *Interpretation of Dreams* he was aware that Von Schubert in *The Symbolism of Dreams* had suggested that dreams could only be understood as forms of wish-fulfillment. Freud also exploited what he had learned from Fleiss. Referred to in Richard Webster, *Why Freud Was Wrong* (New York: Basic Books, 1995), p. 260.

5. Walter A. Stewart and Lucy Freeman, *The Secret of Dreams* (New York: Macmillan, 1972), p. 73.

6. Ibid., p. 152.

7. Quoted in Ibid., p. 73.

8. Ibid., p. 73.

9. Ibid.

10. Margery M. Morgan, *The Shavian Playground* (London: Methuen, 1972), pp. 286–302.

11. *Compact Edition of the Oxford English Dictionary* (1982), pp. 1250–51.

12. Morgan, p. 290.

13. *Collected Plays with Their Prefaces*, ed. Dan H. Laurence (London: Max Reinhardt, 1970–74), 6:783. All quotations from *Simpleton* are from this edition, 6:765–840.

14. Shaw, who referred to Antoine Lavoisier and nitrogen in the Preface to *On the Rocks*, which was written immediately before *Simpleton*, knew that Lavoisier had recognized the element and had named it *azote* because of its inability to support life although it was a constituent of all living matter (*Encyclopedia Britannica* [Chicago: Encyclopedia Britannica, 1974], 7:360). Nitrogen narcosis: The anesthetic of intoxicating effects produced by nitrogen gas when breathed under pressure, as under water, by a diver, results in mild

cases of "intoxicating feeling of lightheadedness, euphoria, . . .carefreeness. The reasoning ability and manual dexterity may next be slowed down" (*Britannica* 7:361). Knowledgeable about the properties of phosphorus as well as nitrogen, Shaw may have the Emigration Officer smell offensive because, ironically, whites have traditionally considered blacks foul-smelling, and phosphorus was first derived from urine, which contains nitrogen. The Emigration Officer, in his dream, inverts the information he may have learned about phosphorus and applies it to himself instead of to the darkskinned Pra and, again remembering the phosphorus, uses it for the name of Iddy.

15. August Strindberg, *Dream Play* (1901), quoted in Morgan, p. 200.

16. Morgan, p. 294. Frederic Berg, in "Shaw's *The Simpleton of the Unexpected Isles:* A New Approach," *Modern Drama* 36:4 (December 1993): 541, suggests that the Young Woman and the Emigration Officer, Mrs. and Mr. Farwaters, and Prola and Pra represent three stages of maturity in the same persons, while the four children and Iddy balance each other.

17. Leon L. Altman, *The Dream in Psychoanalysis* (New York: International Universities Press, 1975), p. 24. Other referents for symbols are based on this book, pp. 22–30.

18. *The Tempest,* V.i.312.

19. Morgan, p. 295.

20. Altman, p. 23.

21. An earlier version of this paper was presented at the International Association for the Study of Anglo-Irish Literature (IASAIL) 1994 Conference, Sassari-Alghero, Sardinia, Italy.

Elizabeth Anne Hull

ON HIS SHOULDERS:
SHAW'S INFLUENCE ON
CLARKE'S *CHILDHOOD'S END*

Arthur C. Clarke deliberately titillated his readers by asking his publishers to add the following statement to the publication facts on the
prefatory pages of the various editions of his novel *Childhood's End:* "The
opinions expressed in this book are not those of the author."[1] When I
had the opportunity to ask Clarke what he meant by this statement, he
momentarily sidestepped the issue by saying, "That was rather naughty
of me, wasn't it!" He explained that he merely wanted people to be
warned that some of the characters would be saying things that he did
not necessarily endorse. Particularly, he said he did not believe that the
alien Overlord Karellen was correct when he said, "The stars are not for
man," and he did not want readers to accept the Overlords' prohibition
against exploring outer space just because Jan does.[2]

But Clarke, like any other writer, need not be taken entirely at face
value when he explains his own work or tries years later to remember
just which sources influenced his artistic choices at the moment of
creation. In response to an earlier draft of this paper Clarke wrote,
"Frankly, the only Shaw I ever read was BTM and M&S—about the other
[plays] you mention, I don't know! (I'm afraid I'm a literary barbarian)."[3]

Shaw reminds us that we fictionalize ourselves and offers this principle
of self-criticism: "Sometimes I do not see what the play was driving at
until quite a long time after I have finished it; and even then I may be
wrong about it just as any critical third party may."[4] In his "Epistle

Dedicatory to Arthur Bingham Walkley" of *Man and Superman,* Shaw says, "I should make formal acknowledgment to the authors whom I have pillaged in the following pages if I could recollect them all."[5]

The principle of "good reasons and real reasons" is also relevant to explain why an author chooses one word or a particular detail or makes a statement that can be understood by unsophisticated readers following a story on one level while initiates will perceive additional implications. Good reasons are ones that we can tell others to cover our true motives for our actions—and sometimes we can even fool ourselves. Moreover, sometimes good reasons coincide with and are real reasons, but even then these good reasons are not necessarily the main reasons. This may apply to Clarke's disclaimer: He did want to disown the Overlords' limitations on humanity, but in a greater sense his disclaimer of the opinions expressed in *CE* is justified by the debt he owes to others, and to Shaw in particular—not just for the plays, but also for the prefaces Shaw wrote to explain his themes, which Shaw felt were too often overlooked or misunderstood by a public that adored him and made him rich and famous.

While Clarke was original and did not simply lift his ideas from Shaw, Clarke took Shaw's ideas and adapted them for his own ends. Shaw himself admitted that, in learning his craft of play writing, "I was finding that the surest way to produce an effect of daring innovation and originality was to revive the ancient attraction of long theatrical speeches; to stick closely to the methods of Moliere; and to lift characters bodily out of the pages of Charles Dickens" (*BTM* 2:x).

Indeed, while reading Shaw's *BTM* and *CE* together it is easy to see that Clarke borrowed heavily from Shaw in order to give embodiment to his epic story. But more importantly, the ideas Clarke expressed differ somewhat in regard to Shaw's concept of the Life Force and Creative Evolution, and differ significantly in regard to the social context of humanity's immediate future. While both Shaw and Clarke challenge mankind to take responsibility for choosing a future that we will wish to live with, Shaw is a cautious optimist, as befits his principal genre of choice, comedy, whereas Clarke is reluctantly pessimistic. Hence the cloudy ending of *CE,* which focuses on Karellen's future on the dark and dusty plain while humanity has evolved and gone on to glory, joining with the Overmind. Childhood's end has meant the end of humanity as we know it, and the pictures Clarke paints of the children before they depart are bleak indeed: "Then Jan saw their faces. He swallowed hard, and forced himself not to turn away. They were emptier than the faces of the dead, for even a corpse has some record carved by time's chisel upon its features, to speak when the lips themselves are dumb. There was no more emotion or feeling here than in the face of a snake or an insect. The Overlords themselves were more human than this" (*CE* 202–3).

Clarke's pessimism is evident much earlier in *CE,* of course, when he describes the results of the Golden Age of peace that the Overlords usher in. In spite of all the material comforts and advances in health and social justice that have resulted from the enforced end of war and strife, both science and art have stagnated and religion has died. Only a few humans still possess initiative, and even those—like Jan, who tries to outwit the Overlords in finding a way to escape Earth and visit the Overlords' home planet—are surprisingly easy to discourage. The elite group of artists and scientists that is the focus of "The Last Generation" withdraws to New Athens (where their primary aim is for each of them to be the best at their chosen field). Yet even this elite colony, the cream of humanity, commits mass suicide in despair when their children take the next evolutionary step without their parents. Clarke's image of "the segments of uranium [rushing] together, seeking the union they could never achieve" (*CE* 188) is particularly intriguing as a metaphor for human isolation; we are born and die alone. Together we might achieve great heights, but no matter how we try to touch each other, we fail because of our very nature. By contrast, Shaw's view of the future in *Tragedy of an Elderly Gentleman* is a Fabian Socialist heaven. Although it is far less detailed and shown mostly off-stage by implication rather than dramatization, the Elderly Gentleman's response of despair at the transformation that he cannot participate in is very similar to the New Athenians' despair at the loss of their own children.

Readers can infer that Clarke admired Shaw since he chose to have the characters in New Athens produce *BTM.* Clarke seems to have been inspired to give embodiment to his own version of Creative Evolution as dramatized in *BTM* and elucidated by Shaw in his commentary. Shaw threw out a challenge to every artist to "produce a masterpiece," and he felt that he had done so with *BTM,* which he proudly claimed a "world classic or it is nothing" (*BTM* 2:xci, cvi).

Clarke accepted this challenge. Some characters are strongly reminiscent of Shaw, like the lovable philanderer George Greggson, who may have been inspired by Tanner/Don Juan from *Man and Superman*— George Greggson is no more in control of the courtship of Jean Morrel than Shaw's protagonist was. Rupert Boyce's beautiful wife Maia might remind the reader of Maya from *The Simpleton of the Unexpected Isles,* despite Clarke's disclaimer that he never read or saw this play. Clarke made his own myths to inspire and challenge his readers to better themselves.

One clear difference between Clarke's and Shaw's vision is that Clarke seems clearly atheistic. Shaw promoted what he called a Lamarckian view of evolution based on the will of the organism to improve or change and discounted belief in a mindless evolution of Darwin as being "blind coarseness and shallow logic" (*BTM* 2:liv) and just too depressing to bear, for "If it could be proved that the whole universe had been produced by such Selection, only fools and rascals could bear to live" (*BTM* 2:lvi). Whereas Clarke shows that atheism is quite bearable in "The Golden Age," saying, "it had always been clear to any rational mind that *all* the world's religious writings could not be true." After the Overlords bring "the fierce and passionless light of truth, faiths that had sustained millions for twice a thousand years vanished like morning dew. . . . All the good and all the evil they had wrought were swept suddenly into the past, and could touch the minds of men no more. Humanity had lost its ancient gods: now it was old enough to have no need for new ones" (*CE* 74–75).

Shaw first tried to show the world what he meant by the new religion of the Life Force and Creative Evolution in *Man and Superman,* which one critic described as "Shaw's . . . most important play in aim and scope," even though "The weakness of the play is that its integrity depends wholly upon a theme too impersonal to be developed as drama."[6] And of *The Simpleton of the Unexpected Isles,* Shaw's attempt at dramatizing an experiment in human development through selective breeding, the same critic concluded, "The play is rich in dramatic content, but not consistent in its dramatic structure, for the protagonist does not fulfill his function, and the tension is either merely amusing and satirical or talked about and abstract, rather than immediate and concrete. It is entertaining, and, in a high degree, moving, but on the whole unsatisfying."[7] This critic has identified two vital weaknesses in stage drama: the difficulty of having to show the audience the action rather than allowing the reader to imagine the unimaginable and wondrous for himself, and the audience's desire for clear lines of conflict, with an identifiable protagonist and antagonist. These are certainly not insurmountable difficulties. Nevertheless, the epic cast of characters proves a challenge to someone reading the plays, and perhaps may be beyond the capacity of most people in an audience to retain, except for the already familiar characters of the myths and legends Shaw incorporates in these plays. Another critic agrees, calling *BTM* "on the whole, a dramatic composition so tedious as barely to support the spectator's attention in the theater."[8]

This difficulty of fragmentation is not completely gone in the novel *CE,* but the reader has a greater control of print, which is not time-bound in the way that a dramatic performance is, and the typical science fiction reader may be even more prepared by the history of the genre to accept the notion that the ideas are more important than any individual character and that themes are more likely to be concerned with the human condition than with individual human behavior. Certainly it is easier to convey the idea of mixed race of the brother and sister, Jan and Maia, in narrative in *CE* than on the stage, where Shaw specifies that the dark Asian Maya and the blond European Vashti in *Simpleton* must be played by two separate actresses. The mixed breeding experiment of the six parents must be explained in dialogue or the concept will be lost to the audience. In fact, in the recent revival of *Simpleton* in London (Orange Tree Theater Richmond, November 1995–January 1996) the two female children were played by two Asian women and the two male children were played by two European men, totally confusing the audience about the genetic heritage of the four children!

It can be argued that Shaw idealized his women characters[9] in these science fiction plays: from Ann Whitefield to Ana, Lilith to Eve, Clara and Mrs. Etteen to Savvy, Prola to Maya and Vashti. All of them are superficial personalities who have funny lines, but live more as legends, myths, and archetypes than as women. (The dramatist does, however, have the advantage in building character that the audience can see the living actors on stage, giving them immediate substantiality.) Clarke also has been criticized for his weak characterization of women in *CE,* and admittedly he takes few pains to draw a believable Jean Morrel, whose name suggests a type, like one of Shakespeare's clowns. At the party hosted by Rupert Boyce (whose name is somehow faintly reminiscent of both Joyce Burge and Lubin from *BTM*) and his new wife, the multiracial Maia, Jean Morrel is characterized chiefly by her cattiness about Rupert's many marriages and her feelings about the nuisance created by the fundamental polygamous nature of men: "On the other hand if they weren't . . . Yes, perhaps it was better this way, after all" (*CE* 79). In George Greggson's philandering and Jean's tolerance of it, there seems to be a mirror role-reversal of Mrs. Etteen's attitude expressed in "A Glimpse of the Domesticity of Franklyn Barnabas" (the part of *The Gospel of the Brothers Barnabas* originally withheld from performance and publication but that saw print in 1932): "Every good wife should commit a few infidelities to keep her husband in countenance. The extent to which married people strain their relations by pretending that there is only one man or woman in the world for them is so tragic that we have to laugh at it to save ourselves from crying" (*BTM* 2:cliii). For both Shaw and Clarke, ideas are clearly more important than individuals. And they both discourage the reader from becoming overly attached emotionally to any of the characters, for as soon as we feel we know them, they are replaced by others.

Jean fulfills her role as the channel that reveals the Overlords' home planet to Maia's wiser brother Jan, but she has little life aside from being the wife of George and mother of the first two children to evolve. She also functions in the plot to echo the apprehensions of the earlier antagonist, Alexander Wainwright, expressing her fears about the Over- lords' goals: "I don't mean they're evil, or anything foolish like that. I'm sure they mean well and are doing what they think is best for us. I just wonder what their plans really are" (*CE* 106).

Shaw's men are just as artificial as his women. John Tanner says the lines that Shaw wants the reader to hear, as do Adam and Cain and Franklyn and Conrad Barnabas. It is the debate that matters, and Shaw trusts his audience to draw its own conclusions, even though he repeatedly laments in his prefaces that his faith in the common man has been misplaced. In fact, he feels that most people are "untaught or mistaught, . . . so ignorant and incapable politically that . . . a statesman who told them the truth would not be understood, and would in effect mislead them more completely than if he dealt with them according to their blindness instead of to his own wisdom" (*BTM* 2:lxviii). Shaw claims, "I have to make my heresies pleasing as plays to extract the necessary shillings from those to whom they are also intensely irritating" (*BTM* 2:xcix), even though he also says, "In writing *BTM* I threw over all economic considerations" (*BTM* 2:xcvi). But Shaw was writing comedy, which demands less plausibility of characterization, relying on funny lines and situations to carry its weight with the audience.

Nevertheless, Clarke takes no more pains to make George Greggson an individual than he does with Maia Boyce and Jean Morrel. George is a man with a wandering eye, basically a good sort who loves and takes care of his family, but left vague enough for the reader to supply the details from his own experience of such types.

While still not completely developed, the two most interesting and well-drawn characters in *CE* are Karellen (who might be taken as the protagonist of the novel, since he is the only individual who is present all the way from the Prologue to the last page) and Jan Rodricks, of whom Karellen says: "Human beings are remarkably ingenious, and often very persistent. It is never safe to underestimate them" (*CE* 104). Even if he is not perceived as the protagonist at this point, Karellen may be functioning as a *raisonneur* for Clarke in this statement, despite Clarke's disclaimer-warning not to believe everything Karellen (or Jan) says.

As Clarke introduces him, Jan is not only very broadly and deeply educated, but also on a long rebound from an unhappy love affair with a woman whom he regards as the "one real love in his life" (*CE* 91). Thus Jan is like Rikki Stormgren in "Earth and the Overlords" in his coolness and detachment from his fellow human beings. As Stormgren makes the ideal loyal working dog for Karellen because of his cold isolation and disinterest in human factions, Jan makes the ideal observer for the Overlords to view the end of the Earth and report to them the way the final moments look to a member of humanity, a species capable of art, which the Overlords are not. Because he is so isolated, the Overlords can let Jan entrap himself in their whale and disgorge him like Jonah when it suits their purpose without risk of a guilty conscience about taking him from his family and loved ones on Earth. Like a dog, he faces the exile from his own species and accepts the companionship of the Overlords as sufficient to prevent him from feeling utterly alone (*CE* 208). The Overlords even reward him by allowing him to achieve his goal at last of becoming the best pianist on Earth, and he willingly dies in fulfilling the Overlords' goals, repaying what he considers his "debt" to the Overlords (*CE* 213).

It is clear, however, that Karellen is not quite so obedient a dog in serving the Overmind. Near the end, Jan begins to realize that "Karellen was involved in some vast and complicated plot. Even while he served it, he was studying the Overmind with all the instruments at his command," and Jan begins to suspect that the Overlords dream of escaping from their peculiar bondage (*CE* 213–14).

We are left finally with Karellen's view: "a sadness that no logic could dispel. He did not mourn for Man: his sorrow was for his own race, forever barred from greatness by forces it could not overcome. . . . Yet, Karellen knew, they would hold fast until the end: they would await without despair whatever destiny was theirs. They would serve the Overmind because they had no choice, but even in that service they would not lose their souls" (*CE* 217–18).

As much as Shaw lectured in his prefaces, he was a successful playwright because he dramatized a situation and let the audience draw its own conclusions. In a reply to Joseph Wood Krutch's assertion that his plays were devoid of meaning, Shaw explained, "I like my patients to leave the hospital without a suspicion that they have been operated on and are leaving it with a new set of glands."[10] Likewise, Clarke does not lecture on human nature. He lets the story reveal the dual nature of humanity, our physical isolation and our social need to join with one another to achieve more than any individual alone can achieve, and above all, our many needs for other human beings—social, psychological, sexual, and physical needs that must be met—in order for individuals and our species to survive, much less to thrive and continue to evolve toward our potential destiny.

Nor does Clarke lecture on the subject of art in *CE* except to note that in the Golden Age, the production of original art has declined along with religion and science. However, he shows how interested the Overlords are in human art, music, literature, and adornment for its own sake, even though Jan discovers on his visit to their planet that the Overlords have no apparent art of their own to join them together. Significantly, the Overlords do not see the same phenomena that humans see when they observe the Overmind.

Shaw uses the largest part of his preface to *BTM* to explain why the art of fiction in particular is necessary. The artist has to create myths that can inspire humanity to rise above its everyday concerns of spinning and digging, to make the changes that take us in the direction of improvement, lest we fall into degeneracy and despair.

In his preface to *Farfetched Fables* (1950), Shaw comments about the necessity of culture for civilization: "Without culture possible in every home democratic civilization is impossible, because equality of opportunity is impossible. . . . Consequently the basic income to be aimed at must be sufficient to establish culture in every home, and wages must be levelled up, not down."[11] Clarke seems to be a little less optimistic than Shaw about the improvability of the common man, in that the Golden Age provides the leisure for culture, but creativity, both in art and science, is stagnant.

Shaw also worried about the mental capacity of the masses, saying, "Most of us so far are ungovernable by abstract thought. Our inborn sense of right and wrong, of grace and sin, must be embodied for us in a supernatural ruler of the universe: omnipotent, omniscient, all wise, all benevolent" (*FF* 460). Clarke, by contrast, trusts humanity (and his readers) to live without God. Clarke makes the Overmind explicitly limited in its powers: it is not God or it would not need the Overlords to carry out its aims.

Pessimistic as he seems, Clarke does offer some hope for humanity. He dramatizes the concept of second-rate minds who can nevertheless achieve their goals: the kidnappers of Stormgren, Pierre Duval (who helps Stormgren catch a forbidden glimpse of Karellen), and Professor Sullivan (who builds the sarcophagus in the whale for Jan).

Finally, Clarke owes Shaw for the picture of the Overmind. Jan asks the Overlord Rashaverak why the powerful Overmind needs the Overlords: "With all its tremendous powers, surely it could do anything it pleased." He is told, "it has its limits. In the past . . . it attempted to act directly upon the minds of other races, and to influence their cultural development. It's always failed, perhaps because the gulf is too great" (*CE* 206).

Shaw felt that a remote, awful, cruel, sinless perfection of a God was unbearable to humanity and further claimed, "to admit that God can err, or that He is powerless in any particular, is to deprive Him of the attributes that qualify Him as God; but it is a very healthy admission for the strongminded. It increases our sense of responsibility for social welfare, and is radiant with boundless hope of human betterment. Our will to live depends on hope; for we die of despair, or, as I have called it in the Methuselah cycle, discouragement" *(BTM* 2:c).

Ironically, the pessimist Clarke challenges his readers to be strongminded, whereas the optimist Shaw invariably left his audience with a comic ending. Shaw claimed, "we must either embrace Creative Evolution or fall into the bottomless pit of an utterly discouraging pessimism" *(BTM* 2:cv). And Shaw concludes, "Discouragement does in fact mean death; and it is better to cling to the hoariest of the savage old creator-idols, however diabolically vindictive than ab[a]ndon all hope in a world of 'angry apes,' and perish in despair . . ." *(BTM* 2:cvi).

Shaw expresses doubts about the general ability of people to govern themselves wisely, saying in his preface to *FF*, "Democracy means government in the interest of everybody. It most emphatically does not mean government BY everybody" *(FF* 6:474). Moreover, he states, "as the majority is always against any change, and it takes at least thirty years to convert it, whilst only ten per cent or thereabouts of the population has sufficient mental capacity to foresee its necessity or desirability, a time lag is created in which the majority is always out-of-date" *(FF* 6:477). This idea (with another twenty years added for good measure) would seem to be behind the fifty-year time lapse that the Overlords demand before they will show themselves.

Clarke would no doubt agree with Shaw that "We must not stay as we are, doing always what was done last time, or we shall stick in the mud" *(BTM* 2:civ), but he is not so willing to reject science as a path for change. Clarke's Golden Age remains a challenge to present-day humanity: we can make the world a paradise if we cease our war and competitiveness against one another, adopting a cooperative attitude of respect that finds the color of a person's skin merely an aesthetic question, not one to determine that individual's "place" in the world.

In *FF*, Shaw saw the advent of atomic weapons as a temporary deterrent to war, only so long as the secret is not shared. Humanity survives—in altered form, able to eat grass or live on air, "free to do what they like instead of what they must" *(FF* 6:506). When the Hermaphrodite in the Fifth Fable wants to be "a mind and nothing but a mind" *(FF* 6:510), Rose (representing all women) agrees, but reminds the Hermaphrodite that this has not yet occurred and that "meanwhile . . . the world must be peopled" *(FF* 6:510). In the final fable, the teacher cautions that "even the vortexes have to do their work by trial and error. They have to learn by mistakes as well as by successes" *(FF* 6:517).

The class is visited by Raphael, who claims to be a re-embodied vortex, tells them that "curiosity never dies" (*FF* 6:520), and then vanishes. The teacher challenges the class to continue to ask questions, but the message seems mixed, considering the fate of the unstable vortex.

Clarke seems to have a more positive attitude toward the sharing of knowledge. His alien Overlords show that there are enough external dangers in the universe to unite humanity. As he makes clear in the Prologue to *CE*, the arms race and the space race are insignificant compared with the human race.

But at the very end of *CE*, Clarke focuses not on the Overmind of which humanity has become a part, but on the noble failure of the Overlords, who continue to struggle to determine their own destiny. Whereas the Overmind seems to be created in the image Lilith describes as a "vortex freed from matter, . . . [a] whirlpool in pure intelligence" (*BTM* 2:261), Karellen can be seen as an evolutionary example of the dead end that Lilith warned of at the end of *As Far as Thought Can Reach*: "I say, let them dread, of all things, stagnation" (*BTM* 2:262).

Of Karellen Clarke says, "his people were no better than a tribe that had passed its whole existence upon some flat and dusty plain. . . . Yet, Karellen knew, they would hold fast until the end: they would await without despair whatever destiny was theirs. They would serve the Overmind because they had no choice, but even in that service they would not lose their souls. . . . No one dared disturb him or interrupt his thoughts" (*CE* 218), and Clarke leaves it to his readers to imagine what those thoughts might be.

In our physical isolation from each other, we are in fact more like the Overlords than the Overmind. While making a myth of a glorious aggregate Overmind that is able to accomplish far more than any puny isolated human being could, Clarke lets us reach the conclusion that we will not likely see any such transformation of our natures in our lifetimes.

The challenge, then, is implicit but clear: we must do the best we can with what we have to work with; we must take the world as we find it and try to change in the direction that might eventually, generations from now, let us reach the place where we would like to be, even if by then our goals may be different. To do otherwise is to be the doggy instrument of others, not ourselves. If we do nothing, we have only ourselves to blame if the changes that will inevitably occur are not in the direction we want to go, toward building the world we would like to live in and the society in which we want our children to mature.

In one thing it seems certain Clarke would agree with Shaw: it cannot be a static utopia, for change is inevitable, whether it be evolution or destruction. Both men challenge their audiences to be among the active few who do not just accept what seems inevitable, but who will shape humanity's future beyond their own limited views. Both recognize that even the best-intentioned of humanity may make mistakes (and learn from them, one hopes), but we cannot choose to remain as we are, or forces beyond us will destroy us. Neither provides comforting answers. Both Shaw and Clarke do what science fiction does best: make the audience continue to ask questions.[12]

Notes

1. Arthur C. Clarke, *Childhood's End* (New York: Ballantine, 1953). Further citations of *CE* refer to this edition and appear in the text in parentheses.

2. Interview at Seacon, Brighton, England, August 1979.

3. Letter to Frederik Pohl and Elizabeth Anne Hull dated 14 February 1996.

4. Bernard Shaw, "Postscript[:] After Twentyfive Years" (following his original preface to *Back to Methuselah*), in *Complete Plays with Prefaces* (New York: Dodd, Mead, 1963), 2:xci. Further citations of *BTM* refer to this edition and appear in the text in parentheses.

5. Bernard Shaw, *Seven Plays* (New York: Dodd, Mead, 1951), pp. 506–7.

6. C. B. Purdom, *A Guide to the Plays of Bernard Shaw* (New York: Crowell, 1963), pp. 265, 271.

7. Ibid., p. 302.

8. Maurice Valency, *"Back to Methuselah:* A Tract in Epic Form," in *George Bernard Shaw: Modern Critical Views,* ed. Harold Bloom (New York: Chelsea House, 1987), p. 171.

9. Sally Peters Vogt, "Ann and Superman: Type and Archetype," in *Fabian Feminist: Bernard Shaw and Woman,* ed. Rodelle Weintraub (University Park: Penn State University Press, 1977), rpt. in *George Bernard Shaw: Modern Critical Views,* pp. 215–32.

10. Bernard Shaw, "The Simple Truth of the Matter," *Malvern Festival 1935* (London: Ad-Visers Ltd., 1935); rpt. in play book for *The Simpleton of the Unexpected Isles* (London: Orange Tree Theatre, [1955]), p. 11.

11. Preface to *Farfetched Fables,* in *Complete Plays with Prefaces,* 6:459. Further citations of *FF* refer to this edition and appear in the text in parentheses.

12. In "Shaw's Science Fiction on the Boards" in this volume, Ben P. Indick provides Clarke's account of his direct correspondence with Shaw (see pages 33–34, above). For Shaw's letters to Clarke dated 25 and 31 January 1947, see *Collected Letters 1926–1950,* ed. Dan H. Laurence (New York: Viking, 1988), pp. 792–93.

John R. Pfeiffer

RAY BRADBURY'S BERNARD SHAW

In 1992 Ray Bradbury published *Green Shadows, White Whale,* a "novel" created from both published and unpublished stories, loosely related to his several-month sojourn in Ireland in 1953 to write the script for John Huston's film version of *Moby-Dick.*[1] In Ireland Bradbury was mostly in Dublin, Bernard Shaw's home town. The connection between Bradbury and Shaw began in the early 1950s. Since then, nobody has paid more attention to that connection than Bradbury himself. My awareness of the Bradbury/G.B.S. connection began when I edited a number of the old *Shaw Review* in May 1973 on the special topic "G.B.S. and Science-Fiction." When I turned up two pieces by Bradbury containing comments on Shaw, Stanley Weintraub acquired Bradbury's permission to publish excerpts from the pieces in the special number. Subsequently I have kept track of Bradbury's writing about G.B.S.

Twenty-two sources reflect Bradbury's connection to Shaw. The earliest is Bradbury's 1953 novella *Fahrenheit 451* where "Shaw" is one of the writers who would be lost in the book-burning dystopia he envisions. Two are interviews with people who have literary relationships with Bradbury. One is a special correspondence with Bradbury on his interest in Shaw. Two are more prose fictional references by Bradbury to Shaw. Four are poems by Bradbury on G.B.S. The other twelve are published essays by or interviews with Bradbury. Bradbury is thus engaged with Shaw in at least two ways. One is a potential chapter in the relatively recently commenced study of Bradbury as dramatist and playwright that would look for the ways in which Bradbury's works show likenesses to Shaw's in form and message.[2] The second is the one described here as explicitly reported by Bradbury in stories, poems, essays, and interviews.

One circumstantial G.B.S./Bradbury connection began in 1979 when Stanley Weintraub, in his role as Director of Penn State University's Institute for the Arts and Humanistic Studies, contacted Bradbury as an "interesting person" to bring to the campus. Bradbury declined (he then would not fly), but after he learned that Weintraub was editor of the *Shaw Review* he sent him a poem, "GBS and The Loin of Pork," which appeared in the *SHAW* in 1982. They have since met several times, and Bradbury has consulted Weintraub a number of times for facts on Shaw, making Weintraub the principal enabler for Bradbury's raids on Shaw. Bradbury has told Weintraub that his earliest inspiration came from Shaw's most elaborate science fiction work, *Back to Methuselah,* but Bradbury has never mentioned the play in print.[3]

Ray Bradbury has said that, beginning in the 1950s, he read all of Shaw, and it is clear from his statements about Shaw that he knows a good deal more about G.B.S. than most people do.[4] In his comments, Bradbury mentions seven of Shaw's plays by name: They are *Major Barbara* (twice), *The Apple Cart* (twice), *Saint Joan* (twice), *Caesar and Cleopatra, Pygmalion, Misalliance,* and *Don Juan in Hell.* He also refers to the "Life Force" (twice), a concept most closely identified with Shaw's *Man and Superman* and *Back to Methuselah.* Bradbury has also consulted the considerable secondary literature about Shaw that has proliferated over the years, but he has not chosen to mention particular authors or titles in print.

As he pronounced emphatically in his 1976 *Writer's Digest* interview, Bradbury considers his relation to Shaw very important. One reason for this may be that Shaw and Bradbury are similar in many interesting ways. Both have expressed satisfaction in escaping a university education. Both owe much to libraries for their post–grammar school education. Shaw's long studies in the British Museum, for which he often congratulated himself, are legendary. Bradbury describes a similar apprenticeship in his article "How, Instead of Being Educated in College, I Was Graduated from Libraries."[5] Then, too, each started a career with astonishing energy in a genre in which he did not succeed. Shaw wrote five unsuccessful novels and began a sixth before he discovered himself as a playwright. Bradbury admired films and wanted to be a playwright. It is not widely known that Bradbury has been engaged as a script writer throughout his career. He regards himself as a very good and successful playwright. Even so, he has achieved great popularity and respect only for his short fiction, best epitomized in the frame-story work, *The Martian Chronicles* (1951).

Both G.B.S. and Bradbury have invested enormous energy in self-advertisement, especially in claiming that their messages and meaning are radical, even inciting to revolution from agendas that, upon exami-

nation, are essentially "enlightened conservative." Both have energetically associated themselves with a famous earlier literary giant. Shaw
invoked Shakespeare elaborately, respectfully, and facetiously, encouraging comparison. Bradbury has invoked Shaw (along with Shakespeare)
respectfully, mischievously, and practically. He has sometimes mailed
letters in envelopes with a sketch of G.B.S. printed on them.[6] Also, in
part because of the energy of self-advertisement, both became enormously popular. In the first half of the twentieth century there was no
more famous playwright than Bernard Shaw. For the mass audience of
science fiction in the second half of the twentieth century, Bradbury is
far and away the best-known writer.

In the works of both, the authorial voices are radically audible.
Whether regarded as a strength or weakness, a characteristic of Shaw's
plays is that many of the characters sound like Shaw. Fortunately, Shaw
was a brilliant discussant most of the time. Similarly, all Bradbury
characters sound like Bradbury. His fiction and playscripts talk with his
voice. It is frequently that of a terribly vulnerable and then surprisingly
persistent whimsy that has enchanted a vast readership. Also, both
writers are humorists and satirists. They seek laughter as a major part
of the response to their works. Shaw's comedy is literal and at the surface
of his texts as well as in the structure of his works. Bradbury's is more
usually in the structure of his stories and more complex than I am
prepared to elucidate here. In both, the comic discourse teaches lessons.
Shaw and Bradbury are explicit in announcing their agenda: The
reader/audience must be made to think, must be dislodged from condi-
tioned ideas and feelings. Both are mischief-makers and culture-chang-
ers, quite intentionally. This is Shaw's appeal for Bradbury. Shaw has
been recorded as regarding his most ambitious work of speculative
drama or science fiction, *Back to Methuselah,* as his masterpiece, his most
important work. Thus, for him, as for Bradbury, science fiction might
be the most important fiction.

Bradbury has explicitly included G.B.S. in fiction or poetry at least
seven times. The earliest was in the dystopian *Fahrenheit 451* (1953):
"Oh, there are many actors alone who haven't acted Pirandello or Shaw
or Shakespeare for years because their plays are too *aware* of the world.
We could use their anger."[7]

The second, "G.B.S.—Mark V" (1976), is the story of spaceship
crewman Charles Willis's preference for the company of a G.B.S. android, "a cuneiform tablet robot of George Bernard Shaw" (68), "dead
but alive, cold but warm, forever untouchable but reaching out somehow
to touch" (69).[8] Appropriately, this Shaw is engagingly "unbearable"
(68–69). Nevertheless, sensitively, he sees the biblical faces of Moses and
Job in spaceman Willis's face. *Saint Joan* is mentioned twice (69, 74), "Life

Force" once (71). Willis likes G.B.S. because of his "electric deliriums of philosophy and wonder" (72). G.B.S. is a "friend" (73), a musician, has "honey-sweet breath" (73), is puritanical about sex, and "falls up"—an antigravitational, psycho-kinesthetic imposition repeated in Bradbury's only other fictional appropriation of the character of Shaw, seventeen years later, in a chapter of the 1992 *Green Shadows*. Quoting and commenting on the central text of "G.B.S.—Mark V," Bradbury has G.B.S. speak a kind of ebullient mysticism (although authentic Shavian discourse is nothing if not virtually always rational and cogent):

> I lodged his psyche in an audio-animatronic robot aboard a starship bound for the Crab Nebula. Each night, while other crew members salivate over their life-size wind-up toy Marilyns, I sneak below machinery stairs to call my electro-playwright awake. Thus summoned, Shaw sits bolt upright, stares at the Milky Way, and shouts:
> "By God, I do accept it!"
> "Accept what, Mr. Shaw?"
> "The universe," he cries. "It *thinks*, therefore I *am!*"
> In just such a fashion, Shaw spoke from pulpits long before our time. With a wit half-full of cynicism and an awe half-empty of atheism, he came to desire the Life-Force to knock him into believing, to drag him kicking into the cathedral of Space, there to free his amiable soul from his sexual if vegetarian body. Later in that same "GBS Mark V" story, I take Shaw up to gaze at the Cosmos and speak on philosophies. Finally I nudge him and whisper:
> "Say it, Mr. Shaw."
> "Say what?"
> "You know what I want to hear. Say it."
> Shaw looks at the distant stars, then touches my elbow, touches himself.
> "What are we? What, in the long night of the Universe, is this creature that happens in Time? Why . . . [no question mark]
> "We are the miracle of force and matter making itself over into imagination and will. The Life-Force, experimenting with forms; you for one, me for another! The Universe shouts: We are the incredible echo. The void is filled with ten billion on a billion bombardments of ignorant light, mindless avalanches of energy, meteor, cosmic snuffs. God exhales: Comets appear. God sneezes—up we jump! Among so much light and ignorance, we are the blind force that gropes like Lazarus from a billion-light-years tomb. We summon ourselves. We cry, O Lazarus Life-

Force, truly come ye forth! So the Universe, a motion of deaths, fumbles to reach across Time to feel its own flesh and know it to be ours. We touch both ways and find each other miraculous because we are One."[9]

This story provides a translation of G.B.S. into a robot, a Bradbury simulacrum—even a Bradbury. This attempt to appropriate a Shavian mana (which Bradbury baldly asserts he finds desirable) results, not in a convincing Bradburyian imitation of the Shavian voice, but in a Shaw that sounds like Bradbury. Bradbury undoubtedly was perfectly happy with this effect.

Bradbury's poem, "GBS and the Loin of Pork" (1982), alludes to Shaw's famous vegetarianism and alleged sexual adventuring.[10] An erudite Los Angeles cabbie told Bradbury about Mrs. Patrick Campbell's remark to Shaw: "Someday you'll eat a pork chop, Joey, and then God help all women!" Bradbury's poem imagines G.B.S. on the threshold of breaking his meat-fast, which would result in his becoming even more predatory upon women—in Bradbury's diction, "our daughters"—than he already was. In the poem, however, after titillating us with mock epic anxiety, Shaw abstains from the meat. "Our daughters" remain "safe." (Bradbury has four daughters.) In a Bradbury poem published in 1974, the title and repeated line is "The Boys across the Street Are Driving My Young Daughter Mad!" Not lost on us, meanwhile, must be this Shaw poem's play on the word "pork," one of the dozens of vernacular synonyms for the male sexual member, featured in the poem's pre-climactic line, "His mind [G.B.S.'s] is all pork!"

One cannot imagine Shaw using the term "pork" in this slang sense. However, almost certainly the Bradburian doggerel diction of this poem, and the ones to be noted next, consciously intend such clumsy impositions.

More philosophical in content, perhaps, is Bradbury's "Shaw/Chesterton: Two Poems Hardly Longer Than Their Titles" ("O' What I'd Give to Hear and See Wry G.B.S., Spry G.K.C." and "Behold the Beast: Shaw/Chesterton"), published in 1984.[11] In the first, "Wry and Spry," Bradbury conjures a fat Catholic/casuist Chesterton arguing with a lean agnostic/positivist Shaw about the personality of who or whatever it was that made the universe. The spectacle and personalities of the two pundits arguing are the focus of this doggerel debate ballad. The poem is strikingly like the African-American poet Dudley Randall's "Booker T. and W.E.B.," his marvelous late-1960s serio-comic debate over how one ought to live between the practical and compromising Booker T. Washington and the idealistic, contentious W.E.B. Du Bois. In Bradbury's poem G.B.S. has mostly rhythmic speeches, Chesterton more

arhythmic ones. This may be an accidental effect, however, since Bradbury's verse often presents rude diction.

In the second poem, "Beast," Bradbury concocts "the beast: Shaw/
Chesterton / Where is its head, its tail?" and the two heads use the poem
to argue about God's purpose in creating the universe. God, in fact, is
interviewed, and we learn that although G.B.S. and G.K.C. decidedly
annoy him with their interminable disputation, God will be patient with
them since they might indeed eventually tell God why he created
the universe:

> Tart Shaw, glib G.K.C.,
> I'd gladly re-baptize the both,
> And sink their souls at sea!
> But that would me the Devil make;
> I'll let them prattle on.
> Perhaps in listening I'll find
> Just what I meant that Dawn
> When I said "Light!" and all *was* light
> When I said: "Firmament!"
> What fancy shaped my birthing Words?

Nevertheless, given a chance to create a new universe, God is not at all
sure that it would include Shaw and Chesterton:

> If Shaw and Chesterton shout, "Go!"
> I just might start again.
> But this time, using Primal Bang
> To advertise my Laws,
> No roustabouting Chestertons,
> No sly, rambunctious Shaws!

One recent fictional evocation of Shaw by Bradbury occurs in chapter
26 of *Green Shadows, White Whale, A Novel* (1992). He includes a story
told by one Heeber Finn, the owner of the watering hole where the
writer (a Bradbury persona) has been taking time out from writing the
script for the John Huston film, *Moby Dick*, which starred Gregory Peck
as Ahab. In contrast to the robot of "G.B.S.—Mark V," *Shadows* 26
presents a Bradburianized flesh-and-blood Shaw character through a
nonsense sketch that has G.B.S. announcing he is a teetotaler, then
reluctantly downing a shot of whiskey (which will account for his
inevitably unShavian antics to come), and then dispensing "wisdom" via
a "Burma-Shave" display of four "half-largish pieces of painted porcelain" (187) that announce "Stop," "Think," "Consider," "Do." These are

translated by this otherwise unusually taciturn Shaw to be a recommen-
dation to go forth and . . . sin. Any advice from the atheist Shaw is sinful
in the mind of the Irish Catholic priest on hand, Father O'Malley, who
accuses Shaw of having done the "devil's job of confusion." G.B.S.
retorts, "Angels confuse, also. . . . Witness the kind wives who, out of
the fineness of their hearts, cause these chaps to run here, biting their
fists and hard at drink, trying to understand that unfathomable sex!"
(194). Shaw continues later, "Home, church, pub, booze, signs. . . . The
sum of it would poison an elephant and kill a herd. I will confess my
guilt, Father, here today if you will do the same with a nod. You need
not speak it aloud. And you will surely not get the women at home to
admit their guilt as sharp as the elbows they hide like knives in their
shawls" (197). Shaw sums up the intellectual and moral confusion of the
Irish (presumably including himself) as follows: "The Irish. From so
little they glean so much: squeeze the last ounce of joy from a flower
with no petals, a night with no stars, a day with no sun. One seed and
you lift a beanstalk forest to shake down giants of converse. The Irish?
You step off a cliff and . . . fall *up!*" (197). Here we recall the antigravitational, rule-breaking behavior named "*fall up!*" (italicized by
Bradbury) that is exactly the behavior of Charles Willis and the android
G.B.S. in "Mark V," when "Laughing, they jumped into the feather tube
and fell *up*" (70). The Irish and Shaw and aficionados of Shaw like Willis
are thus at once whimsical and profound as they break the most
fundamental rule in the universe, the law of gravity.

Bradbury's latest evocation of Shaw is in his 180–line mock-epic
dream vision poem in heroic couplets, *The R.B., G.K.C., and G.B.S.
Forever Orient Express* in 1994.[12] The setting of the poem is a dream by
Bradbury in which he describes himself joined by a company of authors
taking a trip on the Orient Express, the famous luxury train service that
traveled regularly between Paris and Constantinople between 1883 and
1977. The Orient Express setting is not exploited except to invoke the
gilded age era when these writers flourished—the age of the railroad
train. Noteworthy here is that Bradbury also used the portentous arrival
of a circus train to set the scene for his 1962 novel *Something Wicked This
Way Comes*. The points of embarkation and destination of this run of the
Orient Express are not named. Bradbury's ride with the great authors
is what is important. It is a company he has unabashedly announced in
many published forums that he seeks to have the honor to join. The
Orient Express is legendary. Therefore Bradbury begins,

> And when I die, will this dream truly be
> Entrained with Shaw and Chesterton and me?
> O, glorious Lord, please make it so

> That down along eternity we'll row
> Atilted headlong, nattering the way
> All mouth, no sleep, and endless be our day:
> The Chesterton Night Tour, the Shaw Express,
> A picnicking of brains in London dress
> As one by one we cleave the railroad steams
> To circumnavigate my noon and midnight dreams.

Shaw gets easily the most mentions (15) by name in the poem, followed by Edgar Allan Poe (12), G. K. Chesterton and Herman Melville (8), Oscar Wilde (7), Rudyard Kipling (5), Mark Twain (4), Charles Dickens (3), and Bertrand Russell (2). Shaw's personality (after the familiar "G.B.S." in the title, he is always called "Shaw") presides throughout the poem. He is the first to board the train. Immediately he is called, startlingly, "Our Lord": "His voice pure Life Force judge and Mankind's Maker," and "Shaw amidst the mob like statue sits / And maunders up his tongue to launch the Game / His merest cough a shot to walk us lame." Shaw looks on as the company of famous passengers one by one board the train and enter the poem's dream vision. Soon, Shaw "can rave," and his "philosophic crumbs" that Bradbury will "snatch and eat" are "The Hiccoughing of Shaw?" Again, Shaw argues with Chesterton—subject not named. A clamorous conversation among all the passengers mounts "Til Shaw corks all to point where Truth is at," which gives rise to a sublimely energetic discourse, during which Shaw is allowed to "boast." The Bradburyian soiree climaxes with the following marvelous conceit, a segue of Bradbury's script-writing work for the *Moby Dick* film:
We turn to Melville now and seek his Whale,

> This midnight train which rounds the curve ahead,
> Its engine ghostly pale, a loom of dread,
> Then all's not lost, for whether land or sea,
> Old Moby tracks the chase and summons me.
> We doubt all this but crowd the pane to spy
> That locomoting Whiteness, hear its cry?
> With churned St. Elmo's fires, sweet Christ, what sound!
> The sea like God sounds near, we all are drowned.
> As down the nightfall path we raving go,
> Old Moby dragging us, one train of woe.
> "O, bosh!" says Shaw, and sits, to jolt us back,
> "That's Industry's Revolt upon the track!"

Here Shaw's role is to return the company from a truly magnificent hallucination to sobriety and reason so that Bradbury can say, "Much better that than Beast. We sit to eat, / Take tea, a biscuit, bun, or brioche-sweet." This is a shrewd insight about Shaw who, for all the great range of his analysis of the human condition, rarely presents the Melvillian Beast in his works. The biscuit reference meanwhile returns us also to the cordial Shaw met at the beginning of the poem, who now is first to disembark from the train: "At Land's End Lost Time Station, hear the peace, / Where just the other breath our life was words, / Now trees are filled with literature of birds." The Shavian persona hereafter is homogenized in the departing constellation of beatified and canonized dead writers, about whom Bradbury reflects, "Their deaths diminish, words replenish me. / For traveling down the shore in lonely care. / I open wide their books and there they are!" Shaw, described in the routinely sensational and even bombastic poetic diction of Bradbury, is even so a polar star for him, majestically cool, impulsive, cantankerous, cordial, and ethereal by turns. But this Shaw seems to have the job of setting the agenda for mankind—certainly an august and Zeus-like portfolio.

In his essays and interviews over the years, Bradbury has framed the following comments:

1968: "Permit me, like a fourth rate George Bernard Shaw, to make an outrageous statement. And then permit me, like a similar ramshackle Shaw, to try to prove it. Ready? Here it is: Science fiction is the most important fiction being written today."[13]

1971: "Whenever most new, modern, American novels come out, I go read *Rumpelstiltskin* again, because I think the modern American novel is bankrupt of imagination, wit, style, idea on any level. I am a language person. I've loved poetry all my life and my favorite people, whom I visit at the library again and again, are William Shakespeare and Bernard Shaw, and G. K. Chesterton and Loren Eiseley. People with ideas. People with images. People with language. People who romance me with death, and excitement, and make me want to go on living."[14]

1972: "I have always thought that Bernard Shaw deserved to be the patron saint of the American theater. Yet I saw little of his influence here, a true playwright of ideas born to set the world right. Avant-garde in 1900, he remains light years ahead of our entire avant-garde today. My other saint would be Shakespeare."[15]

1972 (December): "Bernard Shaw describes creative evolution as matter and force making itself over into intelligence and spirit. . . . So neither Shaw nor I, if you will excuse me for trotting in his shadow, is here to celebrate the defeat of man by matter, but to proclaim his high destiny and urge him on to it."[16]

1973 (Shortly after seeing *Don Juan in Hell* performed): "I'm a big Shaw fan and I could hardly wait to see *Don Juan* again. It's one of the great plays; it's a beautiful evening; it's hard to destroy that play. I've always had very good taste."[17]

1974: "Most science-fiction writers are moral revolutionaries on some level or another, instructing us for our own good. When Bernard Shaw and Bertrand Russell ventured into the field it could have been predicted (and I did so predict with Lord Russell) that they would pop up as moral revolutionists teaching lessons and pontificating therefrom. Shaw was better at it, of course. Russell came late to the short story, but it *was* science fiction, and was odorous with morality."[18]

1976: "If someone will just let me into the club to have tea with George Bernard Shaw, I'll be very happy, you know? If I come out at the end of my life and someone *breathes* my name in the same rarefied atmosphere with Shaw or with Shakespeare, my God! Just to be allowed into the club."[19]

1977: Commenting in his story "The Fire Balloons," he says that the Martians are highly evolved and "Free of sin, they live in a state of Grace, not unlike that spoken of by Shaw long before I was born [Bradbury's reference is unclear here. It may refer to Shaw's speculations on mankind's future in *Back to Methuselah,* written in 1920 and produced in 1921. Bradbury was born in 1920.] Later in the essay he writes, "My love for George Bernard Shaw being continuous and extreme, I connived to write him into a story titled 'GBS Mark V.'

"Kazantzakis, like Shaw, says much the same. In his finest and greatest work, *The Saviours of God.*"[20]

1979: "Think of it!" cried [Bernard] Berenson, eyes flashing. "*War and Peace* told by an idiot. *Crime and Punishment* remembered by a fool. Machiavelli's *The Prince* mouthed by a numbskull. *Moby Dick* recited by an alcoholic cripple. . . . It was a superb idea. But it has lain in my files for some twenty-five years now. I didn't dare say to Berenson, or perhaps even to myself, then, that it would take a genius who had read, digested, and completely understood the entire body of American and English literature to plow into and create a book like that. . . . But do it? The ghosts of Molière, Pope, Swift, Chesterton, plus Shaw, might just bring it off."[21]

1989: "After half a lifetime of reading Shaw, quite often out loud because I can't help myself, I still have the feeling that if you had run up to him early or late in his life and asked, 'Do you know everything?' he might well have cried, 'But most certainly, yes!' . . . All Shaw ever does is treat us to his uncommon common sense. What he says about children and reading and libraries is, it seems to me, undeniable. . . . Shaw's comment on quality for kids, and the second-rate for adults, hits the nail. . . . Shaw's ghost is in there with them [kids in the library], asking their advice on books that he should scan in order to catch up. Catch up, hell, he's been ahead of us all of our lives. It is we who must do the running"[22]

1992: "[I] first heard of Shaw, in detail, in my early Twenties [early 1940s], and when I saw MAJOR BARBARA, and, of course, fell in love with everything about the film. But I read no Shaw until my Thirties [early 1950s] when I read everything by him, and everything by Molière and the English Restoration playwrights, plus O'Casey and O'Neill. Learning to become a playwright, myself. Here's where Charles Laughton came into my life, teaching me Shaw and Shakespeare!!!

"[I] never saw or met Shaw, more's the pity. I remember some newsreels which were quite amusing. Heard him on the radio, perhaps once, when I was in my teens. Charles Laughton asked me to write a science-fiction operetta for his wife Elsa Lanchester. During that year, around 1955/1956 he was acting in and directing MAJOR BARBARA and THE APPLE CART, so he tried out his ideas on me and stood on his hearth declaiming the best lines from GBS and Shakespeare. He tried out his concepts on LEAR, also, as we swam about his pool. He went over to Stratford and got, as I recall, good to fine notices as LEAR. TIME, I remember, praised him.

"Biggest Shaw event in my life was in January, 1953 in Dublin where my wife and I attended a performance of ST. JOAN with Siobhan Mckenna who was the finest Joan I have ever seen from that year to this. She performed it in Dublin before she went to London and long before she arrived in New York with the production. It is my favorite Shaw. But then as soon as I say this, I think of PYGMALION and MISALLIANCE (if played with the right/light mad touch and with an inspired cast as in San Diego at the Globe ten years ago! [1982]) and then there is CAESAR AND CLEOPATRA and, my God, but why go on? You could play his essays on the stage, by God, if, once again, cast and honed to a proper edge. DON JUAN IN HELL remains one of the most vivid evenings in my life, seen in 1952 with Laughton, Hardwicke, Boyer and Agnes Moorehead. Incredible. PYGMALION remains a favorite in spite of its anti-climax, which carried over into the musical. Should have been cured by then, but never was. Once our heroine has learned to speak properly, the play is over. Even Shaw couldn't pump enough genius in it to keep it running. I have no suggestions on how to cure the last act, save to cut the hell out of it or write a whole new play, which Shaw almost did when he wrote a variation of the last scene or scenes, some years later.

"But, to repeat, if Laughton had not pounded Shaw in one of my ears and out the other, I would not be the half-decent playwright I am today. Language, cried Laughton. You're a poet, he cried, use your talent and your tongue. Be Shaw's shadow. Be Shakespeare's, too!

"No, He's still the greatest of our time and makes most modern

English and American playwrights turn into Singer's Midgets!! He was the great charlatan/vaudevillian-idea-magician. Humor, my God, humor, how we need it to save us from drowning. Discuss ideas, deep ones, broad ones, serious ones but, he said, don't forget to *wink* at me at times!" (Bradbury to John Pfeiffer)

1995: "I [read] all the great poets, Emily Dickinson, Yeats, Frost. I go back to Shaw most often. He's a superb, gigantic pomegranate that explodes all over the place; I love him so much I put him into a science-fiction story called 'GBS Mark V.' I learn from all of these people and bring it over into science fiction."[23]

1996: "I go back to George Bernard Shaw. He wrote some great science fiction, and he believed in the future. He believed in optimal behavior. He believed in our destiny moving out through the universe. He believed that women were the center of everything—which they are. He wrote about all these things, 80 or 90 years ago. Fabulous writer."[24]

From the evidence, the following conclusions seem warranted: For Bradbury, as for most of us, Bernard Shaw is himself a text, as his works are texts or productions or renditions of texts. Furthermore, and perhaps unlike for most of us, for Bradbury G.B.S. seems to be an idea, a lyric motif articulated in a siren discourse composed and performed by Bradbury, to get us to watch Bradbury. His Shaw is mostly an appropriation of the conventional, already caricatured persona that G.B.S. himself frequently retailed but elevated so that it has become a sort of coolly cerebral divine master of ceremonies, or, more appropriately, play director. He has mentioned hardly more than a half-dozen Shavian works by title. His commentary on them is not analytical, nor extended beyond a sentence or two. It is mock-adulatory and encomiastic. And we might predict as much. Bradbury's agenda is too personal to be analyzed with influence by Shaw. The voice of Bradbury's work is distinctive but very different from the Shavian one, Bradbury's being sexually innocent (but not genderless), pre-adolescent, male, middle American, and precipitantly narcissistic. Thus Shaw is less than an influence upon Bradbury, but more than a warm and fuzzy inspiration for Bradbury.

In Bradbury's work Shaw for the most part functions as a stylish alter ego. Yet Bradbury has been granted his passionate wish of twenty years ago: He has gotten us, as musingly attentive readers, to breathe his name in the same rarefied atmosphere with that of Bernard Shaw.

Notes

1. Ray Bradbury, *Green Shadows, White Whale, A Novel* (New York: Alfred A. Knopf, 1992).

2. A beginning has been made by Ben Indick in *The Drama of Ray Bradbury* (Wheeling, Ill.: T-K Graphics, 1977).

3. Stanley Weintraub, Interview (Summer 1992). Thanks, also, to Professor Donn Albright of Pratt Institute, owner and director of the Ray Bradbury archive, who knew of the Bradbury/Shaw connection and was helpful in locating printed material in which Bradbury mentions Shaw.

4. Ray Bradbury to John Pfeiffer (1 September 1992).

5. Ray Bradbury, "How, Instead of Being Educated in College, I Was Graduated from Libraries or Thoughts from a Chap Who Landed on the Moon in 1932," *Wilson Library Bulletin* 45:9 (May 1971): 849.

6. For his seventy-fifth birthday, Bradbury's wife, knowing his affection for G.B.S. and things associated with him, got for him as a gift Bernard Shaw's planting shovel.

7. Ray Bradbury, *Fahrenheit 451* (New York: Ballantine Books, 1953), p. 77.

8. Ray Bradbury, "G.B.S.—Mark V," in *Long After Midnight* (New York: Alfred A. Knopf, 1976), pp. 67–79.

9. Ray Bradbury, "The God in Science Fiction," *Saturday Review of Literature* (10 December 1977), pp. 35, 43.

10. Ray Bradbury, "GBS and the Loin of Pork," *SHAW* 2 (1982), pp. 1–2.

11. Ray Bradbury, "Shaw/Chesterton: Two Poems Hardly Longer Than Their Titles" ("O' What I'd Give to Hear and See Wry G.B.S., Spry G.K.C."; and "Behold the Beast: Shaw/Chesterton"), *SHAW* 4 (1984), pp. 1–4.

12. Ray Bradbury, *The R.B., G.K.C. and G.B.S. Forever Orient Express* (Santa Barbara: Joshua Odell Editions, 1994). Handsomely produced and available only in an 11 × 17½" single-sheet broadside, folded lengthwise and inserted in a dark red, folded, heavy paper cover, the pamphlet's print run was limited to 300 copies, produced to promote a book of collected pieces by Bradbury titled *Journey to Far Metaphor: Further Essays on Creativity, Writing, Literature and the Arts*. Odell has cancelled publication of the book, but Bradbury hopes to add some pieces to the manuscript for future publication.

13. Ray Bradbury, "Science Fiction: Why Bother?" in *A Teachers' Guide to Science Fiction* (New York: Bantam Books, [1968]), p. 1.

14. Ray Bradbury, "How, Instead of Being Educated in College," p. 849.

15. Ray Bradbury, "Introduction" to *The Wonderful Ice Cream Suit and Other Plays* (New York and London: Bantam Pathfinder Editions, 1972), pp. ix-x.

16. Ray Bradbury, "From Stonehenge to Tranquility Base," *Playboy* 19:12 (December 1972): 322.

17. Paul Simon and Dorothy Simon, "Interview with Ray Bradbury," *Vertex* 1:1 (April 1973): 27.

18. Ray Bradbury, "Henry Kuttner: A Neglected Master," in *The Best of Henry Kuttner* (Garden City: Doubleday, 1975), p. xi.

19. Ray Bradbury, "The Writer's Digest Interview," *Writer's Digest* 56 (February 1976): 25.

20. Ray Bradbury, "The God in Science Fiction," pp. 38, 43.

21. Ray Bradbury, "The Renaissance Prince and the Baptist Martian," *Horizon* 22:7 (July 1979): 61.

22. Ray Bradbury, "On Shaw's 'The Best Books for Children,' " *SHAW* 9 (1989), pp. 23–24.

23. Ray Bradbury, "Sci-Fi for Your D: Drive: Bradbury Commits a Classic to CD-ROM," *Newsweek* 126 (13 November 1995): 89.

24. Ray Bradbury, "Ray Bradbury: Views of a Grand Master," *Locus* 37 (August 1996): 6, 73–74.

George Slusser

LAST MEN AND FIRST WOMEN: THE DYNAMICS OF LIFE EXTENSION IN SHAW AND HEINLEIN

> It takes a woman and a man
> To see the beauty of God's plan.
> —Unidentified Reggae Song

A fascinating point of convergence between the work of Shaw and that of Heinlein is their recurrent fascination with the possibilities of life extension, and their speculations on the future that would evolve as a result of the longevity of certain human beings. Shaw's writing, in a sense, operates in the shadow of Darwinism. His lifelong mission, it appears, was to turn his readers away from what he called "the blight of Darwinism," or purposeless "natural" selection, in order to lead them toward a Lamarckian sense of evolution, a willed vitalism. His contemporary Wells also wished mankind to defeat these same blind Darwinian forces, mastering environment and heredity until, in *Things to Come,* the "body of mankind [becomes] a single organism." Shaw, however, chooses a different vehicle for this process of willed evolution—the *single* extended life, the *individual* willed being he called the "Methuselah." With his choice of protagonist, Shaw retreats from Wellsian prophecy and Stapledonian mysticism alike. He places his focus squarely on the conflict, inherent to vitalism, between collective biology and individual will.

The creative force is generated by biology; will is created out of birth. Once born, will strives to live on. Without death, however, what happens to the need for further births? Without these, where does the vital energy come from to sustain Methuselah's life extension?

Prior to evolutionary science, the quest for endless life, or immortality, was occasion for a moral lesson. From Tithonus to the Struldbruggs, eternal life was a monstrous breach of what were deemed the unalterable rhythms of mutability. Youth passed in "natural" fashion; the man became old and, fearing death, found means to forestall the end, thereby condemning himself to eternity in decrepitude.[1] Age and solitude were the wages of personal desire, not the products of evolutionary will. The possibility of rejuvenation remained a magical grail, the lost fountain of youth.

Effective will in relation to longevity first enters the picture, it seems, with Balzac's Centenarian. Protagonist of a juvenile novel *Le Centenaire: ou les deux Beringheld* (1822), this ancient being seeks to prolong life, not by some magic root or potion, but by science.[2] Balzac's figure, like the mythical Cronos, feeds on his progeny, both figuratively, by controlling their reproductive lives, and literally, by feasting on the flesh of virgins, and thus occluding the female from the chain of reproduction, in this case specifically the marriage bed of great-great grandson Tullius. The act of cannibalism, however, has become a scientific experiment, a volatilizing of virgin in retorts and beakers into the powerful elixir that restores fiendish vitality to his decrepit body. Science—in this case the scientific, Frankensteinian will to creation—extends the limits of human life. Shaw sees Darwinian *natural* selection imposing new limits, this time on the longevity of the human species itself. If the nineteenth century's response to the mortality problem bred monstrosities—from Balzac's distillations and Mary Shelley's "new Adam" to Wells's Dr. Moreau and his House of Pain—Shaw sought a solution through experiments in selective breeding and human genetics. In this, he rejoins a predominant theme of twentieth-century science fiction, and the main preoccupation of one of its major figures—Robert A. Heinlein.

Contextually, there are compelling reasons (despite vast disparities in cultural background) for comparing and contrasting Shaw and Heinlein. The differences are obvious: Shaw was a public figure, lecturer, world statesman, Heinlein a recluse; Shaw was a socialist, Heinlein one of those anarchistic libertarians that Shaw railed against on his sole visit to the U.S. in 1933. Shaw, however, whatever his public stance on this occasion, was deeply influenced by two Americans, Edward Bellamy and Henry George. And, although it is hard to imagine Heinlein embracing socialism, the single tax, or any kind of tax, he would surely sympathize with Shaw's impressing of his modern Don Juan, John Tanner in *Man and*

Superman, into a eugenics experiment, where the Life Force is made to serve the advancement of superior beings.

Moreover, Heinlein's self-reliant entrepreneurism could only approve of Andrew Undershaft's dismissal of poverty, in *Major Barbara,* as a disease of the will. Heinlein replays, in a sense, the eugenic love of Ann and Tanner in *Beyond This Horizon* (1942), with a genetically superior hero again reluctant to breed. Here, however, that hero, Hamilton Felix, is brought to the task not so much by a wily and persistent woman as by resistance, and final capitulation, to the ruling line of genetic supermen, whom he agrees to serve. The early Heinlein has no exact equivalent of Undershaft, the munitions maker who sells weapons of death to any fool who wishes to buy them in order to finance his own private utopia based on the sole power of money. However, there is Delos D. Harriman, the private individual who brings nations and societies to their knees, and adopts his own "utopian" designs, by "selling the moon" ("The Man Who Sold the Moon" [1950]). There is also Hugo Pinero, hero of Heinlein's first story, "Life Line" (1939), who upsets insurance companies, the scientific establishment, and common humanity when he invents the means of reading the individual's literal lifeline, thus predicting exactly how long that individual will live and when he will die. Although intolerable to most, this knowledge causes the persecuted supermen to strive for longer lines, more life, both individually and collectively.

The early novella *Methuselah's Children* (1941) combines these strands.[3] The story tells of a concerted eugenics effort on the part of the late-nineteenth-century family, the Howards, to establish a Foundation whose purpose is to breed for longevity. The Howards emerge in a utopian society of an Undershaftian-entrepreneurial sort—the Covenant—that at first encourages their development, then, yielding to growing envy and hatred of the short-lived, begins to persecute them instead. In response to this, a Howard superman arises, the shrewd Lazarus Long, who leads his about-to-be-exterminated people on a diaspora to outer space. By means of near-light-speed travels, moving from world to far world, Lazarus and his people make great scientific advances in a short span of their time in relation to centuries passed back on Earth. Now they prepare to return and reclaim Earth. Miraculously, they find their way back. Quite serendipitously, relativity has worked in their favor as well, for the Earthlings too have had time to make discoveries, notably of bodily longevity. All have it now, and there is no longer a need for envy. And yet their discovery of longevity reveals an even more important difference (or to use Heinlein's word, "gulf") between the stay-at-homes and the travelers. The former discovered the means of long life in the laboratory; the latter however, although genetically predisposed, seem instead to have *willed* it into being. They discover, in almost Shavian fashion, that biological heredity is less important than what Heinlein calls "psychological heredity." What we have here is a mix of Lamarckian evolutionary will and American "positive thinking." As Lazarus and his family learn, a person need only think that he or she can live a long time, and act as if it were so, for it to come to pass. That "person," however, is not any person; willing may make it so, but, as Lazarus proves, a strong will is needed. The stay-at-homes are the chaff, the Howards the wheat.

The power of will works its genetically extensive way through Heinlein's stories and novels until, in *Time Enough for Love* (1973), Lazarus reappears.[4] Howard genes have colonized all known galaxies, and willed longevity is now universal. Yet Lazarus, however much he constitutes a self-made universe, finds that he too must face the classic fate of the long-lived: boredom and solitude. Because there is nothing left to do, there is no vital reason to do it, hence no force to do it with. Heinlein, in 1973, is at the same point Shaw was in 1921, in his "metabiological pentateuch" *Back to Methuselah*. Evolutionary will once again faces the tyranny of human biology, and at a similar point where we find ends exhausted through the inability of human beings to renew the means to those ends.[5] What can will aspire to when there is no longer any need to exercise it?

At the end of the final section of *Back to Methuselah*, "As Far As Thought Can Reach," ghosts of first things, Adam, Eve, Cain, and the Serpent, replay the beginning of things. Doing so, however, they only make evident, in the exhausted nature of the process, the inability of human will to begin again. Only Lilith abides, first woman before good and evil, the primal force who, long before, "brought life into the whirlpool of force, and compelled [her] enemy Matter, to obey a living soul" (300). Lilith sees the problem. The Methuselahs "have accepted the burden of eternal life. . . . Their breasts are without milk; their bowels are gone; the very shapes of them are only ornaments for their children to admire and caress without understanding" (298). She sees generations now frozen like statues. She alone realizes that, if the vital force is to flow again, she must, by an act of creative will, labor and bear once more. Lazarus, in *Time Enough for Love*, is likewise driven back from sterile immobility to the Ur-mother. In this case, it is his own mother, Maureen. And again, here as in Shaw, this same first Mother remains the inviolate first cause, whose inviolability is made all the more clear through Lazarus's futile attempt to travel back in time in hopes of creating himself, thus of becoming the source of his own creative energy, by making love with Maureen.

This failure at self-creation—at which point longevity would become eternal self-perpetuation—marks the moment in Heinlein's work where Maureen begins to loom large until she, not Lazarus, dominates Heinlein's final novel *To Sail Beyond the Sunset*. As with Lilith, the search to control the final cause ends only with a reaffirmation of the life force that began it all, a force beyond male or female hegemony, before Adam and Eve.

Central to both Shaw and Heinlein, over their respective long careers, is a deep concern with the dynamics of life extension. "Dynamics" is the proper word because for Shaw and Heinlein alike the resolution of the process of life—in the sense of achieving eternal life or immortality—is never an option. The stasis of finality is neither possible nor desirable. Instead, however, their sense of life extension is based on a process of imbalance best described in Emersonian terms as the *undulation* of power and form. Lilith, Shaw tells us, brings life into the whirlpool of force; life then, with its propensity to evolve in organic fashion from its *urform,* acts as vector that impels "force" or power, making of an otherwise converging whirlpool an expanding spiraling form, moving outward, in undulating rhythm, from its dynamic center. At the same time, however, life is defined as matter that is *compelled* to obey a living soul. In this sense, this force incarnate as vectored life must experience the burden of its matter, which necessarily increases as life moves farther from its source of power.

Life extension proceeds by means of continuous undulation between will and biology, individual and collective evolution. In both Shaw and Heinlein, however, these terms (and ultimately the terms "man" and "woman" increasingly used today to cover such oppositions) are neither antithetical nor dialectical, but rather undulatory in the Emersonian sense. This means that short-lived characters, in Shaw or Heinlein, are never simply evolutionary stages on the way to Lazarus Long or Methuselah. Nor is it true, if they are women, that their existence is necessarily short-lived, in contrast to an extended, will-driven male life. For in any given evolutionary stage, at any moment, the "mortal"—and especially the women who otherwise appear constrained by their role, as nature short-lived, in the collective biological evolution of humanity—has the power to enter into an immediate, undulatory relationship with the Methuselah, the extended individual male life. Across the Heinlein canon, there arises in organic fashion a rhythmic relation between long-lived Lazarus and "ephemeral" Maureen, a necessarily dynamic and compensatory pulsation between will and biology, center and circumference. Likewise in Shaw, such a relationship exists, if less directly, between long-lived figures like Haslam and the Methuselahs, and an explicitly

short-lived figure like Saint Joan. Excesses in one direction bring resent-
ment in the opposite direction, but the power-form equation must, if it
is to function, remain elliptical, off-balance, dynamically unstable.

Shaw and Heinlein, creating their individual dramas and stories
around this central undulation of biology and individual will, may be
called "constructivist" writers. Such dynamic modeling of the life force
is ever pushing edges and limits in the high tradition of science fiction.
Heinlein's final novel, with its ceaseless movement between center (late-
nineteenth-century Missouri, the author's own birthplace) and a circumference that reaches farther and farther into the "multiverse," bears a
Tennysonian title, To Sail Beyond the Sunset. The wish at least, as with
Tennyson's aged Ulysses, is to strive and explore without end: to seek
and not to find. Likewise, Shaw's final section to Methuselah, As Far as
Thought Can Reach, places no limits, for active thought, an ever-restless
condition, will surely in some later situation pass from the human to the
transhuman. In the wake, however, of what is today called "gender
studies," any such constructivism is challenged. Indeed, all talk of will
and biology has become suspect to the degree that these are seen, not as
physical realities, but as socially determined concepts, thus instruments
of power, in this case of some entity called patriarchal authority. As if
such undulatory logic were not a physical property of evolving life as we
know it, the deconstructivist (as I shall call such a critic) seeks to entrap
this logic in a binary process of statement and counterstatement, whose
two poles are, on one hand, a static male will to power, on the other, an
equally static female absolute.

In today's deconstructivist reading of their fables of human evolution,
Shaw and Heinlein would be cast as proponents of patriarchal domination. The quest for immortality becomes a male strategy for redressing
the fallen condition of the flesh. This, in turn, recriminates the female,
who is at one and the same time the source of the male's vital energy
and the cause of his travails. Once born, the male struggles (of necessity,
for birth is a curse as well as a blessing) to prolong life. In this
interpretation, as soon as they refuse the limits of life in the flesh, both
Shaw's Methuselahs and Heinlein's Lazarus Long do not merely break
with female genesis. Given their existential dilemma that sees both
mortality and the possibility of immortality alike contingent on birth,
they are driven to control to their ends the power that abides in the
female principle. Given this dilemma, the sole course of action, it seems,
is to follow their male ancestor Cronos and devise an autocannibalistic
cycle whereby they sire and devour their progeny. It is not enough for
the solitary patriarch to manipulate or dominate the female life force.
He has literally to breed and then feed upon it in order to sustain his
own extended bodily existence.

Significant in this light is the recurrence of a Pygmalion figure in both Shaw and Heinlein. It is possible to see Pygmalion's actions as a willful and perverse male inversion of natural birth by woman. The female statue he creates, then "brings to life" becomes, in this perspective, a form whose original life has, through manipulations of the artist's will, been vampirically sucked away. Its "animation" is both a travesty of the first female cause, and a means of enslaving that cause, in the sense that the "awakened" woman, as she steps down from her pedestal, is now through the inducement of "love" (in thanks for this "gift" of life) in thrall to her "creator." Seen this way, Pygmalion becomes a myth of defeminizing, in which the artist/scientist would insure the male final cause (through which version of the myth the single man attains the state of God the Father) by seeking to control, through this bizarre form of recycling, original female energy. Natural birth (as well as natural death) is recast as a fantasy of perpetual motion. The female body, seen as the source of entropy, is turned into a machine that now works to defeat entropy. The benefit of this process ensues only for the male who manipulates this force to his advantage—a possible infinite extension of his single-willed life.

In Shaw's play *Pygmalion*, the twist on the myth is that it is not a statue that is brought to physical life, but rather a lower-class woman made into a socially acceptable being. Through diction lessons, another's words are in a sense put in Eliza's mouth, and by the same token her own organic life drawn out. It is necessary to turn the woman into a statue before the statue can be made to speak the proper way, made into a work of social art, and thus into a person the male artist can not just love but "wed" in civilized society. Shaw, it seems, is equating here the creation of a statue with an act of male vampirism. More significant yet, however, is the Pygmalion who appears in the final section of *Back to Methuselah*. The year is A.D. 31,920. Quite the opposite of pro-evolutionary neoteny, human childhood now lasts a scant four years, during which time a being must rid itself of all "human" temptations—in other words, personal aspirations and relationships—before passing on to a higher plane of solitary self-creation. Pygmalion here is such a child. The "figures" he brings to life are two replicas of the old short-lived humanity. We might expect the man and woman to be Adam and Eve, but this is not the case. The man is Ozymandias, the mighty king of Shelley's poem, who in quite opposite manner from Pygmalion sought immortality through his works and a statue, which is found toppled in the dust of an antique land. The female calls herself Cleopatra-Semiramis, the latter half the legendary harlot-queen of Babylon. By giving life to such figures, Pygmalion is doing more than simply raising again, in humanity's far future, the moral question of free will and sin. Instead, he reawakens raw energy in the form of physical lust and violence. In a time suited to puppet shows and theological debates, Semiramis comes alive as an impulsive and violent female who, in a fit of rage, bites the hand of her creator and causes him to die. Death, it seems, is still in Arcadia, although it is rapidly subsumed by long-lived ancients who treat this more as a playground accident than as an unexpected, monitory eruption of primal power, a reminder of the vital force itself. The "automata" after all are only toys, and Pygmalion a careless child, whose more cautious playmates have already eschewed childish pleasures of the flesh or art, and are moving toward disembodiment—immortality as pure thought. A He-Ancient and a She-Ancient may both be present to guide this process. Its course, however, to the deconstructivist critic, points unerringly to the reign of Male Mind or Spirit.

It is Heinlein's Lazarus himself, as storyteller reminiscing about his endless past, who plays Pygmalion in his long-lived world. And he does so in a manner that is openly manipulative of the female life force. However ancient Lazarus may be, in terms of his potential life-span at any given moment, he remains a child, and thus is encouraged by his sense of the future to act with the same rash and impulsive "creativity" as Shaw's Pygmalion. Lazarus's Pygmalion act is to seduce a computer named Minerva to exchange, as proof of "love," machine immortality for life in the flesh. At first glance, compared with the actions of Shaw's Pygmalion figures, things seem to move in an opposite direction. Higgins appears to take life from Eliza in making her a social automaton, just as Pygmalion in *Back to Methuselah* summons his vital female in the form of a disposable simulacrum. These puppets indeed do prove recalcitrant, but in the end Higgins and the Methuselahs are in control— Eliza will bring back those tie and gloves. But just what sort of "life" is Lazarus bestowing on Minerva? The way he tempts Minerva to change its state is to tell tales of his own love for the "ephemeral," now long dead, Dora. The machine is drawn, not to take new flesh, but to inhabit and resurrect, as one might a dead body or form, the flesh of another, who at the time of the seduction no longer has a fleshly locus but exists as the mind fantasy of the male lover. Despite its form as computer—as machine—Minerva before the fall into flesh, surprisingly, acts as one of the most powerful female presences in the novel. Her name is that of a deity—a female name that enfolds the root *mens,* and thus embodies the traits of "mind," "thought," "wisdom." What Lazarus does, in forcing her from her pedestal by making her embrace the "irrational" passions, is to remove her from this purview of the male Logos, to make her woman in the stereotyped sense of a weak and manipulable being. It might seem that, by taking flesh in a future where life extension is ubiquitous, Minerva actually gains in the exchange. But she cannot become a woman in the reproductive sense because her machine origin assures sterility. Nor can she become an individual, the purview of mortal flesh, because in taking flesh, she can only model that flesh on a form of a dead woman that comes to her through the fantasies of Lazarus. Like the simulacra of Shaw's immortals, Minerva is a toy or plaything of the male will, in this case not just a sign of domination, but an object of masturbation.

Read thus, the quest for life extension as we find it in Shaw or Heinlein is not a philosophical investigation of the limits of the human condition, but a male power fantasy. And science fiction, to the degree it claims to present future history as evolutionary history, and insofar as it offers the narrative frame for such an investigation, becomes by extension a vehicle for male dominance. It is to deconstruct both this male myth, and the genre that sustains it, that Sandra Gilbert and Susan Gubar offer a feminist re-vision of the novel usually seen as the first science fiction work: *Frankenstein*.[6] In their reading we see, standing behind the male Pygmalion Victor Frankenstein, the female author Mary Shelley, with her pen re-enacting the fall and redressing it at the same time. In fact, "creation" of the sort practiced by Frankenstein is and can only be a travesty of creation, for their "creatures," whatever their designated sex, have always been a female in disguise. For do we not recognize here, in the condition of this creature at the hands of its creator, the condition of woman herself? Indeed, unlike the face of treacherous beauty worn by Shaw's female "toy," the woman's moral deformity in such an instance is openly displayed in the "monstrous" nature of the creature. Gilbert and Gubar's point is that Mary Shelley, by making Victor's monster a new Eve instead of a new Adam, recriminates God the Father as the archetypal Pygmalion. And in doing so, Shelley exposes the tradition of male manipulation of the female force. Not only does this "coming out" lift the historical burden of women's subservience, but it bestows real power on women. For Shelley's new Eve, however monstrous, is empowered precisely because she has no patriarchal history to answer to. She is no longer (as was the case with Heinlein's Minerva) part of someone else's story. Nor need she fall as a consequence of its telling. Against the patriarchal authority of a Dante, we are now, in this reading, asked to believe Francesca when she tells us that her place in this male-constructed hell is indeed and truly due to "Galeotto and him who wrote it."

Gilbert and Gubar see *Frankenstein* not so much a feminine revolt as a "feminizing" of the myth of Genesis itself, where "for Mary Shelley the part of Eve *is* all the parts." The result of this interpretation, however, is that the reign of this new Eve, as first and only woman, is as solitary and sterile as the reign of the last male patriarchs it would displace. If Victor creating the creature is woman creating woman, this is still, in any case, a creation outside any womb, a creation as re-assemblage of previously assembled body parts. All that has been done here is to replace violation of the womb by male authority in marriage—the act that reduces woman to pain and subservience in birthing—with a feminized version of physical tyranny, in this case the force that holds sway over any such *bricolage,* entropy, the gradual and inexorable loss of vital energy. Vital force runs down as this travesty of creation, the increasing difficulty of "animating" a dead body, plays out in constant repetition. A female tyranny has simply displaced a male one. In either case we have the same result—immobility and stasis. Rather than the myth of a vital force willing a statue to life, we have the countermyth of the life force desiring itself to become a statue.

At the other end of the nineteenth century, I am tempted to see Wells's novel *The Time Machine* as a response to what Gilbert and Gubar see as the universal feminizing of human history in *Frankenstein.* Wells upsets the neat symmetry of first and last, beginnings and endings, by relocating past Eden in what seems a random point in the future, the year A.D. 802,401, into which the Time Traveller falls headlong through a hasty pull of the time machine's lever. The world he finds fits perfectly the description of a feminized Frankensteinian world run down, where creature turns on creator of the same gender, to feed upon it in a desperate search for ever-diminishing vital energy. Moreover, the Traveller's fall into this world is indeed fortunate. For if he is ultimately saved, his "salvation" comes not through reintroducing male domination to a feminized world, that is, by creating a future of gender strife all over again (this is the solution of the 1960 George Pal film), but rather by de-gendering Eden once and for all, by handing human history over once and for all to the *human* forces of biological evolution. By his physical act of *traveling* to the future, Wells's protagonist has chosen *chronos* over *kairos,* has defined spacetime not in terms of beginnings and ends, but as a continuous process of creative evolution.

It simply never occurs to Wells's Traveller, in his future Eden, to ask whether he is an Adam without an Eve, or an Eve without an Adam. Facing the White Sphinx—whose riddle is as much the potentiality of time in the future as the mystery of time past—the Traveller sees himself standing at the Janus-faced crossroads between human history and future possibility. What is more, as an Oedipus in household slippers, he is an androgynous figure in an androgynous land. In neither of the "races" he encounters can he distinguish the sex. Nor can he make a clear delineation between races as stronger ("manly") or weaker. The Eloi are not only effete and futile, but basically genderless—indeed, the Traveller refers to one specifically as "this fragile *thing* out of futurity." But the Morlocks as well, although he surmises they are the tenders of supposedly male technology and descended from the once virile working class, also appear gender-indeterminate—described as albino-like eunuchs with "pale chinless faces," who move with "rustling like wind among leaves." Not only is gender stereotyping thwarted in this world, but its repository of what Gilbert and Gubar's Mary Shelley would surely call "patriarchal" science, the Palace of Green Porcelain, offers the narrator no clear story of domination. If history seems to bear witness to triumph of the feminine principle—for all books, the patriarchal Logos, have turned to dust, and machines lie idle for lack of lubricants— Promethean fire is also present, in the matches the Traveller finds still ready for use in a glass case. Just as setting itself proves ambivalent— what at first appears a classic bucolic landscape soon reveals distinct (and menacing) marks of technology—so is it increasingly impossible to determine a gender role from the Traveller's actions. If he re-enacts male or Promethean liberation of fire, the use he makes of his few matches is increasingly defensive and passive. In order to protect Weena, he appears to replay the male-dominant patterns of chivalry. But the lady he succors here is no culturally-disempowered creature, but a physically sexless being, more pet than human being. In another strangely androgynous travesty of the myth of Genesis, and its putative fall into gender, the Traveller pulls a lever from the steel exoskeleton of a machine as God before drew the rib from Adam. But as with the fire he previously freed from its glass womb, so this club—the "rib" of a machine of no woman born—is not specifically a means of the female again subservient to the male. Beyond any sense of domination or fall, it serves simply as a general *human* means of survival. Club and fire in hand, the Traveller (although in futile manner on the reverse side of the entropy slope) steps out of Edenic history. In this far future, he is thrust back to the pre-historic evolutionary condition of mankind, to wage again the primal struggle of his species. The collapse of all gender myth is complete when, at the Traveller's farthest advance into the future, Wells totally conflates end and beginning, terminal beach and primal ooze.

Potentially, *The Time Machine* will generate endless sequels. For given the capacity of the time machine to carry us anywhere in time, except to some absolute beginning or end, the domain it marks is evolutionary spacetime, where development of the species is not a function of gender difference, but of vital cooperation. In John W. Campbell's rewrite "Twilight" (1934), a time traveler goes to a future where the split between machine and flesh—male technology and female corporeality—is seemingly complete. He acts, however, to break the stalemate and re-open the flow of vital evolution. As with Wells's protagonist, he again effects this by an androgynous act—he programs machines to be "curious." The result, in a sense, is to obviate once again the gender stigma of Adam's rib. For curiosity, in this future where machines toil and human tenders and users alike are gone, is no longer either Eve's sin or the motor for Adam's technocentric drive to power. It is the general defining human trait in evolutionary terms, now re-introduced into post-human forms, as a vital spirit, in order to allow them to continue to advance toward immortality. Shaw, too, in *Back to Methuselah*, de-genders curiosity. We notice that, at the end of a long cycle of apparently male-driven evolution *(The Gospel of the Brothers Barnabas, Tragedy of an Elderly Gentleman)*, it is not Eve but Lilith, as pre-gender woman, who re-evokes the spirit of curiosity. When Lilith tells us, "I gave woman the greatest of gifts: curiosity" (299), it is not to curse woman, but to save her seed, so that it remains the repository for a vital energy that *both* sexes use to propel humanity forward. "I have waited always to see what *they* will do tomorrow," and now Lilith, curious to see tomorrow, will rekindle the force of curiosity to drive life on, now beyond all considerations of male or female, or any such dichotomy: "Of life only is there no end" (300).

Shaw and Heinlein then, in the lineage of Wells, take the otherwise en-gendered question of human immortality and place it in the dynamic context of the extension of *life* as a general human force. In this light, we must re-read their use of the Pygmalion figure. For both writers, Pygmalion is less a male artist who manipulates women, sometimes in masturbatory fashion, than simply the embodiment of youth revolting against old age, in this case the self-isolating, solipsistic existence of the extended Methuselah life. Indeed, in what is an act of creative disruption, Pygmalion "breathes" or infuses the vital force back into static ancient life. In Shaw's play, she- and he-ancients alike, after an ever-shortening period of youth, can proceed to the "creation of self." Each can now swiftly leave behind love, art, even the technological pleasures of reshaping the human body, to engage in the willed shaping *of one's own soul.* This "creation of self" holds out the danger, not only of solipsism, but of the finality of the human form of being, a finality that calls, not for evolution, but for a *leap* to some non-human state. Rather than a durational life force that dynamically integrates opposites, we again face paralyzing dualism. For as with the gender hiatus, we have the even greater danger of a stalemate between human and non-human. Aspiring to a world of pure mind, Shaw's ancients are increasingly unable to communicate with a time and spirit of youth that, in inverse proportion, shrinks in duration as they expand the world of their sole self.

Into such a world, Shaw's Pygmalion interjects a pair of atavisms. As such, his generic man and woman represent imperfect but *clearly more vital* life forms. In a world of sterilizing reason, their uncontrolled emotions mark them as today's humans, the humanity we recognize. The two at once fall to quarreling, fight, are judged and disposed of. But when asked by their judges which one is to blame—in other words, which one should be destroyed—they respond with varying degrees of altruism, revealing much greater species awareness and evolutionary generosity than their ancient judges. The male responds by asking the judges to kill him and spare the female. The female, however, responds that the judges should kill them both, for given their *mutual* passion, one could not survive without the other. Despite the long "Lamarcko-Shavian invective" of the preface to this play, there is a clear element of Darwinian natural selection here. The episode offers a Darwinian antidote to the possible peril of self-willed longevity. For these ephemeral "primitives" give here what is the *sensible* evolutionary answer: as in the past with species extension, at this juncture the dynamics of life extension requires a real vital interplay if humanity is to reach the next step in evolution. Pygmalion has brought back violence, conflict, unpredictability, and, most importantly, energy to the human condition—an act for which he pays with his life. Yet his "youth revolt" is necessary if the next evolutionary step is not to be the final step. Again we have *chronos* not *kairos,* raw energy rather than reasoned telos. The phrase "As far as thought can reach," is not a statement of ends but a call for means, in which youth provides the power, the always-upward-striving monad, that drives the extended form that is thought.

Heinlein's use of Pygmalion, in terms of the dynamics of longevity, is perhaps more complex yet. *Time Enough for Love* is all about an ancient Methuselah who, in revolt against his own condition of static immorality, acts as his own Pygmalion to reintroduce creative uncertainty into an all-too-predictable world. Lazarus does, in the case of Minerva, turn machine perfection into flesh. In a feminist sense, then, he seems to strip away the goddess's male armor to uncover the vulnerable female beneath (we think of Shaw's Saint Joan). However, what he actually uncovers is an atavistic life-force: Eros as dynamic condition of short-lived flesh in the general sense. Lazarus may tell the stories that make Minerva want to become Dora, but the life-force is the one who makes the choice. Minerva's decision to become *this specific form of flesh* is again an act of species-enhancing altruism, for it in turn awakens erotic passion in an ancient man who thought such stirrings long since over. In a sense, Lazarus does the same with his cloned "sister-daughters." Genetically, they are the sisters he never had. And to make them such (with at least a simulacrum of turning back the biological clock), he has them brought to term in host mothers who at the same time are his mistresses. Raised in this erotic climate, these "daughters" soon succumb to the atavistic idea of incest, seducing Lazarus in turn to become their lover. Insofar as they are flesh of his flesh, as they tell him, their love can be nothing more than masturbation, an act without biological consequence. But if this is all (as with Shaw's ancient ones) controlled play, it nevertheless reawakens the creative *possibility* of a return to the random process of selection. Heinlein's term for this is "serendipity." In Lazarus's world it works in strange ways, as in the case of the "twins who weren't," where diploid siblings, after an elaborate ritual of avoidance, suddenly discover they can make love and have children after all. The life force may take strange by-ways, but it must be made to continue to flow.

The dilemma, then, of these long-lived humans seems to be a necessary consequence of their mortal condition. Given one body by birth, they can only extend that body, and in doing so shape and create ultimately a world out of that body. However, such self-perpetuation, it seems, requires that they come to live a non-mediated existence, a contradiction in terms of the life force that generates and sustains them. "We have a direct sense of life," Shaw's He-Ancient proclaims: "We have tapped the central heat [of the Earth] as prehistoric man tapped water springs; but nothing has come up alive from those flaming depths" (288). Within this frame of self-sufficiency, the same parts are replaced over and over. This process of self-replacement, ultimately, must make such parts interchangeable among like beings. The result is that these Ancients, made of like parts, themselves are alike and interchangeable. Shaw's Ancients have no personal names: their "He" or "She" designations do not specify gender so much as the generic nature of their beings. In light of the youth "revolt," their nature, as they endlessly defer the final cause by interchanging parts, becomes one of sterility and loss of direction. As bodies that have become machines, they can perhaps run forever, but all sense of direction is lost because there is no longer a place in their biology for the striving monad that is youth. Heinlein's Lazarus is even more acutely aware of this quandary. The entire novel *Time Enough for Love* recounts the efforts of such a self-perpetuating Ancient to regain a sense of individual purpose in a world whose every part (as the result of his genetico-technological manipulation) has become his "toy"—movable parts of his single being, clones or machines.

A central and abiding aspect of Heinlein's work, moving apace with the quest for longevity, is the Pascalian terror, on the part of our young and dynamic human race, that such stasis or collective stagnation is the necessary price of life extension. Heinlein's Martians are such, most notably in *Stranger in a Strange Land*. Even the "young" Lazarus, in Heinlein's early novel, *Methuselah's Children*, encounters and violently rejects such an "immortal" group entity. His friend Mary Sperling, who despairs of aging, gives herself over to a collective being called The Little People. This is a "transcendent" group consciousness that takes over human bodies and uses them interchangeably as its medium of expression. Lazarus is horrified when he approaches a stranger and hears Mary's voice speaking to him from its mouth. As with Shaw, built into Heinlein's longevity dynamic is a deep, and ultimately creative, tension between youth and age, between the individual as a unique, imperfect, hence non-interchangeable entity, and the collectivity of Ancients, who through their interchangeable parts can prolong life indefinitely, but at the loss of the vital energy of the monad.

Thanks to the publishing medium of science fiction and its "juvenile" novel category, Heinlein devoted a whole decade of his career to creating what Shaw only suggested in the final section of *Back to Methuselah*: full-blown allegories of youth revolt. The best of these is *Have Space Suit, Will Travel* (1958).[7] In this novel, the he-child and she-child are Kip and Peewee, two human "specimens" collected by a race of intergalactic immortals, whose task is to bring renegade ephemeral races to a bar of justice. For these immortals, once a race is judged unpredictable, it is declared dangerous to cosmic equilibrium and "rotated," totally annihilated. Again as in Shaw, short-lived humans (i.e., we) are counters in a lab experiment. Placed in "bugged" quarters on an Elysian planet in the Vegan system, Kip and Peewee are probed for cultural data that will be used against them in court. Their judges form a typical collective entity, and their philosophy is the product of their physical existence: "I am partly machine, which part can be repaired, replaced, recopied; I am partly alive, these parts die and are replaced. My living parts are more than a dozen dozens of dozens of civilized beings from throughout three Galaxies, any dozens dozens of which may join my non-living part to act" (227). The essence of this entity is homeostasis, self-regulation or self-limitation. Young Kip, in defiance, throws in its "face" that mankind, on the contrary, has no limits. Just as surely as when Shaw's artificial woman bites Pygmalion's hand, this outburst of violence condemns them in the judges' mind. Clearly however, the condemnation comes from fear of the potentially disruptive force of the striving monad: "They [mankind] have no art and only the most primitive of science, yet such is their violent nature that even with so little knowledge they are now energetically using it to exterminate each other. Their driving will is such that they may succeed. But if by some unlucky chance they fail, they will inevitably, in time, reach other stars" (235). Faced not only with their destruction but with that of the human race, Kip and Peewee respond with the same puzzling altruism we saw in Shaw's short-lived beings. The girl Peewee this time steps forward first to plead for Kip's life, citing the fact that he risked his own life to save the Mother Thing, the galactic cop who later had them arraigned. Then Kip steps forward to request that, if Earth is to be destroyed, they be sent home to die with it. Heinlein's group mind is stymied. It simply cannot fathom how a being, once given life, can throw it away for the sake of another. This forces them to offer humanity, as a race of short-lived monads, a reprieve. Youth has bought time against age and, in doing so, kept the channels open for possible changes. For in this interim, maybe Kip and others will invent space travel and go out to bring down their judges. In the short run, however, here, as in Shaw, the protest remains a feeble (if violent and disruptive) gesture: the female bites Pygmalion's finger, Kip throws a pie in the face of his home-town bully.

The dynamics of longevity in Shaw and Heinlein, then, demand these constant intrusions of "ephemeral" humans into the general evolutionary process of life extension. They provide stimulus to keep that process open, or at least to keep it from closing on itself in solipsistic selfcreation. Even so, there is ultimately, even as this undulation between youth and age makes its dramatic irruption here and there in the evolutionary drama of mankind, still a sense of inevitable repetition, sameness, and exhaustion that governs the process. Following his own life line, Heinlein gave off writing stories of juvenile revolt and turned to vast novels chronicling the repetitious actions by which ancients like Lazarus seek to perpetuate their world-bodies. In Shaw's pentateuch, too, after the brief episode of Pygmalion's death, we see the other "children" predictably grow up. In rapid succession, they will displace, as so many interchangeable parts, the Ancients they formerly rebelled against. These "revolts" remain predictable blips in a process moving down the entropy slope, with all humans moving ever farther from the first cause, or source of vital energy, toward the final cause of eternity as stasis. For longevity, the horizontal vector of youth-age will not do. If there is to be a *dynamic system,* a vertical axis is needed that allows the Methuselah, like the giant Antaeus, to touch down on earth, make renewed contact with this primal force. And yet, where being is vectored, through the primal push of birth, irreversibly along its time line, how can, *short of death,* such contact ever be made?

Back to Methuselah is a curious title for a cycle of plays that move increasingly into the future. As cycle, however, the set comes around in the end, despite the fact that mankind is said to be "press[ing] on to the goal of redemption from the flesh," to close on a first woman who is in fact the first *human*—Lilith. Shaw's Lilith is not just Adam's first wife, nor an earth goddess, nor a demon. Speaking for her, he presents her not simply as a being beyond differences in age or gender, or good and evil, but as one who exists *before* such differences. She is the cosmic egg, the androgyne that continuously divides itself in the advancement of the race, in order that "the impulse I gave them in that day when I sundered myself in twain and launched Man and Woman on the earth still urges them" (299). However, the image of the cycle as circle dominates here, and one wonders whether Shaw's Lilith wishes to break the circle or draw it in its finality. Although Lilith's words promise life without end, in the next breath she envisions a time when "my seed shall . . . fill [the vast domain of possible worlds] and master its matter to its uttermost confines" (300). Although she sees humanity's "next step" as the "redemption from the flesh, to the vortex freed from matter, to the whirlpool in pure intelligence that, when the world began, was a whirlpool in pure force," the circular imagery used tends to enfold beginnings and ends in a self-contained dynamic quite analogous to the process by which the Methuselah strives to perpetuate the sameness of a singular life. Now it is beginnings and ends themselves that seem to have become interchangeable parts. In terms of dynamics of longevity, the logic of the line and the logic of the circle would seem to be incompatible. Yet whatever is born, once launched, strives to close the circle, on whatever level—be it individual or race or species—so as to create the internal dynamic that may preserve it short of finality. When Lilith asks; "Is this enough, or shall I labor again?" is she proposing to create the new, or re-create the old all over again?

When Heinlein's Lazarus, at the end of his self-created universe in *Time Enough for Love*, turns back to first woman and source of his long-lived seed, his own mother Maureen, he finds that he cannot dominate his first cause, nor even stimulate its whirlpool of force to generate a next evolutionary step—be this a swirl of pure intelligence or something beyond. In the final *da capo* episode of this novel, Lazarus uses time travel to return to pre–World War I Missouri (his birthplace as well as Heinlein's) and in the guise of Sgt. Theodore Bronson, to become the lover of his own mother, Maureen. This soon proves, it seems, to be at least a gesture toward the crowning act of solipsism—the siring of oneself. Lazarus, of course (good science fiction creation that he is), knows all about the grandfather paradox and the barrier it sets on human powers. He does agree, however, in Pygmalion-fashion, to play with the instant of his own creation by inducing mother Maureen to replay with him the setting—if not the exact moment—of his own conception, using the same place, same blankets, same pretexts to make love to his mother. To protect the first cause, however, Lazarus makes sure his time double, himself at age five, sneaks a ride in the car and looks on as another "he" makes love to his mother. This is masturbatory theater, perhaps, but it points to the fact that the self-perpetuating can never be self-generating. Under the iron law of directional Time, Lazarus's first cause remains forever inviolate. In this sense, he cannot go home again.

From this moment, in Heinlein's work, the dynamic of longevity is displaced. Instead of Lazarus's centrifugal movement, we begin to move centripetally, back to Maureen, toward the vital force at the point of origin. In his last novels, her presence looms larger and larger until, in the final novel, *To Sail Beyond the Sunset* (1987), she is the dominant (indeed the sole) figure.[8] In this novel under the sign of Tennyson, we seem to have again, as with the final words of Shaw's Lilith, promise of forward movement and change: "Come, my friends, / 'Tis not too late to seek a newer world." The action of this novel all too obviously undulates between the center—the Missouri world of Maureen's coming of age—and that far-flung circumference of multiverse worlds, parallel spacetime dimensions without end, where Lazarus operated. Like Lilith, Maureen appears to be pure life force and, as such, an almost androgynous presence. Master of spacetime disguises, she is all ages and genders at once. She slips in and out of roles—breeder and intergalactic spy and warrior alike. Yet at the heart of this, Heinlein's final integrative effort, where first cause is stirred in hopes of pushing forward human experience, toward those "newer" worlds that forestall the final moment, we sense a deep rift. In ever longer and more wearying passages, the action drifts back, in obsessive fashion, to that time of origin and childhood, pre-war Missouri. Maureen's many loves and births are chronicled *ad nauseam,* admitting to the impossibility of recapturing the initial moment by merely replaying it. As with Lilith, we have the sense of cycles of birthing that become no more than series of concentric circles around an original, intangible, point. We may call this a vortex, a whirlpool or a spiral, but whatever its transformational possibilities, it can never be free of its first cause. Heinlein's novel ends with what seems a domesticated clone of Lazarus's solipsistic perpetual-motion machine. She does not want to be God; she desires marriages and children without end. Yet doing nothing but producing and nurturing these, everywhere and in every age, as the sole purview of a physically ubiquitous woman, is every bit as self-indulgent and world-enfolding as the spatiotemporal contortions of ancient Lazarus. We remember young Lazarus looking in horror at the group entity The Little People, then growing up to generate a world in which, in analogous fashion, all individual parts have become interchangeable and alike, clones and simulacra of his sole self. We imagine the *first* Maureen—the vital individual girl—gazing with similar horror at the description of the last Maureen's "total marriage contract" on the final page of *To Sail:* "Whom you sleep with . . . is your private business. Ishtar, as our family geneticist, controls pregnancy and progeny to whatever extent is needed for the welfare of our children. So we all joined hands in the presence of our children, and we pledged ourselves to love and cherish our children—those around us, those still to come, worlds without end."

Shaw and Heinlein both construct far-reaching visions of humankind's dynamic striving for longevity. Yet somehow, in their vision, they remain prisoner to a paradox of the human condition that endlessly pits curiosity against boredom, youth against age, first against final cause. The attempt that Shaw shared with science fiction to construct an integrative system always seems to run aground on an irreducible duality that seems endemic to the human condition itself. To British physicist J.D. Bernal, in *The World, the Flesh, and the Devil: An Inquiry into the Future of the Three Enemies of the Rational Soul* (1929), a work that in a sense offers a master narrative for modern science fiction, it is likewise a duality centered in the human mind itself that is the final barrier to "rational" advancement.[9] Technology, to Bernal, can extend both our physical environment ("world") and our physical bodies ("flesh"), but remains powerless before a division in the human "soul" that on one hand drives us endlessly to seek newer worlds and, on the other, to hug the known center. But what Shaw, to some extent, and Heinlein teach us is that endless seeking, short of death or transfiguration to the non-human, tends to the state of a self-perpetuating, hence closed, system. More surprisingly, as Lilith and Maureen show us, the same is true at the level of Bernal's ecological stay-at-homes. Bernal lets nature solve this problem through a "dimorphic" evolution. Yet again each of these "forms," in their struggle to extend life, tends toward a sameness of function. They remain static poles, opposing forms. And yet each, at its pole, isolates itself from the other through the sameness of its internal dynamic.

As we see, the question, in terms of the dynamics of longevity, is not whether we do away with duality altogether (we have seen that a world all of men or of women, of long-lived or short-lived humans, is equally isolated and sterile), but the degree to which these terms may, ultimately, engage in creative dialogue. I turn not to Heinlein but to Shaw for a possible answer. *Saint Joan* (1923) responds, in a quiet way, to the evolutionary sweep of *Back to Methuselah*.[10] In the marvelous Epilogue to this play, the ghost of Joan responds to the ghost of Cauchon, who protests the desecration of his grave. She points to pain as means of transition between the poles of life and death: "Your dead body did not feel the spade and the sewer as my live body felt the fire" (174). Because none of Shaw's or Heinlein's first women or last men make this crossing, none speak with the wisdom of Joan, who in this final scene knows how to balance immortality with mortality. Joan has returned from the grave and hears from ghosts of a future not yet born that she is to be a saint, thus immortal. Having made the passage, however, Joan knows clearly (as Achilles learned in Hades) both sides of the longevity question. Earth will never be ready to receive its saints for the same reason that Joan knows that she can not be unburnt: "And now tell me: shall I rise from the dead, and come back to you a living woman?" (183). During this play, Joan carries on a dialogue with the various roles and forms that humans don in their search for longevity. The living woman from Lorraine is first made to wear the costume of the bourgeois, then the male dress of the warrior, the robe of the martyr, and now finally the mantle of a saint. Her individual life is obliterated in the name of human longevity in the form of institutions such as church and state, royalty and nationhood. In the Epilogue, representatives of all these states finally vanish like shades in the face of Joan's evocation of real life (which is, as it was for Achilles, short and yet intense) on "this beautiful earth." They leave behind, as last to depart, Joan and the ghost of the English soldier who gave her a wooden cross as she burned on the pyre, and who is allowed respite from Hell one day a year. In his case, altruism has served a very different purpose than evolutionary vengeance, or the perpetuation of a single species. It allows transition between mortal and immortal and marks the place of crossing as dialogue between a woman and man who exist in their most basic and fundamental human condition. Perhaps the only response to evolution's drive to longevity—a response that Heinlein did not offer—is this life and death of a saint who wanted to be a mortal person.

Notes

1. In the Epic of Gilgamesh, the hero, unable to pass the test of immortality by prevailing against sleep "for six days and seven nights," is told by the solitary immortal Utnapishtim of a prickly plant that grows underwater and that, when plucked, will give to him who takes it eternal youth. Gilgamesh takes the plant, but only to lose it to a serpent who lay in the pool in which he bathed. The mortal hero passes through several stages of the quest for long life. Utnapishtim is the solitary ancient whose immorality is pure stasis. Gilgamesh, who is bound to the diurnal rhythms of sleeping and waking as part of his human condition, cannot achieve this without unnatural aids. The next (and lesser) possibility is, by means of the plant, the achievement of a rhythm of age and youth, so-called rejuvenation, from which point one must grow old again, then rejuvenate, and so on. The snake, as in the Garden of Eden, acts to disrupt this. The reason here, however, is less the guile of the tempter than the need of the mortal being to break rhythms, to do something different, in an uncharted place. The only "longevity" left to the hero is through symbol and figure—the signs he has engraved on the stone walls of Uruk.

2. Horace de Saint-Aubin (pseudonym of Honoré de Balzac), *Le Centenaire; ou les deux Beringheld* (Paris: Pollet, libraire-éditeur), 1822.

3. Robert A. Heinlein, *Methuselah's Children,* serialized in *Astounding Science Fiction* (July, August, September 1941).

4. Robert A. Heinlein, *Time Enough for Love* (New York: Putnam, 1973). All further references are to this edition.

5. Bernard Shaw, *Back to Methuselah: A Metabiological Pentateuch* (New York: Brentano's, 1922). All further references are to this edition.

6. Sandra M. Gilbert and Susan Gubar, *The Madwoman in the Attic* (New Haven: Yale University Press, 1979).

7. Robert A. Heinlein, *Have Space Suit, Will Travel* (New York: Scribner's, 1958).

8. Robert A. Heinlein, *To Sail Beyond the Sunset* (New York: Ace-Putnam, 1988).

9. John Desmond Bernal, *The World, the Flesh, and the Devil: An Inquiry into the Future of the Three Enemies of the Rational Soul* (1929), revised edition (London: Jonathan Cape, 1970).

10. Bernard Shaw, *Saint Joan* (Baltimore: Penguin Books, 1960).

John Barnes

TROPICS OF A DESIRABLE OXYMORON: THE RADICAL SUPERMAN IN *BACK TO METHUSELAH*

"Radical superman" is a desirable oxymoron, a cliché that expresses the human desire to escape a natural tradeoff by taking both sides of a mutually exclusive dichotomy. Besides "radical superman," other examples of the desirable oxymoron are "science fiction," "liberal democracy," "business ethics," and "academic freedom." We want the people simultaneously to be sovereign and to be free of absolute power; we want economic dealings to maximize both profit and justice; we want the institution most dedicated to finding and enforcing the True against the False to be broadly tolerant. Such imagined escapes, from difficult tradeoffs between positive goods into a greater satisfaction somewhere outside the envelope of possibility, are so common that their names have become clichés.

Because the oxymoron introduces an unresolvable contradiction, it poses a problem in logic but not necessarily in tropics. If the desirable oxymoron is a representamen, it can be dialectically resolved into two aspects of some greater truth. (The representamen corresponds to the signifier, the interpretant to the rule by which the receiver of the sign constructs the signified from the object, and the object to the difference between the signifier and signified.)[1] But in science fiction one of the most common tropes is the depiction of an impossibility. Thus an oxymoronic representamen, in science fiction, may not be the sign of a complex whole, but instead may have to be mapped so that the interpretant must preserve the contradiction as it translates the representamen into a believable unbelievable, or an unimaginable imagined.

In live theater, with its necessary interaction between audience and actors and its elemental representamen of the performed action, a desirable oxymoron like "radical superman" directly engages the audience in the process of synthesizing a thing that cannot exist. Thus to present a radical superman forces the audience, if it wishes to understand the performance, into an exploration and reassessment of the boundaries of what is conventionally thought possible.

Driving the audience to thought by any means necessary, of course, is characteristic of Shaw, so it is hardly surprising that he experimented with the tropics of this particular desirable oxymoron. In *Back to Methuselah*, Shaw struggled to make the concept of "radical superman" take a definite shape through live performance—to create in the audience's mind an object that would correspond to a "real" superman in the service of Shaw's radical politics.

"Radical superman" is actually a double problem in signification when we think of its performance on the stage. First of all, it would be oxymoronic in any discourse, for radical thought is predicated on the equality and malleability of human beings and assumes that the greater part of the capacities and behavior of people derive from their socialization. A world in which supermen come into being and bring about revolutions is exactly opposite a world in which revolution allows the next generation to grow up as supermen. To make the utopian transformation by means of a superman is to negate the premises that make such a transformation desirable to the radical.

But a second problem arises when theater is the medium of signification: the audience must be convinced that an ordinary person, the actor, is a superman. Furthermore, to the extent that the illusion succeeds, it must exacerbate the oxymoron.

It is a remarkable feat for an ordinary actor on the stage to represent a person whose capacities and nature are beyond our comprehension by definition. Shaw was well aware of this, as he noted in a letter to St. John Ervine: "In Methuselah, I could not show the life of long livers because, being a short liver, I could not conceive it. To make the play possible at all I had to fall back on an exhibition of shortlivers and children in contrast with such scraps of long life as I could deduce by carrying a little further the difference that exists between the child and the adult. . . ."[2]

Shaw solves the problem of representing the superman in two ways in *Back to Methuselah*. The more conventional way by which the representa-

men, "an actor playing Haslam," represents "the Superman" is the basic
theatrical principle of reaction: a feigning that some action is important
and unexpected. For example, a skilled actor tries to appear to hear
every line of the actors for the first time, which creates the illusion of
two people in conversation (when in fact they are repeating memorized
words verbatim); an actor who grimaces in apparent pain may actually
be holding her own hair while another actor grips her wrist, but her
reaction to the situation tells us she is being hurt; playwrights "prepare
the stage" by putting minor characters on so that their behavior when
more important characters finally arrive can give information about the
important character. The audience, seeking to understand the actions
before it, then constructs an interpretant in which the representamen
is mapped to "significant surprise" and hence to "important part of
reality"—e.g., the actor stepped back because the unexpected news is
worthy of a strong emotional reaction, or is grimacing and struggling
because she is being lifted by her hair, or flung himself to the floor
because a tyrant entered.

Reaction is frequently used when the superman must be presented in
Back to Methuselah. When Haslam, now 283 years old, enters, the President is inexplicably afraid of him, presumably because of his superiority.[3] Mrs. Lutestring reacts to Burge-Lubin's suggestion of himself as a
sexual partner as if the elderly Burge-Lubin were a child.[4] The Elderly
Gentleman and Napoleon both suffer bouts of "discouragement," despair brought on by close contact with the supermen.[5] A reaction can
also convey information by not happening, as in the atmosphere of
complete normality in Part 5 when a seventeen-year-old girl is born—
speaking, conscious, and able to walk after a few steps—from an egg.[6]
(In this last case, the blasé reactions of the youths—"One would think
nobody had ever been born before"—are a representamen for "It is
routine for functional adult people to hatch from eggs in 31,920 AD.")

As a tool for establishing superiority, reaction works well enough in
Back to Methuselah. But Shaw's concept of Creative Evolution required a
very specific kind of superiority, one that had degrees and gradations
and could increase with time, and reaction could show only that one
character was superior to another, not that a whole class of characters
was superior, let alone that they would grow more superior with time.

This seems to have been one of several problems Shaw discovered
after his first reading of the play in 1918. Granville Barker, along with a
few others, was in attendance for the reading, and Shaw later wrote to
him on 18 December 1918 to say that "I, alas! am worse bored by the
Brothers Barnabas than by their unfortunate family and rector. I shall
have to get the picture better composed."[7] Since he finds it necessary to
describe what eventually becomes of Haslam, Lutestring, Savvy, and

Clara (who does not appear in the final version), it seems likely that the reading was partial and did not include *The Thing Happens,* but his references to "reproducing" Church, marriage, and family "under long lived conditions" would seem to indicate that the essential direction of *Back to Methuselah* was already worked out.[8] To Granville Barker's apparent objection that much of the "Gospel of the Brothers Barnabas" was dull, Shaw responds that "if I make them all satisfactory, the reason for making them live 300 years vanishes. What I have to do is not to make them satisfactory; but to find an artistic treatment of their unsatisfactoriness, which will prevent its being as disagreeable as the real thing."[9]

The problem, then, was that if there was to be a credible impulse toward the superman that the audience could be persuaded to share, the audience must be brought into dissatisfaction with present-day people. Yet if their being unsatisfactory were merely a matter of their being "disagreeable," then they would not make the case for a superman; they would merely appear to be unpleasant characters. Shaw thought such people were "dull and irritating . . . in real life," but the point was not to draw them as they were so much as to show that until the superman was achieved, they could be not better.[10] The audience must be unhappy with the characters but it must not blame the characters for their unsatisfactory qualities; rather, the dissatisfaction must be one that could lead to a quite specific wish for a quite specific something better (much like the wish by which acquirements are inherited in Shaw's outline of Creative Evolution in the Preface).[11]

Shaw had real actors on the stage, limited by their real capacities. Therefore he needed an interpretant that would cause the object the viewer constructed to be a precisely perceptible superiority of supermen characters (played by ordinary actors) to ordinary humans (played by equally ordinary actors). He needed to force the viewer to see the actors in an intellectual forced perspective so that they seemed to be giants of a specific size, which would increase with time.

To do this, Shaw devised a sophisticated and subtle tropic process, deployed in two stages. First an interpretant is established as a convention within the performance by using it to connect a fairly simple and direct representamen (who explains what to whom) with an easily established object (difference in intellectual stature). Second, a representamen that clearly belongs to the same class as the first is presented— but that representamen is chosen so that, according to the now-established interpretant, it points to an object that the audience would otherwise accept only with difficulty, either because it is hard to imagine or because audiences are emotionally predisposed to reject it.

This particular tropic process is accomplished across the entire length of *Back to Methuselah.* The first stage, of establishing the interpretant, is under way as soon as the curtain goes up. In the opening scene of the "pentateuch," Adam and Eve, in Eden, investigate a dead deer.[12] The concept of death is familiar to the audience, and thus we have a "correct" interpretation for every observation Adam and Eve make, so the reaction of the actors playing Adam and Eve establishes them as representamena of "People who don't know about death."

The introduction of the character of the Serpent specifies that interpretant to be applicable to any representamen of the form (person who must have something obvious explained).[13] The necessity of the Serpent's explaining things that everyone in the audience already knows connects it to the object (superiority in greater knowledge or experience). The interpretant is thus established as the rule that the representamen (explainer + character who needs things explained) maps to the object (difference between adult/wise superior and childish/naïve/inferior being).

As we move into Parts 3, 4, and 5, the interpretant that the audience has been encouraged to construct is played against it: the characters who are most like the audience are the ones who must have things explained to them, and thus if the audience continues to play Shaw's game and deploy the interpretant established in Part 1, it is forced to construct the object (superiority to any living person).

Using this interpretant, Shaw then presents a rising succession of demonstrations of superiority: Haslam and Mrs. Lutestring explain matters to the President; Zoo explains things to the Elderly Gentleman; the Oracle explains to Napoleon; finally the Ancients explain things to the Youths. This forms a neat progression. Through this medium of having to have commonsense things explained to them as a demonstration of inferiority, first supermen who have only gradually learned that they are superior are demonstrated to be superior to the President (who is presumably a good specimen of a contemporary human), thus signifying a state of affairs 250 years from now when superiority is manifest and the supermen are at least as far beyond us as we were beyond Adam and Eve in Part 1.

Then in Part 4 a young superman, from a society of supermen, explains things to a cultured and intelligent gentleman, and a middle-aged superman explains things to Napoleon and "solves" his problem by effectively eliminating him. This signifies a state of affairs 3,000 years from now when the very best of contemporary humans is not even capable of bearing (let alone understanding) the explanations of the supermen. In this world Haslams and Lutestrings not only exceed ordinary people, they reach their full potentials, so that the superiority of the superman turns out to be larger than it first appeared.

Finally, in *As Far as Thought Can Reach,* a group of "goodlooking

philosopher-athletes"[14] who are presumably our contemporary idea of
the superman have to have things explained to them by the Ancients—
the "super-supermen," who must explain things to "mere" supermen
and who thus may be supposed to have attained a doubled or squared
superiority to us.

Shaw represents an ever-widening gap between contemporary humans and the superhuman future, until finally the gap has been extended "beyond super" to "As Far as Thought Can Reach," by the
repeated application of a trope:

(representamen = a strangely behaved person explaining the obvious to a person like us)	+	(interpretant = within the scope of this play the persons who have the obvious explained to them are inferior and the person who does the explaining is superior)	+	(object = superiority of the strangely behaved person to people like us)

As the "metabiological pentateuch" ends, Lilith, who began life before
Adam and Eve by dividing herself into male and female, concludes the
play with a swift, startling extension of the trope. In the last few lines
she refers first to the Ancients directly as "these infants that call
themselves ancients," then to being superseded by them, and finally to a
stage that "the eyesight of Lilith is too short" to see.[15] Thus even the
Ancients are dwarfed by Lilith (who apparently cannot explain things to
them because they are unready), and Lilith is dwarfed in turn by the
eventual destiny of the fully living universe that she cannot grasp. The
ascent from naïve humanity (in Part 1) to ordinary humanity (in Part 2)
through the occasional superman (in Part 3), the dominant superman
society (4), and the superseded superman (5) is abruptly extended, in
the last part of Lilith's closing monologue, into a vision of several more
levels stretching beyond the Ancients until finally all that can be said is
that there is something beyond.

Shaw, through Lilith, asserts at the end that "It is enough that there is
a beyond."[16] Having established superiority so thoroughly—if a director
deploys the theatrical tropes discussed above thoroughly and consistently, the illusion should work quite well on stage—Shaw has made his
superman real. But now that the superman is real, is he radical?

The problem is that the whole history of radical thought centers on
the environmental determination of human characteristics so that
greater equality and prosperity will lead to a better and happier breed

of human beings, whether by Kautskyist evolution (so that each generation, in improving the lot of the next, makes the next generation fitter to advance further) or Leninist revolution (so that a small group of visionaries takes over and establishes conditions under which the great majority of the population can advance).

At first Shaw appears to side with Lenin in *Back to Methuselah,* despairing of religion, politics, and education as pathways to reform in the Preface.[17] But if the public arenas of discourse cannot produce better people, then where are the better people for a better world to come from?

Shaw's solution to this is his Lamarckian version of Creative Evolution, an idea whose name he borrowed from Bergson and whose critique of Darwin derives from Butler, but which is for Shaw not a philosophic or scientific concept (as in Bergson and Butler) but a religious and mystical one. The introduction to *Back to Methuselah* argues that because the Life Force wants a species that will do its work, the Life Force will act on human beings by a Lamarckian process to make them produce one.[18] Hence, without the world having to become any better first, the people who can make it better will come to be born and will eventually save the day.

Thus Shaw does not reject only liberal democracy, in which people choose revolutionary change. He also rejects vanguardist democracy, in which an enlightened minority forces people into what they would have chosen had they known their objective interests. Creative Evolution does not act on behalf of human interests at all, but on behalf of the Life Force, which is not yet conscious but seeks to be.

Temporarily Shaw believes that the motion of the Life Force is in the same direction as that of socialism. But Creative Evolution, not radical politics, is primary to him—not just the movements and causes of the moment, but humanity itself, are to be weighed and judged according to the need of the Life Force to replace a universe that was all matter with one that will be all mind. As Lilith says,

Best of all, they are still not satisfied: the impulse I gave them in that day when I sundered myself in twain and launched Man and Woman on the earth still urges them: after passing a million goals they press on to the goal of redemption from the flesh, to the vortex freed from matter, to the whirlpool in pure intelligence that, when the world began, was a whirlpool in pure force. And though all that they have done seems but the first hour of the infinite work of creation, yet I will not supersede them until they have forded this last stream that lies between flesh and spirit, and disentangled their life from the matter that has always mocked it.[19]

This is simply not a radical position. Although it does seek to "wrest a space for Freedom from Necessity," it is specifically *anti*-materialist and escapes rather than synthesizes the dialectic between mind and matter. Further, humanity as we know it *is* both mind and matter, so this would seem to require the end of humanity. Antimaterialist antihumanism is hardly radical at all, as the term is commonly understood. A freedom purely in thought is not won from necessity (which would require a tension with necessity), but is a purely ideological freedom in which necessity is obviated by fiat. This is not radicalism, but mysticism (and Shaw himself repeatedly describes these ideas as religious).

This fits well with the tropic movement toward ever-expanding superiority described above. Haslam and Mrs. Lutestring plainly excel everyone at everything that Shaw thinks ought to matter. In *Tragedy of an Elderly Gentleman,* Shaw invents "discouragement," which happens whenever an unimproved human being has prolonged contact with one of his supermen and seems to be Creative Evolution's way of telling *homo sapiens* to die, get off the planet, and make way for our betters.[20] In the fifth part, set 30,000 years into the future, Shaw sharpens his sting by having virtually all of humanity's intellectual and creative functions or activities become the amusements of the supermen before they are four years old. The Ancients of *Back to Methuselah* do not live in anything that most radicals would recognize as a utopia; on the contrary, they long not to shape matter for human ends, but to abolish matter.[21] The purpose of the Life Force as stated by Lilith is explicitly and militantly inhuman and antihuman, abolishing everything human except a sort of pure apprehension or perception.

The desire for a better world, made by and for humans, which makes the radical superman attractive in the early parts of *Back to Methuselah,* is frustrated by the success of the tropic process by which Shaw induces belief in exponentially increasing superiority. After the struggles of Parts 1 and 2 *The Thing Happens* is a kind of idyll to which Lutestring and Haslam seem like enhancements and ornaments. But the tropic process continues on until humanity is lost and obliterated in an antihuman destiny. The tropics hold up well; the illusion of superiority lasts right to the end. The problem is that the superman devours the radical, and the images devour the people.

This is common enough in science fiction. "Science fiction" itself might be seen as a desirable oxymoron—an expression of the impossible wish simultaneously to have a story and to have knowledge of reality, to live in the realm of myth and the realm of facts, tragically and philosophically, at the same time. But finally a science fiction story must be either a description of reality (science in its extended sense of knowledge) or a story about a place that does not exist (fiction). Either the science will have to be compromised for the fiction, or the fiction will have to be forced back into our mundane world. The representamen of "science fiction" is revealed to point only to a disguised science lesson or (more commonly) to a romance decked out with science.

Thus as Shaw's radical superman grew more superior through his tropic (fictionalizing) process, it became less a philosophic position on what people ought to be (science/knowledge) and more myth (fiction). If Shaw's Creative Evolution really were science, the production of a Mrs. Lutestring (a remarkably able civil servant to rule us for our own good) might be conceived of as a serious pragmatic project. But we do not end up there; we end up with the barely conceivable Lilith telling us that there is something far beyond her, and that "it is enough that there is a beyond."[22] If Shaw's superman must lose radicalism, still it gains a powerful theatrical apotheosis. Regrettable as it is that the radical supermen could not be both superior and radical all the way through, flawed as the concept of the radical superman may be, it is admirable that Shaw chose as he did when the tropic limits finally forced him to come down on one side of that other desirable oxymoron, "science fiction."

Notes

1. For a fuller explanation of the semiotics of Charles S. Peirce, see his letters to Lady Welby, his 1891 article "The Architecture of Theories," and his best-known essay, "How to Make Our Ideas Clear," in Philip P. Wiener, ed., *Charles S. Peirce: Selected Writings* (New York: Dover, 1966).

2. Quoted in St. John Ervine, *Bernard Shaw: His Life, Work and Friends* (New York: Morrow, 1956), p. 490.

3. Bernard Shaw, *Back to Methuselah: A Metabiological Pentateuch* (New York: Oxford University Press, 1947), p. 97.

4. Ibid., p. 115.

5. Ibid., pp. 137, 164.

6. Ibid., pp. 198–200.

7. *Bernard Shaw's Letters to Granville Barker*, ed. C. B. Purdom (New York: Theatre Arts Books, 1957), p. 198.

8. Ibid.

9. Ibid., p. 199.

10. Ibid., p. 198.

11. *Back to Methuselah*, pp. xix-xxi.

12. Ibid., pp. 1–4.

13. Ibid., pp. 6–11.

14. Bernard Shaw, *Man and Superman: A Comedy and a Philosophy,* ed. Dan H. Laurence (New York: Penguin, 1988), p. 216.

15. *Back to Methuselah,* p. 245.

16. Ibid.

17. Ibid., pp. ix-xv.

18. Ibid., pp. lxviii-lxxiv.

19. Ibid., p. 244.

20. Ibid., pp. 160, 174.

21. Ibid., pp. 238–39.

22. Ibid., p. 245.

Julie A. Sparks

SHAW FOR THE UTOPIANS, ČAPEK FOR THE ANTI-UTOPIANS

The continuing argument between utopian writers who prefigure the Millennium and the anti-utopian writers who prophesy the approach of Armageddon is generally assumed to be a struggle between wide-eyed optimism and misanthropic pessimism. But the profoundest thinkers in each camp sometimes find, after a prolonged engagement with their dialogic opposites, that their tents are pitched on common ground—that a Hegelian synthesis has occurred wherein the seemingly irreconcilable positions have merged into a guarded but life-affirming optimism. One such reconciliation can be found in the dramatic dialogue between Bernard Shaw, representing the utopians, and Karel Čapek (1890–1938), a Czech anti-utopian writer with Luddite tendencies and conservative religious views who respected Shaw's work but disagreed with some of its deepest philosophical underpinnings. They began working out their different visions of humanity's future independently, both weighing the unprecedented destructive ferocity of World War I against the great promise of the early twentieth century's technological advances and exploring humanity's prospects in a utopian-dystopian format. Both also employed their own variations on biblical themes—Creation, Armageddon, and the achievement of the Millennium—to illustrate their different conclusions. Eventually, however, they were drawn into a dialogue that focused on a question central to utopian and anti-utopian discourse: Should humanity strive for a secular millennium, struggling to re-create man and society into the image suggested by our brightest hopes, or should we content ourselves with the status quo and wait patiently for divine orchestration to work out our destiny?

Their essential disagreement on this point stems in part from their very different concepts of humankind's progress. As J. L. Wisenthal explains in his study of Shaw's dialectic dramatic method, "His perspective is evolutionary, and he thinks in terms of progress toward goals rather than their actual attainment. In an evolutionary world no stage is final, and in a neo-Lamarckian evolutionary world the human will is always aiming at something higher."[1] In contrast to this evolutionary outlook, Čapek agrees with the prophet of Ecclesiastes that there is nothing new under the sun, and he found evidence for this belief even in a London art museum. In his *Letters from England,* written after his trip there in 1924, he wrote, "How awful a discovery to find the perfection of man even at the very beginning of existence; to find it in the formation of the first stone arrow, to find it in a Bushman drawing. . . . [D]readful is the relativity of culture and history; nowhere behind us or before us is there a point of rest, of an ideal, of the finish and perfection of man; for it is everywhere and nowhere, and every spot in space and time where man has set up his work is unsurpassable."[2] There could hardly be a more radical divergence of perspective than this, and it led the two writers to present very different interpretations of humanity's distant past and hypothetical future, especially when they became aware of each other's work and squared off for a theological battle. Nevertheless, the first arguments in the debate did not begin as such.

Between 1918 and 1920 Shaw labored on an immense work, a five-play cycle called *Back to Methuselah,* in an effort to provide a modern credible religion that could guide us all out of the error and folly that seemed to have brought us so close to the edge of doom during the Great War. The resulting work was his "metabiological pentateuch" which begins "In the Beginning" with a re-working of the Genesis myth and extends "As Far as Thought Can Reach" to a far-distant future when humankind has evolved into god-like Ancients who live for centuries in their serene, intensely intellectual utopia. Although Shaw's history of humankind recognizes the power-mad, wantonly destructive Cain element in our early stages, he shows how the truly vital, creative element finally prevails and pulls humanity onward and upward straight past the tidy millennial societies that the socialist utopian reformers were dreaming about. The last play of the cycle, *As Far as Thought Can Reach,* ends with a prophecy that some super-evolved humanity, discarding the bodies that encumber it, will eventually spread to populate the stars.

Although many critics objected that the utopia of Shaw's Ancients is not a very appealing goal to strive for and that *Back to Methuselah* only demonstrated Shaw's misanthropy, Shaw seriously intended to offer modern man hope that through willing ourselves to be better, we could ascend the evolutionary ladder from the Yahoo to the Houyhnhnm stage of intellectual and spiritual development. Thus understood, Shaw's Creative Evolution is probably the brightest optimism that could be maintained in the aftermath of Neo-Darwinism and the Great War.

In 1920, the same year Shaw finished his utopian pentateuch, Čapek, writing in Czechoslovakia, finished his first anti-utopian play, *R.U.R. (Rossum's Universal Robots)*, wherein he, like Shaw, evaluates twentieth-century millennial ambitions and Apocalyptic fears employing a modern version of biblical motifs. In Čapek's own words, he meant to write "a comedy, partly of science, partly of truth. The old inventor, Mr. Rossum . . . is no more or less than a typical representative of the scientific materialism of the last century. His desire to create an artificial man—in the chemical and biological, not the mechanical sense—is inspired by a foolish and obstinate wish to prove God to be unnecessary and absurd. Young Rossum is the modern scientist, untroubled by metaphysical ideas; scientific experiment is to him the road to industrial production, he is not concerned to prove, but to manufacture."[3]

This scenario develops into a dark cautionary tale. Young Rossum, hoping to free humanity from toil and establish a leisurely millennial society on android labor—and to make a fortune in the process—is at first phenomenally successful. But the utopian scheme creates too much leisure and renders humans obsolete. Recognizing this, the robots rise up and destroy humanity, then realize that they too soon face extinction because they are not designed for reproduction. Yet the play ends with a life-affirming miracle as two of the robots metamorphose into love-struck humans. Ending where *Back to Methuselah* begins, this Adam and Eve go forth to renew and repopulate the earth.

Although the central concerns of *Back to Methuselah* and *R.U.R.* are very different, both feature automatons that are created in a laboratory to resemble human flesh and intellect very closely—more "androids" in the current use of the term than the metallic, mechanical beings usually implied by the term "robot" (a Čapek-coined word from the Czech "robota" for "forced labor, drudgery"), although the robots hold a much more central position in Čapek's play. In *Methuselah* the automatons appear in only one scene of the last play of the cycle, *As Far as Thought Can Reach*, and they live only briefly before they turn vicious, kill their creator, and then die. In Čapek's play, however, the robot revolution easily upstages the human characters' petty concerns, giving the play a more "science fiction" feel and a more coherent focus than Shaw's eclectic, rambling chronicle could achieve.

Despite their differences, the two plays were linked in the public's consciousness when, in 1922, both were given their American debut (it was a world premiere for *Methuselah*) by New York's Theatre Guild— Shaw's in February and March, Čapek's in October. One reviewer with the *New York Herald* noticed an affinity between the two plays immediately, observing that *R.U.R.* "has as many social implications as the most handy of the Shavian comedies," while a reviewer with the *New York American* goes so far as to assert (rather snidely) that "Bernard Shaw did not write *R.U.R.* but he probably will. Possibly later on we shall have a variation of *R.U.R.* by Mr. Shaw and then what we accepted last night as an exceedingly enjoyable and imaginative fantasy will become a dull diatribe."[4] Yet the two playwrights who were being discussed together in New York both insisted later that they remained unaware of each other's work for some time, and the evidence seems to support this.

R.U.R.'s principal motif—man-made automatons that try to overthrow their creators—can be traced back to much earlier influences. One obvious possibility is the medieval Jewish folk-tale of the Golem, a clay manikin brought to life through cabalistic magic to defend the Jews of the Prague ghetto. Since a German film version of this legend was being shown widely in Czechoslovakia in 1920, the year Capek wrote *R.U.R.*, its influence on the play seems probable.[5] Another obvious precedent is Mary Shelley's *Frankenstein* (the *New York Times* critic titled his review "A Czecho-Slovak Frankenstein"). Probably the closest previous literary precedent, however, describes, like Čapek's play, a society that reaches for the utopian ideal of universal leisure by relegating most of the labor to manufactured automatons: Edward Bulwer-Lytton's anti-utopian novel, *The Coming Race* (1871). Although we can only speculate whether Čapek may have had access to this novel, precedents for his robots are certainly in evidence. When Bulwer-Lytton's narrator first encounters the highly advanced society several miles underground, he reports, "In all service, whether in or out of doors, they make great use of automaton figures, which are so ingenious, and so pliant to the operations of Vril [an energy source], that they actually seem gifted with reason. It was scarcely possible to distinguish the figures I beheld, apparently guiding or superintending the rapid movements of vast engines, from the human forms endowed with thought."[6]

We do know that Shaw was familiar with Bulwer-Lytton's novel, and he tells us in a speech he delivered to the Fabians in 1933 that he borrowed from it the idea that one possible key to a utopian society is "mutually assured destruction" at the personal level—that is, if each member of society could kill with a thought, that society would have to make sure it arranged its institutions carefully so that all members would be content with their lot, and the race would have to develop a high degree of self-control and a horror of killing or it would self-destruct in

SHAW AND KAREL ČAPEK

short order.[7] We see this awful power being demonstrated on a small scale in the fourth play of the *Methuselah* cycle, *Tragedy of an Elderly Gentleman,* just before Shaw's "coming race" finally decides that it must humanely but implacably exterminate the more primitive species of humanity that has failed to evolve this power (just as Čapek's robots decide to exterminate the human race). Although Bulwer-Lytton draws a utopia that many socialist reformers (including Shaw) would approve of, his anti-utopian message—that humankind is constitutionally incapable of either establishing or living in such a perfect society—would appeal more to Čapek, as he makes clear in his later dystopian works.

It is important to note, however, that even at this early stage of his career, Čapek seemed to be working with the same biblical motifs Shaw used in his utopian works, and the plot similarities that result between *R.U.R.* and *Methuselah* are striking, particularly in their revision of Genesis. For example, Čapek's robotic Adam and Eve prove their worthiness to take on the grave responsibility of regenerating the species by demonstrating their willingness to die for each other—in a scene with parallels in Shaw's *In the Beginning* and *As Far as Thought Can Reach.* The scene is pivotal in Čapek's play, providing the deus ex machina device that prevents a species-wide tragedy as God mercifully decides to give humankind a second chance despite the disastrous effects of our greed and hubris. Just as the last remaining human, Alquist, has completely given up hope of rediscovering the lost robot formula and despairs that life will perish from the earth, he discovers that a young robot couple, Helena and Primus, seem to have developed a crucial human quality: they are in love with each other. *They* don't know what is happening to them, but it is clear to the audience from their behavior and is proven in a classic test when Alquist tells them he *must* dissect one of them to save the robot race, and each begs to be the sacrificial victim so that the other might live. Finally Primus declares "I won't allow it. You won't kill either of us, old man. . . . We—we—belong to each other." Alquist then sends the pair out into the world with a benediction: "Go, Adam. Go, Eve—be a wife to him. Be a husband to her, Primus." In case we did not catch the biblical allusion, Alquist proceeds to read from Genesis: "And God saw every thing that he had made, and, behold, it was very good." This receives special emphasis because it is Čapek's principal theme, in this and all of his anti-utopian works. Alquist voices Čapek's challenge to the worshipers of technology when he asks (rhetorically, since they are all dead), "[G]reat inventors, what did you ever invent that was great when compared to that girl, to that boy, to this first couple who have discovered love, tears, beloved laughter, the love of husband and wife?" Finally, on his knees, Alquist thanks God that his eyes have "beheld Thy deliverance through love, and life shall not perish!"[8]

Although Shaw's version of Genesis is quite different in many respects, there is a strong parallel to what Alquist describes as "this first couple who have discovered love . . . beloved laughter, the love of husband and wife." In Shaw's Eden these phenomena (and many others) are also discovered, and words are found for them by the very articulate Serpent, who also explains to Eve how they can reproduce their kind. (*This* secret Alquist delicately leaves the robot couple to discover for themselves.) Also like the robots, Shaw's Adam and Eve are faced with the threat of extinction, for we meet them the morning they discover death in the garden. This discovery makes them suddenly terrified for the other's safety, and like Primus, Adam is especially protective: "You must never put yourself in danger of stumbling," he tells Eve. "I will take care of you and bring you what you want."[9] After discovering the feelings of uncertainty and jealousy, the two discover (like the robots) that they belong to each other, so they invent marriage, and the Serpent, like Alquist, supplies the titles "husband" and "wife" (18).

If we skip from the first to the last play of Shaw's cycle, *As Far as Thought Can Reach,* we see another sort of "first couple" that resembles Čapek's: the automatons created by Pygmalion. Although physically superb, they are morally defective, for the most part, as haughty and self-centered as thoroughly spoiled children. When reproached for killing their creator, they respond as the Bible's Adam and Eve do when reproached for their disobedience: they try to blame each other. However, they manage to rise briefly to the level of Helena and Primus when the very superior He-Ancient, taking Alquist's role, presents them with the same ultimatum: "Now listen," he says, "One of you two is to be destroyed. Which of you shall it be?" "Spare her; and kill me," the male figure responds. "Kill us both," urges the woman, "How could either of us live without the other?" (243). As it happens, they do both die, for they are deeply flawed creatures who cannot live among the super-evolved Ancients, but Shaw's play ends on a note that is as emphatically life-affirming as Čapek's. Lilith, another character Shaw has appropriated from biblical legend and radically reinterpreted, sounds a bit like Alquist when she declares, reverently and exultantly, "Of life only is there no end; and though of its million starry mansions many are empty and many still unbuilt . . . my seed shall one day fill it and master its matter to its uttermost confines. And for what may be beyond, the eyesight of Lilith is too short. It is enough that there is a beyond" (262).

Although both plays are in their different ways life-affirming, they clearly take opposite positions on the issue of humanity's role in shaping its own destiny. Shaw does not believe God could really survey creation and declare it "good" in the same sense that Čapek means it, which is to say "quite good enough for us." Like most utopians, Shaw believed that both humanity and human society needed to be vastly improved and that our duty as humans (in his view, gods in embryo) is to strive continually toward that end. Shaw expresses this belief in defending "the divine force of curiosity" in an earlier preface (to *The Doctor's Dilemma*):

> I have always despised Adam because he had to be tempted by the woman, as she was by the serpent, before he could be induced to pluck the apple from the tree of knowledge. I should have swallowed every apple on the tree the moment the owner's back was turned. When Gray said "Where ignorance is bliss, 'tis folly to be wise," he forgot that it is godlike to be wise; and since nobody wants bliss particularly, or could stand more than a very brief taste of it if it were attainable, and since everybody, by the deepest law of the Life Force, desires to be godlike, it is stupid, and indeed blasphemous and despairing, to hope that the thirst for knowledge will either diminish or consent to be subordinated to any other end whatsoever.[10]

Čapek, conversely, seems to be asserting in *R.U.R.* that striving to be "godlike" is not only ill-advised but downright sinful—a classic expression of the kind of willfulness and pride that led to our Fall in the first place. Čapek soon added another anti-utopian play to the argument in his next work, *The Makroupolous Secret*.

In 1922, the same year that the New York Theatre Guild produced *Methuselah* and *R.U.R.*, Čapek's *Makroupolous Secret* had its debut in Prague. Like *R.U.R.*, it was immediately considered in relation to *Methuselah* (especially the third play of Shaw's cycle, *The Thing Happens*) because it demonstrates how extreme longevity would be a curse to humanity. Čapek was rather insistent in the play's preface that he had heard only sketchily of Shaw's play when he was writing his, but the plot similarities suggest otherwise. Both plays feature a woman who has taken a step toward immortality—each can live for three centuries without any decrease in vigor or change in appearance after the first forty years or so—and both plays focus on evaluating whether that miracle would be a blessing or a curse were it more widespread in the race. As before, both playwrights take diametrically opposed positions on the desirability of humankind's striving to achieve this miracle. Shaw believes our survival absolutely depends on our developing the level of maturity and sense of social responsibility that only a very long, vigorous life can provide, while Čapek insists it is not only ill-advised but downright sinful to aspire to more than our traditionally allotted three score and ten—Adam and Eve were, after all, driven from Eden to prevent their eating from that second forbidden tree, the one that would grant eternal life.

Despite the diametrically opposed themes, however, the two plays contain several remarkably similar plot elements. Most striking is the exact period of longevity in both plays: three centuries. It really *looks* as if Čapek was being clever in pretending to arrive as this figure by "coincidence" because Shaw begins the second play of his pentateuch, *The Gospel of the Brothers Barnabas*, with this same coincidence: the two brothers who have been developing their plan for the salvation of humanity decide independently but simultaneously that we must achieve life-spans of three centuries if we are to survive as a species. When Conrad bursts into his brother Franklyn's study with this announcement, Franklyn says, "Now that is extraordinary. . . . The very last words I wrote when you interrupted me were 'at least three centuries' " (37–38). Unfortunately, the two are interrupted before Franklyn can answer his brother's question, "How did you arrive at it?" Could this be another instance of the artists' intuitive synchrony? Or did Čapek appropriate at least this detail from the "resume" of Shaw's play that he says he read in 1921?

The other plot parallels may simply have followed logically from the similar situation depicted. Anyone who lives for a couple of centuries would experience similar difficulties and thus could be expected to respond with similar stratagems if forced to live among people of normal life-spans. Accordingly, we find Shaw's Mrs. Lutestring, who survives from the day of the Brothers Barnabas to the distant future of the next play, *The Thing Happens*, describing problems similar to Emilia's. Both must periodically stage a death and adopt a new persona to allay the suspicions of short-livers; both must suffer the loss of beloved friends and family who age and die in the usual way; both finally become emotionally detached from their numerous progeny and, indeed, from all short-lived people, who begin to seem rather tediously childish; and both acquire a mysterious power of inspiring awe and fear in ordinary mortals, who cannot help feeling their own inferiority in the presence of these majestic, goddess-like women. Perhaps certain other plot details are also inevitable, arising from the conflict between the desire for eternal youth and the fear of the unknown. Thus, both plays contain characters who consider with trepidation how this phenomenal longevity, if it became widespread in the population, would wreck the current political structure; both contain moving passages that describe the unbearable brevity of the traditional life-span and the great potential for human improvement that any significant extension could make possible; both plays refer to a race of "supermen"; and both plays include characters who are not brave enough to face the prospect of a three-century life-span.

Despite all these similarities, the playwrights come down on opposite sides of the question of whether this is a desirable development, whether the possibilities for human improvement that greater longevity could provide—the striving for a nobler quality of life, even an approach to godhead—are worth the risks and the burden involved. In order to present their very different answers to this philosophical question, the playwrights had to present their heroines' characters somewhat differently. Shaw suggests that a longer lifetime would produce wise, goddess-like women by describing Mrs. Lutestring as *"a handsome woman, apparently in the prime of life, with elegant, tense, well held-up figure, and the walk of a goddess. Her expression and deportment are grave, swift, decisive, awful, unanswerable. She wears a Dianesque tunic . . . [T]he men, who rise as she enters . . . incline their heads with instinctive awe"* (113–14). Her interaction with the short-livers bears out this description of her awful magnificence and shows that she is quite capable of bearing the grave responsibility of establishing and maintaining a utopia. When the relatively ineffectual and shallow president, Burge-Lubin, speculates that "The complications must be frightful. Really I hardly know whether I do want to live much longer than other people," Mrs. Lutestring replies regally, "You can always kill yourself. . . . Long life is complicated, and even terrible; but it is glorious all the same. I would no more change places with an ordinary woman than with a mayfly that lives only an hour" (119).

Čapek is more terse in his stage directions than Shaw, so we hear of Emilia Marty's magnificence only from the other characters, but they all rave about her beauty, her charisma, her marvelous singing voice (she is an opera diva), and, as with Mrs. Lutestring, the instinctive fear she inspires. Even without stage directions, however, one director seems to have captured what Shaw describes as the irresistible psychic force that longevity would produce in a woman like this. The effect is reported precisely in Walter Kerr's review of the 1957 New York revival of the play. In describing the scene wherein Emilia is confronted by an old lover of hers, now elderly, Kerr says, "Miss [Eileen] Herlie rests on a chaise-longue, turned thoroughly away from us. The old sport's eyes meet hers. In the intake of a breath, and a few seconds' silence, something happens between them—something strong enough to blow the frail gallant backward, like a windblown dandelion, into the lap of the nearest onlooker."[11] Shaw presents a very similar scene in the fourth play of the cycle, *Tragedy of an Elderly Gentleman*, between an ancient oracle and some presumptuous short-livers who fall to their knees in terror and awe when she is revealed to them.

Despite these similarities, however, Shaw's and Čapek's heroines are very different people. We can see just how different Čapek's heroine is from the "Dianesque" Mrs. Lutestring when Gregor, a character who has been so unfortunate as to have fallen passionately in love with Emilia, raves, "I am terrified of you. . . . There is something dreadful about you. . . . You are vicious, low, awful, you are a callous animal. . . . Nothing means anything to you. Cold like a knife. As if you'd come out of a grave."[12] It is significant that while Shaw invokes the imagery of Greek mythology—and specifically a goddess "chaste and fair" (although really Athena would have been a more appropriate model)— Čapek presents Emilia as a vampire. Both are immortal and awe-inspiring, but only one is admirable. While Shaw's heroine works hard, devotes herself to the future of humankind, and finds the effort "glorious," Čapek's heroine is locked in the tail-chasing aimlessness of narcissism. We are not terribly surprised when we find the other characters pitying Emilia her fate, as Gulliver pitied the Struldbruggs, when Emilia cries, in the last act, "One should not, should not, should not live so long! . . . One cannot stand it. For 100, 130 years, one can go on. But then . . . then . . . one finds out . . . and then one's soul dies." The soul-withering truth she discovers is that "one cannot believe in anything. Anything" (173). Acute ennui has turned to nihilism and the despairing conclusion that "People are never better. Nothing can ever be changed. Nothing, nothing, nothing ever really matters" (174). Considering how Shaw's estimation of modern man had suffered from the grim spectacle of World War I, he could never have preserved his essential hopefulness had he agreed with Emilia on this point. He had to believe *radical* improvement to be possible or despair over the future of the race because, as Stanley Weintraub put it, Shaw had come to believe humanity was engaged in a "race between Utopia and catastrophe."[13]

Considering the striking plot similarities, the diametrically opposed positions the two plays take on utopian aspirations, and that *The Makropulos Secret* was published in 1922, a year after *Methuselah* appeared in print, it is easy to see how Čapek's play could be so widely assumed to be a direct rebuttal of *Methuselah*. Čapek therefore felt it necessary to insist in the preface to his play that he was actually inspired *not* by Shaw but by "the theory of Professor Mecnikov [Metchnikov] . . . that old age is autointoxication of the organism." He mentions this, he explains, "because this winter there appeared a new work by Shaw . . . which so far I know only from a resume, and which also—on a scale apparently much more grandiose—treats the question of longevity."[14] He adds, "This coincidence in subject is entirely accidental, and, as it would seem from the resume, purely superficial, for Bernard Shaw comes to quite the opposite conclusions" (112). It should be noted, however, that Čapek may have first heard of Metchnikov from an earlier Shaw play, *The Doctor's Dilemma*, where Shaw mentions him in discussing the latest theories of immunization, in both the play and preface. Since *The*

Doctor's Dilemma was written in 1906 and first translated into German in 1908, it is reasonable to suppose that Čapek may have read it or seen it performed before he wrote *The Makropulos Secret,* whether he would later remember the Metchnikov discussion or not.

Although Čapek is quite explicit in pointing out that his position on the longevity question differed from Shaw's, he goes on to explain how the two playwrights, although one is utopian and the other anti-utopian, could both be seen as "optimists." Although he acknowledges that "Shaw's thesis will be received as a classical case of optimism" while his will be labeled "pessimism," he mildly explains that

> In my comedy I intended, on the contrary, to tell people something consoling and optimistic. I do not know if it is optimistic to maintain that to live sixty years is bad, while to live three hundred years is good; I only think that to declare that a life of sixty years (on the average) is adequate and good enough is not exactly committing the crime of pessimism. . . . Perhaps there are two kinds of optimism: one which turns away from bad things to something better, even dreams; another, which searches among bad things for something at least a little better, if only dreams. The first looks straight off for paradise; there is no finer direction for the human soul. The second searches here and there for at least some crumbs of relative good; perhaps this effort is not quite without value. (112)

This is a diplomatic effort to reconcile the two opposing attitudes, and indeed some important similarities can be found between the habits of thought and theories of their art professed by these otherwise very different people. There is, for example, the striking similarity in their statements that assert the necessity for artists to reject a simplistic absolutism. In his preface to *Plays Pleasant,* Shaw declares that "the obvious conflicts of unmistakable good with unmistakable evil can only supply the crude drama of villain and hero, in which some absolute point of view is taken, and the dissentients are treated by the dramatist as enemies to be piously glorified or indignantly vilified. In such cheap wares I do not deal. Even in my unpleasant propagandist plays I have allowed every person his or her own point of view, and have, I hope to the full extent of my understanding of him, been as sympathetic with Sir George Crofts [the "villain" of *Mrs Warren's Profession*] as with any of the more genial and popular characters in the present volume" (3:111). Čapek makes a very similar assertion about the kind of morally compli- cated conflict he wanted to dramatize in *R.U.R.* After explaining each major character's particular ideological stance and declaring them all to be "right," Capek explains that

> the most important thing is . . . that all of them are right in the plain and moral sense of the word. Each . . . has the deepest reasons, material and moral, for his beliefs, and according to his lights seeks the greatest happiness for the greatest possible number of his fellow-men. I ask whether it is not possible to see in the present social conflict of the world an analogous struggle between two, three, five, equally serious verities and equally generous idealisms? I think . . . this is the most dramatic element in modern civilization, that a human truth is opposed to another truth no less human, ideal against ideal . . . instead of the struggle being, as we are so often told it is, between noble truth and vile selfish error.[15]

This agreement on objective relativism for the sake of truth in art did not preclude disagreement on other important philosophical issues. Nevertheless, Čapek's report of his first visit to Shaw's flat in London describes the beginning of a friendship that appears to have been warm and respectful on both sides. It is also clear that Shaw's pentateuch was still in Čapek's mind. He describes the great Irishman much as Shaw describes his Ancients: "an almost supernatural personality. . . . He looks half like God and half like a very malicious satyr, who however, by a process of sublimation extending over thousands of years, has lost all that is too closely akin to nature."[16] He confesses to having felt actually afraid since he had "never seen so unusual a being," but he was also charmed, concluding that Shaw "sparkles with life and has heaps of interesting things to say about himself, about Strindberg, about Rodin, and other famous things; to listen to him is a delight coupled with awe" (183). After returning to Prague, Čapek wrote Shaw a letter urging him to "put your interest in our country in order." Referring to their meeting in London, Čapek repeats his original assessment of Shaw's Czech translator, offering to help find a more trustworthy one and inviting him to come and see a Prague production of *Man and Superman*. A later letter indicates that Shaw took this advice about the translator.[17] But their mutual friendship and respect did not bring them any closer to accord on their basic philosophical disagreement about the legitimacy of utopian aspirations, and in 1927 Čapek carried the debate back onto the stage, producing his most emphatically anti-utopian play, *Adam the Creator*.

This time there is no question about coincidental influence. Adam the Creator is clearly a conscious, deliberate refutation of Shaw's entire utopian oeuvre from his treatment of the Superman, to his faith in willed Creative Evolution, to his mystical, human-centered *In the Beginning*. The play opens with the violent end of the world as we know it when the Adam of the title, disgusted with the "petty, miserable human race," writes a manifesto proclaiming "all order, all customs and institutions bad, null, and void . . . every effort to improve or change the world order is cowardly compromise . . . life is a bad habit."[18] Then he loads his Cannon of Negation and blows up the world. The empty wasteland that results disconcerts him somewhat, but he concludes defiantly, "Yes, it was badly made, and I've abolished it" (15). This remark is not allowed to pass: God's voice thunders down a command that as a penalty for his presumption, Adam must create the world anew himself, from the clay on which he kneels. Still in the grip of Darwinism, Adam hurrumphs, "As if one could create life out of clay! It's clear he has no idea of modern biology" (17). Yet when life does not appear spontaneously out of the clay, as he expects, Adam takes on the role of Creator with relish. "Let's skip this monkey-stage of human beings!" he cries, and instead sets out to make a "Superman," then changes his mind and makes a Superwoman instead, named Eve (19). Here we get a reprise of Henry Higgins and Eliza, for once she is completed, the woman turns on her creator and refuses to acknowledge his claims on her, prompting Adam to complain "Why, I with my own hands created her, and all there is in her is my big words; and if you please, she now puts on to me these lofty airs!" (28). None of Adam's other creations turns out any better: the Nietzschean Übermensch, Miles, scorns his creator as an inferior creature and runs off to the hills with Eve; the sweet, womanly little Lilith becomes a tediously clinging wife; and Alter Ego, intended as a friend and collaborator, becomes a critic and a rival (since he is as opinionated and argumentative as Adam).

Alter Ego proves to be Adam's most significant creation, however, because he finally persuades Adam to let him create, too. Operating on different artistic principles, Adam and Alter Ego produce two different races of men. Adam creates artistic, anarchic individualists while Alter Ego manufactures identical, lock-step collectivists who march in step and whistle the same tune, the one Alter Ego whistled as he made them. This essential dichotomy brings intensified discord into this new world because both races have been created with all of mankind's old propensity toward bigotry, so they bicker over which has the greater claim to being "real people." Adam's people claim to be "Personalities," "Souls," "Images of God," while Alter Ego's declare themselves "the New World," "the Mass," and most crushingly (twisting Shaw's hope-inspired religion of Creative Evolution) "creative revolution"! (115).

These blank myrmidons were not at all what Shaw had in mind when he expounded his theory of Creative Evolution, but Čapek, like many other anti-utopians of his time, equated any willful reorganization of the social order with totalitarian uniformity. This places Čapek firmly in the mainstream of his anti-utopian contemporaries because, as Lyman Tower Sargent points out, "[t]he tendency in this century has been to equate utopia with force, violence, and totalitarianism."[19] Sargent adds that "Much of the original basis for the antiutopian position came from anti-communism or anti-fascism. It was transformed first by the coalescence of these two positions into an anti-totalitarian position, and transformed second by the development of dystopia" (26). Accordingly, Čapek's play contains a scene that specifically demonstrates the danger that utopian efforts might pave the way for powerful tyrants: the scene where Miles returns from the hills. This Superman, instead of leading the newly created human race to the highest possible intellectual and spiritual development, drags it back to the level of the angry ape, introducing modern warfare just as Shaw's Cain does in Act II of *In the Beginning,* and as Shaw's Napoleon Cain Adamson continues to threaten in the thirty-first century in *Tragedy of an Elderly Gentleman.* But while Shaw introduced the Cain figure only to show an atavistic type of barbarian to be resisted and eventually left behind, Čapek presents Miles (whose name, derived from the Latin word for "soldier," suggests his inherently bellicose nature) to help drive home his point that the besetting difficulty of changing the world is that we can never eradicate the inherent flaws of human nature: hubris, aggression, lust for power and glory, and even defeatism and misanthropy.

While the Cain type of person is subject to the first two flaws, utopian aspirants like Adam are subject to the latter two. Like all the would-be world-betterers before him, Adam had eagerly written ideas for five different kinds of Golden Ages in little notebooks—he names Plato, Bakunin, and Marx as inspirations—but he becomes demoralized trying to realize his schemes and advises the equally sanguine Alter Ego not to bother: "You can write it down so beautifully; you can write down whatever you want, but the moment you begin to put it into practice—" (84). And that seems to be Čapek's principal theme. Čapek's play is unusual in its expressionistic approach to the subject, but the anti-utopian use of the Edenic motif is not surprising for the period, for as Sargent explains, "Some dystopias . . . can be seen as a continuation of the idea of original sin. Ejected from the Garden of Eden, unable to return and unable to achieve a secularized version of it, [the anti-utopians believe] the human race is incapable of utopia" (26).

But Čapek gives the play an optimistic, comic denouement. When Adam and Alter Ego find themselves in the position God held at the beginning of the play—first denied credit for being Creators, then reproached for the flawed world they produced—they almost decide to destroy the world again but are finally won over by a sublime religious festival of the people (who worship their creators with an abstract, slightly garbled tribute to their real genesis). Humbled and uplifted at the same time, Adam promises God to leave the world as it is. And God, given the last line of the play, says "So will I!" (183). Although *Adam the Creator* failed on the stage, it was translated into English in 1929 and was popular as a book, and it seems fair to assume that at this point in their acquaintance, Shaw would have received his own copy from the author.

In 1932 Shaw produced an odd little novella, *The Adventures of the Black Girl in Her Search for God,* wherein he again takes up the issue that Adam and God wrangle over in Čapek's play and exposes some rhetorical sleights of hand Čapek had used in presenting his case. In Shaw's novel, an intelligent, inquisitive, clear-eyed African girl meets a succession of God-figures who represent stages in the evolution of our conception of the deity. The second of these is the God revealed in the book of Job, and the Black Girl naturally asks him Job's question (which is also Adam's complaint in Čapek's play): "I want to know why, if you really made the world, you made it so badly." And God answers according to tradition (and Čapek): "Who are you, pray, that you should criticize me? Can you make a better world yourself? Just try: that's all."[20] The Black Girl is not abashed as Job and Čapek's Adam are. She points out that this response is not an answer or an argument, "it's a sneer." She adds "I don't mind your laughing at me . . . but you have not told me why you did not make the world all good instead of a mixture of good and bad. . . . If I were God there would be no tsetse flies. My people would not fall down in fits and have dreadful swellings and commit sins" (14). Because he can make no satisfactory answer to this question, she concludes that he is no God but an imposter and continues on her quest. In the postscript, Shaw affirms this conclusion, asserting that "God's attempt at an argument is only a repetition and elaboration of the sneers of Elihu, and is so abruptly tacked on to them that one concludes that it must be a pious forgery to conceal the fact that the original poem left the problem of evil unsolved and Job's criticism unanswered, as indeed it remained until Creative Evolution solved it" (90). According to Shaw's scheme of development, Čapek's deity would probably be classified with Micah's, who tells the Black Girl of a God who requires only that we "do justice and love mercy and walk humbly with Him." She finds this is a great improvement over Job's God, but still insufficient, for he does not provide the answer she seeks. "But doing justice and shewing mercy is only a small part of life when one is not a baas or a judge. And what is the use of walking humbly if you don't know where you are walking to?" she asks Micah (23).

We cannot know what Čapek would have replied to this because he died only a few years later, in 1938, and his widow had to burn his letters to prevent their falling into the hands of the Nazis and implicating Čapek's correspondents in his anti-Fascist agitations. But Shaw was not finished with the argument. Shaw's last utopian play, *Farfetched Fables*, written almost twenty years after *The Black Girl*, returns to the biblical motifs of Armageddon and the Millennium that the Shaw-Čapek debate had employed. Despite his steadfast repudiation of Čapek's anti-utopianism, Shaw's final vision of utopia synthesizes Čapek's appreciation for ordinary humankind with more rarefied Shavian aspirations. Shaw deprecates *Farfetched Fables* as a "few crumbs dropped from the literary loaves I distributed in my prime," but it seems more than coincidence, considering that Čapek's *Adam* had been subtitled "A Comedy in Six Scenes and an Epilogue," that Shaw's last utopia takes the form of six little fables rather than the three- or one-act plays he usually produced. Like Čapek's play, Shaw's begins with a vision of an Armageddon that, although cataclysmic, is not final: the last four fables show how human civilization rebuilds itself from its own ashes.

Despite these similarities, however, the distinction between utopian and anti-utopian remains. While Čapek shows civilization revived with all its flaws, Shaw depicts one that has evolved onto a somewhat higher plane, and this society shares the universe with the Ancients of *Methuselah* who have managed to continue their evolution into disembodied spirits, or "thought vortexes," to use Shaw's term. After the initial Apocalypse, each fable shows how our development progressed from "the dark ages that followed the 20th century," each describing a new strategy for world-bettering: an advanced science for measuring and classifying human potential, improved diet, and eugenic manipulation in the lab to create "the Just Man Made Perfect." The fifth fable revives an idea presented at the end of *Methuselah*, for one of the eugenic scientists decides that "we shall never make decent human beings out of chemical salts. . . . We must get rid of our physical bodies altogether."[21] Like the Ancients, he longs to be a disembodied spirit, a "vortex in thought." It was this theme in *Methuselah* that led critics to declare Shaw a misanthrope since it looks as if he is proposing to empty the universe of human life altogether. Yet this fable ends with a forward-looking assertion that echoes Lilith's and is, in its own Shavian way, life affirming: "The pursuit of knowledge and power will never end" (511).

It may appear at this point that Shaw remains an unrepentant utopian, defying Čapek's contention that ordinary human life is enough, but the final fable is the crucial point in the Shaw-Čapek debate because it contains a synthesis of their two kinds of optimism—their two versions of humanism—and presents the two positions in a way that shows them

to be complementary. The last fable is set in a school for advanced
children where a sort of Socratic schoolmarm conducts a lively anarchic
debate that ranges through epistemology, history, and biology to evalu-
ate the theory of the Disembodied Races, which holds that some of the
highly advanced people we saw in the fifth fable did manage to escape
their bodies to become "Thought Vortexes" although they continue to
interact with ordinary humans, "penetrating our thick skulls in their
continual pursuit of knowledge and power, since they need our hands
and brains as tools in that pursuit" (517). The teacher accounts for the
problem of evil in the world—the Job question—by explaining that "the
pursuit of knowledge and power involves the slaughter and destruction
of everything that opposes it," and the opposition arises because "even
the vortexes have to do their work by trial and error. They have to learn
by mistakes as well as by successes" (517). Then one of the thought
vortexes materializes as "a youth, clothed in feathers like a bird" who
announces that he is Raphael, "an embodied thought. . . . What you call
the word made flesh" (519). His motive is simple curiosity to "know what
it is like to be a body," for even among the immortals, "Curiosity never
dies" (520). After this brief visitation, the curious being vanishes back
into the infinite, and the ordinary human youths and maidens are sent
off to read the Book of Job for next Friday. Since the theory of the
Disembodied Races has at least partially explained the pain and evil that
remain in the world, much of that ancient story's power will, no doubt,
be lost, but the teacher presents it not as a theological text but as an
example of clever rhetoric. Here, then, is the most optimistic vision of
humanity's prospects that Shaw could devise when the destruction of
Hiroshima had provided a preview of Armageddon and the hope was
fading, even for an old Fabian like Shaw, that communism could bring
about a millennial society.

   Things had looked even grimmer in the final years of Čapek's life as
the Nazis swept through Europe and crushed his country. During a
period of despair Čapek wrote *The White Illness* (1937), which Harkins
describes as an anticipation of Fascism's triumph: "half gruesome fantasy, half dystopian image" (150). Yet Čapek absolved himself from "the
charge of pessimism," for he wrote *The Mother* in 1938, a play that ends
with a stirring call to defend the ideals of liberty. He sounds even more
defiantly optimistic in his essay "The Crossroads of Europe," also written
in 1938, wherein he seems to have joined forces with the utopian
idealists in his own country, especially T. G. Masaryk, a friend since the
1920s. With a nationalistic and humanistic fervor that departs radically
from his usual mild, ironic, understated tone, Čapek writes,

> This democratic spirit, this love of liberty and of peace, is part
> and parcel of the very character of the Czechoslovak nation.

Over and above that, however, T. G. Masaryk, the Liberator and
first President of our Republic, made those things the moral and
political program of our people. For him . . . politics represented
a realization of love of our fellow men; in his eyes democracy
and liberty were based on respect for man, for every man; they
issued from recognition of his immortal soul and the infinite
value of human life; for Masaryk the ultimate goal of all honest
politics and all true statesmanship was to bring about the Kingdom of God on earth. . . .[22]

It would be facile to say that his dialogue with Shaw had finally vanquished Čapek's objections to the idea of ordinary humans striving to
establish a millennial society without waiting for divine intervention.
Certainly the influence of Masaryk and the threat of Fascism also had
their impact. But the dauntless hopefulness expressed here testifies to
the power of the sort of optimism Shaw's utopian works continued to
assert. Shaw himself, who lived to see all the brutality of the Holocaust
and the horror of Hiroshima, retained his stubborn belief in humanity's
prospects to the end. His final words on the subject, the last lines of the
"What Is My Religious Faith?" chapter of his autobiographical *Sixteen
Self Sketches,* could be taken as a manifesto for all utopians: "Creative
Evolution can replace us; but meanwhile we must work for our survival
and development as if we are Creation's last word. Defeatism is the
wretchedest of policies."[23]

Notes

1. J. L. Wisenthal, *The Marriage of Contraries: Bernard Shaw's Middle Plays* (Cambridge: Harvard University Press, 1974), p. 9.
2. Karel Čapek, *Letters from England,* trans. Paul Sever (Garden City, N. J.: Doubleday, 1925), pp. 48–49.
3. William E. Harkins, *Karel Čapek* (New York: Columbia University Press, 1962), p. 91.
4. Sam Moskowitz, "Karel Čapek," *Drama Criticism* (Detroit: Gale Research, 1991), 1:54.
5. Ibid., p. 55.
6. Edward Bulwer-Lytton, *The Coming Race or: The New Utopia* (New York: Francis B. Felt, 1871), p. 122.
7. *Bernard Shaw, Practical Politics,* ed. Lloyd J. Hubenka (Lincoln: University of Ne-braska Press, 1976), p. 239.
8. Karel Čapek, *Toward the Radical Center: A Karel Čapek Reader,* ed. Peter Kussi (n.p.: Catbird Press, 1990), pp. 108–9.
9. Bernard Shaw, *Complete Plays with Prefaces* (New York: Dodd, Mead, 1962), 2: 132.

10. Ibid., 1: 30–31.

11. " 'The Makropoulos Secret' Opens at Phoenix Theatre," New York Herald Tribune (4 December 1957), p. 163.

12. Karel Čapek, The Makropoulos Secret, reprinted in Toward the Radical Center, p. 145.

13. Stanley Weintraub, Journey to Heartbreak: The Crucible Years of Bernard Shaw 1914–18 (New York: Weybright & Talley, 1971), p. 295.

14. Harkins, Karel Čapek, p. 111.

15. Ibid., p. 92.

16. Čapek, Letters from England, p. 181.

17. British Library Add Mss. 50519, 50520.

18. Karel Čapek, Adam the Creator: A Comedy in Six Scenes and an Epilogue, trans. Dora Round (London: Allen & Unwin, 1929), p. 10.

19. Lyman Tower Sargent, "The Three Faces of Utopianism Revisited," Utopian Studies 5:1 (1994): 24.

20. Bernard Shaw, The Adventures of the Black Girl in Her Search for God (New York: Capricorn Books, 1933), p. 14.

21. Bernard Shaw, Complete Plays with Prefaces, 6: 510.

22. Karel Čapek, Toward the Radical Center, p. 407.

23. Bernard Shaw, Sixteen Self Sketches (New York: Dodd, Mead, 1949), p. 107.

Susan Stone-Blackburn

SCIENCE AND SPIRITUALITY IN
BACK TO METHUSELAH AND
LAST AND FIRST MEN

Shaw's thinking about the relationship between matter and spirit in humanity is central to *Back to Methuselah*, and its reception by science fiction scholars sheds light on their thinking about the ways in which spirituality and science should be related in a text for it to "count" as science fiction. Psychic powers are frequently featured in science fictional texts that work to keep science and spirituality connected. *Back to Methuselah* is such a text, a monument to a tenuous effort to keep the two linked in evolutionary thought. It was written at a time when Shaw, who had for decades been belittling scientism, was moving toward a more positive view of at least the physical sciences and mathematics, although he maintained his opposition to the orthodox life sciences.[1] At the same time, he made his spiritual commitment to the Life Force even plainer in *Back to Methuselah* than he had years earlier in *Man and Superman*. The nature of the relationship between the spiritual and the scientific in Shaw's most science fictional work makes it most problematic for science fiction scholars. The materialist emphasis of science, which is embraced by most academics, including science fiction scholars, is the dominant factor in the acceptance of some texts that combine scientific and spiritual features into the science fiction canon because they are considered scientific while others are excluded as mystical.

  Some insights into the ambivalent reception of *Back to Methuselah* by science fiction scholars are provided by a comparison of *Back to Methu-*

selah (1921) with Olaf Stapledon's *Last and First Men* (1930). Both
texts speculate about future evolution of humankind. Both oppose
materialism and associate human evolutionary progress with the development of psychic powers. However, Shaw and his text have been
generally considered to be not only unscientific but antiscience, while
Stapledon and his text are widely regarded as faithful to science and
seminal in the development of science fiction. Stapledon thought himself
markedly different from Shaw in this respect, regarding Shaw as "hostile
to science, medicine."[2]

Shaw's influence on a few leading science fiction writers has been
established,[3] but scholars defining and tracing science fiction traditions
often overlook him. In *Explorers of the Infinite,* science fiction historian
Sam Moskowitz mentions Shaw only to establish that Karel Čapek was
not familiar with *Back to Methuselah.* By contrast, he gives a chapter to
Stapledon, whom he describes as "one of the most powerful prime
movers in the history of science fiction."[4] There are several pages of
discussion of "the cosmic sweep and grandeur of the ideas and philosophical concepts" of *Last and First Men,* Stapledon's "extraordinary"
first novel (261), and excerpts from enthusiastic reviewers. Again, Shaw
rates only a footnote in Brian Aldiss's history of science fiction, *Trillion
Year Spree,* where *Last and First Men* has a full page in a substantial section
devoted to Stapledon. Shaw receives some attention in more specialized
studies: Brian Stableford's *Scientific Romance in Britain 1890–1950,* for
instance, has more than a page on *Back to Methuselah,* which he says
contains "one of the most influential images of the future evolution of
man to be produced in the post-war years."[5] By comparison, however,
he gives *Last and First Men* three and a half pages, concluding with the
observation that "it embraces more completely and more effectively than
any preceding work the new cosmic perspective" (203).

In his introduction to "Bernard Shaw and Science Fiction: Why
Raise the Question?" Julius Kagarlitski complains, "It has long been
acknowledged that Shaw consistently and persistently waged war against
science."[6] He goes so far as to say that "the task [Shaw] set for himself
[was] to destroy science" and that *Back to Methuselah* was part of that
effort (62). Science fiction scholars who think that science fiction is, or
at any rate ought to be, a literature allied with and derived from the
principles and findings of science and who share Kagarlitski's perception of *Back to Methuselah* are not likely to rank it highly in the science
fiction canon. Shaw's Lilith, introduced into *Back to Methuselah* solely to
deliver the concluding speech, should qualify as the patron saint of
science fiction because of her assertion that curiosity is "the greatest of
gifts" given to humanity, her urging to "dread, of all things, stagnation,"
and her visionary declaration that "of Life only there is no end; and

though of its million starry mansions many are empty and many still unbuilt, and though its vast domain is as yet unbearably desert, my seed shall one day fill it and master its matter to its uttermost confines."[7] Still, for the science fiction scholar who wants science fiction to be based on science, *Back to Methuselah* seems to fall short.

Both *Back to Methuselah* and *Last and First Men* are generic misfits whose claim to a place in the science fiction canon is presumably proportionate to their inability to fit neatly elsewhere. Shaw's five-play cycle could not be accommodated in the "two hour's traffic of the stage," so it was marked from the outset as a misfit in the theater. *Last and First Men,* initially published as fiction, had a different problem: without characters, it lacked the human interest expected of novels and was even reissued as philosophy rather than fiction.[8]

Four similarities place Shaw's text and Stapledon's virtually in a category by themselves in the period between the two world wars:

1. Both *Back to Methuselah* and *Last and First Men* are tales of future evolution that reach from the present (or, in Shaw's case, from the past through the present) into the far future, showing the process of evolution as well as the results.
2. Both are offered as modern myth, that is, as stories with religious or spiritual significance that are grounded in scientific truth.
3. Both mock the foolishness of unquestioning faith in scientists.
4. Both emphasize the significance of evolving mind or spirit, as opposed to simply material progress, in approaching the human ideal.

Shaw's five-play cycle begins with Adam and Eve and ends in A.D. 31,920. The three middle plays, set in 1920 and in the very near future, in A.D. 2170 and in A.D. 3000, show humanity evolving in the direction of greater longevity and greater intellect, aspiring finally to a time when mind would be freed from body altogether and life "disentangled . . . from the matter that has always mocked it" (261). In the final play, only the first four years of human life are given to the material pleasures of the body and the arts. The Ancients are contemplative and ascetic, indifferent even to simple comforts, and their powers of mind include telepathy and psychokinetic control of matter.

Stapledon's *Last and First Men* ventures two billion years into the future, sketching the evolution of eighteen species of humankind on three planets. Cosmic and microbiological accidents, radical environmental changes, and human creation and self-destruction produce erratic changes in humankind. Despite the general impression of randomness about evolutionary change, however, there are parallels between the development from the First Men—that is, ourselves—to the admirable Fifth Men on Earth and the development from the Four-teenth to the Sixteenth Men on Neptune. These, together with the impression that the Last Men are the greatest of all, provide a sense of direction toward ideal humanity. The ideal includes spiritual community as well as advanced intellect. Telepathic communication is both the key to spiritual community and the means of advancing intellect beyond individual limitations.

Both writers conceived their narratives as modern myth. Shaw de-scribed *Back to Methuselah* as "a contribution to the modern Bible" of Creative Evolution (xix), and the opening revision of Adam and Eve's story effectively establishes the mythological nature of his play. Staple-don's foreword to the original American edition of *Last and First Men* records his conviction that only "a new vision" can save us from becom-ing lost "in a vast desert of spiritual aridity." He provides that vision, asserting in his preface that "his aim is to achieve "neither mere history, nor mere fiction, but myth" (9).

The "modern" part of modern myth acknowledges that in the twenti-eth century, scientific credibility is essential for myth that purports to explain an evolving human race. This weighs against the argument that Shaw was anti-science. Stapledon acknowledged that his myth "must take into account whatever contemporary science has to say about man's own nature and his physical environment" (11). Shaw, offering a "genuinely scientific religion" (xix), described himself as an "artist-biologist" whose drama is meant to "take biology a step forward on its way to positive science from its present metaphysical stage in which the crude facts of life and death . . . defy the methods of investigation we employ in our research laboratories" (xcvi).

Although both Shaw and Stapledon acknowledge the importance of science, both mock uninformed veneration of scientists. Shaw opposed the prevailing tendency of nonscientists to accept current scientific theory on faith, and the persistence of this stance in his writing accounts in large part for his "anti-science" reputation. Moreover, he was pro-foundly antimechanist at a time when positivistic science was in vogue and scathing in his comments in the Preface to *Back to Methuselah* on scientists who persisted in conducting experiments that were both stupid and cruel to search for biological truths that they could have discerned by looking at the life around them (liii–lvi).

Stapledon is also withering about veneration of scientists in *Last and First Men*. He depicts materialism and mystification of science as the twin causes of the downfall of our own species, the First Men. He portrays a near-future world religion featuring scientist-priests who worship a legendary founder of atomic physics. When the social order collapses from the exhaustion of coal and oil, and the scientist-priests who are supposedly in possession of the scientific secret that will save the world fail to produce it, the wrath of the duped propels the destruction of civilization and humanity.

The obverse of both writers' attacks on unquestioning faith in science and materialism is their emphasis on evolving mind or spirit to approach an ideal humanity. In a study of utopian fictions of the late nineteenth and early twentieth century, Susan Ablon Cole comments on the scarcity of utopian texts that focus on mental and spiritual evolution while the vast majority center on technological change.[9] Both Shaw and Stapledon depict a humanity that determines to change itself, not merely its physical environment or its social organization.

Shaw's He-Ancient says, "The truth [is] that you can create nothing but yourself" (249). The ideal is pure intelligence, and the process is depicted as movement toward dispassionate contemplation, away from emotion-incited conflict and pursuit of material pleasures. Human progress depends on individual acceptance of moral responsibility for the future—which is facilitated by a life-span long enough to give the individual a personal stake in the future. In turn, a long life-span allows full development of intellectual potential. Shaw's spirituality lies not so much in his emphasis on the intellectual component of mind as in his concept of a Life Force that is expressed in and through all forms of life and that directs evolution toward increase of intellect. For the most part, Shaw replaces the "Life Force" of *Man and Superman* with the term "Creative Evolution" in *Back to Methuselah,* from Henri Bergson's 1907 book of that title. Bergson's term has more scientific resonance than "Life Force"; it sounds less vitalist and more Darwinian. Shaw explains Creative Evolution in detail in the Preface to *Back to Methuselah;* in the play itself the concept is touched on in various kinds of discourse that evolve with the passage of time. "The Voice" in the garden of the first play seems identifiable with the voice of God, although that identification is complicated by Eve's assertion that the garden is "full of voices" and by Adam's and the Serpent's that the voice Adam hears is his own inner voice (4, 5). In the second play, there is reference to "the tremendous miracle-working force of Will nerved to creation by a conviction of Necessity" and a reminder that all great efforts are made with reluctance under inner compulsion (84). In the last play, the struggle of the scientist Pygmalion to create protoplasm is an effort to produce a material that will fix and conduct "high-potential Life Force" (229–30). These three passages use first religious, then humanist, then scientific discourse to explain the Life Force, but because it links the individual consciousness with an immanent consciousness, Shaw's Life Force is essentially spiritual.

Stapledon's Second Men move beyond the limitations of the First Men's "spiritual isolation" (102) and their belief in a physical basis for everything real (58). They advance both in the power of dispassionate cognition and in the power to love one's neighbor as oneself (103), twin ideals throughout *Last and First Men*. Spiritual community is attained among the Fifth Men by telepathic communication, which enables participation in the experience of others. The evolution of the Fourteenth to the Eighteenth Men is described in terms of "almost steady progress towards spiritual maturity" (206). The Sixteenth Men, like the Fifth, have telepathic community that resolves conflict, and they can enter minds of the distant past. Also like the Fifth—and Shaw's Ancients— their life-span is thousands of years long. The Eighteenth Men reach a new mode of consciousness with a brain that can fuse with others' brains. Their final attainment is a state in which the individual becomes the mind of the race, sharing the physical bodies and the perceptions of all individuals through the time and space inhabited by species of humankind. Stapledon's narrator explicitly compares the experience with that of mystics among the First Men, but he specifies that the methods of the Eighteenth Men are intellectual (229). The goal is philosophical understanding of the nature of space and time and of mind and its objects.

In Shaw and Stapledon we have two portrayals of future evolution designed to combine scientific truth with spiritual significance, both of which mock blind faith in science and emphasize the significance of evolving mind or spirit. Why do they have such different receptions from science fiction scholars? Why are not both dismissed as mystical or both accepted as science fiction classics? Their innumerable differences, some more significant than others, play a part in their contrasting receptions by science fiction pundits.

One is a difference in the corpus of the two writers, which affects perception of a single text. Shaw is well known as the most successful and prolific dramatist of the twentieth century, but his writing as a whole is not science fiction. Stapledon, on the other hand, wrote several books besides *Last and First Men* that reinforce his position as a canonical science fiction writer, and he is best known for these books.

The contrasting styles of the two texts is a minor factor. Shaw's joyously irreverent writing about science is doubtlessly hard to swallow for those who are earnest about science, while Stapledon's sober satire of the worship of scientist-priests and his often clinical style are more in the scientific mode. Balancing that, however, is that Shaw rarely writes in terms of the spiritual, focusing in *Back to Methuselah* on intelligence, which is exactly to the taste of science fiction scholars, while Stapledon's writing is laced with references to the spiritual.

More significant is a third difference in the two writers' ways of relating science and spirituality. Shaw deconstructs the science-religion binary, working to point out the mystification of science and to demystify religion. He declares that "every genuine scientist must be, finally, a metaphysician" (lxxiii), and he equates scientific miracles and mysteries with metaphysical speculation (cv). He calls religion "the science of metabiology" (lxxxviii) and describes his modern religion of Creative Evolution as the best "hypothesis" yet devised, although it is still "provisional" (cv). Shaw's approach to science and religion recalls the Martians in Heinlein's *Stranger in a Strange Land* who do not distinguish among the concepts we call religion, philosophy, and science and who work what we would call miracles by our reckoning.[10] Shaw suggests that this is purely a matter of different discourses: "Let the Creator say, if you like, 'I will establish an antipathetic symbiosis between thee and the female, and between thy blastoderm and her blastoderm,' " says one of his characters (78). He may well be right with respect to science fiction. Certainly Stapledon, who consistently describes evolution in terms of changes in "germ plasm," is generally counted as more scientific than Shaw, who describes it in terms of a "Force" that, being immaterial, can be identified with religion as easily as with science.

Unlike Shaw, Stapledon tries to preserve a distinction between science and religion. His twin evolutionary goals seem to divide neatly between the two: advance in dispassionate cognition pertaining to science and advance in sympathy with others pertaining to religion. Although he satirizes unreasoning faith in science, Stapledon takes proper science very seriously. While Shaw has a good deal of fun deconstructing the binary that privileges science over religion, Stapledon soberly casts all advances in scientific terms. "Psycho-physics," the bedrock of the Fifth Men's knowledge, reveals the fundamental identity of the principles of the physical universe and the principles of humanistic pursuits such as art (173). Stapledon seriously asserts the distinction between the Eighteenth Men's culminating attainment of instantaneous perception of all time and space and the identical effect of mystical experience in our own past and present. Although they reach the same conclusions, the Eighteenth Men do so by means of intellect while the First "deceive themselves with comfortable fantasies" (229). Most readers of science fiction probably take that without a blink while they balk at Shaw's challenge to the supremacy of science among epistemes.

A fourth difference is Shaw's complete separation of the essence of life from matter. Shaw's response to the materialism of his age is typically polemical, and it places him radically apart from the beliefs of most science fiction readers. Stapledon, on the other hand, keeps a balance between matter and spirit. In *Last and First Men* material progress is dependent on mental and spiritual progress, not divorced from it. In fact, his narrator declares, "the spirit . . . is but the flesh awakened into spirituality" (245). Still, *Back to Methuselah* is a stage play filled with material bodies and settings and props, so its concluding vision of humanity as a vortex cannot strip the play itself of material interest.

Although all these factors presumably play some part in the reception of Shaw's and Stapledon's texts, most science fiction scholars would focus on the accounts of how evolution works in these texts to explain why *Last and First Men* is counted more substantially science-fictional than *Back to Methuselah,* so it is here that the relationship between science and spirituality is most pertinent. Darwin's chief contribution to evolutionary theory may have been to provide a purely material basis for evolution and thereby allow it to be placed securely in the domain of science, safely removed from religion. That Stapledon aligned himself with Darwinians and Shaw did not is probably sufficient in itself to account for the difference in reception by science fiction scholars, but that distinction grossly oversimplifies the question of what might count as scientific when it comes to evolution. Biologist Alistair Hardy is on Shaw's side when he declares, "Few ideas have had a greater influence on the intellectual world of today than the supposition that the doctrine of Darwinian evolution must lead inevitably to a materialistic interpretation of life," a supposition that Hardy sees as "an intellectual scandal of the academic world."[11] Anything that smacks of religion has been suspect as an account of evolution from Shaw's day to our own, and Shaw was openly a vitalist in his evolutionary thought. That he opposed orthodox religion at least as vehemently as he did orthodox science could not save him from the scorn of the materialists.

Paleoanthropologist Misia Landau's *Narratives of Human Evolution* is of considerable interest with respect to fiction about future evolution although Landau discusses only scientists' accounts of past evolution. She applies Propp's *Morphology of the Folktale* to the various accounts of human evolution, viewing all such accounts as versions of the heroic tale in which Man triumphs in a struggle against various challenges. Since there are only a few key fossil finds, she presents any anthropological narrative of human evolution as myth constrained by the rules of art as much as theory constructed around the facts.[12]

The key narrative function in Landau's Proppian approach to differentiating accounts of evolution is the "donor," the figure in folktales who gives the hero the magic gift that enables him to triumph against the odds. Darwin's donor is natural selection. Stapledon's donor is natural selection in the early stages of human development and biological manipulation in later stages. (He does not call it genetic manipulation, but that can easily be "read in" now to his accounts of changes made in "germ plasm," which the O.E.D. defines as "the essential part of a cell that determines the nature of the individual that grows out of it.") Shaw's donor is the Life Force, which means that he was out of step with the accepted scientific theory of his day—and still is. Perhaps worse, his donor is more spiritual than material in nature despite the care he took to put the proposition that "The Eternal Life . . . wears out Its bodies and minds and gets new ones, like new clothes" (75) into the mouth of a professor of biology in *Methuselah*'s second play and to link the Life Force to such other forces as gravitation, atomic attraction, electricity, and magnetism in its fifth play (228).

Not enough attention has been paid to the distinctions that Shaw drew between Darwin, with whom he had no significant quarrel, and the neo-Darwinians, with whom he did, or to the difference between Lamarck's discredited position and Shaw's, which he calls neo-Lamarckian (xi, xxii). Although his detailed argument appears in the Preface and not in the play, it is clear even in the play that the *conscious* will of the individual plays no part in the workings of Creative Evolution, which distinguishes Shaw's theory from Lamarck's. Shaw's presentation of the Ancients' psychokinetic power—mental control of matter—may seem to confuse the Creative Evolution issue because here individuals do consciously will biological change, manipulating their own flesh as they practice their powers of mind. This is not the process of Creative Evolution, however, but an effect of it. Shaw's lack of interest in how such powers might work contributes to the unscientific effect of his drama. Landau's account of Darwin's theory supports Shaw's contention that Darwin offered natural selection as *one* means of evolutionary change, not the only one or even the chief one (Landau 15; Shaw, xlvii). Darwin left an opening for the operation of Shaw's Life Force in what Darwin thought of as random events. What Shaw objected to were the more restrictive views of his followers. Shaw was not anti-science except in the sense that he did not believe that a search for truth should be limited to the material world of the laboratory. Thus, one of his characters declares that "The most scientific document we possess at present is . . . the story of the Garden of Eden" (75), asserting that the persistent attraction of that story "whilst hundreds of much more plausible and amusing stories have . . . perished . . . is a scientific fact; and Science is bound to explain it" (78). However, Shaw's "metabiology" would have fared better with science fiction scholars if he had claimed affiliation with Darwin on whatever pretext— perhaps on the grounds that natural selection favors intelligence—and if he had specified something material through which the Life Force might operate, like Stapledon's "germ plasm."

Stapledon was committed to Darwinian natural selection, and he struggled to accept cruelty, suffering, and evolutionary regression dispassionately, to "rise above" such concerns. In his study of Stapledon, Leslie Fiedler identifies "*amor fati*, the ice-cold worship of whatever is" as the *leitmotif* of *Last and First Men*.[13] Shaw, on the other hand, opposes Darwinism for precisely the reason that it has had the effect of suppressing humane considerations. Writing in the aftermath of World War I, he observes, "At the present moment one half of Europe, having knocked the other half down, is trying to kick it to death, and may succeed: a procedure which is, logically, sound Neo-Darwinism" (xii). What produced "the barren cruelty of the laboratories [of] Darwin's followers" was that "their only idea of investigation was to imitate 'Nature' by perpetrating violent and senseless cruelties, and watch the effect of them with a paralyzing fatalism which . . . established an abominable tradition that the man who hesitates to be as cruel as Circumstantial Selection itself is a traitor to science" (liii). Finally, Shaw declares, "What damns Darwinian Natural Selection as a creed is that it takes hope out of evolution, and substitutes a paralyzing fatalism which is utterly discouraging. As Butler put it, it 'banishes Mind from the universe' " (c). That Shaw's critique of Darwinism is grounded in hope and even faith that humanity can improve makes the critique itself no less rational. Fiedler suggests, after all, that Stapledon's fascination with the cruelties of life and his lifelong struggle to find them somehow acceptable, even beautiful, may be grounded not in a commitment to scientific objectivity but in "a streak of sado-masochism" verging on "the pathological" (12)!

Declaring an evolutionary goal as Shaw did runs counter to the prevailing idea of natural selection as blind mechanism. Stapledon was more subtle since his very roundabout evolutionary route to the Eighteenth Men does not obviously suggest purposeful evolution. However, Stapledon has humanoids re-emerging even from rabbitlike descendants of humanity on Neptune, and intellect and compassion are repeatedly sought and realized by his various species of humanity, which suggests directed evolution although he does not acknowledge it. Stapledon's uncertain grasp of evolutionary theory has not gone unnoticed—Brian Stableford describes it as "at best vague and at worst mistaken" (203)—but exhibiting proper deference to Darwinian theory and providing a material basis for his evolutionary processes are sufficient to establish Stapledon as a true science fiction author. In contrast, Shaw understood the evolutionary theory of his day quite well but challenged its materialistic bias in a way that left his spirituality without the material counterweight that Stapledon's had. Neither *Back to Methuselah* nor *Last and First Men* appears on science fiction course reading lists with anything like the frequency of Wells's *Time Machine*, which is unencumbered by any spirituality at all and thus seems to appeal more to a materialistic age.

It is tempting to conclude that acceptance of spirituality in science fiction depends entirely on an author's willingness to surround it with a fiction that is at least superficially deferential to the reigning scientific theory of the day and that offers enough of material interest to permit the typical science fiction reader to overlook the spirituality. The vision that concludes *Back to Methuselah* reduces life to something that is difficult for the Western mind to distinguish from nothing: a vortex of pure intelligence freed from matter. Many years later, in *Farfetched Fables* (1948), Shaw re-established a balance between mind and matter by having Raphael, a youth clothed in feathers who is recognizable to readers of *Back to Methuselah* as a product of evolution beyond even the Ancients, announce himself as "an embodied thought, . . . the word made flesh," and explain that "evolution can go backwards as well as forwards. If the body can become a vortex, the vortex can also become a body."[14] *Back to Methuselah* certainly influenced Arthur C. Clarke and Ray Bradbury and possibly Robert Heinlein as well as other science fiction writers. However, Shaw's was a single vision of the future, while Stapledon's immense range and variety provided rich source material for later science fiction writers—rich enough that materialists can ignore the spirituality and still value Stapledon's work. Weighing against the temptation to conclude that spirituality is acceptable in science fiction only if it is thoroughly camouflaged is Samuel Delany's observation that "virtually all the classics of speculative fiction [a term that includes science fiction] are mystical."[15] Many stars among science fiction writers, including Asimov, Clarke, Heinlein, Sturgeon, Bester, Herbert, and LeGuin, have written such texts. This suggests that under the right conditions, spirituality in a science fiction text has very powerful appeal.

The key condition seems to be one that ties the spirituality into an unsolved scientific problem, and the more tantalizing, the better. What works for Stapledon—and for many of the other writers of science fiction classics—is the way that psychic powers manifesting a link between an individual and a greater consciousness are tied into a probing of the nature of time, which is arguably the reigning unresolved philosophical and physical puzzle of the twentieth century. Since conjectures about thought transmission in the form of radiation have lost scientific credibility, the most intriguing hypotheses are linked to scientific speculations about the nature of spacetime. Stapledon exploited this mystery, but Shaw did not.

In "Shaw, Einstein and Physics," Desmond McRory notes that Einstein became an international celebrity just as Shaw was writing *Back to Methuselah,* when the General Theory of Relativity was verified by a British expedition that recorded the deflection of light from a star by the sun's gravity in November 1919.[16] By 1930 Shaw, like Stapledon, had no doubt about the importance of Einstein's work, but although *Back to Methuselah* contains a reference to "space-time," (230) the strangeness of Einsteinian time plays no part in the drama. Stapledon's narrator, one of the Eighteenth Men, speculates that time is not simply one-directional but links past and future in a mutually interactive causality (229–41). Events pass in one mode of time but are eternal in another, and while we—and even the Eighteenth Men—are most cognizant of passage from Beginning to End, "there is a vaster span, stretching beyond the End and round to the Beginning. Of the events therein we know nothing, save that there must be such events" (230). The attention Einstein focused on the strangeness of spacetime, rather than on particulars of his theory, shows in *Last and First Men*. Stapledon adapts the Einsteinian account of the gravitational attraction of light curving spacetime to an idea that centers on mind rather than matter: "the occurrence of mentality produces certain minute astronomical effects. . . . These effects increase slightly with the mere mass of living matter on any astronomical body, but far more with its mental and spiritual development." Here the narrator solves a mystery left earlier in the text with a surprise revelation: "Long ago it was the spiritual development of the world-community of the Fifth Men that dragged moon from its orbit." The Eighteenth Men have developed instruments that are sensitive to such effects and yield most of their knowledge about minds in other worlds (230–31). Stapledon both exploits the mysteriousness of Einsteinian spacetime and keeps the mystery connected to the concreteness of scientific materialism.

Still, twentieth-century evolutionary theory rather than twentieth-century astrophysics has supported the perception that *Last and First Men* is more scientific than *Back to Methuselah*. Stapledon may have simply been lucky in that the next giant step past Darwin in evolutionary theory, tying genetics into the process, appeared only seven years after *Last and First Men* in Theodosius Dobzhansky's *Genetics and the Origin of Species* (Landau, 145), so Stapledon's changes in "germ plasm" are supported by twentieth-century evolutionary theory. Stapledon did incorporate the ideas of biochemist J. B. S. Haldane on adaptability of man to other planets and on possibilities of biological engineering into *Last and First Men,* so he was in fact following the science of the day, which certainly assists luck in anticipating scientific developments.[17] The twenty-first century, however, may yet see Shaw as ahead of his time rather than behind it. Colin Wilson concludes his book on Shaw with his belief that Shaw will yet be seen as the prophet of a revolution that turns attention to evolution of consciousness. Wilson mentions Alistair Hardy and a number of other prominent people in various fields whose work moves us toward the development of an evolutionary psychology, including

Abraham Maslow, Robert Ardrey, Arthur Koestler, Michael Polanyi, and Maurice Merleau-Ponty.[18] Consciousness research has continued to gather momentum in the quarter century since Wilson recorded his conviction of the significance of Shaw's Creative Evolution, and the research has strengthened the argument that mind affects matter in ways that we do not yet understand.

Back to Methuselah and *Last and First Men*, however suspect to the minds of many academic science fiction critics for their departures from materialism, are major landmarks in the development of a theme that has always been strong in science fiction: speculation about powers of mind and its place in the workings of the universe. Shaw's text and Stapledon's, which did not fit comfortably even into the late nineteenth-century tradition of scientific romance, and still less into any other literary genre, challenged the generic boundaries of literature as well as the materialist boundaries of neo-Darwinian evolutionary theory. The challenge to literary boundaries helped to create the twentieth-century genre of science fiction. As the end of this century nears, the term "speculative fiction" is being used increasingly to sidestep academic arguments about what text does or does not qualify as "scientific," with science fiction as a subset of speculative fiction and "SF" a conveniently ambiguous acronym for both. In a literary realm reconceptualized as speculative fiction, *Back to Methuselah* and *Last and First Men* are both incontestably classics. While evolution as a concept no longer dominates science fiction as it did early in the century, the interplay between science and spirituality continues to figure significantly in science fiction, and as the twenty-first century approaches, the possibilities of consciousness evolution retain their fascination.

Notes

1. Desmond J. McRory discusses this transition in "Shaw, Einstein and Physics," *SHAW* 6 (1986): 33–68, as does Arthur H. Nethercot in "Bernard Shaw, Mathematical Mystic," *Shaw Review* 12:1 (January 1969): 2–25.

2. Robert Crossley, quoting from Stapledon's manuscript notes for a lecture on science and literature, "Olaf Stapledon and the Idea of Science Fiction," *Modern Fiction Studies* 32:1 (1986): 26.

3. See articles by Daniel J. Leary, Ray Bradbury, and J. R. Christopher in *Shaw Review* 16:2 (May 1973), special issue on "G.B.S. and Science-Fiction."

4. Sam Moskowitz, *Explorers of the Infinite* (Cleveland: World Publishing, 1963), p. 262.

5. Brian Stableford, *Scientific Romance in Britain 1890–1950* (New York: St. Martin's Press, 1985), p. 262.

6. Julius Kagarlitski, "Bernard Shaw and Science Fiction: Why Raise the Question?" *Shaw Review* 16:2 (May 1973): 59.

7. Bernard Shaw, "Back to Methuselah," *Complete Plays with Prefaces* (New York: Dodd, Mead, 1963), 2:262. All subsequent references to *Back to Methuselah,* its Preface, and its Postscript are to this edition.

8. Olaf Stapledon, *"Last and First Men" and "Star Maker"* (New York: Dover Publications, 1968), p. 203. All subsequent references to *Last and First Men,* its Foreword, and its First American Preface are to this edition.

9. Susan Ablon Cole, "The Evolutionary Fantasy: Shaw and Utopian Fiction," *Shaw Review* 16:2 (May 1973): 89.

10. Robert Heinlein, *Stranger in a Strange Land* (New York: Berkley Medallion, 1961), p. 133.

11. Alistair Hardy, *Darwin and the Spirit of Man* (London: Collins, 1984), pp. 11, 23.

12. Misia Landau, *Narratives of Human Evolution* (New Haven, Conn.: Yale University Press, 1991), p. 2.

13. Leslie Fiedler, *Olaf Stapledon: A Man Divided* (Oxford: Oxford University Press, 1983), p. 66.

14. Bernard Shaw, *Farfetched Fables,* in *Complete Plays with Prefaces,* 6: 519–20.

15. Samuel Delany, "About 5,750 Words," *The Jewel-Hinged Jaw* (New York: Berkley Windhover, 1977), p. 34.

16. McRory, pp. 33–34.

17. Stableford, pp. 156–57; Landau, p. 145.

18. Colin Wilson, *Bernard Shaw: A Reassessment* (New York: Atheneum, 1969), pp. 296–97.

Tom Shippey

SKEPTICAL SPECULATION AND *BACK TO METHUSELAH*

Shaw's Preface to *Back to Methuselah* begins, not uncharacteristically, with an error that one feels he could and should have avoided. In his opening anecdote Shaw recounts that he saw, one day early in the 1860s, "an elderly man, weighty and solemn" go up to the counter of a Dublin bookstore and ask pompously for "the works of the celebrated Buffoon."[1] Shaw's point is about the way that knowledge degrades. At the time of his writing the Preface, "the celebrated Buffoon" has been completely forgotten, his fame eclipsed (Shaw thinks, unfairly) by that of Darwin. But even at the time of the anecdote the second-hand nature of bourgeois knowledge is demonstrated, Shaw implies, by the fact that the pompous gentleman does not know the real name of the author he is asking for, George-Louis Leclerc, Comte de Buffon (1707–88).

However the book-buyer of the anecdote was in a way right, and Shaw's reaction not exactly wrong, but certainly superficial. The history of words in English ending in *-oon* is by no means clear. They certainly derive from Romance languages, but often one cannot tell whether from French, Italian, Spanish, or Portuguese. *Buffoon* for instance could come from French *buffon* or Italian *buffone,* while the strong maritime or military associations of other words in this class (*pontoon, doubloon, maroon, platoon, musketoon, spontoon,* etc.) might well suggest derivation from Spanish or Portuguese during the era of Anglo-Spanish warfare in the West Indies. This latter possibility is strengthened by such place-names as Tiberoon Bay in the West Indies (quite clearly from Spanish *tiburón, shark*), or from the conservative Royal Navy habit of always pronouncing words like *caisson* as *cassoon*.[2] There is however in the history of these words in English a strong Irish streak, or more accurately a strong Gaelic streak. Perhaps encouraged by the common Gaelic place-names which end in *-oon* (Doon, Troon, Dunoon, and the fictional Brigadoon), Gaelic speakers whether Scottish or Irish have tended to keep or to invent words of this class. Bourbon whiskey in Scotland is still sometimes pronounced *burboon* (on the rare occasions when it is mentioned at all), and one can tell that the pronunciation is an old one from the habit of early caricaturists of presenting the Bourbon dynasty as a tribe of baboons: at one time the pronunciation of both words was almost identical. The word *gossoon* (from French *garçon*) is recorded by the *O.E.D.* only in Irish contexts after its first introduction, coincidentally in a work titled *Epilogue to Lacy's Sir H. Buffon.* It is very likely, in short, that Shaw's pompous old bourgeois (almost certainly an Irishman if he was in a Dublin bookstore) knew perfectly well who the Comte de Buffon was, and was merely using an authentic and characteristically Irish pronunciation of the name. Shaw, who often relied strategically on his Irishness, and who boasts within the Preface itself of his own prodigious awareness of words (*BTM,* p. xxvii), should have known that, but he preferred an easy jibe to any deeper understanding.

One could, and with more damaging effect, say the same thing about the central biological argument of the Preface. The main thrust, both of Shaw's play and of the long polemical Preface to it, is to reject Darwin's theory of evolution and of natural selection in favor of what Shaw calls, following Henri Bergson's book of 1907, Creative Evolution. The main positive prop for Shaw's argument, in play, Preface, and elsewhere, is his thesis about the acquisition of habits. If a mere weight-lifter can "put up a muscle" without knowing how he does it, by will and by training, Shaw asks (*BTM* p. xviii), why can other physical or intellectual organs not be developed in the same way? Nor need this be a gradual matter. What happens when you learn to ride a bicycle? One day you cannot do it, Shaw asserts (*BTM* p. xxiii), but the next day you can, and this shows that you have developed an organ somewhere or other, "some new bodily tissue" that you never knew you had. Shaw returns to this bicycle analogy too often, one may think, trying it on H. G. Wells in his ribald commentary on Wells's co-authored *The Science of Life* of 1930. Shaw's marginalia to this (which he sent to Wells) read in part,

> He [Wells] knows very well that I was the first great biologist to make an end forever of the silly controversy about acquired habits by reminding the squabblers that to the evolutionist all habits are acquired habits, and that those who do not see this are still in the Garden of Eden. To solve the riddle of the

apparent division of habits into inherited and uninherited I
applied the scientific method of experiment and observation. I
acquired a habit (balancing on a bicycle) and observed the
process. I inferred the acquirement of habit by infinitesimal
increments, their establishment as fully inherited habits, and
their end as prenatal recapitulation. . . . I pointed out that
acquirement by practice was a delusion. . . .[3]

One need not take this over-seriously (especially Shaw's claim to be a
"great biologist"), but it is not surprising that Wells, keen cyclist although
he himself was, did not bother to argue the matter but wrote back
simply, "You're the same G.B.S. as ever & I quite believe your statement
that you've read nothing about biology since you were sixteen" (*Shaw/
Wells*, p. 149). If one cared to make Wells's reply for him, it would no
doubt center on the fact that nothing in Shaw's cycling activities showed
that anything he had learned was or would be inherited, any more than
the weight-lifter's muscles—or, indeed, the cut-off tails of the mice of
August Weismann's experiment, about which Shaw so often waxed
indignant. And after all, Weismann had at least done an experiment to
test a theory and accepted that something could be learned from
negative results, a scientific method of inquiry that Shaw never en-
visaged.

It is amusing that in the same exchange with Wells, Shaw records
meeting the formidable J. B. S. Haldane (1892–1964) at the Fabian
Society (to be distinguished from his biologist father, J. Scott Haldane
[1860–1936], whom Shaw also knew from the Fabian Society and whose
views he respected) and asking him whether he would consider either
Shaw or Wells not a scientist, but a "man of science": "He said at once
that I was not, as I had never performed any laboratory experiments,
but after a long and painful hesitation he said that he thought you had
worked in a laboratory at the School of Mines or somewhere; and
therefore he wouldnt like to say" (*Shaw/Wells*, p. 142). Dismissing Wells's
year at Imperial College under his idolized Professor Thomas Huxley
(whose grandson Julian was one of Wells's co-authors for *The Science of
Life*) as "the School of Mines or somewhere" was of course yet one more
complex barb for Wells to writhe on, but Shaw does at least repeat
Haldane's point: science is a matter of experimentation, not just hypoth-
esizing. He seems elsewhere, however, not to grasp it, arguing (*BTM*, p.
1) that Creative Evolution cannot be disproved (but a hypothesis not
susceptible of disproof has no scientific value), repeating very nearly *ad
nauseam* his remark that "to the Evolutionist all habits are acquired
habits" without at any time explaining what it meant, and eventually
falling back on the last resort of the outmatched polemicist, the circular

claim that all sensible people agree with him, put forward in *Back to Methuselah* by both Savvy and Professor Conrad.

Shaw's promotion of Creative Evolution was always wrong, always shallow, and often rather cheap. It is admittedly possible to find some excuses for the negative side of his arguments, especially the refusal to be convinced by Darwin. During the decades on either side of 1900, genuine difficulties had accumulated over the Darwinian model of natural selection, ranging from Lord Kelvin's apparent demonstration (as far back as 1868) that the Earth was simply not old enough for evolution to work according to the Darwinian theory, to the continuing difficulty of biologists in pointing to anything that might qualify as the mechanism for random and "infinitesimal" differences to originate. Wells's co-author Julian Huxley indeed refers to this period as "the eclipse of Darwinism" in his book *Evolution: The Modern Synthesis*, a title picked up and its force much extended by later scholarship.[4] The point of eclipses, however, is that they are temporary: the sun and moon come out from occultation or shadow as bright as they were before, as (Huxley argues) did Darwin from the 1890s. Shaw, however, his knowledge of evolution largely resting on Samuel Butler's books of the 1870s or Bergson's *Évolution Créatrice* of 1907, and as Wells points out never updated, might be forgiven in 1921 for not having noticed the end of the Darwinian eclipse (a *fait accompli*, according to Julian Huxley, by 1925).

Just the same, it is impossible to take Shaw's claim to being a "great biologist" or even a deep biological thinker at all seriously, and this is not simply the result of hindsight strengthened by seventy years of genetics, "chromosomes and hormones,"[5] and the discovery of DNA. Even his contemporaries found Shaw easy to dismiss on this level. J. B. S. Haldane, for instance, had the breadth of mind in 1932 to praise both Wells and Olaf Stapledon for their biological speculations—he himself had ventured in the direction of speculative fiction in his essay "Last Judgement" of 1927—but nevertheless wrote off Shaw's long-livers of Part 5 of *Back to Methuselah* with the austere remark that "To a biologist they are unconvincing."[6] On p. 105 of *The Eclipse of Darwinism*, Peter J. Bowler remarks that "Shaw seems to have felt that he was part of a new wave of support for Lamarckism, but in fact his claim that it represented the spiritual salvation of the evolution movement was no longer fashionable even outside science." Shaw's chronology of the whole Darwinian and anti-Darwinian movements seems to have been astray. He was sure Darwin was abandoned by all but the most stubborn in 1921, just as the "modern synthesis" of neo-Darwinism was about to sweep the field. Conversely he has "the neo-Darwinians . . . practically running current science" in 1906, when both Huxley and Bowler saw them as in eclipse (*BTM*, p. xi). Shaw's biographer Michael Holroyd feels that in his opposition to Darwin, Shaw allowed himself to go beyond exaggeration into "factual error."[7] And the best that the modern evolutionist Richard Dawkins can say of Shaw is that his case was based upon "emotional loathing" rather than "biological knowledge," but was nevertheless "bewitching" enough rhetorically to hold back Dawkins's appreciation of Darwinism, to his own shame, "for at least a year."[8]

One has to conclude that in most respects Shaw's arguments in Preface and play alike are false, ill-informed, unfair, shallow, scientifically disproved. The other side of the coin, however, is that they appear to have been amazingly productive in the areas of theme, plot, and speculative fiction. Again and again in the science fiction of the past seventy years, one comes across novels or stories that seem designed to illustrate some point or other of Shaw's *Back to Methuselah* thesis. How does one acquire a new ability, Shaw asks, and illustrates his answer by the ability to balance on a bicycle. A much more dramatic and striking example provides the starting point and central datum for Alfred Bester's classic science fiction novel *The Stars My Destination* (1956). This time the ability is teleportation, or "jaunting," an ability discovered entirely by accident when a laboratory worker sets fire to himself and in dire emergency teleports himself (before witnesses) to the fire extinguisher. His colleagues then set out deliberately and in Weismann-like style to kill him, theorizing that only the danger of death can trigger this unconscious process. They prove to be right. They learn how the laboratory worker, Jaunte, "jauntes," and learn how to do it themselves.

Bester then illustrates the point by an oddly Shavian dialogue between a representative of the Jaunte Schools and a reporter playing stooge, as it were, to the representative's Shaw.

> [REPRESENTATIVE]: Jaunting is like seeing; it is a natural aptitude of almost every human organism, but it can only be developed by training and experience.

Exactly as with bicycles, one might say. The dialogue then continues:

> REPORTER: But how do we do it?
> [REPRESENTATIVE]: How do we think?
> REPORTER: With our minds.
> [REPRESENTATIVE]: And how does the mind think? What is the thinking process? Exactly how do we remember, imagine, deduce, create? Exactly how do the brain cells operate?
> REPORTER: I don't know. Nobody knows.

[REPRESENTATIVE]: And nobody knows exactly how we teleport either, but we know we can do it.[9]

Is this "new faculty" associated with some "new bodily tissue as its organ," as Shaw would have it with cycling? In a report that Bester ascribes to "Sir John Kelvin"—reminiscent of the real and Victorian Kelvin whose calculations helped to breed the "eclipse of Darwinism"—we are told that "the teleportative ability is associated with the Nissle bodies, or Tigroid substance in nerve cells. . . . Where the Tigroid Substance does not appear, jaunting is impossible. Jaunting is a Tigroid Function." Yet the Substance and the Function, and the potential ability to "jaunte," all existed (as Shaw would have pointed out) long before the ability was demonstrated. "Jaunting" is an acquired habit, just like music, mathematics, chess, or shorthand in the examples Shaw gives of prodigies in his section "The Miracle of Condensed Recapitulation" (*BTM,* pp. xxv–xxix).

Condensed Recapitulation itself, however, is a feature of stories other than Bester's. Perhaps the most prominent example is James Blish's novel *A Case of Conscience* (1958), an extraordinary work very clearly emanating from exactly the same background of Victorian resistance to Darwin as Shaw's play and Preface. Blish's work came out indeed on almost the hundredth anniversary of the most luckless of the many attempts to confute Darwin, provocatively revived by Blish, Philip Gosse's book *Omphalos* (1857). Gosse's tragedy has been told several times.[10] He was both a biologist and a Plymouth Brother. When he heard in advance about Darwin's forthcoming *Origin of Species,* he hastened into print with a book arguing that the Almighty had created the world according to the schedule of Bishop Ussher and the literal word of the Bible, but had embedded in it evidence of geological creation and fossil record just because the world ought to have that sort of thing, exactly as Adam (although unborn himself) had had a navel or omphalos because a perfect man naturally would have. The scornful reaction from all sides bewildered and embittered Gosse. But a hundred years later an author was prepared to accept his thesis, if only in fiction, and to take it to a logical extreme tested by experiment. If the world of Lithia, which appears to show in the lives of its dominant intelligent race exactly the Darwinian (and Shavian) principle of condensed recapitulation, is genuine, then Darwin must be right, and God and the Bible wrong. Since the Bible cannot be wrong, reasons the Jesuit biologist on the space expedition, Lithia cannot be genuine, but must be an illusion or "sending" of the Evil One. He exorcises it—and it blows up, although whether this is a result of the exorcism or of an uncontrolled nuclear experiment is in true Todorovian style not revealed to us. Shaw had attempted such an experiment, on a much smaller scale, when he invited the Almighty to blast him for his unbelief (*BTM*, pp. xxxiii–xxxv), although a Jesuit would have little difficulty in showing that Blish's experiment is a much more penetrating one than Shaw's. Meanwhile a further development of "condensed recapitulation" forms the basis and background for Charles Sheffield's three more recent novels, *Sight of Proteus* (1978), *Proteus Unbound* (1989), and *Proteus in the Underworld* (1995). Sheffield is himself a professional scientist, to whom (one would have thought) Shaw's ideas about reaching longevity by the power of will alone would seem ludicrous. However, Sheffield suggests that will-power needs, essentially, a magnifier in the form of "bio-feedback machines." If people can learn to control autonomous functions like their heartbeat by practicing bio-feedback (as to some extent they can), then maybe they could some time in the future learn to alter their bodily forms, give themselves wings or gills, creating "some new bodily tissue" as Shaw puts it, and doing it "solely by willing" (*BTM*, p. xxiii).

The whole issue of artificial longevity is meanwhile taken up by several science fiction works, including the first work in Blish's *Earthman Come Home!* series, his *They Shall have Stars* of 1957, James Gunn's *The Immortals* (1962), and John Wyndham's *The Trouble with Lichen*, also of 1957. There is a comic scene in *The Gospel of the Brothers Barnabas* when Lubin suddenly stops and asks,

> LUBIN: Citizens! Oh! Are the citizens to live three hundred years as well as the statesmen?
> CONRAD: Of course.
> LUBIN: I confess that had not occurred to me [*he sits down abruptly, evidently very unfavourably affected by this new light*]. (*BTM*, p. 82)

And this forms in a way the basis for Wyndham's entire novel as the female discoverer of the life-extending lichen struggles to find a way to propagate her elixir without causing total social chaos or her own violent death. In a further echo of great power and great significance for the science fiction genre, we see Shaw proclaiming, in 1921, both in Preface and in play (pp. xvii, 72) that Flinders Petrie's 1911 thesis of "eight successive periods of civilization," each ending in collapse, is established fact. It is hardly that, even within the limited confines of Egyptian civilization, which is all that Petrie would commit himself to, but the ideas of cyclic history and recurrent collapse have proved irresistible to science fiction writers from Isaac Asimov's early short story "Nightfall" (1941) and the early works in the same author's *Foundation* sequence (1942–50) on through several works by Heinlein to Frank Herbert's famous *Dune* (1965) and its successors. It is said, indeed, although the story is probably apocryphal, that the immensely influential science fiction editor John W. Campbell had in his possession a book detailing the secrets of cyclic history that he would lend out to his favorites. If such a book existed, it would have been a successor to Petrie's.

This list of echoes and analogues could be much extended. The "Vital Force" to which Shaw appeals in "The Homeopathic Reaction against Darwinism" cannot but remind a modern reader of the Force so often appealed to in *Star Wars*. Shaw's idea of a "scientific religion" has been played with by author after author, usually in hostile mode. The idea that if God did not exist He would have to be re-invented, or His place taken by Satan, is the very basis for Blish's novel *The Day after Judgement* (1971), the sequel (!) to his *Black Easter* (1968), which ended with the literal and one might have thought unfollowable death of God, but compare again Shaw on "The Brink of the Bottomless Pit" (*BTM*, pp. xliii–xlv). Even Shaw's cranky aside in *The Brothers Barnabas* about "the ferocity which is still characteristic of bulls and other vegetarians" has been picked up and made the foundation of a novel by Poul Anderson, *Satan's World* (1969), while Shaw's 1887 review of Samuel Butler's *Luck or Cunning?* sets up a question, whether luck can be an inherited survival quality, to be answered only by the character of Teela Brown in Larry Niven's *Ringworld* (1970). One can say in brief that a case can be made for *Back to Methuselah* in particular among Shaw's works as a compendium of future science fiction plots and developments.

This is, in a way, a coincidence. I do not think it likely that any of the authors above (except probably Blish) used Shaw as an actual literary source, to be re-read, considered, used, and answered as they use each other and as many science fiction authors have always used Wells. However, although a coincidence, it is not a meaningless one. The fact is that Shaw placed himself in a sense in the middle ground of science fiction by writing the argument that he did. Later authors participating in the argument are then bound in some way or other to brush against him, as against his antagonists in the "eclipse of Darwinism" debates. One might say that while there is good reason for arguing that science fiction takes its rise from the "fabril" tradition of physics and engineering, dealing with weapons, artefacts, and spaceships as pioneered by Wells's "Land Ironclads" or Martian Fighting Machines,[11] there is equally good reason for arguing that it came into being as an attempt to theorize not the machines so much as the new and mechanistic conception of humanity that lay behind them: that science fiction has a root in *The Island of Doctor Moreau* just as much as in *The Time Machine* or *The War of the Worlds*, while "fabril" and "evolutionary" origins are furthermore by no means mutually exclusive.

To show this line of development for science fiction, one needs to go back to Shaw's central and most shocking thesis (the negative prop of his argument as "acquired habits" were the positive one). This is that Darwin was ultimately responsible for World War I. Shaw's own statement, set in the context of his own life history from "the celebrated Buffoon" to the present in 1920, is that by 1916, "Neo-Darwinism in politics had produced a European catastrophe of a magnitude so appalling, and a scope so unpredictable, that as I write these lines in 1920, it is still far from certain whether our civilization will survive it" (*BTM*, p. xi). Later on, in an even more frequently quoted sentence, Shaw declares, "Thus did the neck of the giraffe reach out across the whole heavens and make men believe that what they saw there was a gloaming of the gods" (*BTM*, p. xliii). In between, Shaw writes of the "abyss of horror" that his own post-Darwinian anecdotes reveal (*BTM*, p. xxxvii), of the "hideous fatalism" of the Darwinian process, its "ghastly and damnable reduction of beauty and intelligence, of strength and purpose, of honor and aspiration," so that "when its whole significance dawns on you, your heart sinks into a heap of sand within you" (*BTM*, p. xlii). Now, as with Shaw's pseudo-biological statements, it would be easy to make fun of this belief that intellectual conviction will lead and has led to political and personal disaster. As C. S. Lewis wrote mockingly of a similar *Geistesgeschichte* statement (this time the once-familiar one about the brutality of the Middle Ages giving way to a Renaissance dawn ushered in by Copernicus), "as if a new hypothesis in astronomy would naturally make a man stop hitting his daughter about the head."[12] As if a new hypothesis in biology (one might translate) would cast Europe into despair and start its politicians plotting world war! Nevertheless, the negative prop of Shaw's argument carries weight where the positive one does not. It has also been astonishingly productive in the field of science and speculative fiction.

Lewis himself, to begin with, has a fondness for bringing into his fiction exactly that sense of the "abyss of horror" that Shaw presents, and reactions to it that at least parallel Shaw's argument for a new "scientific religion." In Chapter 12 of his children's book *The Silver Chair* (1953), Lewis presents three characters trapped far underground and persuaded by magic that there is no other world than the dark geology in which they find themselves, and for which they have the immediate evidence of their senses. One of them, however, turns on the witch and declares that even if there is no evidence at all for the brighter world in which he believes, nevertheless he proposes to believe in it, simply because his "made-up" world, if made up it is, is more attractive than her real one. He agrees in a way with Shaw in saying that it is necessary to have a faith even if it defies reason, if only for purposes of morale. Lewis's character is proclaiming allegiance to what Shaw says we must invent, namely "a delightful stock of religious folk-lore on an honest basis for all mankind" (*BTM*, p. lxxix). In Chapter 15 of his adult novel *That Hideous Strength* (1945), Lewis creates a similar scene when a weak and undecided character is invited, in prison and in serious danger, to insult a crucifix as a test of loyalty. Lewis's character is an atheist. He has no motive of belief for refusing to do the safe thing, but at the critical moment he asks himself a Shavian question: "If the universe was a cheat, was that a good reason for joining its side? . . . Why not go down with the ship?" He turns on his interrogator, and says, "It's all bloody nonsense, and I'm damned if I do any such thing." Lewis entirely disagrees with Shaw over the nature of Christianity. Both agree, however, that if the choice is between a false belief and no beliefs at all, then the "abyss of horror" of a pointless and design-less universe is to be rejected.

One might describe the fictional scenes above as centering on an "Existential Moment," when a character is faced with the destruction of faith by reason and falls back on some illogical inner resolve. It is not a common, but a repeated scene in later science fiction, especially in that sub-genre known as "the enclosed universe story." Wells, as usual, set the paradigm for this with his 1904 story "The Country of the Blind." This is a particularly obvious Darwinian fable. Just as Darwin had considered the case of the blind fish in the Kentucky caverns, and the way in which they proved "fitter" for their environment than their sighted relatives, in Chapter 5 of *The Origin of Species,* so Wells imagines a lost valley where the human population has gone blind slowly enough to set up a society adapted for blind people, and in a way that makes their blindness (like the fishes') hereditary. Into this generations-old society, a sighted mountaineer penetrates by accident. When he realizes the situation, the words come into his mind, "In the country of the blind the one-eyed man is king." His attempts to make himself king, however, totally fail. Like Lewis's characters in the underworld, the blind people have no evidence for the existence of sight and a belief-system that denies it. In the end they decide to operate, taking out the mountaineer's (to them) swollen and distorted eyes to cure him of his madness. The point of the story lies in the demonstrated impossibility of persuading people out of a belief for which they genuinely do have overwhelming evidence. This point has often been misunderstood. Self-assuredly certain that the sighted mountaineer is right and the blind people wrong, and that this must be obvious, Bernard Bergonzi wrote in 1961 that the whole story is a fable of the gifted artist or "free spirit" failing to convert the benighted bourgeoisie.[13] In that case the fable would cease to have any Darwinian connection, while also lost would be Wells's central ironic point that, after all, the blind people are not stupid, but (like Wells's contemporaries) honestly drawing logical conclusions from all the evidence they have. Their evidence may be inadequate, but then so may ours. It is in the nature of inadequate evidence that there may be no internal sign of its inadequacy.

Wells's point has been taken far more intelligently by a number of successors. As science fiction progressed, the traditional setting for an "enclosed universe" story became not the isolated valley but the "generation starship," a giant ship or hollowed asteroid sent off at sub-light speeds to cross interstellar space in such a way that the descendants of the original pioneers would arrive at another star. But then, would the ship-born descendants believe in a world outside any more than Wells's blind men? This scenario is used with many twists and alterations in Robert Heinlein's *Orphans of the Sky* (1941), Brian Aldiss's *Starship* (1958), James White's *The Watch Below* (1966), Harry Harrison's *Captive Universe* (1969) and several others, including in a way Orwell's *Nineteen Eighty-four* (1949). The turning point of these stories is, however, nearly always some form of what I have called above the "Existential Moment": the moment when a character finds all the evidence against him and pointing to a total dissolution of faith—Shaw's "abyss of horror"—and either reaches inside himself for some inner and ultimate conviction, or else refuses and rejects the evidence in favor of inherited belief.

In Heinlein's story, characters go both ways. Hugh, the hero—in terms of the Ship a hard-boiled realist who merely pretends to faith—is forced to realize that the "religion" of his world, full of references to "the Trip," is true after all, only literally rather than allegorically. He responds first with horror at the new enormous perspectives opened up in space and time, but then with conviction and commitment: in Shaw's terms he would be a neo-Darwinian, a sincere disbeliever. Others, however, see the same evidence, use it, but make it only a basis for "practical [i.e., genocidal] politics": like Shaw's European politicians, insincere disbelievers. Still others, sincere believers, prefer not to move at all, to die in the faith of their fathers rather than live in the "abyss": Shaw's anecdotal clergymen. No one finds a middle path.

Ripostes to and variations on this central Wells/Heinlein theme have been frequent. Brian Aldiss repeated Heinlein's scenario in *Starship*, in some ways closely, but with the addition of Freudianism, and also with a dogged return to the problem Shaw discusses of "Paley's watch," for Aldiss argues that it is inconceivable that people living inside an artefact could simply not notice the difference between the *natural* and the *made* (Aldiss's emphasis, Part II, Chapter 2). Daniel Galouye created a kind of hybrid between Wells, Heinlein, and even Lewis in *Dark Universe* (1961) by imagining a society lost in lightless underground survival caverns, but still managing to exist by echo-casting like bats, and still retaining confused religious beliefs of a world outside. A highly consistent and unexpected point about nearly all variations, however, is that instead of being stories about radical heroes confronting smug bourgeois (the Bergonzi image), they center on conservative heroes who find the new world outside their enclosed ones totally desolating. Jared, the hero of Galouye's *Dark Universe,* indeed breaks away once rescued and goes back underground, driven there by the "horrors of infinity" revealed by sight. All the science fiction stories agree that the conflict of reason and faith, or science and religion, is not one of truth and virtue against superstition and vice. Superstition is only a truth based on inadequate evidence and (very strongly in these stories) degraded information, while vice can appear on either side. Central to the plot shared beneath all the disagreements and variations is the idea of the well-intentioned believer brought to the very "brink of the abyss"—as Shaw puts it, looking into a "gulf of despair," a "bottomless pit," the "horrors of infinity"—and having to find a way through.

No science fiction author accepts Shaw's solution of Bergsonian or quasi-Lamarckian belief in an *élan vital.* They do, however, accept and take seriously his question whether any ethical sense can survive the universe of pointlessness, cruelty, and "blind chance" apparently revealed by Darwin. Other Victorians took the matter as seriously as Shaw, if with quite different conclusions. Tennyson for instance is quoted as saying that "If I ceased to believe in any chance of another life, and of a great Personality somewhere in the Universe, I should not care a pin for anything."[14] Their descendants outside science fiction seem very often to have merely pigeonholed the question, falling back on law and a sense of rights rather than of right. What is perhaps surprising about Shaw is that he wrote some ninety pages of Preface and almost three hundred more of play without mentioning what must be the other major post-Darwinian statement on his topic, the two essays "Evolution and Ethics" and "Prolegomena to Evolution and Ethics" by Wells's revered teacher Thomas Huxley. In these Huxley soberly confronts the abyss of cruelty brought before us by the struggle for survival, an abyss to which he was himself no stranger, as his own life and even his moving epitaph bear witness. Huxley lost his eldest son to scarlet fever in 1860, the year of his triumph over Bishop Wilberforce; and his agnostic epitaph reads, "Be not afraid, ye waiting hearts that weep;/ For still He giveth his beloved sleep,/ And if an endless sleep He wills, so best." Huxley concludes that the answer to the abyss lies not in denial, or abandonment of all principle, or the creation of false religions, but in dogged, principled, one might even say Manichaean rejection. There is no "sanction for morality in the ways of the cosmos," he concludes: human beings must provide their own sanction. "Social progress means a checking of the cosmic process at every step and the substitution for it of another, which may be called the ethical process . . . we should cast aside the notion that the escape from pain and sorrow is the proper object of life."[15] Huxley's influence on Wells has always been clear. In recent years it has been shown how much he affected, for instance, Joseph Conrad. Kurtz's famous utterance "the horror! the horror!" is a Huxleyan statement by one who has gone down into the abyss and managed to retain only this final ethical judgment."[16]

At the start of *Antony and Cleopatra*, Act V, Caesar, told of the death of Antony, declares, "The breaking of so great a thing should make / A greater crack," and one may feel the same about the Victorian and post-Victorian crisis of faith. Shaw's post–World War I anxieties seem outdated now, like the post–World War II conviction that all would be ended by the Bomb. Yet neither set of fears has been set completely at rest. One may feel that we are still in some ways in quest of a solution, a firm standpoint from which to make ethical judgments, and a conviction alluring enough to motivate altruism. Shaw's prognosis may have been wholly or partially rejected, but his diagnosis has retained force for a series of writers up to the present day. It was remarked above that his influence can rarely be shown to be direct on authors like Aldiss or Blish or Heinlein (or even Wells). In counterbalance, however, one can point to a remarkable concatenation of authors writing on "evolution and ethics" in England in the early twentieth century and note Shaw's position close to the heart of it. Thomas Huxley was Wells's professor. Shaw seems to have had no contact with him, but clashed with both Wells and Julian Huxley, Thomas's grandson, over *The Science of Life*. It is not known what Aldous Huxley, Julian's brother, thought of Shaw, but his *After Many a Summer* (1939) takes up exactly Shaw's issue of human longevity, if in deeply ironic mode. The biologist John Scott Haldane meanwhile was a colleague of both Shaw and Wells in the Fabian Society. It was his son J. B. S. Haldane who refused Shaw the title of "man of science" for never doing any experiments. It was the same J. B. S. Haldane's essay on "Man's Destiny," together with Stapledon's fiction, that prompted C. S. Lewis to savage satire in *Out of the Silent Planet* (1938), when an inadequate translator tries to put Haldane's abstractions into "real" or non-abstract language. Lewis later changed the object of his satire to Wells in the vulgar, self-important, catspaw figure of Jules in *That Hideous Strength*.[17] Meanwhile, J. B. S. Haldane associated and compared himself, Shaw, Wells, and Stapledon in *The Causes of Evolution*. Stapledon was a member of the Merseyside Fabian Society, not quite the same thing as the London Fabians, but nevertheless in outer orbit round it.[18] Outside this group of allies/relatives/antagonists, all active between the wars, are further clusters. J. B. S. Haldane's sister is better known as

Naomi Mitchison, author of *Memoirs of a Spacewoman* (1962). Lewis is connected not only with Tolkien but also with other war-veteran fantasy authors, including Orwell and Golding, as possessed as Shaw or Conrad by a sense of the abyss. Haldane's connections with later science fiction are movingly described by Arthur C. Clarke.[19] Links between these authors in terms of literary "sourcing" are not always easy to make out, any more than the links between Shaw and the later, and mostly American, science fiction authors of "enclosed universes" discussed above. It does seem valuable, however, to see them in terms of a cluster connected by shared interests, if divided by conflicting solutions. It is unlikely that any of the Huxley family/Haldane family/Fabian Society concatenation can ever have been quite unaware of all the others. In his *Scientific Romance in Britain 1890–1950*, Brian Stableford remarks on the power of the speculative non-fiction produced in England between the wars, discussing several of the writers named above, although he gives little space to Shaw, and others including Bertrand Russell (who observed Shaw telling Henri Bergson what he should have meant by Creative Evolution and who wrote a comic account of it many years later).[20] Stableford concludes, "They were all, in their fashion, sceptical appraisers of the state of contemporary civilization, and analysts of its prospects."[21] This is certainly a description that one could apply to Shaw, and as certainly if more indirectly to the string of science fiction authors who followed, if not his lead, then at least his path.

Notes

1. *The Collected Works of Bernard Shaw, Vol. XVI, Back to Methuselah* (New York: William Wise, 1930), p. ix. All further references are to this edition, abbreviated *BTM*.

2. The points above were made to me by the late Ted Hope, Professor of Romance Philology at the University of Leeds, although the following theory about Gaelic influence is my own.

3. *Selected Correspondence of Bernard Shaw: Bernard Shaw and H. G. Wells*, ed. J. Percy Smith (Toronto: University of Toronto Press, 1995), pp. 147–48. All further references to *Shaw/Wells* are to this edition.

4. See Julian Huxley, *Evolution: The Modern Synthesis* (New York: Harper, 1942), pp. 22–28, and Peter J. Bowler, *The Eclipse of Darwinism: Anti-Darwinian Evolution Theories in the Decades around 1900* (Baltimore: Johns Hopkins University Press, 1983).

5. This rather contemptuous phrase is used by Shaw in the "Postscript" to the World's Classics edition of *Back to Methuselah* brought out by Oxford University Press in 1945. The *O.E.D.* recorded neither word before its *Supplement* of 1933, but then found "chromosome" used in something like its modern sense in 1907, "hormone" in 1905.

6. See J. B. S. Haldane, *The Causes of Evolution* (London: Longmans Green, 1932), p. 165, and (for his more speculative essays) *Possible Worlds* (New York: Harper, 1927).

7. Michael Holroyd, *Bernard Shaw, Vol. 3: 1918–1950: The Lure of Fantasy* (New York: Random House, 1991), p. 40.

8. Richard Dawkins, *The Blind Watchmaker* (New York and London: W. W. Norton, 1986), cited here from the Norton paperback reprint of 1987, pp. 291–92.

9. Since there are no standard editions of most science fiction works (many of them continually reprinted in different formats), I cite date of first publication and give references where necessary by chapter rather than page. This quotation and the one that follows come from the "Prologue" to Bester's novel.

10. Most notably by his son Edmund Gosse, *Father and Son: A Study of Two Temperaments* (London: Heinemann, 1907). The full title of Philip Gosse's book is *Omphalos: An Attempt to Untie the Geological Knot* (London: J. van Voort, 1857).

11. As I have done in the "Introduction" to my anthology *The Oxford Book of Science Fiction Stories* (London: Oxford University Press, 1992). Note that there I explicitly extend the "fabril" tradition to biology, as shown by the last story in the collection, David Brin's "Piecework."

12. *"De Descriptione Temporum:* An Inaugural Lecture," in C. S. Lewis, *They Asked for a Paper* (London: Geoffrey Bles, 1962), p. 10.

13. See Bernard Bergonzi, *The Early H. G. Wells: A Study of the Scientific Romances* (Manchester: Manchester University Press, 1961), p. 80.

14. Cited by Humphry House, "The Mood of Doubt," in G. M. Trevelyan, ed., *Ideas and Beliefs of the Victorians: An Historic Revaluation of the Victorian Age* (London: Sylvan Press, 1949), p. 76.

15. James Paradis and George C. Williams, eds., *Evolution and Ethics: T. H. Huxley's "Evolution and Ethics" with New Essays on Its Victorian and Sociobiological Context* (Princeton: Princeton University Press, 1989), pp. 111, 139, 144.

16. See Allan Hunter, *Joseph Conrad and the Ethics of Darwinism* (London and Canberra: Croom Helm, 1983), pp. 18–27.

17. Both Stapledon and Haldane are explicitly mentioned as provocations by Lewis. See W. H. Lewis, ed., *Letters of C. S. Lewis* (New York: Harcourt, Brace and World, 1966), p. 160, and Humphrey Carpenter, *The Inklings* (London: George Allen & Unwin, 1978), p. 66. Neither Carpenter nor A. N. Wilson in *C. S. Lewis: A Biography* (New York: W. W. Norton, 1990) mentions the Wells parody in *That Hideous Strength*—both are weak on the background of popular science—but it seems self-evident, especially in Chapter 15/V of the unabridged version.

18. See Robert Crossley, *Olaf Stapledon: Speaking for the Future* (Syracuse, N.Y.: Syracuse University Press, 1994), for Stapledon's links with the Fabians, Haldane, Mitchison and Wells, respectively pp. 14, 190–91, 201–3, 210–15. Shaw has relatively few mentions in Crossley's biography.

19. Arthur C. Clarke, "Haldane and Space," in K. R. Dronamraju, ed., *Haldane and Modern Biology* (Baltimore: Johns Hopkins University Press, 1968), pp. 243–48.

20. Bertrand Russell, "George Bernard Shaw," in *Portraits from Memory and Other Essays* (New York: Simon and Schuster, 1956), pp. 75–80. Russell describes Bergson's rage at Shaw's confident misinterpretation of him on p. 78.

21. Brian Stableford, *Scientific Romance in Britain 1890–1950* (London: Fourth Estate, 1985), p. 165.

Peter Gahan

BACK TO METHUSELAH:
AN EXERCISE OF IMAGINATION[1]

[I]magination is the beginning of creation.
You imagine what you desire; you will what you imagine;
and at last you create what you will.[2]

Bernard Shaw was one of the most ambitious writers of this century, and
it is gradually being realized that his art was a far more consciously
crafted one than was suspected in his own lifetime. Shaw himself called
Back to Methuselah his *magnum opus.* Embedded in it is a poetically
structured theory of imagination, one intimately bound up with an
awareness of death. The science of metabiology that the Preface in
particular seems to be calling for is nothing less than a science of the
imagination. *Back to Methuselah* is an allegory in which the old promise
of longer life and man's victory over death is to be taken as a hope that
his imaginative capacity can be expanded. But Shaw, as a didactic artist
having built up with great care this imaginative construction, the play-
cycle *Back to Methuselah,* had also to show that imagination must go
beyond itself. It must continue to work on the imaginations of its
spectators and readers, outside the theater, in their direct experience of
life. And that imagination—and language through which it works—must
eventually lose its basis in metaphor in order to acquire a greater
perception and understanding of reality.

Back to Methuselah is crucially concerned with the metaphorical aspect
of imagination; it is, in effect, a great dramatic poem by a writer who
considered himself not only a playwright, but also a dramatic poet. As

Franklyn Barnabas suggests in Part 2, "the poem is our real clue to biological science" (5:422), and a poem is above all an artefact of the imagination. "Find me a word for the story that Lilith imagined and told you in your silent language" asks Eve in Part 1. "A poem," answers the Serpent (5:349). And be it noted, Lilith, the first mother, is the presiding imaginative principle of *Back to Methuselah* itself.

The growth of Shaw's own imaginative response to the catastrophe of war became a deliberate project in which he encapsulated his general conclusions about imagination based on his experience of confronting the questions raised by the Great War (1914–18).[3] The response that *Back to Methuselah* calls for, both from its particular readers and audience and from humanity in general, is a similar growth of imagination as the solution to the problems of civilization. This is what Creative Evolution means. In effect, Shaw completely rethought his position as an artist as a result of the war, and for seven years, all his writings were concerned with its implications. His nondramatic pieces, from the outbreak of war and during the writing of the first draft of *Back to Methuselah*, are colored by his work on it, and they, equally, provide a gloss to the play.

Shaw's first response to the war was a pamphlet entitled *Common Sense about the War* containing a devastating attack on militarism, of both the German and English variety. It portrayed the war as the inevitable product of a militaristic, Junker-class mentality shared by both sides. Rather than attack militarism on its weakest ground, Shaw writes of the failure of Napoleon, the highest case of military genius: "Napoleon conquered and conquered and conquered; and yet, when he had won more battles than the maddest Prussian can ever hope for, he had to go on fighting just as if he had never won anything at all. . . . Nothing can finally redeem militarism. When even genius itself takes that path its end is still destruction."[4]

This theme reappears in Part 4 of *Back to Methuselah*, in which Napoleon is reincarnated as General Aufsteig, Cain Adamson Charles Napoleon, Emperor of Turania, who puts his dilemma to the Oracle in this form: "If you kill me, or put a stop to my activity (it is the same thing), the nobler part of human life perishes. You must save the world from that catastrophe, madam. War has made me popular, powerful, famous, historically immortal. But I foresee that if I go on to the end it will leave me execrated, dethroned, imprisoned, perhaps executed. Yet if I stop fighting I commit suicide as a great man and become a common one" (5:538).

The problem that militarism poses for civilization is the principal question that Shaw will tackle in Part 2, *The Gospel of the Brothers Barnabas*, the first part of the play cycle to be written. In *Common Sense*, not only does he state the problem of militarism, but he also plants the seed of the solution that would bear fruit six years later as *Back to Methuselah* by advocating "*a general raising of human character*[5] [my italics] through the deliberate cultivation and endowment of democratic virtue without consideration of property or class."[6]

This is one of the clearest and most noble statements of Shaw's long-held belief that the key test for any social system must be complete intermarriageability, unhindered by class considerations, which would create the best conditions for the development of human beings and bring about a situation in which the unconscious, creative force of Life would be able to maximize its opportunities. Here is the link between his socialism and his "metabiology" or religion, Creative Evolution; a link made explicit in Part 2 when Conrad Barnabas, the biologist advocate of the new Gospel of Creative Evolution, asks the ex-Prime Ministers, Burge and Lubin (satirical portraits of Lloyd George and Asquith), "in the character of a laborer . . . would you allow your son to marry my daughter, or your daughter to marry my son?" (5:412). The politicians dismiss this as not being a political question, and indeed the audience might be puzzled as to its relevance. What *Back to Methuselah* adds to this, with its emphasis on the imaginative side of human experience, is an elaboration of what precisely "a general raising of human character" means. There is a problem here analogous to the order of priority of the chicken or the egg: will we get "a general raising of human character" as a result of social reorganization, or will social reorganization be the result of "a general raising of human character"? The answer, like the answer to the chicken and the egg, is that they must evolve together as the result of "the tremendous miracle-working force of Will nerved to creation by a conviction of Necessity" (5:433).

In *Common Sense*, war and the triple failure of social organization, government, and religion are seen as the major problems facing civilization. Shaw is particularly critical of established religion, which has resulted in "The privation of faith, and the horror of the soul, wrought by the *spectacle* [my italics] of nations praying to their common father to assist them in sabring and bayoneting and blowing one another to pieces; and of the church organizing this monstous paradox instead of protesting against it."[7]

So for the following year he made a study of the New Testament and wrote a treatise which was, as he puts it, "a criticism (in the Kantian sense) of an established body of belief which has become an actual part of the *mental fabric* [my italics] of my readers" (4:565). This Kantian critique of the "mental fabric" Shaw is speaking of is easier for us to appreciate after our exposure to such disciplines as psychoanalysis, Marxist interpretations of ideology, and structuralist studies of mythology, all of which are concerned with the necessary mental interactions through the medium of language of the individual with the community. It is as part of the individual's "mental fabric" that he shares with his community that Shaw considered religion necessary, but it must also be credible. This "mental fabric" must be changed or renewed, but first Shaw must show why Christianity, among other established religions, is inadequate.

He should not have been surprised that his conclusion, published in December 1915 as the Preface to *Androcles and the Lion,* caused almost as much outrage as *Common Sense.* He argued that there has never been a society based on Christian principles although that was precisely the type of society needed in a world of large multi-national, multi-ethnic empires or communities of nations: "Government is impossible without religion: that is, without a body of common assumptions . . . [T]here is nothing in the teaching of Jesus that cannot be assented to by a Brahman, a Mahometan, a Buddhist or a Jew, without any question of their conversion to Christianity" (4:577–78). In recognizing this necessity for a religion compatible with science and Christ's basic teaching, Shaw, in his capacity as playwright, would contribute *Back to Methuselah* to promote a credible modern "mental fabric" for western civilization.

Becoming increasingly isolated and with popular feeling running against him, he started writing a play about despair and its overcoming on 4 March 1916. "Heartbreak" is a symbolic and psychological process, as Captain Shotover says to Ellie:

> CAPTAIN SHOTOVER. Heartbreak? Are you one of those who are so sufficient to themselves that they are only happy when they are stripped of everything, even of hope?
> ELLIE [*gripping his hand*] It seems so; for I feel now as if there was nothing I could not do, because I want nothing.
> CAPTAIN SHOTOVER. That's the only real strength. That's genius. That's better than rum. (5:148–49)

Heartbreak would be a minor theme of *Back to Methuselah,* but its psychological and symbolic function would be fulfilled there by the idea of the prospect of death. He did not finish *Heartbreak House* until more than a year later in May 1917, an extremely long gestation for a Shaw play.

1918 began badly: the sons of two of Shaw's close friends, Lady Gregory and Mrs. Patrick Campbell, were killed in the war. On 28 February 1918, he wrote to Charles Trevelyan, a long-time Fabian, to suggest that he should now consider himself a potential Labour prime minister. Shaw followed up with another letter to Trevelyan on 14 March in which there is a sad account of how, because of his publications on

the war, he had lost, to his friend Sidney Webb, access to the main
organs of influence for a Socialist thinker: the journal the *New Statesman*,
which he had helped to found with the Webbs, and the committee of the
new Labour Party. In language anticipating that of Franklyn Barnabas to
the politicians, and in an echo of his Preface to *Androcles and the Lion*, he
wrote that a government party

> must have a common religion, which nowadays means a philoso-
> phy and a science, and it must have an economic policy founded
> on that religion. Well, I contend that such a nexus exists; a
> quite sufficiently definite and inspiring religion of evolution. Its
> crystallization has been taking place everywhere. . . . Here you
> have a body of doctrine on which a party could be built literally
> over a whole epoch. What is more, it is now evident that as the
> human mind and spirit and *imagination* [my italics] have jumped
> that way, it will be the basis of the coming party sooner or later
> consciously or unconsciously.[8]

This was the immediate genesis of *Back to Methuselah*. Five days later,
Shaw started writing his new play in which prominent politicians, caricatures of Asquith and Lloyd George, consult a highly influential religious
and social thinker, Franklyn Barnabas, about the way ahead. Barnabas
in the play preaches to them the same message that Shaw had preached
to Trevelyan.

Early in 1919 he interrupted his playwriting to publish *Peace Conference Hints* with his advice for the Versailles Peace Conference, in which
he warned against "The greed and rancour which abuse victory by
grasping at plunder and vengeance with both hands open and *both eyes
shut* [my italics]. There is only one force that can beat both; and that
force is the entirely mystic force of evolution applied through the sort
of living engine we call the man of principle. Principle is the motive
power in the engine: its working qualities are integrity and energy,
conviction and courage, with *reason and lucidity* [my italics] to show them
the way."[9]

In June 1919, in the middle of his radical revisions of Part 2, he wrote
in the Preface to *Heartbreak House* that, during the war, "there was a
frivolous exultation in death for its own sake, which was at bottom an
inability to realize that the deaths were real deaths and not stage ones"
(5:33). This, our inability to realize the full implications of death or our
inability to imagine death, is central to an understanding of *Back to
Methuselah*. He continued, "It is impossible to estimate what proportion
of us, in khaki or out of it, grasped the war and its political antecedents
as a whole *in the light* [my italics] of any philosophy of history or

knowledge of what war is. I doubt whether it was as high as our proportion of higher mathematicians" (5:35–36). But it was precisely this type of person that Shaw saw as necessary for the salvation of civilized life. And such capacity would be itself a spur to even greater imaginative efforts.

Later in November 1919, he interrupted his writing of *Back to Methuselah* to compose a long lecture on modern religion in which he again confronts the problem of a credible religion for a modern empire, commonwealth, or community of nations. This problem of governing a supernational entity such as an empire runs through Parts 2, 3, and 4 of the play cycle, but, more significantly, Shaw draws the parallel between the physical eye and the mind's eye in the evolutionary process: "There is some force you cannot explain, and this force is always organizing, organizing, organizing, and among other things it organizes the physical eye, in order that the mechanism can see the dangers and avoid them, see its food and go for it, can see the edge of the cliff and avoid falling over it. And it not only evolves that particular eye, but it evolves what Shakespear called *the mind's eye* [my italics] as well; you are continually contriving to know, to become more conscious, to see what it is all driving at."[10] This metaphor of vision and the mind's eye plays an important part in the concept of imagination in *Back to Methuselah;* the allegory of long life can be interpreted as the evolution of the mind's eye.

Having created a tetralogy like Wagner's *Ring,* he subsequently added a fifth play to make it a pentalogy—or, as he subsequently called it, "a metabiological pentateuch," finishing the first draft of the five plays in May 1920, more than two years after he had begun. It was the end of six years of extraordinary mental and spiritual effort during which, like the Serpent of his play, Shaw shed his old skin in order to be born anew. This transformation produced, in the form of a new skin, the play-cycle *Back to Methuselah,* in which we can see the preoccupations of his other writings during this period all brought together.[11] In the Preface, written during the summer of 1920, he warns us about how we should read *Back to Methuselah.* "Legend, parable and drama are the natural vehicles of dogma; but woe to the churches and rulers who substitute the legend for the dogma, the parable for the history, the drama for the religion" (5:328). Indeed, we must be careful not to confuse the drama of *Back to Methuselah* and its aspirations toward an extension of human life expectancy with the "religion" Shaw is proposing. Critics have been confused by this central conceit; but, in the context of his drama, it is only a conceit. Shaw did not expect it to be taken literally as part of his science of metabiology, even if it is a biological possibility.

At the end of 1918 (when he was in the middle of the first draft of *Back to Methuselah*) he wrote, in response to a suicidal letter from an

Indian boy, that if God is omnipotent, then "he is responsible for everything that happens in the universe, and the fact that there is cruelty in the world proves him cruel, injustice proves him unjust, and mortality proves him futile to people like yourself who have so *little imagination* [my italics] that they want to live forever."[12]

Shaw wanted more imagination in confronting such problems as mortality, and his parable of prolonging human life-span is to be taken allegorically as a measure of increasing the capacity of human thought in its fullest sense, of creative imagination. In the context of the play, the realization of the full implications of death is the spur to imagination. If this interpretation of the allegory is correct, then in the play it must also be the spur to living longer. That it is we can surmise from the very first image of the entire play-cycle, a vision of *a vision of death*, the theater audience staring at Adam staring in consternation at the dead body of a fawn. "What is the matter with its *eyes* [my italics]?" says Eve. They slowly realize that the fawn is not asleep, that it will not wake up, that it is *dead* (a new word), and that what happened to the fawn could happen to them. They find the dead fawn putrid and disgusting, just as Eve will later find the "secret" of sex disgusting because of the proximity of the genital and excremental areas. It is as part of his poetic or structural method that Shaw, in connecting these similar reactions of disgust, makes a telling metaphorical association between sex and death, with both leading to new life. Adam dumps the carcass of the fawn in the river—a metonymic association of death and water drawing on the symbolism implicit in the Christian rite of baptism that becomes a burlesque symbol of rebirth in Part 3 when the Archbishop tells that he repeatedly had to fake his death by drowning. In the new consciousness of their own mortality, Adam and Eve decide, with the help of the Serpent (the rational principle), to set the duration of human life at one thousand years, which, in terms of the allegory, is more imagination than anyone could ever want. However, the rot sets in with the next generation of Cain and Abel who, building on their parents' invention of death, invent killing and murder, with the result that by what we would call historical time, life-spans have been reduced to three score and ten, with our imaginative capacities reduced accordingly.

The final image in the play-cycle is an analogue of a vision of death. Lilith, the personification of the creative principle herself, speaks of her hopes for the future and concludes, "And for what may be beyond, the *eyesight* [my italics] of Lilith is too short. It is enough that there is a beyond" (5:631). She vanishes, leaving the stage in darkness, Shaw significantly shutting off the eyesight of his audience. Imagination can do no more; it is a metaphorical death like the others we have encountered through the play, but this time it extends beyond, to its audience—as a spur to its imaginative capacities if it has grasped the full implications. Throughout the text, the following metaphors are repeatedly associated with creative imagination: eyes, vision, images, mirrors, telescopes, dreams, sleep, sculpture, art, stories, poetry, death, water, rebirth. Also the varied geological, botanical, and lepidopteral metaphors throughout the play are all indications of the levels, varieties, and stages of human life, all the deaths and rebirths that must be experienced as part of the development of creative imagination.

In *The Perfect Wagnerite*, Shaw described Loki in Wagner's *Ring* as "Logic and Imagination without living Will,"[13] and that is the function of the Serpent in Shaw's drama of Part 1, *In the Beginning*, as it is also the function of the writer, Bernard Shaw. The Serpent learned to speak from Adam and Eve (as a child learns to speak from its parents), but is constantly inventing new words to account for their rapidly dawning awareness of experience, their eating of the tree of knowledge. It was from the Serpent that Eve learned the new word *dead* to describe what happened to the fawn. She is a variation of Hegel's principle of negation, the principle of reason: "I tell you I am very subtle. When you and Adam talk, I hear you say 'why?' Always 'why?' You see things, and you say 'why?' But I *dream* [my italics] things that never were; and I say 'why not?' " (5:345).

The Serpent explains to Eve how Lilith, the first mother, created Adam and herself: "She *saw death* [my italics] as you saw it when the fawn fell, and she knew then that she must find out how to renew herself. She *imagined* [my italics] it as a marvellous story of something that never happened to a Lilith that never was" (5:348). At this point the Serpent speaks the lines that lie at the heart of the entire play-cycle: "*imagination* [my italics] is the beginning of creation. You imagine what you desire; you will what you imagine; and at last you create what you will" (5:348). Note, however, that for Shaw it is imagination (not desire, which is logically inferior) that is the beginning of creation. Desire without imagination cannot create.

Here are the four moments of the dynamic of creative imagination: desire, imagination, will, creation. The term the Serpent uses to describe this process is "to conceive." That is the word that means "both the beginning in imagination and the end in creation," and Lilith's marvelous story is "a poem." Already we can see how imagination is intimately linked to language and poetry and how Shaw has built up Lilith's marvelous story which is a poem from the "silent language" of Lilith and the Serpent; to Adam and Eve's spoken language; to their new capacity for understanding their own experience following the death of the fawn and the Serpent's capacity for creating new words to match their dawning consciousness.

In Part 2 Franklyn Barbabas, the religious ex-clergyman, has the dream of longevity that is reinforced by the science of his biologist brother, Conrad; it becomes their gospel. Franklyn, like Eve's visionary children, can dream but cannot will his dream into existence. The "silly" rector and the socially "inferior" parlormaid (both specific farcial "types") have deeper, unconscious reasons for prolonging their lives, for expanding their imaginative capacities. At the end of Part 2 we learn that the politicians' own sons had been killed in the war, as had Franklyn's, but nobody mentioned them. They had all forgotten them except for the silly clergyman: "*I* didnt forget, because I'm of military age; and if I hadn't been a parson I'd have had to go out and be killed too. To me the awful thing about their political incompetence was that they had to kill their own sons" (5:437). In Part 3 the transfigured parlormaid, the Domestic Minister Mrs. Lutestring, relates how she used alcohol to stave off suicide. "You people can have no *conception* [my italics] of the dread of poverty that hung over us then, or of the utter tiredness of forty years' unending overwork" (5:472).

The failure of imagination to grasp the reality of death is the problem, and the imaginative response is the solution. However, imagination is a concept that Shaw always saw as double-edged. In his Preface to *Misalliance,* he makes this quite clear in his distinction between romantic and realistic imagination:

> The power to imagine things as they are not: this I call the romantic imagination. The other is the power *to imagine things as they are without actually sensing them* [my italics]; and this I call the realistic imagination. Take for example marriage and war. One man has a vision of perpetual bliss with a domestic angel at home, and of flashing sabres, thundering guns, victorious cavalry charges, and routed enemies in the field. That is romantic imagination and the mischief it does is incalculable. The wise man knows that imagination is not only a means of pleasing himself with romances and fairy tales and fools' paradises, but also a means of *foreseeing* [my italics] and being prepared for realities as yet unexperienced, and of testing the possibility and desirability of serious Utopias. (4:138–39)

In the second act of Part 4, Napoleon claims to have this rare gift of being able to see things as they are. The oracle wonders if that means he has no imagination, to which he replies, "I mean that I have the only imagination worth having: the power of imagining things as they are, even when I cannot see them" (5:536). But Napoleon's tragedy, as we have seen, is that realistic imagination is confused with romantic imagination, especially that of his followers. It is romantic imagination from which most of the shortlivers (which is to say, most of us) suffer, and it is realistic imagination that the play champions. The politicians of Part 2 and, most tragically, the Elderly Gentleman in Part 4 all suffer from romantic imagination. It is tragic in the Elderly Gentleman's case because it is mixed up with realistic imagination in a language of dead thought, which is why he dies after his exposure to the long-livers, possessors of realistic imagination *par excellence*.

Cain, who visits his now-old parents in Act II of Part 1, is a typical example of the destructiveness of romantic imagination. "Stay with the woman who will give you children. I will go to the woman who will give me *dreams* [my italics]," Cain announces to his father. However, he wants his mother "to create more men and more women, that they may in turn create more men. I have *imagined a glorious poem* [my italics] of many men. . . . I will divide them into two great hosts. . . . And each host shall try to kill the other host. Think of that! all those multitudes of men fighting, fighting, killing killing! . . . That will be life indeed: life lived to the very marow: burning overwhelming life" (5:363). But Eve angrily responds to Cain's romantic dreams of military glory: "You cannot taste life without making it bitter and boiling hot: you cannot love Lua until her face is *painted* [my italics]. . . . You can feel nothing but a torment, and believe nothing but a lie. You will not raise your head to look at all the miracles of life that surround you" (5:366). She places her hope in those of her children who are dreamers: "They tell beautiful lies in beautiful words. They can remember their *dreams* [my italics]. They can dream without sleeping. They have not will enough to create instead of dreaming; but the Serpent said that every dream could be willed into creation by those strong enough to believe in it" (5:374). But Cain, whose flights of imagination led him to invent murder and dream of military glory, flings the accusation in their faces: "Who invented death?" And they have to admit their guilt, the inadequecy of imaginations that could not bear the thought of a life of more than a thousand years.

For Shaw, the dramatist, every character is right from his or her point of view, even the romantically imaginative but murderous Cain, whose inner Voice has persuaded him that "Death is not really death: it is the gate of another life: a life infinitely splendid and intense; a life of the soul above" (5:370). This is symbolically true and is a recurring theme throughout the play-cycle; however, another constant theme is the warning not to mistake the metaphor for the reality, the gravest defect of the romantic imagination, which can be attributed to the nature of language itself.

In Part 2, Burge, the Lloyd George caricature, boasts of "a certain power of spiritual *vision* [my italics], because I have practised as a solicitor. A solicitor has to advise families. He has to show them how to provide for their daughters after their deaths" (5:434–35). Although this is a burlesque variation of Cain's "gateway to another life, splendid and intense," Shaw is making a serious point about death being a gateway to a life of the imagination. In this second part, Shaw cleverly gets the two statesmen, both of whom served as Prime Minister during the most catastrophic war in history, to condemn each other by pointing out each other's deficiencies. Burge accuses Lubin, the Asquith caricature, of having no conscience, significantly using a mirror metaphor: "you have a mind like a *looking-glass* [my italics]. You are very clear and smooth and lucid as to what is standing in front of you. But you have no foresight and no hindsight. You have no continuity; and a man without continuity can have neither conscience nor honor from one day to another" (5:418). Burge has already boasted of his own visionary capacity, but Lubin angrily, and with some condescension, responds by accusing him of having "mere energy without intellect and without knowledge. Your mind is not a trained mind" (5:418).

As Shaw indicated in the Prefaces to *Misalliance* and *Heartbreak House,* imagination must be informed by both knowledge and a philosophy. In Part 4 the Elderly Gentleman makes a point about how imagination can be distorted by knowledge if it is acquired without conscience, and which makes play with size in a fashion similar to Swift's *Gulliver's Travels:*

> I maintain that it is dangerous to shew too much to people who do not know what they are looking at. I think that a man who is sane as long as he looks at the world through his own eyes is very likely to become a dangerous madman if he takes to looking at the world through *telescopes and microscopes* [my italics]. The moment men made telescopes, their belief perished . . . they could no longer believe in their deity, because they had always thought of him as living in the sky. . . . Whatever the scientific people may say, imagination without microscopes was kindly and often courageous, because it worked on things of which it had real knowledge. But imagination with microscopes, working on a terrifying spectacle of millions of grotesque creatures of whose nature it had no knowledge, became a cruel terror-stricken, persecuting delirium. (5:514–15)

Shaw's horror, evident here (he is thinking particularly of man's torturing other animals), cannot be exaggerated. What makes it most reprehensible for him is that it is done in the name of science. It is another violent consequence, with war, of social, religious, and educational systems that inculcate imagination without conscience.

Perhaps the area of greatest confusion for romantic imagination is where the desire for beauty and the desire for sex become confused, leading to a loss of self-control, the possession of which is the greatest evolutionary virtue for Shaw. In Part 1 we have seen how Eve disparaged Cain in his relation with his wife, Lua, as a "poor slave of a painted face and a bundle of skunk's fur." (As Shaw is making the familiar Puritan point against the deceiving senses, skunk has to be the most appropriate fur for Lua.) In Part 2, for instance, the political war-monger Lubin cannot remember having met Conrad because "Your pretty niece engaged all my powers of vision" (5:401). In Part 3 this romantic distortion of imaginative capacity is expressed comically in the President's infatuation with the Minister of Health, a handsome Negress, but when accused of it, the President protests that his relations with her are purely "telephonic, gramophonic, photophonic, and, may I say, platonic" (4:477).

Again Shaw makes a serious point comically; a sex affair between two people who have never met in the flesh is conducted through instruments that are extensions of the senses exemplified by the large television screen. In other words, it is an affair of the imagination divorced from reality. Shaw should, perhaps, be given more credit for his emphasis on the importance of imagination in human sexuality. Within the dialectic of the play this can be either bad or good: bad, if imagination divorced from reality leads to a loss of self-control (which it palpably does in this case); but good if it leads to greater imaginative capacity. And in this one respect only the President is contrasted favorably to his Chinese chief secretary, Confucius, a reincarnation of the Serpent, who reacts to the President's infatuation with disgust similar to Eve's reaction when she learned the secret of sex from the Serpent. "For me a woman who is not *yellow* [my italics] does not exist, save as an official" (5:448). Confucius's color prejudice is a symptom of inadequate imagination. Later in the act there is a much more poetic example of the vagaries of romantic imagination. After two hundred fifty years, the silly clergyman and the parlormaid meet again, this time as Archbishop and the Domestic Minister, the formidable Mrs. Lutestring. They will leave at the end to mate in order to become the Adam and Eve of a new race of long-livers. In a strange anticipation of this (and as an ironic echo of Cain's "gate to another life"), they have this dialogue:

THE ARCHBISHOP. This *vision* [my italics] of a door opening to me, and a woman's face welcoming me, must be a reminiscence of something that really happened; though I see it now as an angel opening the door of heaven.

MRS. LUTESTRING. Or a parlormaid opening the door of the house of the young woman you were in love with?
THE ARCHBISHOP [*making a wry face*] Is that the reality? How these things grow in our *imagination* [my italics]. (5:469–70)

What makes this so wonderful, in this most satirical of the five plays, are the reverberations set up that extend throughout the play cycle, from Adam and Eve, through Haslam and Savvy, the Archbishop and Mrs. Lutestring, and beyond them; opening a door to Heaven presages a better future. It also tells us something about imaginative truth. Imagination may distort reality, but it can also illuminate the significance of such prosaic reality as the everyday duties of an early-twentieth-century parlormaid.

Part 5, with the creation of the automata, Ozymandias and Cleopatra-Semiramis, is Shaw's most extreme satire on romantic imagination as determinism. These apparently splendid examples of humanity can react only to stimuli, and, since they completely lack realistic imagination and that "highly developed vital sense" of self-control of which it is a function, they have no other way of responding when their romantic illusions are destroyed and their vanity is pricked than violence. They are the victims of their self-interest and self-conceit. The result, of course, is that they completely lack creative imagination. As the He-Ancient puts it, "These things are mere automata: they cannot help *shrinking from death at any cost* [my italics]. You see they have no self-control, and are merely shuddering through a series of reflexes" (5:608).

At the end of Part 5, this theme makes its final appearance in the last line before the epilogue, which is spoken by the art lover, Ecrasia. Shaw returns to romantic imagination, but here it is an imagination of hope, as it was in the Archbishop's "vision" of the parlormaid. Ecrasia, finding no one to spend the night with, exclaims, "Must I spend the night alone? After all, I can *imagine* [my italics] a lover nobler than any of you" (5:627). She is left alone with her imagination to dream dreams, a reincarnation of the serpent and one of those children in whom Eve put her faith for a better world.

An ancillary theme to this is the more prosaic reality of procreation. When Lilith renewed herself, she divided herself in two, into Adam and Eve, so that they could share the burden of procreation between them. But, in fact, Lilith left a preponderance of the burden on the woman whom she made in her own image. And, whereas man is supposed to be in woman's "power through his desire," the reverse happened when Cain the provider, the false superman, the modern military macho man comes along and declares, "When I have slain the boar at the risk of my life, I will throw it to my woman to cook, and give her a morsel of it for her pains. She shall have no other food; and that will make her my slave. . . . Man shall be the master of Woman" (5:364).

This physiological and social imbalance is one of the things within the play's scheme of themes that has to be rectified, just as the problems of government and social organization have to be solved if we are to allow imaginative capacity of either women or men to flourish. So, as we follow the allegory of long life as an indication of expanded imagination, we can see how the burden of childbearing is progressively lifted from women. By Part 5, women do not give birth any more; oviparous methods of reproduction have somehow come about. Once the unequal burden of childbearing has been lifted, then the necessity for this aspect of romantic imagination disappears.

Another aspect of imagination that can be traced through the play is the development of the metaphor of looking that Shaw elaborated from his analogy between the physical eye and the mind's eye. At first it is merely reactive, as when Adam and Eve stare at the dead fawn or when Eve admires the Serpent's new hood. By Part 3, when we meet the first long-livers, a change is taking place. To convince President Burge-Lubin that she is indeed two hundred seventy-four years of age, Mrs. Lutestring *"turns her face gravely towards him"* and tells him to "look again." He looks *"at her bravely until the smile fades from his face, and he suddenly covers his eyes with his hands."* The activity of looking has seemingly changed from a reactive to a proactive process. In fact, Shaw is only making a point which has since become a commonplace of the psychology of perception. As he puts it in his 1944 Postscript to the play in speaking about visual perception, "Attention is the first symptom of thought" (5:699). In other words, all perception and thought are proactive; it is only a question of how much.

There are two examples in Part 4 of this proactive power of looking. The first is in the confrontation between Napoleon (General Aufsteig, Emperor of Turania) and the Oracle, a long-liver in her second century. Although he has the strongest "mesmeric" field she has ever encountered in a short-liver, when she uncovers her eyes and looks at him "face to face" he staggers, covers his eyes, and shrieks, "Help! I am dying" (5:533–34). Another moment of symbolic farce: Napoleon, the soldier, dies and is reborn as a coward; he goes off to gibber impotently at the statue of the discoverer of the precept that "cowardice was a great patiotic virtue," Sir John Falstaff. The second occasion, near the end of Part 4, is analogous to Gulliver's description of his position when he has to leave the land of the Houyhnhnms: "That the certain prospect of an unnatural death was the least of my evils: for, supposing I should escape with life by some strange adventure, how could I think with temper of passing my days among Yahoos, and relapsing into my old corruptions, for want of examples to lead and keep me within the paths of virtue?"[14] For Yahoos, read short-livers. The Elderly Gentleman's version of this is, "They have gone back to lie about your answer. I cannot go with them. I cannot live among people to whom nothing is real. I have become incapable of it through my stay here" (5:562).

When the Oracle tells him that he will die of discouragement if he stays, he asserts, "It is the meaning of life, not of death, that makes banishment so terrible to me". The Oracle *"looks steadily into his face. He stiffens; a little convulsion shakes him; he falls dead"* (5:563). Shaw, thus, in his ordering of the examples of Napoleon and the Elderly Gentleman in his drama, reverses Hegel's adage that history repeats itself: first as tragedy; second as farce.

But, as always, we must not confuse Shaw's metaphor or allegory with the reality that he is proposing. What he is illustrating visually in his "symbolical farce" is the intimidation of an inferior civilization by a superior one. For example, when so-called primitive people encounter western civilization, their culture seems to crumble from within without the necessity for the full colonial apparatus. This becomes a major theme in Part 4, when the big political question of the day for the long-livers is whether they should colonize the rest of the world or remain isolated "a race apart": if they choose to colonize, then short-livers who come in contact with long-livers will simply choose to die. The term the long-livers use to describe the inability of short-livers to live with them is "discouragement," what we might call existential despair. The ultimate result is death: "He simply dies. He wants to. He is out of countenance" (5:529).

However, proactive vision can enoble as well as discourage, as in Part 5 when the Ancients confront the automata made by the Infants. The automata have no self-control, and after they have killed their creator, Pygmalion, they are terrified of what the Ancients might do to them, so, to propitiate them, each immediately suggests that the other be killed. The Ancients, with Solomon-like wisdom, put to them the question, "One of you is to be destroyed. Which of you shall it be?" The stage directions tell that the Ancients take the automata by one hand and place the other on their heads, and after a slight convulsion, during which their *"eyes are fixed"* on the Ancients, the automata make their answer. Although similar to the Oracle's encounter with the Elderly Gentleman, the result of the Ancients' action is "to put a little more life into them." Released from their stimulus/reaction determinism, the automata, by making an imaginative leap, can see beyond their own self-interest. Ozymandias suggests that he be killed, but that Cleopatra-Semiramis be spared, while she asks that they both be killed: "How could either of us live without the other?" In Part 4 it is the Oracle who shows pity to the short-liver; here, the imaginations of the short-livers (for that is what the automata are) are raised to recognize the implications of life, and they embrace pity. Again Shaw was being extremely prescient. He was far from blind to the role played by either "natural selection" in evolution or "behaviorism" in our mental lives, his point being precisely that we have become prisoners of ingrained behavioral habits. But he would have accused behaviorism, as he accused Darwinism, of "banishing mind from the universe" in the words of Samuel Butler. We can only become imaginative when we break through such behavioral patterns. And it is of this, above all, that the Ancients speak when they talk about escaping from the tyranny of their bodies.

If our ability to conceive death is the spur to our imaginative capacity, then the much more difficult ability to conceive of the full implications of life is what imagination means in the widest sense. This we can gather from the Ancient's response to the Youth's taunt of living a miserable life: "Infant: one moment of the ecstasy of life as we live it would strike you dead" (5:567). Apart from critical or realistic imagination, and defective or romantic imagination, there is this more important aspect to imagination: creative imagination, the type of imagination the Serpent announced when she declared that "imagination is the beginning of creation." This is the principal subject of the final play, *As Far as Thought Can Reach*. The Infants exercise their imaginations in love, art, science, and nature, but these are found wanting: "Art is the magic *mirror* [my italics] you make to reflect your invisible dreams in visible pictures. You use a glass mirror to see your face: you use works of art to see your soul. But we who are older use neither glass mirrors nor works of art. We have a direct sense of life" (5:617).

We must be careful to note the distinction that Shaw makes between two metaphorical antitheses involving the concept of life: life/death and life/matter. The first refers to our imaginative capacity irrespective of space and time; the second refers to our perceptions of the spatial-temporal world. This is similar to Kant's division between reason and understanding, or between Plato's world of ideas and world of appearances. In Part 5 Shaw shows the Infants in full celebration of the life/matter antithesis, the world of the senses. It opens with the infants dancing when an Ancient "with his eyes closed" (5:564) appears sleep-walking, lost in intense thought *(dreaming)*, and interrupts the festivities. More and more the Ancients aspire to a liberation from the world of the senses toward a world of thought, where language would lose its metaphoric basis.

Shaw, and *Back to Methuselah* is eloquent testimony to this, is a fully paid-up subscriber to the philosophy of the *logos*, which has dominated western thought since Plato. To Derrida and the deconstructionists logocentrism, as they call it, is anathema. For them, thought is a special case of writing rather than the other way around. What is interesting about Shaw is that, in a sense, he anticipated the objections of the deconstructionists to logocentrism and left traces of these doubts scattered through the text of *Back to Methuselah*. It is noteworthy, for instance, that Lilith devises her poem of creation before the creation of spoken language, in a silent language that would correspond to Derrida's concept of arche-writing. But, most notably, it is here, in dealing with the metaphorical nature of language and imagination, that Shaw seems to realize the limits of the theory of imagination that he has so carefully built up to this stage of the play-cycle. The problem lies in the concept itself, and Shaw deconstructs it, as it were, before the fact. Imagination requires the ability to imagine, to make images in the mind, but at a certain point, if imagination is highly enough developed, that ability becomes redundant. It is replaced by "a direct sense of life," as the She-Ancient puts it, thought without language. It loses its meaning, in the same way as Lilith foresees her own legend's losing its meaning. "Dead thought" is what the long-livers of Part 4 call it. However, this does not mean that it is sterile, but rather that this loss of meaning is part of the dynamic of creative imagination that must lead it beyond itself.

Ironically enough, by means of this deconstruction, this final part of the play-cycle proposes a platonic ascent. By taking the eye out of the metaphor of "the mind's eye," and image out of the concept of imagination, by stripping metaphor from language, Shaw is left with Platonic thought contemplating reality, the result of the process that began in a small way in Part 3 and became a major theme in Part 4. In Parts 3 and 4, some words had lost their meaning, such as *parlormaid* and *landlord*. But by Part 4, one of the great differences between the long-livers and the short-livers is in their use of metaphor. In a discussion with Zoo, the Elderly Gentleman, as a reincarnation of a true nineteenth-century liberal, gives a highly metaphorical description of human progress at which Zoo explodes with laughter:

> ZOO. Oh, Daddy, Daddy, Daddy, you are a funny little man, with your torches and your coral insects and bees and acorns and stones and mountains.
> THE ELDERLY GENTLEMAN. Metaphors, madam. Metaphors, merely.
> ZOO. Images, images, images. I was talking about men, not about images. (5:517)

In Part 5, then, these visual metaphoric attributes of language, the imaginative side of language, are superseded in a platonic ascent from the senses to pure thought, the world of ideas. Imagination in art is a metaphor for imagination in life, which is why the Ancients leave art behind them when they leave their childhood. This is the point of the Ancient's parable of the rag doll. The child's love for its rag doll is transferred in adulthood to replacements for it. We desire realistic images and stories (art) to such an extent that we want to recreate reality itself, which is why the Infants create the automata (making their own dolls). However, this cannot be done. It will always be mere machinery and, thus, dissatisfying. Turning to nature, friends, and lovers is, ultimately, equally dissatisfying. Eventually, "It leads to the truth that you can create nothing but yourself" (5:616). As the She-Ancient says, "It was to myself I turned as to the final reality. Here, and here alone, I could shape and create" (5:619). However, in her search for bodily perfection, she found that "I could not create it: I could only imagine it . . . [and so] This body was the last doll to be discarded" (5:617). The Ancients discovered that their bodies, over which they had such control, were only enslaved automatons, and since, Hegelian fashion, the slave becomes the master when the master cannot live without him, they were only slaves of a slave, the body. In another variation of Cain's dream, they complain, "Whilst we are tied to this tyrannous body we are subject to its death and our destiny is not achieved. . . . Our destiny to be immortal. . . . The day will come when there will be no people, only thought. And that will be life eternal" (5:620).

After the Ancients describe the life of thought without bodies to which they aspire, when they will possess eternal life, the Infants in a kind of reprise discuss the implications of this in their own language. Ecrasia, the art lover, exclaims, "No limbs, no contours, no exquisite lines and elegant shapes, no worship of beautiful bodies, no poetic embraces in which cultivated lovers pretend that their caressing hands are wandering over celestial hills and enchanted valleys." Acis, the nature lover, interrupts her disgustedly: "What an inhuman mind you have, Ecrasia! Why don't you fall in love with someone? Love is a simple thing and a deep thing: it is an act of life and not an illusion. Art is all illusion." To which the sculptor, Arjillax, replies, "That is false. The statue comes to life always." But his master, Martellus, feels that "Nothing remains beautiful and interesting except thought, because the thought is the life" (5:621–22).

This can be interpreted as a desire to liberate the constraints on imagination by the material world that exists in space and time (the world of images), but there is also something here in Shaw's view of history that is related to Yeats's concept of the gyres. History is circular, civilization advances and retreats; there appears to be no progress, no evolution; that is why the Fabian utopia of Part 3, in which social problems have been solved but where duration of human life (i.e., imaginative capacity) has been circumscribed, is a false utopia. The He- and She-Ancients of Part 5 are very similar to Adam and Eve of Part 1. But there is a difference. Adam and Eve were not capable of bearing the burden of immortality. The Ancients are, and indeed want to go beyond it. The difference is their power of imagination, which started with Adam and Eve staring at the dead fawn. So, if history is circular, it is also spiral-like as men develop a greater capacity for imagination. The last word on this is left to the creative principle herself, Lilith: "I shall see the slave set free and the enemy reconciled, the whirlpool become all life and no matter. And because these infants that call themselves ancients are reaching out towards that, I will have patience with them still; though I know well that when they attain it they shall become one with me and supersede me, and Lilith will be only a legend and a lay that has lost its *meaning* [my italics]" (5:630–31). The Ancients are striving to become one with the creative imagination and to go beyond even that. Shaw himself is looking forward to the time when his legend of Lilith may be superseded, when the metaphorical aspect of his imaginative effort in creating this dramatic poem of Lilith and her descendants will have lost its meaning and a new level of reality will have been reached in which our language, our mental fabric, will have been transcended.

An integral part of the thematics of language and imagination in the play-cycle is the interaction between the play and its audience. The allegory of imagination can be taken on many levels: social, psychological, poetic, and theatrical. At the theatrical level, Shaw wants it to work on the spectator in analogous fashion to the way the Great War worked on him in prompting him to write it and the way the idea of death prompted Adam and Eve to develop their imaginations. He therefore designed *Back to Methuselah* in such a way that, if it was to be appreciated, the act of appreciation itself would be the result of a developing imagination: "as far as the theatre is concerned [it is] all quite impossible except for a very thoughtful and advanced audience."[15]

Shaw decided against character-based drama, of which he had just written his finest example in *Heartbreak House,* and, by transmuting Captain Shotover's seventh degree of concentration into the Barnabas brothers' gospel of longevity, he elaborated a multipart fable in the manner of a medieval morality play, even to the extent of having biblical characters. This time Shaw was not interested in evoking a simple artistic response; he wanted to stimulate his audience as Brecht later would stimulate his audiences by breaking away from character-based drama in his way. If imagination is the primary subject of the play, it applies outside it as well. He wanted to stimulate the imagination of his audience by fascinating it and making it think. He wanted to educe the change in human imagination he was advocating in a way analogous to the proactive power of vision of the long-livers. In his next play he reverted to character-based drama, with Saint Joan becoming the very incarnation of Shaw's gospel of imagination.[16] But later, in the 1930s, he would continue his formal experiments initiated in *Back to Methuselah* in such plays as *Too True to Be Good* and *The Simpleton of the Unexpected Isles*.

To understand his technique, three other aspects of the work apart from allegory must be taken into account. The first is his technique of symbolic farce, which was quite different from, although developed from, the forms of drama he had made his own up to this stage: the problem play, the play of ideas, and the disquisitory play. However, he had been experimenting with different forms in such works as *Fanny's First Play* and some of the shorter plays. In creating *Back to Methuselah*, he veered away from the tragic undertones of *Heartbreak House* but retained aspects of its symbolic comedy. Part of this symbolic farce is the way in which characterization involves the reincarnation of certain personifications in the different parts of the play-cycle. Using the same actors to depict similar character types in different contexts throughout the play-cycle enabled Shaw to expand the conceptual possibilities of his drama. In a letter to Lawrence Langner he identified these doublings as follows:

> Adam, Conrad, The Accountant General, the Envoy (unsympathetic character actor)
> Eve, Mrs Lutestring, the Oracle, the She-Ancient (dignified leading lady)
> Cain, Burge, Burge-Lubin, Napoleon, Ozymandias (Brilliant swagger and geniality)
> Lubin, Confucius, Elderly Gentleman, Pygmalion (Must have a gentle and very distinct voice)
> Savvy, Zoo, The Newly Born
> Franklyn, The He-Ancient.[17]

The second aspect of his technique is the musical recurrence of concepts or themes throughout the work; concepts such as rationality, laughter, language, imagination, love, art, wisdom, conscience, creativity, civilization, militarism, good government, empire, history, science, religion, evolution, immortality, death, sex, and even the importance of good manners. Shaw introduces these themes in different contexts, developing them, varying them, and sometimes inverting them: "I don't think it will come to a Socratic dialogue pure and simple. . . . To the end I may have to disregard the boredom of the spectator who has not mastered all the motifs, as Wagner had to do."[18] This is significant, not only because of the reference to Wagner's system of Leitmotiven, but because Shaw associates it with the dialogue form of platonic philosophy. However, he is clear that he is writing a drama, not simply a philosophical dialogue. The logic of the development of his themes is musical-dramatic rather than strictly philosophic.

The third aspect of Shaw's method is that of allusion: *Back to Methuselah* constantly alludes, in both form and content, to people, historical events, and books external to it, not unlike Joyce's *Ulysses*. This allusiveness is an integral part of Shaw's dialectical method: his work is part of his particular cultural context; it reflects it and can only proceed out of it; his thought can only have meaning as part of the Westernized Judaeo-Christian tradition, that "mental fabric" from which it springs. Appreciation of that must be part of the spectators' and readers' response. In loose Hegelian terms, they are invited to make a synthesis from their experience of Shaw's drama (antithesis) in the light of their own experience and knowledge of history (thesis).

This allusiveness appears in the title, *Back to Methuselah: A Metabiological Pentateuch*. For a drama that looks forward so much, it is ironic that its title insists on going back, but this does imply the cyclical aspect of history implicit in the play. Methuselah, the biblical character from Genesis, suggests the prophetic aspect of Shaw's work, and the slogan itself is an ironic adaptation of Rousseau's "Back to Nature." Rousseau, a leading figure of the eighteenth-century enlightenment, is described in the play as "a sort of Deist" (5:426), Deism being a kind of clockwork Christianity, a mechanistic view of the world inimical to Shaw's. Finally, there is the neologism "metabiological," which is to biology what metaphysics is to physics (Newton enabled Locke to do away with metaphysics in the same way that Darwinism enabled science to "banish mind from the universe"). For Shaw, a living religion cannot be in conflict with contemporary biological theories. The etymology of "metabiology" includes the Greek word *logos,* which means word, but it also means reason, discourse, knowledge, science, and concept, and it is allied to idea (in Plato's sense).

The title of Part 1, *In the Beginning,* quotes not only the first words of Genesis but also the first words of the gospel of St. John, "In the beginning was the Word." As Shaw explains in his Postscript, "the Thought was what the Greeks meant by the Word [Logos]." And Thought is incorporated into the immodest title of the final part, *As Far as Thought Can Reach.*

The personification of the Word "in the beginning" is Lilith, who is the principle of Creative Imagination, as Shaw makes quite clear in the conversation between Eve and the Serpent in Act I. The Serpent tells Eve that Lilith created Adam and herself. "How did Lilith work this

miracle?" asks Eve. "She imagined it," answers the Serpent. Thus not
only did Lilith create Adam and Eve, but she is the creative principle
behind the play itself, behind Shaw's writing of it. We do not see Lilith
at the beginning. We can only infer her existence from the fact of the
text/drama as a work of imagination itself.

In form, the allusiveness of *Back to Methuselah* lies in the specific
models Shaw draws on for his drama. With Wagner's *Ring,* the most
notable are the Bible, Plato's *Republic,* Bunyan's *Pilgrim's Progress,* Swift's
Gulliver's Travels, Blake's prophetic Books (in particular, *Jerusalem*), Nietzsche's *Thus Spake Zarathustra,* and, perhaps, Hegel's *Phenomenology of
Mind.*

The allusions and the themes and motifs that recur in the play are all
concepts or ideas, and a dialectic develops, more or less, after Plato and
Hegel. So, for instance, those concepts that are part of the dialectic of
creative imagination are desire, thought, language, knowledge, conscience, will, vision, curiosity, hope, and dream. This play of ideas is his
dramatic form, a Shavian dialectic; but in Plato, Hegel, and Shaw,
dialectic has a double nature. The play of concepts, the development of
ideas, involves experience, the experience of an individual in the world.
So, for instance, in Plato's *Symposium,* the experience of sexual desire
leads to, or gives way to, a "platonic" or spiritual desire for beauty. In
Heartbreak House, the experience of heartbreak leads to the "beginning
of wisdom." Within *Back to Methuselah,* "death"—the concept of death
and the experience of death in life, which are both acts of imagination
and catalysts for imagination—is at the root of his dialectic in this play.
This aspect of his design makes the allegory equating human life-
span with creative imagination, or the increase of life expectancy with
heightened imaginative activity, not as arbitrary as it might otherwise
appear.

Having created his drama of imagination and its characters from the
realm of the fantastic, it is worth bearing in mind Shaw's warning against
the assumption that the giants and gods in Wagner's drama, *The Ring,*
were superhuman. "The danger is that you will jump to the conclusion
that the gods, at least, are a higher order than the human order. On the
contrary the world is waiting for man to redeem it from the lame and
cramped government of the gods. . . . Unless the spectator recognizes in
it an image of the life he is himself fighting his way through, it
must needs appear to him a monstrous development of the Christmas
pantomimes."[19] Thus, in *Back to Methuselah,* we should be prepared to
see the long-livers and the Ancients, as well as the biblical characters, the
short-livers, infants, and automata, as only aspects of ourselves, as
incomplete moments in the drama of becoming more fully human. In
this dialectical drama of creative imagination, the play itself acts as a

catalyst for the imagination of the audience. If we respond to it fully, it will involve an understanding, a certain sympathy of Shaw's playing with ideas, in the play that most closely mirrors his own mind. That understanding is not a simple one. It is not simply a question of understanding his themes and his techniques. It also means entering into the playing with ideas ourselves, in the context of our own experience; it requires creative imagination of its audience. This is the same imaginative effort that is required of all of us if we are to overcome the problems of civilization that led, for example, to the First World War. In spite of the Ancients' disparagement of art, this is a highly complex artistic and theatrical achievement that goes some way to justify Shaw's hope that "Back to Methuselah is a world classic or it is nothing" (5:703).

Notes

1. This essay is an expanded version of a talk given at the Bernard Shaw Summer School held in Dublin in June 1991. Indispensable guides to the labyrinthine construct of the imagination that is *Back to Methuselah*, which I have found particularly illuminating, are Martin Meisel, *Shaw and the Nineteenth-Century Theater* (Princeton: Princeton University Press, 1963); Margery M. Morgan, *The Shavian Playground* (London: Methuen, 1972), pp. 221–38; Valli Rao, "*Back to Methuselah*: A Blakean Interpretation," *SHAW* 1 (1981): 141–81; Daniel Leary, "*Too True to Be Good* and Shaw's Romantic Synthesis: A Religion for Our Times," *SHAW* 1 (1981): 183–203; and John A. Bertolini, *The Playwrighting Self of Bernard Shaw* (Carbondale: Southern Illinois University Press, 1991), pp. 131–36.

2. *Collected Plays with Their Prefaces*, ed. Dan H. Laurence (London: Max Reinhardt, 1970–74), 5:348. Subsequent references appear in parentheses in the text.

3. Stanley Weintraub, *Journey to Heartbreak: The Crucible Years of Bernard Shaw 1914–1918* (New York: Weybright & Talley, 1971), has the best biographical account of Shaw at this period.

4. Bernard Shaw, *Common Sense about the War*, originally published on 14 November 1914 as a supplement to the *New Statesman*, reprinted in *What I Really Wrote about the War* (London: Constable, 1930), p. 103.

5. This is an example of Shaw's mind at work. In Part 4 of *Back to Methuselah*, this "general raising" becomes one of the names for the Napoleon character, General Aufsteig (*aufsteigen* is German for "to raise").

6. *Common Sense about the War*, p. 94. By italicizing certain words in quotations I intend to stress the importance for Shaw at this period of the concept of imagination, its related metaphors of vision, and its significance for human development.

7. Ibid., p. 96.

8. *Collected Letters 1911–1925*, ed. Dan H. Laurence (London: Max Reinhardt, 1985), pp. 542–43.

9. Bernard Shaw, "Peace Conference Hints," in *What I Really Wrote about the War*, p. 315.

10. See *The Religious Speeches of Bernard Shaw*, ed. Warren S. Smith (New York: McGraw-Hill, 1965), p. 77.

11. See Charles A. Berst, "In the Beginning: Poetic Genesis of Shaw's God," *SHAW* 1 (1981): 5–41, where he suggests that Shaw made a similar effort in the 1890s at formulating his religion.

12. *Collected Letters 1911–1925,* pp. 576–77.

13. Bernard Shaw, *The Perfect Wagnerite* (London: Constable, 1898; revised, 1913), p. 31.

14. Jonathan Swift, *Gulliver's Travels* (London: Penguin, 1967), p. 329.

15. Letter to Sasha Kropotkin-Lebedeff, *Collected Letters 1911–1925,* p. 701.

16. See Bertolini, p. 144.

17. *Collected Letters 1911–1925,* p. 727.

18. Ibid., p. 575.

19. Bernard Shaw, *The Perfect Wagnerite,* pp. 31, 1.

REVIEWS

The War of the World-Betterers

Selected Correspondence of Bernard Shaw: Bernard Shaw and H. G. Wells. Edited by J. Percy Smith. Toronto, Buffalo, & London: University of Toronto Press, 1995. xxv + 242 pp. Index. $40 (Canadian).

Shaw the inveterate stage manager was always on the lookout for fellow "world-betterers" to cast in the Fabian drama, and in H. G. Wells he hoped he had found a star. Seemingly possessed of Shavian "realism," Wells drew satiric portrayals of the world as it is, envisioned a better world, and gave scary warnings of what would happen if the vision was not achieved in such a powerfully imaginative way that many additional supporters were won to the cause of reform. The Wells act needed polish and practice. He was no public speaker, and Shaw worked hard to "make a decent public man" of him (66), but generally Shaw approved. Shaw was much taken aback, however, whenever Wells revealed that he was also one of the many Peter Pans of this period, trapped in adolescent patterns of behavior that defeated his own ends. When, for example, Shaw admonished him to "grow up" to the responsibilities of a world-betterer by seeing his ideas through, Wells often replied with letters that were little more than sophisticated tantrums, which only drew further scoldings and ridicule and contributed to the defeat of Wells's principal practical attempt at reform. The Shaw and Wells relationship is well displayed in a correspondence between them that sometimes seems an exercise in quarreling, but a fascinating read it is, and thanks to the expert editing and glossing of J. Percy Smith, Professor Emeritus at the University of Guelph, we now have a collection that gets to the heart of the conflict.

Part of "The Selected Correspondence of Bernard Shaw" series, *Bernard Shaw and H. G. Wells* follows the series goal of presenting accurate texts of mostly unpublished letters and situating them in the context of Shaw's life and career. Smith's "Introduction" starts things off with a judicious summary of the Wells-Shaw relationship, balancing the quarreling aspect of the correspondence with an acknowledgment of their common cause in reforming a world they intensely disliked. They seemingly had good intentions toward one another, for the most part, and often good relations as well, most of their jibes being of the playful and teasing sort. Wells signed one letter "H. G. B. Shawells" as a concession to their common purpose (41), but at times the relationship looked more like a Punch and Judy show than a model of camaraderie. Shaw can share some of the blame for this in that, when Wells attacked the Fabian Old Gang, he advised Wells, "It is only by placing ideas in clear opposition that any issue can be created. It is our business & yours to create an issue; and if you consider your feelings or ours in the matter you are simply unfit for public life and will be crushed like a trodden daisy" (27). Wells was temperamentally disinclined to consider the feelings of others anyway, although easily hurt himself, so Shaw here was simply advising Newcastle to import coal.

Smith organizes the correspondence chronologically, occasionally including letters by others when germane, but his glossing, with headnotes before letters and annotations after, highlights the themes and issues in a way that facilitates thematic or topical study. The central issue was the cause of world-betterment, which had several facets and phases, not the least of which was the attempt to keep up a personal friendship between families in the midst of a sometimes ugly power struggle between the men, Charlotte Shaw being the chief peace-maker. It is fair to say that Wells picked the fight and Shaw gave better than he got. In fact, Shaw thought that "it was like boxing with a novice who knocked himself out in every exchange" (212).

Shaw's main tactical concern was to keep up a united front in the reform movement. "The idea must not get about that the Wellsians and the Shavians have any differences," Shaw summed it up late in life. "They are in fact the same body" (190). The elderly Wells replied, "our minds move in sympathy" (191). However, Wells had often seemed reckless of public solidarity, wreaking havoc among carefully built coalitions through a condemnatory, insulting style that brooked nothing short of unconditional, ignominious surrender of his opponents, in imitation of the war games that Wells doted on as a child. When Wells in

1930 became embroiled in a libel suit with the Society of Authors, Shaw counseled Wells to "be content with victory without blood and humiliation of the vanquished" (158).

Twenty years before Wells took up political agitation, Shaw as a young gadfly had learned the hard way that "You must study people's corns when you go clog dancing" (30), becoming at last an excellent committee man who could play the Fabian like a fiddle. He had few peers either on the debating platform or in smoothing ruffled feathers. As Smith states, Wells was "no match for Shaw in either oratorical or parliamentary skills" (45). When Wells attacked the Fabian Executive in 1905 in his usual insulting fashion, an exasperated Shaw finally hit back with such an impressive array of forensic weapons that Wells was made to look rather a fool, which just sent Wells off into ever more towering tantrums and vituperative rages. Some of his letters are nothing more than extended name-calling. J. Percy Smith asks, "why, if Shaw and Wells so liked each other and their minds moved in sympathy, did they so often bash each other about?" (xvi). He speculates that the part that was good-natured sparring was probably much enjoyed for its own sake, but there is a darker side to this correspondence that suggests enjoyment was sometimes no factor. At times it was like a war of the worlds, but in this case earthling Shaw was so much better equipped that Wells's inept Martian attack had no chance.

The correspondence begins, in this collection, with a 1903 letter in which Wells critiques Shaw's recently published *Three Plays for Puritans* and defends his own work, *The War of the Worlds*, against an earlier critique of Shaw's, an exchange of works and criticism being customary throughout the relationship. When Wells would sometimes skip the "constructive criticism" in favor of just trashing the work and the author, Shaw would reply, "I want help, not cheek" (83). The most charitable way of putting this aspect of the correspondence is that they were both concerned that their partner in world-betterment not disgrace or compromise the cause with inferior or misleading art. Ironically, although Wells at first hob-nobbed with such high-art types as Henry James, Joseph Conrad, and Ford Madox Ford, Shaw ultimately comes off as more concerned with artistic quality than Wells, who grew increasingly didactic and preachy in his novels as Shaw generally became less so in his plays, Shaw having hit upon the device of the preface to separate the polemic from the parable, as he advised Wells to do (123).

The next issue in the correspondence is currency reform as an aspect of Wells's proposal for a world state, but Shaw's long critique of that reform as useless in itself ends with a sudden shift to the damning of science, Wells's favorite remedy, as "abject credulity." Shaw concludes, "These doctors all think that science is knowledge, instead of being the very opposite of knowledge: to wit, speculation" (8). Wells immediately shot back, "Science is neither knowledge nor speculation. It is criticism ending in Wisdom" (10). Thus was launched the War of the World-Betterers, Shaw never budging in his debunking of what he saw as an outdated mechanistic science that stood in the way of real reform by substituting technological progress for moral growth and Wells never ceasing to dream of a perfect and perfecting science, however ambivalent he was about certain applications of science. It was inevitable too that they should take opposite sides on the issue of evolution, Wells playing the pessimistic Darwinian to Shaw's optimistic Lamarckian. As they debated the role of biological evolution in the cause of world-betterment, both wondered whether evolution was a destroyer or preserver, but Shaw had faith in the benevolent purposefulness of the universe in the long run while Wells rather doubted any purposefulness, benevolent or otherwise. Naturally, they heatedly disagreed about the use of animals in experimentation, Shaw arguing that it was immoral for a higher species to abuse a lower while Wells enthusiastically supported the likes of Pavlov. To summarize their views on science and evolution, Smith has provided Shaw's marginal comments on Wells's *Science of Life* in a form that reads like a dialogue (143–48).

The issue that led to the most acrimony was Wells's ambitious plans, launched in 1905, to overhaul the Fabian Society to make it more influential in politics. Shaw had enticed Wells to join in 1903 in hopes that Wells would demonstrate the leadership capabilities that would allow Shaw, the Webbs, and others of the Old Gang on the Fabian Executive to retire. It was Shaw in fact who invited Wells to attack the Fabian status quo and even explained how it should be done, but here Shaw had overreached himself, trying to stage manage the unmanageable. Many of Shaw's letters are patient expositions of how Wells must acquire the committee habit (39), learn how to get documents through a corporate body (29), and above all avoid insulting the very people he is trying to work with: "The energy that wastes itself in senseless quarrelling would reform the world three times over if it could be concentrated and brought to bear on Socialism. The whole thing is so ridiculous that if you once let your mind turn from your political object to criticism of the conduct and personality of the men around you, you are lost. Instantly you find them insufferable; they find you the same; and the problem of how to get rid of one another supersedes Socialism, to the great advantage of the capitalist" (38). Wellsian ideas were not the problem so much as Wellsian behavior. The man simply did not know the etiquette of public debate.

With the advantage of hindsight one can see that Wells's plan to expand the Society Fabian and perhaps even make of it a political party somewhat on the order of the Social Democrats might have nipped the Labour Party in the bud and so utterly changed the nature of the socializing of Britain that a Thatcherite reaction would not have been possible. Still, there was much wisdom in the original Fabian policies of keeping its membership small and relatively manageable, independent of any party, and dedicated to slow, peaceful enlightenment of the body politic and permeation of the government with socialist ideas. Thus the Old Gang did not deserve the slamming that Wells gave it (or the later bitter satire in Wells's *New Machiavelli* [1910]). Given that the Executive itself had called for reform, it was simply socially inept of Wells, as Charlotte Shaw put it, to "try the Executive; with the foregone conclusion that we were to be condemned" (33). At one point Wells had sufficient support among Fabians, especially the young, to accomplish his revolt, and the Old Gang longed to be replaced by younger leaders, but his intolerant, impatient nature betrayed him, and his support vanished as Shaw stood to debate him.

Although Wells could magnificently inspire solidarity among reformers, he seemed to know little of, or perhaps care little about, the engineering of it, especially of the tact, diplomacy, and strategy needed to keep like-minded but idealistic people bonded in common effort, which was Shaw's special skill. In his second marriage, Wells left tact and most of the other social graces to his wife Jane, but in the Fabian Society he must not have listened to her any more than to Shaw.

Wells was essentially an "idea man" and "motivator," his mistake being to attempt to go beyond the general to the specifics of management and installation, and when the inevitable enormous gap opened up between idea and action, it made his ideas seem merely grandiose, without practical application, and made him "a novelist bombinating in vacuo" (39). Wells loved the excitement of intellectual battle and could inspire others to think globally and cosmically, but he had little grasp of how to put grand ideas to work. When Wells entered the scene of practical politics with his assault upon the Fabian Executive as the first step in a swift revolution toward a world state, Shaw, growing tired of such politics, had long since concluded that, as Smith puts it, "the way to betterment meant much more of patient toil than of exciting drama" (xiv), and he had come to think of reform as a slow, steady process by determined reformers who were not loathe to confront the smallest of details.

The impatient, lofty-minded Wells and the relatively patient, practical-minded Shaw were separated not only by temperament but by vastly different experiences. Shaw tried to share what he had learned. Many of his letters reflect his concern to educate Wells in the ways of reform, which he knew by long experience and Wells had only looked at from outside. Reform just was not as easy and obvious as Wells thought. In one letter Shaw commented, "I believe you are so spoiled by living in a world of your own invention, peopled by your own puppets, that you have become incapable of tolerating the activity or opinions or even the phrases of independent individuals. . . . Jane is greatly to blame. She spoils you in a perfectly disgusting manner" (14).

One issue related to the Fabian brouhaha was the effect of Wells's open adultery and advocacy of sexual reform upon both the cause of world-betterment and his family. Wells is notorious for his philandering, and his emotional development seems to have frozen, as indicated by his conducting his adult sex life like a romantic but randy sixteen-year-old. A great charmer, he seems to have been very successful in starting and sometimes even in developing lengthy relationships with certain women, mostly young and mostly of the New Woman sort, who shared his romantic fantasies up to a point, but he seemed unable to keep up a responsible adult sexual relationship over the long haul or to maintain much respect for the female as a sex. Like Peter Pan, Wells always wanted to be "free." With some of the women that was not much of a problem since sexual freedom was what they wanted, too, and some had actually been the aggressor, but it was definitely a problem for whoever was his wife, particularly the wife who lasted the longest, second wife Jane, who, serving as hostess during his first great blaze of fame, had to keep up a smiling front in the face of his publicized adultery. It is a tribute to his powers of persuasion that he was able to talk Jane into granting him freedom to philander, but that came at the cost of much damage to his reputation and perhaps to her psyche as the private Jane grew ever more estranged from the public Jane. The crucial example of infidelity occurred just as he was trying to take over the Fabians, and the combination of his public flaunting of conventional marriage morality and his insulting behavior toward the Old Gang was more than most Fabians could stomach, thus contributing to his defeat. In his letters the author of *The Philanderer* and "The Revolutionist's Handbook" made it clear, however teasingly, that he was in agreement that sexual mores needed radical reform, but Shaw as usual advocated tempering such radicalism with practical considerations, such as the need for Wells to be fairer to his wife and more discreet with the public.

Wells's desire to be free of sexual responsibility found parallels in other phases of his life, such as his wish to be free of the responsibilities of his reform of the Fabian and of his world-bettering in general. He was always asking for the impossible, and Shaw could never get Wells to see that it was unfair for him to be so angry with people who could not gratify his impossibilism. Wells disarmingly had glimpses of the fact that Never-Never Land was too often his principal address, his many househuntings, house-buildings, and house-movings, with usually a corresponding switch of sex partner, being symptomatic of his inability to get external reality to accord with his dream world. That realization, however, usually came only after he had deeply offended most of his friends, allies, and sex partners by declaring them the deluded ones in as insulting a language as he could muster. That his considerable charm and boyish enthusiasm often won him forgiveness does not cancel the fact that he often went out of his way to make forgiveness necessary. Shaw forgave him many times, but there is an unusual edge to some of Shaw's letters that reveals that Wells took him closer to the brink of nastiness than perhaps any other correspondent. Knowing the magnanimous good humor that prevails in most of Shaw's correspondence, one appreciates that only a very exasperating person could have brought this out in Shaw. Not that Shaw did not exasperate Wells as well. Shaw's characteristic refusal to play along with Wells's death kitsch upon the occasion of Jane's slow dying of cancer was couched in polemical terms that Wells viewed as tasteless and insensitive, leading to a major cooling of their relationship.

Two such practitioners of overstatement were, it seems, fated to clash, especially when each took the other too literally. Shaw, being the more playful of the two, needed allowances to be made, but Wells was too in earnest to accomplish that. For example, Shaw sometimes played at being infallible, but Wells in reading Shaw's letters forgot the twinkle in the eye that would have accompanied such playing in person. Then Wells would reply with a ferocious display of his own infallibility, especially when angry at being thwarted or criticized, and the thunderbolts were awful to behold. That there was obviously little hope of either Infallibility converting the other perhaps accounts for the ferocity of their attacks on each other. Nothing less than storming the citadel would do. But it was mainly Wells who wanted complete capitulation. Shaw, always the dialectician, better understood that theirs was not an identical view of the world but rather a complementary one: "These differences between us are very fortunate; for our sermons complement instead of repeating one another; you must read us both to become a complete Wellshavian" (216). Wells, however, insisted on the surrender of Shaw's will to his. The Shavian must give way to the neo-Shavian or Wellsian.

The quarrel went well beyond the epistolary. It seems to be embedded in much else that Shaw wrote. In fact, I am left with the growing belief that Wells was a profounder influence on Shaw's playwriting than is generally acknowledged. There is at least a book in exploring this influence, starting with what *Man and Superman* and *Back to Methuselah* owe to Wells's "scientific romances." The influence was of course often dialectical, as in the way Shaw uses the character of 'Enry Straker to satirize Wellsian notions of the technocratic New Man. Straker represents the new scientifically-trained engineering classes that Wells hoped would take over the leadership of the coming world state, but Shaw shows this "advanced" individual to be surprisingly atavistic in his familial and tribal loyalties, no Superman he. And the character of Jack Tanner may owe more to Wells than to its announced model, H. M. Hyndman, Wells's *Anticipations* finding many echoes in "The Revolutionist's Handbook," especially on the topics of sex, marriage, and eugenic breeding, which are given a Shavian twist. Then, too, the crazy weekends at Wells's various country houses remind one of the action of *Heartbreak House,* and Captain Shotover is very Wellsian in his weapons inventions and wish for a magical death-ray. I can read hardly anywhere in these letters or in Wells's works without noticing ideas, characters, situations, problems that later pop up in Shaw's plays in different guises.

I can find little fault with this book. The statement that "When [Shaw] and Wells met [Shaw] had had almost two decades of working at socialism, intellectually and practically" (xv) seems inaccurate in light of the 1895 date cited as the date they first met and 1882 seeming to be the year that Shaw first gave socialism much of a look. Occasionally something is left unglossed that one wishes had not been, as in the reference to Wells's "thesis of the Resentful Employee" (94), and the glossing of the mulberry tree reference may incorrectly refer it to Milton (213). In the Mike Wallace *Biography* film, Shaw, planting a tree, says that he is not going to be outdone by Shakespeare, who had "a vulgar mulberry tree." Also, it is unfortunate that considerations of length kept out the large number of letters written to newspapers as contributions to public debates on a wide range of issues. Although there is little to complain of here, there is much to ponder and enjoy.

R. F. Dietrich

Indefatigable!

Selected Correspondence of Bernard Shaw: Bernard Shaw: Theatrics. Edited by Dan H. Laurence. Toronto, Buffalo, & London: University of Toronto Press, 1995. xxv + 241 pp. Index. $40 (Canadian).

"Theatrics," Dan H. Laurence tells the reader in his Editor's Note, is an American usage: "Theatrical effects or mannerisms, histrionics," says the *American Heritage Dictionary.* A purist on the Eastern Seaboard of the

Atlantic—a latter-day Shaw, shall we say—may be inclined to resist a title that lacks the sanction of the Queen's English, but, there being no standard word that quite fits the bill, "theatrics" may be accepted as saying precisely what this selection of 182 letters is about: Shaw following his profession as a playwright; Shaw of the "histrionic instinct," of "theatrified imagination" (Laurence's phrases). It brings to mind the compelling anecdote with which Michael Holroyd concludes the third volume of his biography. "Well," G.B.S. says, waving goodbye to a famous actress he had been entertaining in the garden at Shaw's Corner, "Did I give a good performance?"

His performance in *Theatrics* is what one would expect: sparkling, witty, impish, ferocious, shrewd, wise: Shaw in top form dealing with what mattered to him most: plays, the theater, actors and actresses. But the book raises the question whether this selection as Shaw's encore—the encore being for his "performance" in the *Collected Letters*—is strictly necessary, given that the *Collected Letters* already amply represents him in all his theatrical guises. The question hovered unanswered during the reading of the first few batches of letters. The first, dated 21 June 1889, to Janet Achurch is a case in point. It was Shaw's second letter to her, and he had already declared his undying passion (the day after meeting her) on 17 June (*Collected Letters* 1: 215–16), and it shows a young and not entirely insincere Shaw honing his craft as an epistolary lover. Which is all very well, except that the *Collected Letters* shows this side of him more than adequately. Much the same applies to the letter to Elizabeth Robins (No. 3): nothing especially new in it. Also the letter to Ellen Terry missing from Christopher St. John's collection. She was ill, she became quite seriously ill with the flu, but "that theatre must be kept open," she told Shaw on 30 January 1897, particularly as it was the opening night—a revival—of W. G. Wills's *Olivia;* and Shaw, responding the next day with the letter featured in *Theatrics* (No. 15), raved about the play, indirectly about her playing—and said not a word about her illness. Nothing new in this either. And the three letters to Mrs Beatrice Mansfield, a large quota in a volume as selective as this (115 correspondents), about sundry possibilities for Shaw's plays in America, also amount to very little of significance because nothing came of all these overtures.

One could go on like this—and miss the point entirely. *Theatrics* is not an "encore" but a necessary supplement to what is already in print. The letters in the collection are of great intrinsic interest, as they are bound to be; there is more than enough for scholars to get their teeth into because Shaw is always quotable, always saying something worth while; and what is more, the letters, lifted as they have been from Shaw's other activities, thus highlighted, accumulate, one by one, to provide a series of self-portraits, generally unwittingly, of what may be seen as the three phases of Shaw in the theater: the thwarted genius of 1889 to 1904, writing plays furiously, seeking opportunity here, there, everywhere, and failing to make headway in London; then the emergent, assertive, more firmly entrenched maestro of 1904 to 1920, conducting with dazzling virtuosity the ever-developing, ever more complex Shavian concerto as its music spread over the globe; and finally from 1920 to 1950 the colossus, the Grand Old Man of the Theater, his wit as sharp as ever, his mind keenly focused, his manner increasingly benign. This hidden "autobiography" is the subtext of the collection, its cohering principle; and it is a safe assumption that Dan Laurence was guided in his selection, at least in part, by this consideration.

So, then, Shaw's letter to Oscar Wilde in 1893 (No. 5), given in its entirety, is not here only to make good the truncated version in *Collected Letters* (1:384), but also to underscore the way Shaw projects himself—it may be more accurate to speak of the role he assumes—when addressing an acquaintance who at that time was well ahead of him as a literary celebrity. It is a strained effort; and the more Shaw tries to relax, the more strained he becomes: "I hope soon to send you my play 'Widowers' Houses,' which you will find tolerably amusing, considering that it is a farcical comedy. Unfortunately I have no power of producing beauty; my genius is the genius of intellect, and my farce its derisive brutality." Shaw's correspondence with Henry Irving in the same period (1896, Nos. 10 & 11) about the possible production of *The Man of Destiny*, is distant, courteous, and unambiguous about the terms he was asking, and it reveals, if not the same straining after effect as with Wilde, an apologetic stance that one finds hard to reconcile with the "G.B.S." of the *Saturday Review*. "I am heartily sorry that the play is so trivial an affair; but when I wrote it I had no idea it would be so fortunate. Even now I am not quite persuaded that it is more than a fancy of Miss Terry's." This is in the first letter; in the second he has recovered his *savoir faire* and, having made it clear that he will not be fobbed off with £50 and vague promises of a production *and* the false position this will land him in, tells the great actor that, "[I]f you will excuse my saying so, I'm hanged if I'll be put off for Shakespear. Take him away: he lags superfluous." All that came of this was disappointment; more disappointments followed, but he continued to try hard, willing himself to be almost aggressively positive about prospects that remained bleak, going so far as to speak to Janet Achurch about a syndicate for forming a "Shaw theatre, where we could all seriously learn our business" (No. 14).

Yet there were moments when repeated failure induced a more somber frame of mind. On the sixth day of the new century, a time of re-assessment for all, he told the actor, Frederick Kerr, about the plays he had written and his failure to have them accepted for the London stage (No. 24): The managers "sometimes thought they wanted a play by me until they saw the prompt book; and then they knew well enough that they didnt want *that*. So I published the plays, and gave up the theatre as a bad job."

Four years later the theater became a very good job when the second phase of his career beckoned from the stage of the Royal Court Theatre. Here in next to no time he became the most talked about, the most controversial, and, for a while, the most fashionable of contemporary playwrights. Suddenly the busy but abortive theatrics of the years before becomes the busy productive theatrics of full engagement. It all seems pell-mell, and although a glance at the dates indicates that the selection of letters takes one through the months and years at a sober pace, the image Shaw projects is of a man rushing at opportunities, now that they have come at last, with indefatigable zest. One minute he is telling Granville Barker that it would be very bad business to produce *Rule Britannia* (the working title of *John Bull*) before Parliament meets again (No. 32): "In fact, it mustnt be done. You will sell a lot of stalls to the political people; and the Irish M.Ps will fill the pit." And the next, as the seasons get under way, he is telling his Candida, Kate Rorke (No. 35), "The last act—*your* last act—was immense: if I had met you immediately after it I should simply have eaten you; so I ran away." He could not stop himself from being a ferocious Casanova (at a safe distance) with his younger prettier actresses, although later he was less inclined to gobble this particular delectable up (No. 39): "James is very exasperating; but oh, my dearest Kate, couldnt you pretend to love him just a little for my sake?" Then there was Louis Calvert, his successful Broadbent in *John Bull,* threatening to make a mess of Undershaft in *Major Barbara* (No. 44): "I don't complain of anything except the end of the second act; but for that I have no words strong enough to describe your atrocity: you will scream through endless centuries in hell for it, and implore me in vain to send you ices from heaven to cool your burning tongue." No words strong enough? For Shaw? He always had the words.

Meanwhile, there were his translators to keep an eye on. His 1908 account of the trouble many of them had caused him quite conceivably persuaded his correspondent, fellow playwright Henry Arthur Jones, to draw back from forays on the Continent (No. 58): "My European reputation was engineered systematically on a heroic scale. . . . The results have been very varied. At best, as in Germany, the translator [Siegfried Trebitsch] took no advances & sent me £500 a year in half fees & half prices for translated essays, articles &c &c. Sweden [Hugo Vallentin] has also been a great success. The opposite extreme is France, where I have had to extricate my translator [Augustin Hamon] (an

Anarchist) from debt, build a large house for him on mortgage, and lend him the money to pay me the interest, besides advancing him more than he is ever likely to repay. . . . The trouble, including occasional lawsuits, is sometimes so devilish that I curse the day when international copyright was invented. . . ."

As these middle years went by and play succeeded play and Shaw's position as the dominant English playwright was consolidated to a point where even the carping and quibbling of the critics could not hurt him, one venerable institution held out against his reputation—the stage censorship. *Mrs Warren,* refused a licence in 1898, and *Blanco Posnet,* refused in 1909, were still proscribed, and the reader of plays at the time (1916) would not budge. There are two private letters to the Lord Chamberlain, Lord Sandhurst, on the subject (Nos. 88 & 89). Shaw did not write letters to the Lord Chamberlain in the 1890s or even 1909 about the censorship; he wrote to the papers instead. Things had changed since then. "Some day," he told Sandhurst after giving him a courteous, controlled earful on the subject, "you will have a Reader of Plays with some knowledge of the [White Slave Traffic] and some conscience as to the guilt of the nation in the business. We shall both be dead by that time, probably." Not as pugnacious as in years gone by, almost resigned to the fact of invincible institutional stupidity, but he argues his case with the same old pertinacity and clarity, pursues his crusade with the same commitment.

He told the American actor William Faversham in 1917 (No. 91), "What my plays need is . . . energy, vivacity, impetuosity of delivery, brightness and high spirits. The man I dread is the actor who thinks that Shaw is 'intellectual drama,' and that he must play it as if there were a sick person in the house, the result being that the whole audience presently consists of sick persons." Perhaps this defines the personality rather more comprehensively than it does the plays, and the wonder is that as he entered into what are referred to as "declining years," these qualities remained with him, infusing the letters of his third phase with everything that is enduringly quintessentially Shaw.

He attended a performance of *Geneva* during its first run in 1938 and wrote to H. K. Ayliff (No. 152), "What a horrible horrible play! Why had I to write it? To hear those poor devils spouting the most exalted sentiments they were capable of, and not one of them fit to manage a coffee stall, sent me home ready to die." A mere eighty-two, he was far from ready to die; and the world still needed him. In 1942 he gently corrects a young actor, Patrick Crean, who as Bohun in *You Never Can Tell* had dared to blow a whistle to silence the quarrelling Clandons, instead of shouting at them as directed (No. 158): "Obviously the whistle will get a laugh. I should probably join in if I were in the audience; BUT

I should at once class you as a crude low comedian and not as a serious actor. An actor can always get a laugh in the theatre by doing something absurdly silly; but whether it pays him to do so depends on whether he desires to get future engagements as a clown or as a serious comedian. . . . I should not engage a clown, however gifted, to play any part in You Never Can Tell. . . . " Responding to a query from F. Aicken in 1948 (No. 174): "I never write with my tongue in my cheek. Your view of Arms and the Man is correct. Played farcically for the laughs, they will not come; and the performance will be a failure. Played melodramatically it will be dull and ridiculous and disappointing. Played sincerely as serious 'anti-romantic' comedy it never fails." To his old companion in arms, his first Magnus, Cedrick Hardwicke, who wanted to act in and direct *Caesar and Cleopatra* (No. 175): "But you must not produce as well as act. . . . [P]roducing [directing] is the ruin of an actor: instead of thinking of his own part he watches the others all the time and ceases to be an actor. That is what happened to Granville-Barker. As to the scenery you will be up against the Pascal film: a bad film except for the scenery. . . . " By this time (1949) he had long given up attending the theater, but he had no need to: all theater he desired was in his mind.

The other wonder is that his age and inordinate fame did not turn him into a curmudgeon. He would stick to his guns in matters of business and could be sharp if he reckoned he had to be (and indeed there were times, not reflected in *Theatrics,* when he was "difficult"), but the over-riding impression is of a sage willingly dispensing the wisdom of fifty and more years of experience, at least to those who struck him as deserving of attention. Shaw always had largeness of mind, but there is more than this here, not always evident in the first and second phases of the career—largesse of spirit.

Two constants run through these letters: the first is Shaw dealing with his actors and actresses, advising them on their playing, correcting, chiding, encouraging, and as often as not, almost incidentally, dropping remarks about his plays that an aspirant stage director could and should distill from these pages as a Ready Guide to Shaw's Plays in Production. A few examples have been given; there are many more. The second constant is Shaw dealing with his business interests. There may seem to be too many of such letters—about royalties, the licensing of plays, the possibility of this or that production at this or that theater, refusing to waive royalties for charity performances (on unexceptional grounds, it may be said)—but in this, as much as in the more purely "theatrical" component of the selection, gaps are filled in, the career is enlarged. "You should never think of anything else but money: I never do," he told an erring American lady (No. 94). Never? Not quite.

There are gaps in the collection. Two major ones are explained:

Archer and Murray will feature in future volumes of the series; but theatrical Shaw without these two essential members of his audience depletes the book. Grein in the early 1890s and Daly in the early 1900s, neither of whom is well represented in the *Collected Letters,* are also missing. Shaw would almost certainly have corresponded with them during these crucial periods of his career, and the fact that nothing has surfaced to augment the little available in print seems to indicate permanent loss—important letters mislaid by a neglectful Grein, cast aside by a casual Daly. As for the continuing absence of anything from Thorndike-Casson in the 1920s and 1930s, it looks as though nothing survived the London blitz. We may be sure that, had any letters to these four still been around, Dan Laurence would have tracked them down by now.

The editing is everything one would expect from a scholar recognized by a generation of Shavians as an information-retrieval system of unparalleled swiftness and accuracy. The breadth and depth of knowledge Dan Laurence brings to his comments and explanatory notes makes any quibble fractious—nit-picking of minuscule proportion. Nevertheless, a few nits may be picked, one or two puzzlements mentioned, without detracting from the achievement. The postscriptal editorial comment to Shaw's letter to Lord Sandhurst (No. 88) names E. F. S. Pigott as the original reader of plays to whom Shaw refers; the reference seems more likely to be to Pigott's successor, Redford. In a letter of 23 March 1920 to Viola Tree (No. 105), Shaw mentions *Blanco Posnet* as having been fully licensed; yet the licence permitting London productions was issued only in 1921 (p. 127). The error is probably Shaw's (mistaking the 1916 Liverpool production of the play as *carte blanche* for wider presentation, which it was not); an editorial comment to remind one of this anomaly would have helped. Daly in London in 1911 producing *Arms and the Man* is described (p. 112) as a "luckless performer." It is a matter of interpretation, but Daly would seem to have deserved no more and no less luck from Shaw than he got. C. B. Purdom (No. 154) is introduced as "a journalist, author, and stage director, who at one time operated a theatre in Welwyn Garden City." As among the first independent producers to stage Shaw's plays outside London (in 1909) and as a pioneer in Shavian-Barker studies, Purdom deserves more than this, notwithstanding the rule of brevity governing editorial entries. The same rule no doubt prevented Laurence from filling in an entertaining detail in Shaw's set-to with the *Daily Express* when that paper published unauthorized information about *The Doctor's Dilemma* ahead of production in 1906 (No. 49). The editor refused to tender an apology, as Laurence reports, but he did place a rave notice of the play on the front page and a large glamorous picture of Lillah McCarthy as Mrs Dubedat on an inside page of his paper—placating gestures that did nothing to placate Shaw.

Shaw wrote to his old Independent Theatre associate Grein in 1933 (No. 140), "I wonder why the devil you and I, being respectable men of fair abilities and reasonable conduct, should have succumbed to the craze for the most absurd and disreputable of human institutions." Thank heavens he did succumb; and here, thanks to Dan Laurence, Shaw celebrating his craze for that disreputable institution is given deserved currency. *Theatrics* helps launch the new series of letters in fine style.

Leon H. Hugo

Wit, Common Sense, and Prophetic Vision

Bernard Shaw. *The Complete Prefaces, Volume 2: 1914–1929.* Edited by Dan H. Laurence and Daniel J. Leary. London: Allen Lane, 1995. ix + 626 pp. Index. $45.00.

The appearance of Shaw's collected prefaces in the monumental and masterful three-volume edition by Dan H. Laurence and Daniel J. Leary is a cause for celebration. Surely one of the three or four great twentieth-century collections of prose, the prefaces are a literary and intellectual marvel. A wonderfully eclectic potpourri of observation and argument, politics and religion, autobiography and anecdote, they are infused with the moral and artistic vigor that characterized Shaw himself. Sweeping across a dizzying mountain of concerns, the prefaces totter thrillingly on the precipice of sheer genius, and from that rarefied vantage point the view is glorious.

Yet historically the prefaces are also a curiosity, voluminous append-ages often related obliquely to the work they precede. To account for his prefatory impulse, in a preface (of course!) to a 1928 series of reprints of prefaces to his plays, Shaw placed himself in a literary tradition dating back to Dryden. Claiming that the only connection between the prefaces and the plays was that "they have hitherto kept company within the same book covers," he saw no difficulty in separating one from the other. Like the shipwright who builds a house with the material left after building his ship, Shaw constructed prefaces, his "houses," with his superfluous but good material, and "you can inhabit them without ever having seen the ships, just as you can travel in the ship without knowing anything about the house." In yet another preface to prefaces (this time the 1934 one-volume edition), Shaw once again yoked his verbal profligacy to frugality: "a simple desire to give my customers good value for their money by eking out a pennorth of play with a pound of preface," which ended in a volume "which is all preface and no play."

Shaw's penchant for prefaces was not confined to his plays, however. He also appended prefaces to his prose writings great and small (including collections of his correspondence), as well as to literary and non-literary efforts by others. The second volume of the Laurence and Leary comprehensive edition consists of more than three dozen prefatory pieces written from 1914 to 1929. Ordered chronologically, they range from the familiar to the unpublished, from the massive prefaces to *Misalliance, Androcles and the Lion,* and *Back to Methuselah* to the brief and previously uncollected prefaces to a labor yearbook, a volume by Cecil Chesterton, and a catalogue of an exhibition of illustrations for T. E. Lawrence's *Seven Pillars of Wisdom.*

The writings provide an invaluable cultural commentary by an omnipresent and penetrating contemporary observer, one who accurately identified himself as "a castigator of morals by ridicule." Three quarters of a century later Shaw's stunningly lucid prose explodes with energy and wit as the new, the unpopular, even the dangerous view are fearlessly voiced. In a previously unpublished preface, he alludes to the nearly universal vilification unleashed by his pamphlet *Common Sense about the War,* noting that he was denounced by the Germans until the Allies called him pro-German. But whether considering the prospects of Christianity or the role of socialism, whether supporting the trade unionism of clerks or exposing the conventions of the pseudo-sex play that mistakes duels, divorces, and the "Trade unionism of married women" for sex, Shaw challenges the assumptions of his audience. That intended audience is composed of literate, intelligent readers prepared—even eager—to tackle lengthy argument, appreciate moral complexity, understand nuanced language, and recognize satire. The blockhead, the blind ideologue, and the literalist are condemned to the hell of misinterpretation and misreading.

Although he always dwells in this world and offers plentiful advice about human relationships in the here and now, the threat to western civilization posed by the Great War hovers over Shaw's hopes and fears concerning the future of the human race. Envisioning a new world order of highly evolved superbeings, he traces biology and theology, history and myth as he spins out prophecy and embroiders his themes. In the 1919 preface to *Heartbreak House,* he provides a retrospective on the political and moral failings leading to the recently concluded war.

He also suggests the disastrous effect the war had on the theater: an audience of soldiers could be pleased not only with "a bevy of pretty girls and a funny man," but even with "a bevy of girls pretending to be pretty and a man pretending to be funny."

Two years later in the preface to *Back to Methuselah*, he decries the flimsiness of civilization in a Darwinian world. Rejecting the "poison" of Darwin for the vitalism of Lamarck, extolling self-control over appetite, Shaw cites the imperative for Creative Evolution. For him it is not a question of a new religion, "but rather of redistilling the eternal spirit of religion and thus extricating it from the sludgy residue of temporalities and legends that are making belief impossible." Although no one ever tires of stories of miracles and saints, "healthy enjoyment" requires that "no one shall believe them literally."

Ever a missionary in the cause of advancing the human race, Shaw continues his discussion of evolution, religion, and miracles in the Preface to *Saint Joan*. He cites forces at work that use individuals for transcendent purposes, but he accounts for Joan's voices and visions by calling her "a Galtonic visualizer," one who saw "imaginary saints just as some other people see imaginary diagrams and landscapes." Here he refers to Cambridge biologist Francis Galton, who conducted investigations in heredity and eugenics, and when Shaw wrote that "the street is full of normally sane people who have hallucinations of all sorts," he was referring to himself as well as to Joan. He also described himself when he asserted that Joan's ideal biographer had to be capable of regarding woman "as the female of the human species, and not as a different kind of animal with specific charms and specific imbecilities." Her historian could not be an anti-feminist and had to believe women "to be capable of genius in the traditional masculine departments." Quite ahead of his time (and of some in our time), he thought that the exemption of women from military service was founded "not on any natural inaptitude that men do not share, but on the fact that communities cannot reproduce themselves without plenty of women. Men are more largely dispensable, and are sacrificed accordingly."

Shaw posits that Joan might have been canonized sooner had she not been an "unwomanly woman." A decade earlier his feminist sympathies were articulated in the Preface to *Androcles and the Lion*, where he cites the tyranny of parents who condemn their daughters to wait in genteel idleness for a husband instead of acquiring a profession. An advocate of economic independence, he thought that marriage should be as "easily dissoluble as any other partnership." As it was, women "for the sake of their children and parents, submit to slaveries and prostitutions that no unattached woman would endure." When he extends the call for "One

Man One Vote" to include "One Woman One Vote," he alludes to
Scripture, putting universal suffrage and equality of income in the
ethical and Christian context his audience would find persuasive.

Shaw's ethical concerns are illuminated differently in "Killing for
Sport," which could have appeared in today's *New York Times* magazine
instead of *Hearst's Magazine* in 1914. Here Shaw denounces as an idiot
the person who kills animals merely to pass the time, and not even out
of villainy or passion or greed. Rather endearingly, he admits to talking
to animals, to feeling gratified that robins sometimes treat him with
confidence, and to viewing two lions at the Regent's Park Zoo quite
differently and personally—one was a morose brute who deserved to be
shot if he broke loose, another seemed a lovable St. Bernard. In the
Androcles preface, he claims to have petted the cordial beast. Shaw
possessed what he praised: "the broad outlook and deepened consciousness which admits all living things to the commonwealth of fellow
feeling."

Still topical is the preface to Sidney and Beatrice Webb's *English Prisons
under Local Government.* Shaw labels as blood sports those punishments
such as flogging that provide pleasure to the spectators. Even though
demoralizing to the public, he argues that such savagery is not as cruel
as imprisonment. Again Shaw's views could have come from a current
newspaper or magazine article as he inveighs against retribution (another word for vindictiveness) and insists that deterrence comes from
the certainty of punishment, not its severity. Although he finds reform
irreconcilable with retribution, he favors capital punishment since society has a right to defend itself against "intolerably mischievous human
beings."

Naturally Shaw has much to say about artistic matters. His theory of
translation is expounded in the Preface to *Jitta's Atonement,* his adaptation of the play by his German translator, the novelist and playwright
Siegfried Trebitsch, who had done much to further Shaw's reputation in
Germany. Shaw's desire to translate was not at all inhibited by his slight
knowledge of German, which was, it seems, limited to several holidays at
Bayreuth and getting his way in shops and railway stations. When he
discovered that Trebitsch used words not in the dictionary—at least not
in *his* dictionary—Shaw managed "to divine, infer, guess, and co-invent"
the story of Jitta. He also discovered that "when it comes to translating a
play the mere translation is only the tiniest fraction of the business," so
he translated the audience as well with Vienna becoming London and
New York, as he translated "one theatrical epoch into another." However
Trebitsch's "melancholic delicacy" could not withstand Shaw's "barbarous and hilarious occidental touch," which Trebitsch found not very
hilarious as he complained of the liberties Shaw took but would never

have forgiven had they been perpetrated upon his own work. Yet Shaw's translation was entirely consistent with his playwriting practice. Whether turning the final act of Shakespeare's *Cymbeline* into *Cymbeline Refinished*, casting the Bard in his own play (*The Dark Lady of the Sonnets*), or depicting Napoleon, Caesar, or Joan, Shaw always employed the "translator's treacheries" in interpreting his characters, themes, and actions.

One reason Shaw remains such lively reading is a prose style liberally sprinkled with vivid autobiographical vignettes, slices of life that offer insight into the man and his personality. We see the terror-stricken small boy placed on a frisky pony by a malicious relative, and the man concludes that "the right to liberty begins, not at the age of 21 years but of 21 seconds." The frightened young boy who felt forced by his own braggadocio to come to the rescue of a friend's pet goat becomes the man who turns that adventure into an exemplum illuminating the impostures of parents and schoolmasters. We see Shaw in the 1880s in the British Museum Reading Room observing Thomas Tyler, a man so disfigured by goiter that he was shunned by virtually everyone. Shaw, not one "to be frightened or prejudiced by a tumor," struck up a warm friendship with Tyler, and the two often talked of literature and "things of the spirit."

There is a revealing glimpse of Shaw one showery day at the exact moment he comes upon a stern William Archer, appearing eight feet tall, draped in a buff-colored mackintosh, with a small comely woman clinging to his arm. Shaw "feared the worst," and "sure enough" he was introduced to the future Mrs. Archer. At times movingly, he uses the occasion of this preface, written in 1927 for the posthumous publication of Archer's *Three Plays*, to sketch his most complete account of his relationship with his stalwart friend: "I still feel that when he went he took a piece of me with him."

In another vein, there is Shaw's tale of a bachelor party one evening in about 1878. The men entertained themselves by hotly debating whether it was true that the Secularist Charles Bradlaugh had taken out his watch and challenged the Almighty to strike him dead in five minutes if He existed. To decide the matter, to the horror of everyone present, Shaw took out his watch and threatened to utter the same challenge. His host was forced to intervene and forbid the experiment, for "when thunderbolts were in question there were no sceptics." Nevertheless Shaw thought the leader of the evangelical party seemed a bit preoccupied until the five minutes had elapsed.

Brilliant as a meteor shower, the prefaces are an intellectual pyrotechnics where glimpses of Lawrence of Arabia, Catherine the Great, or Jack the Ripper are just as likely to burst into view as those of Shakespeare, Ibsen, or Wagner. Yet the inspired and visionary wit is grounded in a savvy wisdom. There are aphoristic sayings. "The secret of being misera-ble is to have leisure to bother about whether you are happy or not. . . . A perpetual holiday is a good working definition of hell" (Preface to *Misalliance*). There are famous definitions: "A genius is a person who, seeing farther and probing deeper than other people, has a different set of ethical valuations from theirs, and has energy enough to give effect to this extra vision and its valuations" (Preface to *Saint Joan*). There are pronouncements on art: "It is ridiculous to say . . . that art has nothing to do with morality. What is true is that the artist's business is not that of the policeman" (Preface to *Overruled*). To "the wiseacres who repeat the parrot cry that art should never be didactic," Shaw delightedly boasts that "great art can never be anything else" (Preface to *Pygmalion*).

Both those readers familiar with the prefaces and those introduced for the first time to the unique pleasures of Shaw's prose will welcome this meticulous edition. To maximize the collection's usefulness, the editors generously and scrupulously supply a cornucopia of important information—identifications, annotations, datings, clarifications, back-ground—either concisely and unobtrusively in brackets in the text or in thorough (but never overwhelming) explanatory footnotes. The editors' persistence and energy in tracking Shaw's references and quotations (or none-too-accurate paraphrases) to their sources invite great admiration. Most certainly we owe them a debt of gratitude for lavishing so much time and care to ensure that we have the complete prefaces, so com-pletely edited.

In the Preface to *Heartbreak House* Shaw consigns the great thrones of Europe to ephemeral history, the Solons and Caesars to failure and obscurity, "but Euripides and Aristophanes, Shakespear and Molière, Goethe and Ibsen remain fixed in their everlasting seats." So, too, forever fixed is Shaw, playwright and preface writer.

Sally Peters

Intersections

Stanley Weintraub. *Shaw's People: Victoria to Churchill.* University Park: Penn State Press, 1996. 255pp. Index. $29.50.

"Unless you can shew me in the context of my time, as a member of a very interesting crowd," Shaw once told his biographer Archibald

Henderson, "you will fail to produce the only thing that makes biography tolerable." If the dozen personalities Stanley Weintraub has assembled as "Shaw's people" do not exactly constitute a crowd, they certainly are interesting—even a loser like Shaw's inept German translator, Siegfried Trebitsch. Literary figures predominate: Wilde, Mencken, Yeats, Joyce, Frank Harris, T. E. Lawrence, O'Casey. But there are also Edith Adams, who inspired Jennifer Dubedat in *The Doctor's Dilemma;* "General" William Booth, founder of the Salvation Army; Winston Churchill; and Queen Victoria.

Actually Shaw never met the Queen who, in turn, Weintraub speculates, may have mercifully gone to her rest without having heard of the socialist renegade, George Bernard Shaw. Yet Shaw was hardly an iconoclast where the Queen was concerned. He could criticize the pomp and circumstance of the Diamond Jubilee or the grotesquely prolonged funeral ceremonies inflicted upon Victoria's corpse; the Queen herself, however, won his admiration. Her clear voice and precise English, regal carriage, impeccable manners, and air of authority made her in the coming playwright's eyes a consummate actress on the political stage. Their values, too, were not fundamentally dissimilar. Both believed in the virtues of civilized behavior and the benign exercise of power; both were optimists who believed in progress and, although often surrounded by fools, the perfectability of human nature. Paradoxically Shaw, the prophet of a new order, could with truth call himself "an old Victorian."

One could further speculate (although Weintraub does not) that Queen Victoria chiefly gripped Shaw as a mother figure. It was one of her most puissant images: Great Mother, not only to the nine children she bore but to the nation and the British Empire. Starved for attention and affection from his own mother, Shaw must have subconsciously drawn comfort from the nurturing presence of a devoted wife and mother on the throne. "You will notice that Queen Victoria, even when she was most infatuatedly in love with Prince Albert, always addressed him exactly as if he were a little boy of three and she his governess," he wrote to an actress struggling to capture Ann Whitefield's superb ladylikeness. How, one feels, he would have liked being that little boy of three. Victoria exemplified what he had missed in his own life: a commanding, stable mother-figure who was, above all, loving. Weintraub persuasively identifies the Queen's influence on *Caesar and Cleopatra, Man and Superman, The Doctor's Dilemma,* and even *Pygmalion.* One could argue that all Shaw's vital female geniuses owed their creation in part to the image of the powerful Queen who shaped the young Shaw's world.

Shaw never met Queen Victoria; similarly, it was William Booth's *In Darkest England and The Way Out* that influenced him rather than the man himself. He never met H. L. Mencken, who wrote the first critical assessment of Shaw's plays in 1905, nor did he ever cross paths with his ex-Dubliner compatriot James Joyce. Although Shaw had actual friendships with Yeats, O'Casey, Harris, and Churchill, the curious effect of *Shaw's People* is to underline Shaw's essential isolation, giving weight to the gibe attributed to Oscar Wilde, "Shaw has no enemies, and none of his friends like him."

Partly this isolation was due to Shaw's own personality—a fastidious shyness masked by a garrulous, ex-cathedra way of laying down the law, neither of which encouraged intimacy. Shaw's isolation was also due to his ability to countenance people of very different persuasions. Although Winston Churchill, for instance, was Shaw's vital genius incarnate, the hard-drinking politician and the playwright seldom saw eye to eye; nor, for all Churchill's personal charm, did Shaw care to hobnob with him at Mayfair dinner parties or country houses. Similarly, although Yeats was his countryman, Shaw felt less than sympathy for the poet's Celtic mysticism, while Yeats deplored what he considered Shaw's machinelike mind. Often Shaw's great success got in the way of friendship. Joyce's works may bristle with Shavian allusions, as Weintraub demonstrates, but personally the struggling writer seemed to have regarded G.B.S. chiefly as a potential subscriber at three guineas to *Ulysses.* (Shaw declined to buy.) O'Casey felt genuine affection for Shaw, but the poverty he concealed from G.B.S. as play after play failed at the box office made true intimacy with the millionaire impossible. Shaw's virtue also made him a hard man to know. Compared with his godlike magnanimity, "Shaw's people" often look shabby indeed: Mencken turning surly about his former idol in print; Frank Harris whining and begging; Joyce having a negative review of *The Shewing-up of Blanco Posnet* sent to Shaw with the request that he promote *Dubliners;* Siegfried Trebitsch whining and begging. But then a god *is* lonely.

Not that Shaw is all saint by any means. "Why," asks Weintraub, "did Shaw suffer a donkey of a translator for nearly fifty years?" Did he feel in Trebitsch's debt? Did he enjoy insulting the barely adequate translator? Did he like bantering with him in German? Did he pity him? All of the above; yet surely there is another reason that Shaw encouraged bad translators like Augustin Hamon and Trebitsch: his obsessive need to control. Had he hired talented translators, his plays might have slipped out of his hands, taking on—as with all good translations—artistic lives of their own. With Trebitsch and Hamon he could play the schoolmaster, correcting and recorrecting their work, certain that his version would remain the work of genius. Shaw put up with an execrable biographer for the same reason: although Archibald Henderson failed utterly to capture Shaw on the page, Shaw had the satisfaction of controlling the biography, as he did Hesketh Pearson's later and far better version of his life.

Like Churchill, Weintraub is "a master at extracting mileage from his material": although revised, updated, and in some cases largely rewritten, eleven of the twelve essays in *Shaw's People* have previously appeared in print. It is useful, however, to have the revisions collected here under one cover. And although occasionally one may wish for deeper probing, Weintraub's knowledge of Shaw's life and the other lives that it intersected is prodigious, while the cross-pollinations he discerns and explores invariably illuminate. *Shaw's People* effectively combines biography and literary criticism; one closes the volume feeling educated in unexpected ways about Shaw, Shaw's associates, and his world.

Margot Peters

The Latest Biography of Shaw

Sally Peters. *Bernard Shaw: The Ascent of the Superman.* New Haven and London: Yale University Press, 1996. xvi + 328 pp. $28.50.

To my knowledge Sally Peters's *Bernard Shaw: The Ascent of the Superman* is the first biography of Shaw to have appeared since Michael Holroyd's monumental four-volume *Bernard Shaw.* One might have questioned the need for another biography so soon, but Peters shows that a book like hers is justified, a book that gives a thorough, sympathetic, and in-depth account, focusing upon the facets of Shaw's mind and psyche rather than upon his multifarious activities in many realms. Peters's book is not all-inclusive (she has little to say about Shaw after 1920, for example, but this is understandable since Shaw's attitudes and beliefs were firmly established by then). Her restriction of focus and coverage allow her to explore minutely Shaw's persona and values as they had developed to their maturity. Her careful scholarship and the concentration of her presentation lend her work authority so that we are led to accept tentatively her conclusions even when we may not want to give complete assent to all of them. The documentation is exhaustive but not obtrusive; she relies for the most part on published sources, and her work reveals how much can be done using the vast number of primary sources now in print.

She is concerned, above all, in demonstrating how closely the life and the work are connected and then how revealing the written record is in illuminating the man and his ideas. Her discussion is not confined to Shaw's sexual beliefs and experiences, but this aspect of her book is its most original and arresting. In fact, she has much to say about standard Shaw subjects such as vegetarianism, Jaeger clothing, the "new woman," Fabianism, the rivalry with Shakespeare, vaccination, and the medical profession, to mention some. She uses available materials to give us new insights into these familiar matters.

Peters follows Rosset, O'Donovan, and Holroyd in her discussion of the early Dublin years. She views these years as formative for Shaw but, on the whole, as traumatic. She regards Bessie Shaw as unsympathetic and her lack of affection and solicitude as having a profoundly negative impact on her son. Peters also regards Vandeleur Lee as a disruptive influence upon the family. Shaw did respect Lee's devotion to music and his decisiveness, Peters feels, at the same time that he felt much rivalry toward him. In London Shaw was grateful to Lee for the opportunity to write musical reviews for the *Hornet* while Lee's inability to do so fed Shaw's sense of superiority to a rival. In Dublin Shaw had been an outsider, and he continued to be one in London. There, however, he wanted to demonstrate that with the arts it was he who was the insider. Over the years, Shaw, not without controversy, did manage to prove himself to be such an insider.

Shaw was attracted in the 1880s and later to a number of women in London, ingratiating himself with them but managing to evade commitment to any one of them. Shaw also projected his ambivalent attitudes toward women at this time through the central male characters in his novels, who express both attraction and repulsion toward the women who interest them. Shaw's own relationships with women, then and later according to Peters, follow a similar pattern, woman being viewed alternatively as "forbidden temptress" and "unattainable goddess," as "punishing fury" and "nurturing virgin," as signifying "flesh, blood, and mortality," in contrast to an ethereal reality toward which the appreciative male continually aspires. So the early relationship with Alice Lockett is marked by tension rather than devotion, Shaw needing to dominate her and to prove his masculinity but also to elevate the relationship to a transcendent, universal realm.

Peters extends her discussion of Shaw's sexual psychology in her thorough analysis of his consummated affair with Jenny Patterson. Peters establishes the fact that Shaw was not an avid lover and that he was sometimes critical with Jenny to the point of cruelty. According to Peters, Shaw revealed a fear of being absorbed in female flesh at the same time that he enjoyed the sexual experience and felt the need to establish through it his masculinity. While he wished to dominate Jenny, he also felt aversion to her insistent demands, reacting like a stereotypical Victorian woman in an aversion to sex, feeling a sense of violation approaching rape. He did not wish to satisfy all Jenny's sexual demands or else was unable to do so, Peters maintains, and in any case, his treatment of her reveals his sadistic and masochistic tendencies toward women. At the same time he championed the rights of women in *The Quintessence of Ibsenism,* advising them to rebel against the compulsion to honor the call of duty, including the sexual obligations that marriage entails. In his other significant relations with women in the 1880's and 1890's (with Grace Gilchrist, Grace and Constance Black, Eleanor Marx, Annie Besant, Edith Bland, Janet Achurch, Bertha Newcombe, Florence Farr, and May Morris) he revealed that he did not crave the flesh-and-blood woman so much as the romantic, idealized image of her created by his imagination. Such a complex of attitudes underlies the famous erotic correspondence with Ellen Terry, the letters dwindling after the two actually met.

It is possible, Peters says, that Jenny Patterson may have been the only woman with whom Shaw had sex. Peters observes that such sexual constraint can be observed in three types of men: the religious, the ascetic, and the homosexual. This is the first time she uses the word homosexual (half-way through her book), and much of the rest of the book is devoted to the exploration of homosexual tendencies in Shaw. She does not use the term but infers that Shaw was a closet homosexual, whether he knew it or not (she does refer to him at one point as "a closet Urning," Edward Carpenter's term for a homosexual). Her interpretation of Shaw's psyche is suggestive and in large part convincing, mostly because she presents her evidence without insisting upon her interpretations of it. She alleges that if Shaw had been born a century later he would have been better able to understand his nature and to have come to terms more forthrightly with it. While Peters is generally persuasive, I also regard Shaw's celebration of ecstatic heterosexuality and his denial of homosexuality in "To Frank Harris on Sex in Biography" (in *Sixteen Self Sketches*) as a strong statement. If nothing else, it may indicate how deeply divided Shaw's psyche actually was.

In her presentation of Shaw's eroticism, *Candida* plays an interesting role. The burden of the play, Peters asserts, is simply this: "art offers salvation, sex damnation." At the end, Marchbanks seeks transcendence rather than physical fulfillment in sex in a highly allusive atmosphere, which suggests, Peters says, a coded homosexuality. Shaw denied any connection between himself and Marchbanks, but the warmth of the denial, Peters thinks, would indicate some autobiographical basis for Marchbanks.

Shaw's views on sex and allied matters bear the impress of two radical thinkers whom he knew, Edward Carpenter, who was a homosexual writer and publicist, and Havelock Ellis, who was heterosexual, married to a lesbian, and wrote about sexual "inversion" in his *Psychology of Sex*. Although Shaw did not follow Carpenter in his theories that there was a "third sex" (homosexuals) and that artists were of necessity homosexuals, he was sympathetic to Carpenter's views of the aspiring nature of "Urnings" and of the artist as a special individual or "genius." From Ellis Shaw derived an idea that appealed to him: the contrast between two types of inversion, that of "the noble invert" versus that of the degraded "pervert." Shaw could relate to Ellis's concept of the noble invert while he regarded the sexual practices of the pervert with abhorrence. It is possible, too, that the homosexuality of Samuel Butler, an idol of Shaw's, may have been an unconscious influence upon him from the background. In a chapter in Peters's book entitled "Ascent of the Naked Skeleton," Peters cites a letter to Janet Achurch (14 April 1896) in which Shaw describes an ecstatic experience he had had out-of-doors in the South of England and from which he, as artist and genius both, could derive guidance henceforth for the conduct of his life. Peters regards this episode as central to the establishment for Shaw of his identity: "Crucially, for his self-identity as man and artist, he now bore the secret brand of the invert." The intense aspiration of the "noble invert" Shaw also regarded as germane to the superman, the ideal individual toward whom he aspired and toward whom the race ought also to aspire.

Peters has a revealing chapter on Shaw's marriage to Charlotte Payne-Townshend. Peters emphasizes the casual manner in which Shaw "accidentally" became a husband. Lacking from the beginning was passion, which was replaced by a sense of personal drama that made him rather than his bride the center of the affair in his publicizing of it. Charlotte did not frighten nor threaten him because she made no sexual demands, Peters concludes, and the abstention from sex in their relationship was as much Shaw's wish as hers. The couple's decision not to have children may also have been as much Shaw's as Charlotte's since the children of the "noble invert" (a class to which Shaw had apparently begun to realize that he belonged) were, according to Ellis, likely to be "neurotic" and "a failing stock." At least Shaw and Charlotte seem to have been reasonably satisfied with their rather unusual marriage.

One of the most interesting friendships that Peters explores is that between Granville Barker and Shaw. From the first it was a close and affectionate relationship, and Peters feels that there were at least homosexual elements in it, even if they may not have been acknowledged as such by the principals. For example, Shaw used coded homosexual terms to describe Barker to Ellen Terry: "genius," "noble soul," and "handsome Italian." The situation may also represent the "idealized" Greek love of an older for a younger man, "the higher order of love appropriate to the aesthetic artist." Shaw never did get over the break with Barker, a break instigated by Barker's second wife, Helen Huntingdon, whose antipathy to Shaw was intense, as was Shaw's toward her. This was the one triangular relationship in Shaw's life (between himself, Barker, and Helen) that did not work out in his favor (if we except the triangle with himself, Charlotte, and Mrs. Patrick Campbell). Peters also cites interesting connections between the Shaw-Barker relationship and *Heartbreak House*. She finds a parallel between Hector Hushabye and Barker, viewing them both as having been seduced by a woman and money into an unproductive, idle existence, Shaw as it were warning Barker to avoid such a life of drift. In Barker's contemporary *The Secret Life*, the unattainable love between Joan Westbury and Evan Strowde may mirror, Peters thinks, the frustrating love the two playwrights felt for each other.

What on balance can we say of Peters's book? Throughout she maintains a dispassionate yet sympathetic attitude toward Shaw as she attempts to untangle and synthesize the various facets of his mind and persona. Her accumulation of evidence to support her conclusions is impressive and gains our partial or complete credence, depending upon how we react to it. In this review I have been able to cite only a portion of the sources she uses for documentation. She presents new or forgotten aspects of Shaw's life, personality, beliefs, and interests for us to consider as she weaves them into a novel, complex, and coherent pattern. The drift of her book suggests the need to reconsider Shaw's erotic life; the significance that she attaches to her evidence of Shaw's inversion is difficult to ignore. The texture of the book is dense; almost every page induces us to pause and ponder. Peters's deep and intense immersion in her project results in a profound critique that is certain to alter in some degree the way in which we think of Shaw.

Frederick P. W. McDowell

Shards of Shaw

Martha Fodaski Black. *Shaw and Joyce: "The Last Word in Stolentelling."* Gainesville: University Press of Florida, 1995. xvi + 445 pp. $49.95.

It would be manifestly unfair (and unkind) to begin a review of *Shaw and Joyce: "The Last Word in Stolentelling"* by quoting Tanner's comment

to Mendoza in Act III of *Man and Superman:* "You are sacrificing your
career to a monomania." But it has to be said that this book does display
an exaggerated devotion to one subject. "[M]y book," the author tells
us, "is about literary borrowings of storyteller James Joyce heretofore
unexamined in depth—his 'stolen-telling' from George Bernard Shaw"
(1). To call its argument overstated would be almost an understatement,
for its claim is nothing less than this: that (apart from Joyce himself)
Shaw is the predominant presence in Joyce's work. Something of the
book's atmosphere of excited dedication is conveyed by a sentence in its
preface: "I also want to express my gratitude to a graduate student
whom I met in Vancouver, who already knew that Joyce encoded Shaw
as 'fish' in the *Wake* (I've misplaced his name. Sorry!)" (xii). Then
Chapter I introduces the pervasive Shavian element in *Finnegans Wake:*

> Shaw's influence on his "somewhat dreamy" double is perhaps
> most obvious in his first and last prose works, *Stephen Hero* (the
> first version of *Portrait*) and *Finnegans Wake.* When Joyce found
> his own voice in *Dubliners, A Portrait of the Artist as a Young Man,*
> and *Ulysses,* he assimilated Shavian theory into literary practice
> almost antipathetical to Shaw's. However, in the *Wake* the kinship
> and the polarity of the two Irishmen become, I believe, almost
> an obsession to Joyce. After my epiphanic realization that Joyce's
> "NIGHTLETTER" (308.21), never sent to Shaw, begins to make
> sense as a parodic portrait of Shaw, I overcame my resistance to
> the "Allmaziful" text by admitting that G.B.S. is a major pres-
> ence at the wake. (18)

This lengthy, devoted piece of literary detective work is a case of
Possession—and in fact Byatt's novel is alluded to at one point.
    Contrary to the ordering of its title, *Shaw and Joyce* is very much a
study of Joyce rather than of Shaw. It is published as part of the Florida
James Joyce Series, and it makes no claim to illuminate Shaw's work. It
does aspire, however, to benefit Shaw's literary reputation by associating
him with Joyce. "I also hope," the author says, "to shine Shaw's tarnished
halo by indicating his relevance to the acknowledged master of modernist fiction" (5). Shaw "has been passé among the literati," and this study
is, among other things, an attempt to make him respectable among
sophisticated readers. Shaw can be revalued as the major influence on
the modernist master, but he is certainly no modernist himself. Martha
Fodaski Black's Shaw is a logocentric, and indeed phallocentric, conveyer
of political and social messages. "Although Shaw has been passé among
the literati, perhaps because we remember him as a white-bearded,
twinkly-eyed leprechaun in a television documentary or because his

writing seems too logocentric, his wit and wisdom are as germane to us as they were to Joyce, who was, as some of my readers may be, discomfited by the thought of admitting the value of his incorrigible sallies into the realm of ideas" (23). (One of Black's sources for quotations from Shaw's writings, by the way, is a 1965 volume entitled *Bernard Shaw: Selection of His Wit and Wisdom.*) Shaw's wit and wisdom do not, unfortunately, seem to give rise to particularly good plays. His "talky dramas debate issues" and convey "the social messages that we think of as Shaw's métier" (112, 194). Altogether, he is a writer who lacks Joyce's subtlety and complexity.

> Whereas Shaw's writing is often discursive and digressive and his plays are sometimes interminably talky, Joyce's carefully honed prose is fertile ground for literary archaeologists who delight in delving into the Talmudic intricacies of texts. Shaw's prose does not demand or repay the hermeneutic exegesis under which Joycean texts often deliver up treasure. Despite his persistent attacks on nineteenth-century theater and mores, Shaw's writings are in many respects a carryover from the phallocentric prose of the nineteenth century, aiming to provoke thought and discussion through clarity of expression. (4)

An interesting, valuable way of relating Shaw and Joyce might be to consider modernist, Joycean elements in Shaw's plays—some of the late plays in particular—but that is not what is being attempted here.

The connection between Shaw and Joyce that will first come to most people's minds, I think, is Shaw's refusal to subscribe for a copy of *Ulysses* in 1921. It is also well established that Joyce read *The Quintessence of Ibsenism;* that he owned and had read a number of Shaw's other works; that he reviewed the Dublin opening of *The Shewing-up of Blanco Posnet* for an Italian newspaper in Trieste in 1909; that he blamed Shaw (erroneously) for the rejection of his play *Exiles* by the Stage Society in 1918; and that in the same year his English Players Company in Zurich put on unauthorized performances of *Mrs Warren's Profession* and *The Dark Lady of the Sonnets,* for which he was rebuked by the Society of Authors on Shaw's behalf. All of this is in *Shaw and Joyce,* as it was in previous sources, including Stanley Weintraub's 1986 article in the *Journal of Modern Literature,* "A Respectful Distance: James Joyce and His Dublin Townsman Bernard Shaw." But here in *Shaw and Joyce* the story of their connections is background to Joyce's borrowings from "his literary sire."

The method of the book is to go through each of Joyce's works, discovering references to Shaw and his plays—to read and reinterpret

Joyce "by Shawlight," or, in another of the author's favorite phrases, to examine Joyce's works "by the Shavian arc light." The assumption is that Joyce's "real sympathies were Shavian" (4), but that he felt compelled to conceal his debt to Shaw, mainly for fear of alienating his avant-garde supporters such as Ezra Pound. This means that "as secret sharer Joyce was condemned to loneliness and a guilty secret that ate at him" (414–15). It also means that most of the Shavian allusions in Joyce's work are not obvious, and must be dug for. "In my digging," Black says, "I kept coming up with shards of Shaw. Hence this book to share my discoveries" (4). The biggest and richest archaeological site by far is *Finnigans Wake*, which is combed over in a gargantuan 145–page chapter, but Black also finds concealed allusions to Shaw, or reflections of his ideas, in *Stephen Hero, A Portrait of the Artist, Dubliners* (in which each story is examined in detail), and *Ulysses*. Patterns that other readers might place in the wider context of the early-twentieth-century culture of individual rebellion are firmly and specifically attached to Joyce's "secret mentor." Shaw's "covert disciple" is also his Oedipal rival, and father-son relationships in Joyce's work are connected with Joyce's anxiety of influence. Harold, one might say, takes his place beside Leopold.

Black's determination to uncover shards of Shaw leads to some strained readings of texts. In *Dubliners,* Mahony's catapult in "An Encounter" is glossed at some length with reference to Shaw's views on killing for sport (122), while in "A Painful Case" Mr. Duffy's "taste for Nietzsche links with Shaw's interest in the superman" (136). Polly in "The Boarding House," it is seriously suggested, might have enjoyed a different destiny if she had only managed to see a performance of *Getting Married* (168–69). And the awful Mrs. Kearney in "A Mother" becomes a feminist hero: "Thus, contrary to critics like Walzl who believe that Mrs. Kearney is an obnoxious, pushy mother, the story reveals, in the Shavian arc light, sympathy for the betrayed mother, who is far more courageous and purposeful than the muddling male supremacists who are in charge" (146–47). In the discussion of *Ulysses* (in which Leopold Bloom shares qualities with Shaw and with characters in his plays) we are informed that Shaw would not have approved of Molly's manner of dressing (244–45), and Bloom's desire to improve transportation out of Dublin for vacationists provokes this comparison: "Equally concerned with transportation, in his Fabian tracts Shaw promoted linking up 'entire manufacturing districts with a network of electric trams which will enable English to work in towns whilst their children grow up in the country instead of the slums' " (232; there are three errors in the quotation from Shaw's text).

The heart of the book, and its most valuable part, is the chapter on "Methuselah at the Wake," which uncovers vast numbers of Shavian allusions (some undeniable, some likely, some debatable) in *Finnegans Wake*. The identifications go far beyond the numerous allusions noted by Joyce scholars such as Adaline Glasheen (*Third Census of "Finnegans Wake,"* 1977, p. 261) and those subsequently proposed in Weintraub's article. For Black, Joyce's last work is "the Irish dish whose main ingredients are Shaw and Joyce," and Shaw "might have been astounded to discover that Joyce's duplicitous book is based in large measure on the five plays which make up *Back to Methuselah*" (395, 262). The character Shaun is Shaw, and so partly is H.C.E. Here is one example of the kind of elaborate exegesis that yields such conclusions:

> Joyce's druidic Balkelly is described by an Oriental voice that sounds like Confucius of part 3 of *Methuselah*. "The Thing Happens": "he savvy inside true inwardness of reality . . . Rumnant Patholic, stareotypopticus, no catch all that preachybook, utpiam" (611.20–25). An avatar of the Shaw/Shaun character, the archdruid Balkelly is not a Roman Catholic but a pathetic and pathological contemplative ("Rumnant patholic") all too like the remnant Catholic who thought of Shaw as a twin, because Joyce too had contemplated a religious life, one very different from the one he simultaneously approved and disdained in Shaw's Methuselan vision. Joyce's Protestant bishop is a "stareotypopticus"—a starry-type pop, a stereotype and stereopticon maker of a "preachybook," a three-dimensional utopian ("utpiam") vision about how to atone, from the Latin *ut* plus *piamen*. It is a vision that not everyone "caught." The "preachybook" is simultaneously *Methuselah* and the *Wake*, Joyce's at-one-ment with himself and Shaw regarding his sins against the old playwright. (306–7)

Black does demonstrate that in *Finnegans Wake* Joyce drew copiously from *Back to Methuselah*, along with many of Shaw's other works as well as Frank Harris's and Archibald Henderson's biographies and contemporary newspaper reports of Shaw's activities. In her research, she has not only examined Joyce's books thoroughly from her point of view, but has also looked carefully through a wide range of Shaw's work in order to identify the shards, and we should be grateful to her for this assiduous digging. Her book has its virtues, but a sense of proportion is not one of them. Although the book does reveal that Joyce had a strong (and mostly hostile) interest in Shaw that manifests itself in *Finnegans Wake*, in the end this study does not provide real evidence that he built his literary career on a monomania.

J. L. Wisenthal

John R. Pfeiffer*

A CONTINUING CHECKLIST
OF SHAVIANA

I. Works by Shaw

Shaw, Bernard. *The Adventures of the Black Girl in Her Search for God* (excerpt). See *Simpleton of the Unexpected Isles* in Books and Pamphlets, below.

———. *Bernard Shaw and Gabriel Pascal.* Edited by Bernard F. Dukore. Toronto: University of Toronto Press, 1996. Publishes 268 pieces of correspondence by the two writers, including 109 previously unpublished items by Shaw. Dukore's introduction provides a full account of the Shaw/Pascal relationship. To be reviewed in *SHAW* 18.

———. *Bernard Shaw's Book Reviews, Volume 2: 1884–1950.* Edited by Brian Tyson. University Park: Penn State University Press, 1996. To be reviewed in *SHAW* 18.

———. *The Columbia Book of Bernard Shaw Quotations.* Edited by Bernard F. Dukore. New York: Columbia University Press, 1997. Not seen.

———. *The Complete Prefaces, Volume 3: 1930–1950.* Edited by Dan H. Laurence and Daniel J. Leary. London: Allen Lane, 1997. The third of three volumes. To be reviewed in *SHAW* 18.

———. Extract from autograph note signed "G. Bernard Shaw," written on cropped conclusion of a printed statement. "It may amuse you to learn that the Belgians themselves appreciated my view of this case so well that they came to me to state it for them to the United States." No date given in catalogue description. In *Remember When Auctions, Inc.* Catalogue number 40, part 3 (30 October 1996), item 3444. $150–$250.

———. Extract from autograph postcard of 23 February 1916 signed "G. Bernard Shaw"

*Thanks to Richard E. Winslow III for discovering and supplying page copies for a number of entries in this list. Professor Pfeiffer, *SHAW* Bibliographer, welcomes information about new or forthcoming Shaviana: books, articles, pamphlets, monographs, dissertations, films, videos, reprints, and the like, citations of which may be sent to him at the Department of English, Central Michigan University, Mount Pleasant, MI 48859.

to bookseller Hugh Rees, asking to be sent *A Short History of England* by G. K. Chesterton, "& charge to my a/c." In *Occasional List No. 3*, 1996: Michael Silverman, P. O. Box 350, London SE3 OLZ. Telephone: 0181–319–4452. £295.

———. Extract from letter. One page typed, signed letter, May 1948 (day of date obliterated by punch-hole through the original page). The content, in part: "The exploitation of the Pygmalion film is governed by my agreement with GENERAL FILM DISTRIBUTORS LTD. . . . This agreement is a limited license and not an assignment of rights. . . . I remain the sole owner of all rights in the play and the scenario founded on it. . . ." Readable photo included in catalogue. *Remember When Auctions, Inc.* Catalog number 39 (1–2 June 1996), item 480. $750–$1,000.

———. Extract from letter of 6 June 1913 (one page) on 10 Adelphi Terrace letterhead to James B. Pinker, signed "G. Bernard Shaw." About selling printing rights for *Caesar* to an American magazine and an American production of *Androcles*. Readable photo of letter provided. *Remember When Auctions, Inc.* Catalogue number 40, part 3 (30 October 1996), item 3442. $800–$1,200.

———. Extract from postcard of 30 May 1946, signed "GBS" and addressed in Shaw's hand to Symon Gould, Jr., American Library Service. Contains a printed message stating that he cannot write prefaces for unpublished works. *Remember When Auctions, Inc.* Catalogue number 39 (1–2 June 1996), item 481. $200–$300.

———. Extracts from seven letters and cards signed (one a receipt) to theater director B. Iden Payne (one to Mrs. Eve Strindberg). *Sotheby's Catalogue LN6412 "NOAH"* (11 July 1996), p. 163. Shaw comments about British and American productions of his plays, including *Doctor's Dilemma* ("not yet available"), *Philanderer* ("Withheld because of the difficulty of finding a cast"), *Mrs Warren's Profession* ("will only get you into hot water"), *Pygmalion* ("three languages are required"), and others. There are also comments on various actors and producers (Daly, Barker, Mrs. Patrick Campbell, Mona Limerick, and others) and later (1937) on his version of the last act of *Cymbeline* at Stratford: "The horrible dissolution of all the characters into happy-ending sentiment is what makes the act so dull. I have simply kept them alive and kicking vigorously. . . ." Asking price: £800–£1,000.

———. "From Shaw to Us." *New York Times Magazine* (14 April 1996), sec. 6, p. 88, col. 1. Reprinted from *New York Times Magazine* (1 June 1941), p. 15. The original "message from George Bernard Shaw to America, with gestures" (in nine accompanying photographs) begins, "Citizens of the United States of America, the whole 130 millions of you, I am sending you my old plays, just as you are sending us your old destroyers. Our Government has very kindly thrown in a few naval bases as well; it makes the bargain perhaps more welcome to you." Shaw's message counters the statement of "the German humorist" Goebbels "that England has sold her colonies for scrap iron." This had appeared in *PM's Weekly* in January and in *Variety* in May (C3394). It is reprinted as "Spoken preface to the film version of *Major Barbara*, 1941, for American audiences" in *Collected Plays with Their Prefaces* 7:64–65 (A296).

———. "Pygmalion." *Scholastic Scope* 43 (10 February 1995). An adaptation of Shaw's play. Not seen.

———. Quoted in *The Faber Book of Christmas.* London: Faber, 1996. Not seen. The *TLS* review (22 November 1996) presents an excerpt of Shaw on Christmas: "An indecent subject; a cruel gluttonous subject; a drunken, disorderly subject; a wasteful, disastrous subject; a wicked, cadging, lying, filthy, blasphemous, and demoralizing subject. Christmas is forced on a reluctant and disgusted nation by the shopkeepers and the press: on its own merits it would wither and shrivel in the fiery breath of universal hatred; and anyone who looked back to it would be turned into a pillar of greasy sausages" (p. 14).

————. *SHAW: The Annual of Bernard Shaw Studies: Unpublished Shaw.* Volume Sixteen. Edited by Dan H. Laurence and Margot Peters. University Park: Penn State University Press, 1996. Included are a "General Introduction" by Laurence and Peters and a number of unpublished pieces by Shaw introduced by various hands, as follows: "Narrative Verse Fragment" (1877) introduced by Richard Nickson; "Contemporary Art Viewed from behind the Age" (1878), "Oakum Picking" (1878), and "Asides" (1889) introduced by Dan H. Laurence; "Conductors and Organists" (1879) and "Unconscionable Abuses" (1879) introduced by J. L. Wisenthal; "On the True Signification of the Term Gentleman" (1879) introduced by Margot Peters; "A Reminiscence of Hector Berlioz" (1880) introduced by Jacques Barzun; "Exhausted Arts" (1880) introduced by Norma Jenckes; a review of H. B. Pritchard's *George Vanbrugh's Mistake* (1880), "The Future of Marriage" (1885), "A Socialist's Notion of a Novel" (1887), "Found at Last—A New Poet" (1887), and "That Realism is the Goal of Fiction" (1888) introduced by Brian Tyson; "Open Air Meetings" (1885), "Proudhon—CH IV. Propositions I–V pp 126–153" (1886), "Ten Reasons Why Women Should Support the Progressives at the Borough Council Elections" (1903), and "Lady Day Speech" (1929) introduced by Stuart E. Baker; "Socialism and the Family" (1886) introduced by John A. Bertolini; "A Prizefighter on Prizefighting: The Seamy Side of the Ring" (1888) introduced by Sally Peters; "Why Not Abolish the Soldier?" (1899), "Appeal for the Second U. S. Liberty Loan" (1917), "Replies to Questionnaire" (1920), "Message to the World League for Peace" (1928), "Self-Drafted Interview at Durban" (1935), "How to Talk Intelligently about the War" (1940), and "Bernard Shaw on Peace" (1950) introduced by Alfred Turco, Jr.; and "The Superman, or Don Juan's Great Grandson's Grandson" (1901), "The Man Who Stands No Nonsense: A Drama" (1904), and "The Trinity v Jackson" (1912) introduced by Charles A. Berst.

————. "Shaw's *Saint Joan*, Inscribed and Signed First Edition." Sale listing of *Saint Joan: A Chronicle Play in Six Scenes and an Epilogue.* London: Constable and Company, 1924. Small octavo, original light green cloth, original dust jacket, uncut. Signed on half-title: "This is also a first edition. You had better sell it. G. Bernard Shaw. 26th November 1925." *Bauman Rare Books, New Acquisitions and a Summer Selection of Rare Books and Autographs* (1995), p. 72. New York Gallery: The Waldorf-Astoria, Lobby Level, 301 Park Avenue, New York, New York, NY 10022. Telephone: (212) 759–8300.

————. "Wagner as a Dramatic Poet." Reprinted from *World* (17 January 1894). In *The Alternative Listener: Three Centuries of Music Criticism.* Edited by Harry Haskell. Princeton: Princeton University Press, 1996; pp. 195–99. The text is not complete. Shaw's article, representing 19th-century criticism, is one of one hundred selections in this anthology. Haskell writes, "The close of the century was dominated by the great Wagner-Brahms debate, which found lasting expression in Shaw's exuberantly polemical prose and in the erudite writings of his . . . antagonist, Eduard Hanslick."

II. Books and Pamphlets

Abel, Sam. *Opera in the Flesh: Sexuality in Operatic Performance.* Boulder, Colo.: Westview Press, 1996. Enlists Shaw's commentary in support of a prevalence of intense and even perverted representations of sexuality in dramatic productions. "But as . . . Shaw argues in his exploration of the morality of prostitution, *Mrs. Warren's Profession*, all life in modern society demands that we sell ourselves one way or another. And when we are not selling ourselves, we are (if we have the means) buying others. A service- and labor-based economy depends on the sale of human bodies. Sexual desire and money are the two most powerful means of exchange that we have, and opera trades heavily in both." Et cetera.

Allen, Thomas B. See Polmar, Norman, below.

Baker, Stuart E. See *SHAW* in Works by Shaw, above.

Barnouw, Erik. *Media Marathon: A Twentieth-Century Memoir*. Durham: Duke University Press, 1996. In telling of his adaptation of Thornton Wilder's *Our Town* for *Theatre Guild on the Air*, Barnouw remembers Theatre Guild director Homer Fickett's account of Shaw's reluctance to have his scripts altered for radio presentation.

Barzun, Jacques. See *SHAW* in Works by Shaw, above.

Beckson, Karl. *London in the 1890s: A Cultural History*. New York and London: W. W. Norton, 1992. Many pages are devoted to judicious explanation of the work and influence of G.B.S., with references to *Arms, Candida,* "A Degenerate's View of Nordau," "The Difficulties of Anarchism," *Doctor's Dilemma,* "Don Juan in Hell," *Fabian Essays, Fabianism and the Empire,* "Fragments of a Fabian Lecture 1890," *Immaturity, John Bull,* "Literature and Art," *Major Barbara, Superman, Mrs Warren, Our Theatres in the Nineties, Perfect Wagnerite, Philanderer, Plays Pleasant, Press Cuttings, Quintessence, Sanity of Art, Widowers' Houses,* and *You Never Can Tell.*

Belford, Barbara. *Bram Stoker: A Biography of the Author of Dracula*. New York: Alfred A. Knopf, 1996. Presents many references to Shaw, including Chapter 13: "Shaw's Dilemma," which gives an account of the relationship of Stoker, Ellen Terry, and G.B.S. in the context of Stoker's job as theater manager for Henry Irving.

Berst, Charles A. *Pygmalion: Shaw's Spin on Myth and Cinderella*. New York: Twayne, 1995. To be reviewed in *SHAW* 18.

———. See *SHAW* in Works by Shaw, above.

Bertolini, John A. "Guided Tour Through *Heartbreak House*" (review of *Heartbreak House: Preludes of Apocalypse* by A. M. Gibbs). *SHAW: The Annual of Bernard Shaw Studies.* Volume Sixteen. University Park: Penn State University Press, 1996.

———. See *SHAW* in Works by Shaw, above.

Bradbury, Ray. *The R.B., G.K.C. and G.B.S. Forever Orient Express*. Santa Barbara: Joshua Odell Editions [1994]. 180–line dream-vision, mock-epic poem in heroic couplets, published as a pamphlet. Shaw presides as train-conductor/moderator of the fantastic conversation of a gilded-age literary company of passengers that include Poe, Chesterton, Melville, Twain, Wilde, Dickens, and Kipling.

Brian, Denis. *Einstein: A Life*. New York: John Wiley & Sons, 1996. The mutual admiration between Shaw and Einstein was intense. This account presents a substantial sample of the record of the friendship. Shaw on Einstein: "I must, in the name of British culture and science welcome the foremost natural philosopher of the last 300 years." Einstein on Shaw: "You, Mr. Shaw, have succeeded in winning the affection and joyous admiration of the world while pursuing a path which led others to martyrdom. . . . By holding the mirror before us, Mr. Shaw has been able, as no other contemporary, to liberate us and to take from us some of the burdens of life. For this we are devoutly grateful to you."

Britton, Andrew. *Katharine Hepburn: Star as Feminist*. New York: Continuum, 1995. Notes that Hepburn's father, Dr. Thomas Norval Hepburn, became a friend of Shaw after distributing, through the Connecticut Social Hygiene Association, a translation by Charlotte Shaw of a Eugène Brieux play about syphilis. He was, with Hepburn's mother Katharine Houghton, an American Fabian. This biography of Hepburn does not inform readers that Katharine Hepburn read virtually all of Shaw's plays in her early years. She played Epifania in *Millionairess.*

Bryden, Ronald. See *Devil's Disciple*, below.

Burke, Carolyn. *Becoming Modern: The Life of Mina Loy*. New York: Farrar, Straus & Giroux,

1996. A fin-de-siècle English painter, *vers libertine* poet, and visual artist who read and liked G.B.S. He was "against shams."

Butler, Hubert. *In the Land of Nod*. Dublin: Lilliput Press, 1995. Not seen. Quoted on G.B.S. in a *TLS* review (28 June 1996): "Deploring the way that Ireland has 'become immensely unimportant, unimportant even to herself,' he sees, in an unusually penetrating essay, how this explains Shaw's grotesque political conduct: 'His tributes to Hitler, Mussolini, Stalin, his defence of the Italian invasion of Abyssinia, are appalling in their tasteless frivolity, unless one thinks of Shaw as a genius shaped like Joyce by a small community to be its gadfly but pitchforked by fate into being a World-Figure' " (p. 14).

Callow, Simon. *Orson Welles: The Road to Xanadu*. New York: Viking, 1995. Welles was involved with a lot of Shaw early in his career. This account includes many references and mentions *Candida* and *Heartbreak House*.

Carter, Violet Bonham. *Lantern Slides: The Diaries and Letters of Violet Bonham Carter, 1904–1914*. Edited by Mark Bonham Carter and Mark Pottle. London: Weidenfeld & Nicolson, 1996. The review in *TLS* (24 May 1996) notes that Carter, eighteen in 1905, went to a number of plays by Shaw during the years recounted in these diaries (p. 33).

Cheyette, Bryan. *Constructions of "The Jew" in English Literature and Society: Racial Representations, 1875–1945*. Cambridge, England: Cambridge University Press, 1995. Paper reissue of the 1993 hardcover. Includes a chapter, "The 'Socialism of Fools': George Bernard Shaw and H. G. Wells."

Cole, Lloyd. *The Philosophy of George Bernard Shaw*. Concord: Paul & Company Publishers Consortium, 1995. Not seen.

Cowley, Robert, and Geoffrey Parker, eds. *The Reader's Companion to Military History*. Boston: Houghton Mifflin, 1996. The entry on "Representation of War in Drama" includes mention of *Arms*, *Saint Joan*, and *Heartbreak House* "which ends with a Channel bombardment" (actually it ends with a Zeppelin raid).

The Devil's Disciple: Shaw Festival 1996 (Shaw Festival Program, 1996). Includes "Director's Notes" by Glynis Leyshon and "A Republican Hamlet" by Ronald Bryden, which reconstructs Shaw's writing of *Disciple*, remembering that Shaw wrote the play for the actor William Terris as something like Hamlet "on popular lines."

Dietrich, Richard Farr. *Bernard Shaw's Novels: Portraits of the Artist as Man and Superman*. Gainesville: University Press of Florida, 1996. On the dust jacket Dan H. Laurence says, "Imaginatively—sagaciously—conceived, Dietrich's book succeeds where all the Shaw biographies have failed: it offers the first genuine materialization we have ever had of the youthful Dublin emigré yearning for the recognition of his innate genius and unsuspectingly creating in his five early novels a composite portrait of himself as he was and as he wished to be." To be reviewed in *SHAW* 18.

Dukore, Bernard F. See *Bernard Shaw and Gabriel Pascal* in Works by Shaw, above.

Dunaway, Faye, with Betsy Sharkey. *Looking for Gatsby: My Life*. New York: Simon & Schuster, 1995. Dunaway mentions Shaw several times: "I spent the summer in Boston and became one of the Harvard Summer Players, winning the role of Hypatia in George Bernard Shaw's *Misalliance*. . . . Jane Alexander, who now heads the National Endowment for the Arts, was in that play too. She played an aviatrix who was used to standing up and taking a bow with her hand flung upwards in the air. There was a moment in the play where she was dozing off on the sofa and someone said her name, the Great Aviatrix, and she leapt up with her hand in the air as if she were taking a bow—and she was so funny. The audience always loved it." Another example: "Shaw's essays on Duse and Sarah Bernhardt, in which he compared their performances, had such an impact on me. Duse's performances were so alive and so real, very much what we call Method acting. Sarah Bernhardt, considered one of the great stage actresses of that time, was representational; she would pretend to feel. Duse *experienced* the role. It was the kind of performance that drew the audience in. You were caught up in the rapture of watching her go through an experience right there onstage in front of you."

Eisenstein, Sergei. *Beyond the Stars: The Memoirs of Sergei Eisenstein.* Translated by William Powell. Edited by Richard Taylor. London: British Film Institute, 1995. Six references and three notes mention G.B.S. with great respect. Sample: "Let a description of my visit to Bernard Shaw in London, 1929, follow here. This happened after he had sent me a cablegram which overtook me exactly half way across the Atlantic Ocean when I was sailing to America. He proposed that I film *The Chocolate Soldier,* 'on the condition that the entire text be altered not one jot.' Hence, retrospective interpretation of that tireless atmosphere of persuasive charm, which he showed me throughout my stay. The great honour of this proposal, coming as it did pointblank, and from someone who had never, for any sum, sold anyone the right to film one of his works. On a par with Maxim Gorky, another major writer whose proposal to film one of his works I 'turned down.' "

Foot, Michael. *The History of Mr. Wells.* Washington, D. C.: Counterpoint, 1995. Contains a number of references to the Shaw/Wells relationship, concluding, "Wells appreciated better than Shaw had ever done the lasting appeal of Thomas Paine and Thomas Jefferson."

Foster, Janet, and Julia Sheppard. *British Archives: A Guide to Archive Resources in the United Kingdom.* Third edition. London: Macmillan, 1995. Entry "604 London Borough of Camden Local Studies and Archives Centre, Address: 32–38 Theobalds Road, London WC1X 8PA" enumerates holdings for Shaw that include "biographies, his works (many first editions), pamphlets by him and on him, news cuttings, playbills, ephemera, records, photographs, original letters." Entry "670 Royal Academy of Dramatic Art, Address: 62–64 Gower Street, London WC1E 6ED" locates forty albums of press cuttings on Shaw. Shaw was a member of the Council for RADA.

"George Bernard Shaw." *Annual Bibliography of English Language and Literature for 1993.* Volume 68. London: Modern Humanities Research Association, 1995. References about forty books and articles that deal with Shaw, a couple of which have not been mentioned in this Checklist.

Gibbs, A. M. See *Simpleton of the Unexpected Isles,* below.

Grant, Judith Skelton. *Robertson Davies: Man of Myth.* Toronto: Viking, 1994. Includes a number of references to Shaw plus mention of *Arms, Dark Lady, Devil's Disciple, Ellen Terry/Shaw Correspondence, John Bull, London Music in 1888–89, Pygmalion,* and *Joan.*

Griffith, Gareth. *Socialism and Superior Brains: The Political Thought of George Bernard Shaw.* New York: Routledge, 1996. Not seen.

Halperin, John. *Eminent Georgians: The Lives of King George V, Elizabeth Bowen, St. John Philby, & Nancy Astor.* New York: St. Martin's Press, 1995. The section on Astor presents a number of pages on the Astor/ G.B.S. relationship: "It looked like an impossible friendship. . . . She really had no idea what he thought about anything."

Herzog, Chaim. *Living History: A Memoir.* New York: Pantheon, 1996. Herzog notes that he attended Wesley College, an English-style Protestant school once attended by Shaw. Herzog remembers the story that the school on its centenary asked Shaw for a message. After three requests, Shaw replied, "If you don't stop pestering me, I will write what I *really* thought about the place."

Hoare, Philip. *Noël Coward: A Biography.* New York: Simon & Schuster, 1995. Many references to Shaw, including mention of *Androcles, Apple Cart, Pygmalion,* and *You Never Can Tell.*

Horsley, Lee. *Fictions of Power in English Literature: 1900–1950*. London and New York: Longman, 1995. Lots of treatment of Shaw, including a chapter section in "Heroic Action: Narratives of Imperialism" on "Jesters and Heroes: Chesterton, Shaw and Napoleon," and in "Superhuman Arts: Narratives of Nationalistic Faith" on "Martyred Prophets: Buchan's *Prester John* and Shaw's *St. Joan*." Also discusses *Methuselah, Caesar, Everybody's Political What's What?, Fabianism and the Empire, Man of Destiny*, and *Perfect Wagnerite*.

Ingrams, Richard. *Muggeridge: The Biography*. San Francisco: HarperSanFrancisco, 1995. This life of Malcolm Muggeridge mentions bits of Shaw's association with Russia, including that Shaw had been duped by Stalin and citing Gareth Jones, political secretary of Lloyd George, as saying that next to Stalin, the most hated man in Russia was Bernard Shaw. "Malcolm's most enduring memories of the Soviet Union were of prominent visitors like Shaw, taken round by Intourist guides—all blind to the nature of what was going on. These pilgrims, suitably caricatured, were to feature prominently in his novel *Winter in Moscow*."

Jablonski, Edward. *Alan Jay Lerner: A Biography*. New York: Holt, 1996. Not seen. Carol Peace Robins in the *New York Times Book Review* (3 March 1996) says that one of the best parts is the chapter on *My Fair Lady*, but most of this biography is a watering-down rewrite of Lerner's *Memoir* (p. 19).

Jenckes, Norma. See *SHAW* in Works by Shaw, above.

Kahlenberg, Richard D. *The Remedy: Class, Race, and Affirmative Action*. New York: Basic Books, 1996. The single reference to Shaw appears in the first chapter, "The Early Definitions of Affirmative Action," acknowledging his moral authority by quoting from Richard Kluger's *Simple Justice: The History of Brown v. Board of Education* (New York: Knopf, 1975), which had cited him for a similar purpose: "George Bernard Shaw, writing seven years after *Plessy* [which provided the "separate but equal" ruling], exclaimed: 'the haughty American Nation . . . makes the negro clean its boots and then proves the moral and physical inferiority of the negro by the fact that he is a boot black.' "

Kiberd, Declan. *Inventing Ireland*. Cambridge, Mass.: Harvard University Press, 1996. Not seen. The *New York Times Book Review* (17 March 1996) refers to "overly ingenious discussions of Wilde and Shaw" (p. 6).

Kinney, Harrison. *James Thurber: His Life and Times*. New York: Henry Holt and Company, 1995. In June 1956 the Thurbers saw *My Fair Lady*, and Thurber was entranced and moved close to tears. "It was one of the wonderful experiences of our life . . . the finest use to which comedy and music have been put in thirty years. It took a great Irishman [Shaw] and a talented cast of English actors to bring dignity back to the American comedy stage" (p. 989). Thurber's efforts to publicize the musical are also described.

Laurence, Dan H. See *Complete Prefaces*, and *SHAW* in Works by Shaw, above.

Lawrence, T. E. *Lawrence of Arabia, Strange Man of Letters: The Literary Criticism and Correspondence of T. E. Lawrence*. Rutherford: Fairleigh Dickinson University Press, 1993. Not seen. Stephen E. Tabachnick's review in *ELT* 39:1 (1996): 128–30, excerpts Lawrence: G.B.S. "never bothers to go underskin. His characters . . . have only one mind amongst them."

Leary, Daniel J. See *Complete Prefaces* in Works by Shaw, above.

Leavis, F. R. *F. R. Leavis: Essays and Documents*. Edited by Ian MacKillop and Richard Storer. Sheffield, England: Academic Press, 1995. From the undergraduate notes of Charles Winder between 1957 and 1960 on Leavis's seminars at Downing College, Cambridge: "Frank Harris. Why did Shaw and Wells retain a tender feeling for him? It's the period. [¶] Shaw; some distinguished journalistic dramatic criticism.

Arrested development, emotional unrest. Taken to see Shaw's 'Pygmalion' in 1917 when on leave; the indignation, the rage, the disgust at being exposed to this. Insufferable except at the pamphleteering level. In his plays when he tries to be serious you can't stand it. Comedy very amusing. A journalist and a pamphleteer but not a creative artist. A gross flatterer of the lower middle-brow in a very obvious way."

Leyshon, Glynis. See *Devil's Disciple*, above, and *Simpleton of the Unexpected Isles*, below.

McDowell, Frederick P. W. "Bernard Shaw: Socialist and Dramatist" (review of *George Bernard Shaw and the Socialist Theatre* by Tracy C. Davis). *SHAW: The Annual of Bernard Shaw Studies.* Volume Sixteen. University Park: Penn State University Press, 1996.

Milton, Joyce. *Tramp: The Life of Charlie Chaplin.* New York: HarperCollins, 1996. Alleges lots of meetings, with anecdotes, between Shaw and Chaplin, but recounts none here.

Misalliance, A Playgoer's Supplement (The Pearl Theatre, 80 St. Mark's Place, New York, NY 10003, production program, 1996). Includes a caricature of G.B.S. as superman by Lia Nickson, a drawing of the aviators Joey and Lina by Maureen Pitz, "What Makes Shaw 'Shavian?': Nothing but Shaw" by Richard Nickson, "The Themes: Shaw's 'Family Values' in *Misalliance*" by Leah Puelle, "An Actor Prepares . . ." by Mona Koppelman, "Shaw's Alfabet" by Angela Tucker, and "Shaw and His World."

Nickson, Richard. See *Misalliance*, above; and *SHAW* in Works by Shaw, above.

Nilsen, Don L. F. *Humor in Irish Literature: A Reference Guide.* Westport, Conn.: Greenwood Press, 1996. Has a number of references to Shaw, including a twenty-page entry on "George Bernard Shaw" in Chapter 6: "Humor in 20th Century Irish Literature: Early Authors." The 45 entries in the "George Bernard Shaw Bibliography" are current only to 1987 (except for one 1991 item by Nilsen).

Parker, Geoffrey. See Cowley, Robert, above.

Paterson, John. *Edwardians: London Life and Letters, 1901–1914.* Ivan R. Dee, 1996. Not seen.

Peters, Margot. See *SHAW* in Works by Shaw, above.

Peters, Sally. See *SHAW* in Works by Shaw, above.

Pierce, David. *Yeats's Worlds: Ireland, England and the Poetic Imagination.* New Haven and London: Yale University Press, 1995. Many references to G.B.S. Nothing new.

Pine, Richard. *The Thief of Reason: Oscar Wilde and Modern Ireland.* New York: St. Martin's Press, 1995. Numerous references to Shaw, including a consciously formed "Celtic School" by Wilde and Shaw, with mention of *Methuselah, Disciple, Fanny, John Bull, Philanderer, Widowers', Quintessence*, and "Sanity of Art."

Polmar, Norman, and Thomas B. Allen. *Spybook: The Encyclopedia of Espionage.* New York: Random House, 1997. Shaw is mentioned in the entry "Black Book," the name given by the British to *Sonderfahndungsliste G. B.* (Special Search List Great Britain) compiled as part of the German plan to invade Britain. Absent from this list of 2,820 people was Bernard Shaw, "whom the Germans apparently saw as a potential friend because he had written a pro-peace essay a month [*sic*] after the war began."

Puelle, Leah. See *Misalliance*, above.

Rand, Ayn. *The Letters of Ayn Rand.* Edited by Michael S. Berliner. New York: Dutton, 1995. One reference to Shaw in a 13 January 1950 letter to Nathan Blumenthal: "A good dramatist is not necessarily a good thinker. Just take a look at the political ideas of Tolstoy , or Dostoyevsky, or Mark Twain or Bernard Shaw."

Richardson, Elliot. *Reflections of a Radical Moderate.* New York: Pantheon, 1996. Richardson headed four Republican cabinet departments. His single reference to Shaw samples the minds of modern politicians who read Shaw. On the messiness of democracy he writes, "Our disorderliness offends, for example, 'self authoritarians' like Lee Kuan Yew, . . . prime minister of Singapore. In November 1992, Lee . . . gave a speech . . . opining that 'The exuberance of democracy leads to undisciplined and disorderly conditions which are inimical to development.' When I paid a call on him in 1992, he immediately launched into a reprise of this theme. Suppressing the impulse to respond in kind, I asked if he was familiar with the dialogue in hell in Shaw's *Man and Superman.* He was. 'I hope then,' I said, 'that you and I will someday have time for that kind of dialogue.' "

Rockman, David. *Pygmalion: Monarch's Notes on Shaw's Plays.* Indianapolis: Macmillan, [1996]. Not seen.

———. *Saint Joan: Monarch's Notes on Shaw's Plays.* Indianapolis: Macmillan, [1996]. Not seen.

Saunders, Max. *Ford Madox Ford: A Dual Life. Volume I: The World before the War.* Oxford and New York: Oxford University Press, 1996. Several references to Shaw. Ford produced novels that "demonstrate his superiority as an artist to Galsworthy . . . and even to Shaw." Saunders knows the Shaw/Ford connection but adds nothing new to existing accounts.

Sharkey, Betsy. See Dunaway, Faye, above.

"Shaw /'shò/, George Bernard." *Merriam-Webster's Encyclopedia of Literature.* Springfield, Mass.: Merriam-Webster, 1995; pp. 1020–21. Provides an outline of Shaw's life, mentioning nineteen of his works. Separate entries, cross-referenced, are provided for eleven plays: *Mrs Warren, Arms, Candida, Caesar, Superman, Major Barbara, Doctor's Dilemma, Pygmalion, Androcles, Heartbreak,* and *Saint Joan.* There is a separate entry, cross-referenced, for "Higgins, Henry," but not for "Doolittle, Eliza." The entry for Shakespeare has thirty-six cross-referenced works; Ibsen and O'Neill, twelve each; and Molière, seven.

"Shaw, T. E." [T. E. Lawrence]. Letter of 12 October 1932 signed "T. E. Shaw" to Benham, offered for sale for £1,850. In *Occasional List No. 3,* 1996: Michael Silverman, P. O. Box 350, London SE3 OLZ. Telephone: 0181–319–4452. Letter comments on the status of the publication of *Seven Pillars of Wisdom.* A second letter to Benham, dated 15 November 1932 and signed "T. E. Shaw," reads "Keep the book [*Seven Pillars*] as long as you like—the probable owner is in Wales. It takes months to wade through."

Shepherd, Simon, and Peter Womack. *English Drama: A Cultural History.* Oxford: Blackwell, 1996. Among its several comments on G.B.S. the book mentions *Arms, Devil's Disciple, Three Plays for Puritans,* and *Major Barbara,* noting that Shaw virtually "engendered a new golden age in the British Theatre." Another sample of the discussion of Shaw: "The rationale for the title [*Three Plays for Puritans*] is roughly this: being constitutively in earnest, the English bourgeoisie have no idea how to play. Either they are seriously in pursuit of edification, in which case they go to church, or else they are seriously in pursuit of pleasure, in which case they go to the music-hall or worse. English drama is therefore hopelessly compromised; seeking to please everyone and offend no one, it ends up with a mixture of vapid sensuality and sentimental moralism which is both ethically and intellectually corrupting. The only exit Shaw can see from this sink of grim depravity is to bid frankly for the earnest audience—to abandon feeble pleasure-seeking, declare the theatre a place of edification, and confide in the moral seriousness and spiritual energy of the Nonconformist middle class. Hence the need to write plays for Puritans. Shaw's argument, like Wilde's play [*The Importance of Being Earnest*], is a complicated cross-cultural tease, but unlike the play, it sheds most of its ironies by the end: Shaw, as a self-styled 'dramatic realist,' really is proposing the birth of serious English drama from the union of theatre and the Puritan tradition."

Sheppard, Julia. See Foster, Janet, above.

Simon, Neil. *Rewrites: A Memoir*. New York: Simon & Schuster, 1996. One mention of Shaw: In *The Star Spangled Girl* "she and the student were no longer equals, even though I had learned from G. B. Shaw always to make your protagonist and antagonist equal adversaries, so that the audience was always in doubt as to who was right and who was wrong."

The Simpleton of the Unexpected Isles: Shaw Festival 1996 (Shaw Festival production program, 1996). Includes "Director's Notes" by Glynis Leyshon and "Theatre of Surprise: *The Simpleton of the Unexpected Isles*" by A. M. Gibbs, in which the play's character Prola is seen as the chief torch-bearer of the Life Force, devoted to the "surprise and wonder" of the future. Moreover, *Simpleton* is a play about "Empire, colonialism, and the uses of religion as a front for imperialist exploitative activities." There is also a one-page excerpt from Shaw's *Adventures of the Black Girl in Her Search for God*.

Sloan, John. *John Davidson, First of the Moderns: A Literary Biography*. Oxford: Clarendon Press, 1996. Not seen. *TLS* review "Farewell Despair" by Patrick Crotty (2 February 1996) recounts a Shaw/Davidson connection, instancing Shaw's gift to Davidson of £250 to enable him to write a play, *The Game of Life*. Davidson was not, at last, grateful: "You could cut six Shaws out of me and there would still be a splendid Davidson left" (pp. 3–4).

Smith, Adrian. *The New Statesman: Portrait of a Political Weekly, 1913–1931*. London: Cass, 1996. Not seen. John Turner, "When Sharp Was the Word," *TLS* (15 March 1996) notes that Shaw was a shareholder and contributor to the magazine—mitigating somewhat the dullness of the numbers of its earlier years (p. 13).

Smith, Bruce R. *Roasting the Swan of Avon: Shakespeare's Redoubtable Enemies & Dubious Friends*. Washington, D. C.: Folger Shakespeare Library, 1994. Represents Shaw's "antipathy to the Bard" from a number of sources, including G.B.S.'s "Afterword" to Tolstoy's book on Shakespeare, essentially a reprint of a review of *Cymbeline*.

Spoto, Donald. *Rebel: The Life and Legend of James Dean*. New York: HarperCollins, 1996. One reference states that Dean "tried to pattern his career on that of Brando, whose Broadway credits had included a 1946 production of Shaw's *Candida*. . . ." Mildred Dunnock was planning yet another revival and was working with playwright Eric Bentley. Longing to play Brando's role of the sensitive but fierce poet Marchbanks, Dean met with them, "but Bentley and Dunnock agreed he was inappropriate for the role. 'He arrived wearing the sort of ill-fitting, secondhand clothes one could buy from a sidewalk salesman,' according to Bentley. 'He was earnest, but this role was, we thought, beyond him.' Said Dunnock, after Dean had departed, 'He looks more the part of a gas station attendant than an English poet.' "

Steiner, George. *No Passion Spent: Essays 1978–1995*. New Haven and London: Yale University Press, 1996. Among wide-ranging comments on literary tradition, addresses the serious Edwardian concern that "Shakespeare's sheer weight and precedent was crushing the life out of English verse and out of any attempts to renew serious drama in the English language. . . ." Shaw's "niggling attacks on Shakespeare's amateurish dramaturgy, Shaw's peremptory rewriting of *Cymbeline* to demonstrate how the thing 'ought to have been done,' are giggly in tone and leave all parties mildly embarrassed. Far more searching, but masked and feline in its cautionary tactics, is T. S. Eliot's dissent. . . ."

Turco, Alfred, Jr. See *SHAW* in Works by Shaw, above.

Tyson, Brian. *The Story of Shaw's Saint Joan*. Ann Arbor: Books on Demand, [1996]. Not seen.

———. See *SHAW* in Works by Shaw, above.

Vendova, Tomas. *Alecksander Wat: Life and Art of an Iconoclast*. New Haven and London:

Yale University Press, 1996. A poet and political pundit, Wat's influence helped the rejuvenation of Polish and East European letters after the Stalinist era. A curiosity of the history of the Sovietization of Poland in World War II is produced in the description of a Polish newspaper *Czerwony Sztandar* (The Red Banner) with which Wat was briefly associated. The newspaper practiced a Stalinist newspeak, and so the names of Goethe and Dickens were given in Latin letters but according to Russian (Soviet) transcription as "Gate and Dikens." Also, "A prominent place was assigned to Hitler's speeches and to the pacifist musings of an English writer introduced as 'Bernard Szou.' "

Warren, Donald. *Radio Priest: Charles Coughlin, the Father of Hate Radio.* New York: Free Press, 1996. One reference, globalizing the perceived influence of Shaw and Wells: Coughlin became a defender of the Catholic Faith against the attacks of such major literary personalities.

Weintraub, Stanley. "Benn Levy and Shaw" (review of *The Plays of Benn Levy: Between Shaw and Coward* by Susan Rusinko). *SHAW: The Annual of Bernard Shaw Studies.* Volume Sixteen. University Park: Penn State University Press, 1996.

———. "Shaw and the American Theatre." In *Cambridge Guide to American Theatre.* Edited by Don B. Wilmeth and Tice L. Miller. New York: Cambridge University Press, 1993; pp. 426–28. Presents information about the production of Shaw's plays in America and the influence of Shaw's works on American playwrights.

Wisenthal, J. L. See *SHAW* in Works by Shaw, above.

Womack, Peter. See Shepherd, Simon, above.

III. Periodicals

Ackroyd, Peter. "Superman in a Jaeger Suit" (review of *Bernard Shaw: The Ascent of the Superman* by Sally Peters). *The Times* (25 April 1996), p. 36.

Adams, Elsie B. "Shaw Correspondence" (review of *Bernard Shaw: Theatrics*, edited by Dan H. Laurence). *ELT* 39:4 (1996): 501–4.

"Additions to Archives." *Theatre Notebook* 50:1 (1996): 53. Includes item: "*British Library, Department of Manuscripts*: William Hudd, actor: letters from G. B. Shaw and T. E. Lawrence: his visitors' book (Deposit 9308)."

Allen, Brooke. "Misalliance." *New Criterion* (December 1995): 64–69. In part a review of *Bernard Shaw and H. G. Wells*, edited by J. Percy Smith.

Allet, John. "Bernard Shaw and Dirty Hands Politics: A Comparison of *Mrs. Warren's Profession* and *Major Barbara*." *Journal of Social Philosophy* 26 (Fall 1995). Not seen.

Auer, James. "Chamber Theatre Puts on Smooth-as-Silk Staging of *Arms and the Man*: Vintage Shavian Farce Is Attacked with Undisguised Gusto" (review of Milwaukee Chamber Theatre production). *Milwaukee Journal Sentinel* (19 February 1996), p. 5B.

Bartlett, Sally A. See "George Bernard Shaw," below.

Bemrose, John. "Theatre: Diabolically Good Diversions" (includes review of the 1996 Shaw Festival production of *Devil's Disciple*). *Maclean's* (10 June 1996), pp. 62–63.

Berson, Misha. "Shaw Thing" (review of the Intiman Theatre [Seattle] production of Jeffrey Hatcher's *Smash!*, an adaptation of *Unsocial Socialist*). *American Theatre* 13:7 (September 1966): 9–10.

Bevir, Mark. "Fabianism, Permeation and Independent Labour." *Historical Journal* 39 (March 1996): 179–96. Not seen.

Blum, David. "As Sure as Shaw." *BBC Music Magazine* (August 1966), pp. 37–39. Shaw's writings on music amounted to more than 1,750 pages and are "a stellar benchmark in the field." They "remain as fresh today as they were a hundred years ago. His satire and drollery—balanced by integrity and wisdom—served as an antidote to the music criticism of the time, which was often, as he put it, 'refined and academic to the point of being unreadable and often nonsensical.' . . . For readers who are tired of today's 'new musicology' with its trend toward psychosexual 'analysis,' Shaw's writings offer relevant, enlightened sanity."

Bryden, Ronald. "Dragging Shaw out of the Closet" (review of *Bernard Shaw: The Ascent of the Superman* by Sally Peters). *Globe and Mail* (15 June 1996).

Cardus, Neville. See Sherbo, Arthur, below.

Carpenter, Charles A. "A 'Dramatic Extravaganza' of the Projected Atomic Age: *Wings Over Europe* (1928)." *Modern Drama* 35 (1992): 552–61. The play, by Robert Nichols and Maurice Browne, appears to have borrowed prominent elements of Marchbanks in *Candida* for its character Francis Lightfoot. Nichols and Browne as Cambridge graduates would surely have read *Back to Methuselah*, which would account for certain elements present in *Wings*. The genre of "extravaganza" can as well handle serious ends, as evidenced by "Bernard Shaw's late-period plays, several of which he called Extravaganzas." "As a dramatized hypothesis (however extravagant) of political and ethical problems that might arise at the onset of a nuclear age, the play [*Wings*] not only adopts Shaw's use of drama as 'a means of foreseeing and being prepared for realities as yet unexperienced'; it also incorporates a notable degree of his thoughtfulness and earnest concern."

Carroll, Mary. Review of *Bernard Shaw: The Ascent of the Superman* by Sally Peters. *Booklist* (15 March 1996).

Crawford, Fred D. "Lowell Thomas on Bernard Shaw." *Independent Shavian* 33:2–3 (1995): 35–36. A summary of accounts of Shaw by Thomas, which provide no evidence the two ever met or corresponded. Included is "Bernard Shaw," the two-minute script of Thomas's sixty-first *Best Years* radio spot.

———. "Shaw on Proverbs" (review of *The Proverbial Bernard Shaw: An Index to Proverbs in the Works of George Bernard Shaw* by George B. Bryan and Wolfgang Meider). *ELT* 38:2 (1995): 243–48.

Cunningham, Valentine. "Don Juan in Hell" (review of *Bernard Shaw: The Ascent of the Superman* by Sally Peters). *New York Times Book Review* (2 June 1996), p. 7.

Dekkers, Odin. "Robertson and Shaw: An 'Unreasonable Friendship.' " *ELT* 39:4 (1996): 431–49. "Shaw had the measure of Robertson. He respected his friend and adversary for his scrupulous honesty, but he also saw clearly that Robertson was no match for him when he tried to impinge on his own special style of rhetoric, his blend of Rationalism and whimsy. It is perhaps here, even more than in all kinds of ideological divergences that the true cause for the widening gap between the two men lies. Their approaches could not be more different. Robertson was always the hard-headed rationalist, . . ." to the extent that he described his relationship with Shaw "unreasonable." "Shaw found in Robertson one of the few critics who could outdo him in erudition and reasoning power, while Robertson may have been stimulated more by Shaw's rhetorical brilliance than he was willing to admit. Their personalities may often have clashed resoundingly, but from the point of view of intellectual stimulus there was finally nothing 'unreasonable' about this friendship."

Delacorte, Valerie Pascal. "How Shaw Gave 'Pygmalion' to Broke Director" (response to 3 November 1995 letter about Shaw's granting of film rights to Gabriel Pascal). *New York Times* (18 November 1995), p. 16 (N); 20 (L); col 5. Not seen.

Drabelle, Dennis. Review of *Bernard Shaw: The Ascent of the Superman* by Sally Peters. *Washington Post* (7 July 1996), p. 8.

Dukore, Bernard F. " 'Responsibility to Another'? Graham Greene's Screen Version of Bernard Shaw's *Saint Joan*." *Theatre History Studies* 16 (June 1996): 3–13. "Despite

Graham Greene's having taken offense at the charge that director Otto Preminger employed him to deProtestantize the film version of Bernard Shaw's *Saint Joan*, despite his denial that he altered any line by Shaw to water down Shaw's Protestantism or to insert a Catholic view, and despite his insistence that he made none of Shaw's miracles look more authentic than Shaw made them look, the evidence of the 1957 movie version of Shaw's play, for which he composed the screenplay, indicates that consciously or not, he did all of these. He did not retain what he claimed he kept: 'a sense of responsibility' to the play he adapted."

Einsohn, H. I. Review of *Bernard Shaw: The Ascent of the Superman* by Sally Peters. *Choice* 34 (September 1996): 129.

———. Review of *Shaw's People: Victoria to Churchill* by Stanley Weintraub. *Choice* 34 (September 1996): 131.

Elley, Derek. "*England My England* (British)." *Variety* (20 November 1995), p. 44. Elley's review of this mammoth "biopic" (*Variety*'s term for a biographical film) about Henry Purcell notes that it includes reference to actor Simon Callow "in hammiest mode" when Callow was "first seen treading the boards [as Charles II] in G. B. Shaw's *In Good King Charles' Golden Days* [*sic*], directed by one Tony Palmer at the Royal Court."

Elliott, Donald A. "Shaw Dramas Presented at Arena Stage." *Independent Shavian* 33:2–3 (1995): 29–33. Reading the Washington, D. C., Arena Stage records, Elliott finds that eleven Shaw plays have been presented there between 1950 and 1995, during eighteen seasons. He sees a loose correspondence between the political message of various plays and the party of the president in office, with no Shaw play during Nixon's administrations.

Emeljanow, Victor. "Chapter VIII: Nineteenth Century, Section V: Victorian Drama and Theatre." *The Year's Work in English Studies*. Volume 74 (1993). Oxford: Blackwell, 1996. Discusses W. D. King's *Henry Irving's Waterloo* and Jill Davis's "The New Woman and the New Life," in Vivian Gardner and Susan Rutherford, eds. *The New Woman and Her Sisters: Feminism and Theatre 1850–1914*; and Fredric Berg's "Simpleton: A New Approach," *Modern Drama* 36 (1993): 538–46.

Evans, T. F. Review of *George Bernard Shaw and the Socialist Theatre* by Tracy C. Davis. *Theatre History Studies* 15 (1995): 230–33.

Fryer, Jonathan. "Was He, Wasn't He?" (review of *Bernard Shaw: The Ascent of the Superman* by Sally Peters). *Tablet* (4 May 1996), pp. 585–86.

Garebian, Keith. "Revisionism: The 1995 Shaw Festival." *Journal of Canadian Studies/ Revue d'études canadiennes* 30:4 (Winter 1995–96): 162–71. Includes reviews of the productions of *Six of Calais*, *Philanderer*, and *You Never Can Tell*.

"George Bernard Shaw." *Journal of Modern Literature* 19:3–4 (Spring 1996): 526. This entry in "Individual Authors" section of the *JML* annual bibliography offers two items, one of which has not been listed in this Checklist: Sally A. Bartlett, "Fantasy as Internal Mimesis in Bernard Shaw's *Saint Joan*," *Notes on Modern Irish Literature* 3 (1991): 5–12.

Gibbs, A. M. " 'Giant Brain . . . No Heart': Bernard Shaw's Reception in Criticism and Biography." *Irish University Review* 26:1 (Spring/Summer 1996): 15–36. "The history of Shaw's reception has followed divergent paths in different arenas of cultural discourse and activity. In the theatrical world, Shaw is normally regarded without question as belonging to the company of such dramatists as Ibsen, Strindberg, Chekhov and Pirandello as a creator of some of the classics of the early modern dramatic repertory. His plays have proved to be solidly durable and fresh in the theatre. . . . The Shaw Festival at Niagara-on-the-Lake in Canada is the second largest theatre repertory company in North America. The theatre and the general public have clearly acknowledged him as a major figure. In the academic sphere, however, his position has been much less secure. In what follows I do not attempt to deal with the extensive body of specialist critical study of Shaw. This essay is concerned rather with the subject of his image and reception in broader literary-critical domains, and with the ways in which Shavian biography relates to those subjects."

Griffiths, Trevor. "Chapter XIV: Twentieth Century, Section III: Drama." *The Year's Work in English Studies*. Volume 74 (1993). Oxford: Blackwell, 1996. Remarks on a few Shaw references. No mention of *SHAW*, unlike many earlier volumes of *YWES*.

Gross, John. "The Body of the Text: John Gross on the Puzzling Sex Life of George Bernard Shaw" (review of *Bernard Shaw: The Ascent of the Superman* by Sally Peters). *Sunday Telegraph* (21 April 1996).

Hampton, Wilborn. "Ibsen and Shaw Have Their Say on Women's Rights" (review of Ibsen's *Lady From the Sea* and Shaw's *Major Barbara*). *New York Times* (19 February 1996), p. C16.

Hughes, Alan. Review of *Henry Irving's Waterloo* by W. D. King). *Theatre Survey* 36:2 (November 1995): 98–100.

"Irish Dramatists: Heroes and Humans." *Economist Review* (18 May 1996), pp. 15–16. Includes a review of *Bernard Shaw: The Ascent of the Superman* by Sally Peters.

Isele, Elizabeth. "Peters' Biography of Shaw: 'A Work of Art' " (review of *Bernard Shaw: The Ascent of the Superman* by Sally Peters). *Middletown Press* (5 April 1996), p. B5.

Jaques, Damien. "Chamber Theatre's Double Bill Is Light but Lively Entertainment" (review of productions of *Six of Calais* and *Androcles* by the Milwaukee Chamber Theatre). *Milwaukee Journal Sentinel* (26 February 1996).

Jenner, Brian. Review of *John Bull's Other Island* as an Audio Book. *Guardian* (19 April 1996), sec 2. p. 7, col. 4.

Johnson, Malcolm L. "The Hidden Life of Bernard Shaw in the Circumstantial 'Ascent' " (review of *Bernard Shaw: The Ascent of the Superman* by Sally Peters). *Hartford Courant* (18 August 1996), p. G3.

Leary, Daniel. "Budgetary Crisis in Elizabethan England and Nearer Home." *Independent Shavian* 34:1–2 (1996): 6–7. Shaw wrote in the preface for a book on William Morris in 1936, "Queen Elizabeth [told] her council that if they turned her out in her petticoat she could make her living with the best of them." Leary writes that she defied not her Privy Council, but her Parliament, and that Elizabeth's moment of confrontation, in Shaw's account, can be seen as a striking parallel to President Clinton's on-going show-down with Congress.

Lewan, Kristin. "Ontario on Stage: Stratford, Shaw Festivals Headline Exciting Theater Options." *Michigan Living* (May 1996), p. 41. A one-page tourist information article.

Lofland, Norman L. Review of *Shaw and Joyce: "The Last Word in Stolentelling"* by Martha Fodaski Black. *English Language Notes* 34:1 (September 1996): 90–91.

MacCaughren, Samantha. "Fair Lady Rescues Shaw's Home." *Evening Herald* [Dublin] (3 May 1996), p. 14. Short news report of Frances McCarthy, who founded the Shaw Birth Place Advisory Council, which bought Shaw's former home (next door to McCarthy's) in 1990. Dublin Tourism took over the project in 1992, and the house is now restored with "painstaking" accuracy. Photo of McCarthy accompanies.

MacFarquhar, Neil. "Baghdad Journal: Iraq at Play: Eliza Doolittle Is Now a Belly Dancer." *New York Times International* (11 October 1996), p. A4. This review of an Arabic production of *My Fair Lady* ("Sayadati al Jamila)" that may run for eighteen months includes the following: "Postwar sentiments also prompted the writers to throw out the happily-ever-after ending. The now lovely pupil, swathed in a pink pantsuit and straw chapeau instead of her belly dance spangles, feels so unloved by her soulless professor that she spurns him and swears to return to her village." See Willment, A. C., below.

Magidson, Svetlana. "Bernard Shaw and His *Pygmalion* Today" (review of production directed by Valentin Goft, starring Galina Volchek). *Moscow News* (15 September 1995), p. 18.

Martin, J. H. "GBS and Women." *TLS* (24 May 1996), p. 19. Response to John Sutherland's 3 May 1996 review of Sally Peters's *Bernard Shaw: The Ascent of the Superman*, correcting Sutherland's misattribution to Ellen Terry of Mrs. Patrick Campbell's comment about the effect that eating meat might have on Shaw's sex drive.

Marx, Bill. "George Bernard Shaw's Suffering Superman" (review of *Bernard Shaw: The Ascent of the Superman* by Sally Peters). *Boston Globe* (2 May 1996), p. 78.

McDonnell, Mary. "Reader Notes on *The Best of Friends* by Hugh Whitemore" (review of PBS Masterpiece Theatre production). *T. E. Notes: A T. E. Lawrence Newsletter* 7 (September 1995): 10–11.

McDowell, Frederick P. W. "Comprehensive Reading of *Pygmalion*" (review of *"Pygmalion": Shaw's Spin on Myth and Cinderella* by Charles A. Berst). *ELT* 39:3 (1996): 379–80.

Mimken, Judy. Review of *Shaw's People: Victoria to Churchill* by Stanley Weintraub. *Library Journal* (15 May 1996), p. 63.

Molenaar, Jacob. "Reikhalzend uitzien naar *Superman*" (review of *Bernard Shaw: The Ascent of the Superman* by Sally Peters). *Homologie* (June 1996): 43–44.

Morley, Sheridan. "Come to the Cabaret . . ." *Spectator* (2 November 1996), pp. 63–64. Includes a review of the Lyric Hammersmith production of *Mrs Warren*.

Murphy, Donn B. "The Opening of Shaw's Closet Door" (review of *Bernard Shaw: The Ascent of the Superman* by Sally Peters). *Washington Times* (26 May 1996), Special section: University Presses.

Nadler, Paul. "Pastoral Elements in *John Bull's Other Island*." *Modern Drama* 38 (Winter 1995): 520–24. "Shaw achieves *John Bull's* unique tone in part by a brilliant combination of genres, specifically of his trademark 'Ibsenist' well-made play structure with the traditional English pastoral." Nadler bases his analysis on explanations of pastoral provided by Edwin Greenlaw and Northrop Frye.

Pearce, Sandra Magoogian. " 'On the Nature of Evidence': Miami Joyce Conference: 2–4 February 1995." *James Joyce Quarterly* 33 (Fall 1995): 17–21. The Ninth Annual Miami James Joyce Conference included a talk noting the G.B.S. references in *Finnegans Wake*.

Peters, Sally. "Ingrid Bergman, *Saint Joan*, and G.B.S." *Independent Shavian* 1–2 (1996): 9–12. Describes with accompanying details the meeting of Shaw and Bergman and G.B.S.'s unsuccessful invitation to Bergman to play Joan in Shaw's version.

Poole, Steven. "They Had No Minds" (review of the Orange Tree Theatre production of *Simpleton*). *TLS* (15 December 1995), p. 18.

Puelle, Leah. "A Begrudged Debt." *Pearl* (September 1995–May 1996), p. 2. Shaw derided the French playwright Scribe but owed an enormous debt to him. *Widowers' Houses*, *Candida*, *Disciple*, and *Arms* bear remarkable resemblances to the work of Scribe. The influence, however, was limited to structure because Scribe was a champion of conservative, bourgeois values and the status quo.

Rae, Lisbie. Review of *SHAW* 14. *Essays in Theatre/Études théatrales* 14 (May 1996): 195–96.

"Ray Bradbury: Views of a Grand Master." *Locus* 37:2 (August 1996): 6, 73–74. Includes the following comment on Shaw: "I go back to George Bernard Shaw. He wrote some great science fiction, and he believed in the future. He believed in optimal behavior. He believed in our destiny, moving out through the universe. He believed that women were the center of everything—which they are. He wrote about all these things, 80 or 90 years ago. Fabulous writer."

Review of *Bernard Shaw: The Ascent of the Superman* by Sally Peters. *Publishers Weekly* (24 January 1996), p. 92.

286   JOHN R. PFEIFFER

Robb, George. "The Way of All Flesh: Degeneration, Eugenics, and the Gospel of Free Love." *Journal of the History of Sexuality* 6:4 (April 1996): 589–604. Prominent thinkers such as Wells, G.B.S., and Havelock Ellis blamed Victorian sexual roles for a decline in the British race and posited a theory of eugenics to replace it. For some the problem was marriage. Some feminists and suffragists were opposed to free love because they were concerned with the burden that childbearing presents to women. Not seen.

S., J. "Biography" (review of *Shaw's People: Victoria to Churchill*). *TLS* (12 July 1996), p. 32.

Scheck, Frank. "Wit, Comedy Sparkle at Canada's 35th Shaw Festival." *Christian Science Monitor* (1 August 1996), p. 10. Includes review of the *Devil's Disciple* production.

Seaton, R. M. "Shaw Biography Artful, Insightful" (review of *Bernard Shaw: The Ascent of the Superman* by Sally Peters). *Sheridan Wyoming Press, Options* (26 April 1996), p. 7.

"Shaw." In "Victorian Bibliography for 1994," edited by Edward H. Cohen. *Victorian Studies* 38:4 (Summer 1995): 770–71. Twenty-six listings retrospective to 1992, a few of which have not appeared in this Checklist.

The Shaw Festival Online. CyberPlex Interactive Media (22 October 1996). Describes Shaw Festival.

"Shaw, George Bernard (1856–1950)." *1993 MLA International Bibliography of Books and Articles on the Modern Languages and Literatures*. New York: Modern Language Association of America, 1994. Lists about twenty items, including those from the subject list. Several have not appeared in this Checklist.

"Shaw, George Bernard (1856–1950)." *1994 MLA International Bibliography of Books and Articles on the Modern Languages and Literatures*. New York: Modern Language Association of America, 1995. Lists ten items, plus five more in the subject list, four of which have not appeared in this Checklist.

Sherbo, Arthur. "Two Overlooked Reviews of Shaw." *Notes and Queries* 241:1 (March 1996): 55–56. One by Henry Somerville is quite negative toward Shaw's *Intelligent Woman's Guide* in *Studies: An Irish Quarterly of Letters, Philosophy, and Science* 17 (September 1928): 455–65. The other, by Neville Cardus, praises the Shaw he finds in Dan H. Laurence's edition of Shaw's *How to Become a Musical Critic* in *Encounter* 16 (April 1961): 82–84.

Siegel, Ed. "Berkshire Valleys and Peaks: Un-Shavian Shaw, Molière with Sparkle." *Boston Globe* (7 August 1996), p. D4. Includes a review of the Stockbridge Berkshire Theatre Festival production of *Jitta's Atonement*.

Siskel, Gene. " 'Lady' Proves Rex is No Ordinary Man." *TV Guide* (23–29 November 1996), p. 18. Special applause for Rex Harrison's obnoxious Professor Higgins, "one of the great performances in musical *and* film history," on the occasion of the film's Thanksgiving 1996 airing on CBS.

Somerville, Henry. See Sherbo, Arthur, above.

Sutherland, John. "The Wilder Loves of Shaw" (review of *Bernard Shaw: The Ascent of the Superman* by Sally Peters). *TLS* (3 May 1996), p. 26. See Martin, J. H., above; Weintraub, Stanley, below.

Sydenstricker, Glória. "The Shaw/Maeterlinck Touch in Granville-Barker's Drama." *Independent Shavian* 34:1–2 (1996): 13–16. In Granville-Barker's drama there are certain identifications with Shaw's social-political concerns and with Maeterlinck's mystical overtones.

Watson, George. "Never Blame the Left: The Left Is Perceived as Kind and Caring, Despite Its Extensive History of Promoting Genocide." *National Review* (31 December 1995), pp. 35–37. Claims that G.B.S., Marx, and Wells are among the socialists who supported genocide. Not seen.

Weales, Gerald. "Shaw's American Inheritors." *Journal of American Drama and Theatre* 6

(Spring/Fall 1994): 1–11. "For American playwrights Shaw is not a direct influence. He is simply a presence—even now, after all these years." Weales reaches this conclusion by surveying the variously tenuous connections of Shaw to American playwrights such as Edward Sheldon, Rachel Crothers, Eugene O'Neill, Robert Sherwood, S. N. Behrman, Clifford Odets, Maxwell Anderson, T. S. Eliot, Tennessee Williams, Edward Albee, and Richard Nelson. This graceful essay is a model of the clear distinction between knowledge of and influence by the works of one writer upon other writers.

Weintraub, Stanley. "GBS and Women." *TLS* (31 May 1996), p. 17. Response to John Sutherland's review of *Bernard Shaw: The Ascent of the Superman* by Sally Peters: Shaw's definitive word on the subject was not to Frank Harris but to sculptress Kathleen Scott (later Lady Kennet): "No woman born ever had a narrower escape from being a man. My affection for you is the nearest I ever came to homosexuality."

Willment, A. C. "Iraqis Make Shaw, but Not 'Iggins, 'Appy." *New York Times* (16 October 1996), p. A16. Letter to the editor pointing out that the *Pygmalion* ending in which Eliza walks out on Higgins actually anticipates the Iraqi production of *My Fair Lady* that ends the same way, noting as well that it is "Odd that an anti-feminist, 'backward' society" would bring the play closer to Shaw's original intent. The letter responds to the review by MacFarquhar, Neil, above.

Wilson, A. N. "Well, Was He?" (review of *Bernard Shaw: The Ascent of the Superman* by Sally Peters). *London Review of Books* (20 June 1996), p. 11.

The Independent Shavian 33:2–3 (1995). Journal of the Bernard Shaw Society. Includes "International Arbitration for Peace: A Speech by Shaw," "Shaw Dramas Presented at Arena Stage" by Donald A. Elliot, " 'Leonine Courage': Vincent Sheen on Shaw," "Shaw by a Sonneteer," "*The New York Times* Snuffs GBS," "Lowell Thomas on Bernard Shaw" by Fred D. Crawford, "Shaw Initiated aux Subtilités du Tango," "Shostakovich Decries Famous Humanists," "Dawn Powell on Shaw: For a Genius to Be a Genius," "Bernard Shaw Describes His New Works: 'The Great Actresses Are All on My Side,' " "Brigid Brophy (1929–1995): Eminent Independent Shavian," "Shaw: Socialist and Imperialist?" "Shaw and Maurice Chevalier: Even Steven," "GBS and His Critics: A Laughing Interview," "Raquel and Shaw's Epifania," "Stalls Must Go," "Seeking Shavian Levity," "An Evening with Shaw and Wells" by William Gerhardi, "Shaw at Kingsway Hall," "Shaw on the Post of Poet Laureate," "The Shaw Manuscripts: An Appreciation" by Herbert Frew, "Not Pygmalion Likely!" "Book Review" by Richard Nickson (review of *The Complete Prefaces, Vol. 1: 1889–1913*, edited by Dan H. Laurence and Daniel J. Leary; *Bernard Shaw and H. G. Wells*, edited by J. Percy Smith; and *George Bernard Shaw and the Socialist Theatre* by Tracy C. Davis), "Book Review" by John Koontz (review of *Shaw and Joyce: "The Last Word in Stolentelling"* by Martha Fodaski Black), "The 1995 Shaw Festival," "Shaw Smells Drama," "A Protest from Authors: A Distinctly Shavian Protest," "GBS and Tasmania," "Shaw Having His Final Say about Christmas," "Letter from England" by T. F. Evans, "Notice," "Shaw as Viewed by His American Publisher," "A Great Number of Bernard Shaws According to James Stephens," "Shavian Shavings from Bits of Benchley," "While the Supply Lasts," "News About Our Members," "Jeremy Brett," "John W. Marvell," "Society Activities," and "Our Cover." See also, Crawford, Fred D.; and Elliott, Donald A., above.

The Independent Shavian 34:1–2 (1996). Journal of the Bernard Shaw Society. An Index to Volume 33 (1995) is supplied as an insert. Includes "Shaw on Royalty," "Budgetary Crisis in Elizabethan England and Nearer Home" by Daniel Leary, "A Shavian Postage Stamp?" "Shaw and Busoni," "Ingrid Bergman, *Saint Joan*, and G.B.S." by Sally Peters, "Joyce Grenfell and G.B.S." by Douglas Laurie, "A Palm to Screenwriter

Shaw," "The Shaw/Maeterlinck Touch in Granville-Barker's Drama" by Glória
Sydenstricker, "Rebecca West and Uncle Shaw," "Notice," "English Socialist Socie-
ties" by Bernard Shaw, "Letter from England" by T. F. Evans, "G.K.C. on G.B.S.,"
"Shaw in Bronze," "Shaw on the Air" by Stuart Hibberd, "The Changing Face of
Village Life According to Villager Shaw," "Shaw in Israel," "Shaw as Cape Town
Music Critic," "Some Reminiscences of Shaw" [1959] by Maurice Evans, "Shaw
Playlets Handsomely Performed," "An Interview with Mr. Shaw" [1948] by Jean
Dalrymple, *Wilde About Wilde*: An Anniversary," "Shavian Theatre: A Factory of
Thought?" "Book Review" by Daniel Leary (review of *Bernard Shaw: The Ascent of
the Superman* by Sally Peters), "Book Review" by Richard Nickson (review of *Bernard
Shaw: Theatrics*, edited by Dan H. Laurence), "Book Review" by Rhoda Nathan
(review of *The Complete Prefaces, Vol. 2: 1914–1929*, edited by Dan H. Laurence and
Daniel J. Leary), "Greer Garson," "Sophia Delza Glassgold," "News About Our
Members," "Society Activities," and "Our Cover." See also, Leary, Daniel; Peters,
Sally; and Sydenstricker, Glória, above.

Shavian 7:7 (Winter 1995–96). The Journal of the Shaw Society. Mailed with a January
1996 *Newsletter*. Includes "Editorial," "Obituary," "Letter to the Editor," "First
Impressions," "Shaw and the Wildes" by Joy Melville, "Our Theatres in the Nineteen-Nineties," "A Japanese View: Impressions of Shaw in Britain and Ireland,
1994–95" by Yoshikazu Shimizu, "Shaw in His Letters" by John Levitt (review of
Bernard Shaw and H. G. Wells, edited by J. Percy Smith and *Bernard Shaw: Theatrics*,
edited by Dan H. Laurence), "Theory and Passion" by John Stokes (review of *SHAW*
15), "Theatre and Fashion" by Frances Glendenning (review of *Theatre and Fashion:
Oscar Wilde to the Suffragettes* by Joel H. Kaplan), "Literary Survey," "Scraps and
Shavings," and "Notes of Meetings."

Shavian 8:1 (Autumn 1996). The Journal of the Shaw Society. Mailed with an Autumn
1996 *Newsletter*. Includes "Editorial," "Obituary," "Only One Deadly Disease" by
Bernard Shaw, "A Debate Recreated," "The Dublin Summer School," "Our The-
atres in the Nineteen-Nineties," "What Price Fame?" by Betty Hugo (review of
Bernard Shaw: The Ascent of the Superman by Sally Peters), "A Note on Reviews,"
"Mount Weintraub" by T. F. Evans (review of *Shaw's People: Victoria to Churchill* by
Stanley Weintraub), "Literary Survey," "Scraps and Shavings," and "Notes of
Meetings."

IV. Dissertations

Dolgin, Ellen Ecker. "So Well Suited: The Evolution of Joan of Arc as a Dramatic Image
(George Bernard Shaw, Bertolt Brecht, Germany, Maxwell Anderson, Jean Anouilh,
France, Lillian Hellman)." New York University, 1995. *DAI* 56 (October 1995):
3951A. "For them, Joan was not solely an historical character, but a forerunner of
the modern woman, working to enlarge her sphere and participate in important
work. . . . Each . . . contributed to twentieth-century visions of Joan as literary icon,
and secular symbol of steadfastness, commitment and heroism. . . . Shaw's *Saint
Joan* (1923) presents a charismatic, spunky girl who is a born leader. Brecht adds
vulnerability of such people to a corrupt society. Anderson balances character as
part saint and part helpless young girl. Anouilh and Hellman show the power of
corruption like Brecht, but also celebrate the rarity of people like Joan. All these
pieces came in the time between two world wars, the rise of the 'new woman,' the
struggle for suffrage, and distrust of institutions that condemned Joan."

Lisker, Donna Eileen. "Realist Feminism, Feminist Realism: Six Twentieth-Century American Playwrights." University of Wisconsin, Madison, 1996. *DAI* 57 (January 1996): 34A. "In my first chapter I return to the origins of modern realism in Henrik Ibsen and Bernard Shaw, recognizing the radical potential they found in the form and questioning whether that potential still exists in contemporary realist drama."

V. Recordings*

Androcles and the Lion (1952 film starring Alan Young, Jean Simmons, and Victor Mature, 100 minutes, remastered), #22–5805, $29.99. Movies Unlimited, 3015 Darnell Road, Philadelphia, PA 19154. Telephone: 1–800–466–8437. Lists also *Caesar and Cleopatra* (1945 film starring Claude Rains and Vivien Leigh, 129 minutes), #47–1301, $14.99; *Major Barbara* (1941 film starring Rex Harrison and Wendy Hiller, 131 minutes), #22–5438, $39.99; *Pygmalion* (1938 film starring Leslie Howard and Wendy Hiller, 90 minutes, remastered), #22–5806, $24.99; *The Millionairess* (1960 film starring Peter Sellers and Sophia Loren, 90 minutes), #53–8529, $19.99; *My Fair Lady* (1964 film starring Harrison and Hepburn, 170 minutes), #04–1682, $19.99, (letterbox version), #04–2875, $19.99; *My Fair Lady Gift Set*, restored letterbox format (adds a separate documentary on making of the film, a portfolio of Cecil Beaton's costume designs, a book, "Cecil Beaton's Fair Lady," and a set of 70 mm. film frames taken from the original negative), #04–2875, $79.99; and *George Bernard Shaw Gift Set* (includes *Androcles*, *Major Barbara*, and *Pygmalion*, as immediately preceding), #22–5808, $79.99.

Brooks, Harold F. Presents Shaw in a series of audiotapes intended to "relate writers to drama tradition and their society." Sussex Publications, Freepost, London W9 2BR. £11.00. Not seen or heard. Noted in the Shaw Society (London) *Newsletter* (April 1996).

Caesar and Cleopatra (1945 film starring Claude Rains, Vivien Leigh, 123 minutes), #SKHMK020053, $14.95. Critics' Choice Video, P.O. Box 749, Itasca, IL 60143–0749. Telephone: 1–800–367–7765. Lists also *The Millionairess* (1960 film starring Sophia Loren and Peter Sellers, 90 minutes), #SKFLA001230, $14.77; *My Fair Lady: 30th Anniversary Edition* (1964 film starring Harrison and Hepburn, 190 minutes), #DKFOX000974, $19.95; *My Fair Lady* (same as immediately preceding, but in letterbox format), #SKFOX000975, $19.95; and *My Fair Lady: Gift Set* (same as letterbox, but includes 60–minute documentary with out-takes from the original film and a portfolio of costume designs by Cecil Beaton), #SDFOX008167, $59.77.

———. See *Androcles*, above.

George Bernard Shaw Gift Set. See *Androcles*, above.

*Professor Bernard F. Dukore offers the following comments that may be applied to the many Shaw pieces being offered for sale in videotape formats: "The 123–minute video of *Caesar & Cleo* you cite [in the *SHAW* 16 Checklist] is one of the American prints. At their premières, the U. K. print supposedly ran 134 minutes, the U. S. print 127 minutes. . . . The publicists or whoever write running times are notoriously unreliable. For instance, the label of my videotape says 129 minutes, but I clocked it at 128. *Bernard Shaw and Gabriel Pascal* [pp. 188–89] indicates one cut made for the U. S. print (a line some idiotic American distributor thought might be construed as anti-Semitic), but Lord knows what others were made or how long the U. K. sequence was that contained the line. Another example: on the relatively recent video of *Major Barbara*, which runs 137 minutes, the box says 145 minutes (this tape is no longer for sale: the one for sale now is 131 minutes)."

Home Improvement. Dir. Andy Cadiff. Fox, 23 September 1996 [original network is ABC]. Rerun of Tim Allen sitcom episode. Script excerpt from non-network videotape:

> JILL [*Tim's wife, referring to a conversation she had with her father in which she told him she did not like the book he has written*]: Look what happened when I told him the truth. Maybe I should have just kept my mouth shut.
>
> WILSON [*the gnomic next-door neighbor to the Allen family, visited in each episode, whose face is never seen*]: Well, George Bernard Shaw wouldn't have thought so. He said, "We must not stay as we are, doing always what was done last time, or we shall stick in the mud."
>
> JILL: Well, I'm stuck in something deep here, Wilson, but it ain't mud.

John Bull's Other Island (with Christopher Benjamin and Patrick Duggan). HarperCollins Audio Books. £7.99. *Pygmalion* (with Michael Redgrave, Michael Hordern, and Lynn Redgrave) is also offered by HarperCollins at £7.99. Not seen or heard. Noticed in the Shaw Society (London) *Newsletter* (April 1996).

"The Kelloggs: Corn Flakes Kings." *A & E Biography* (21 January 1997). This documentary of the lives of Dr. John H. and W. K. Kellogg lists G.B.S. among "frequent visitors" to John Kellogg's Sanatorium in Battle Creek, Michigan. Shaw never visited Battle Creek, but in February 1936, during a two-day layover in Florida, he did dine with John Kellogg, who had relocated his sanatorium in Miami Springs. See *Collected Letters 1926–1950*, ed. Dan H. Laurence (New York: Viking, 1988), p. 425.

Major Barbara. See *Androcles*, above.

The Millionairess (1960 film starring Sophia Loren and Peter Sellers, 90 minutes), #51271, $19.99. The Video Catalogue, P.O. Box 64267, St. Paul, MN 55164–0267. Telephone: 1–800–733–2232. Fall 1996 Catalogue.

———. See *Androcles*; and *Caesar and Cleopatra* (Critics' Choice Video), above.

My Fair Lady. See *Androcles*; and *Millionairess* (Critic's Choice Video), above.

Photograph portrait of Shaw, 9″ × 11″ black and white, inscribed by him "G. Bernard Shaw, 9/11/29, to Messrs Targ and Sordick." Caption says that the photographer pencil-signed the photo (indecipherable in picture reproduced in catalogue). *Remember When Auctions, Inc.* Catalog number 39 (1–2 June 1996), item 479. $1,250–$1,750.

Pygmalion. See *Androcles* (Movies Unlimited); and *John Bull's Other Island*, above.

VI. Other Media

Dyson, Will (1880–1938). Exhibit of caricatures, cartoons, drawings, and satirical prints at Australia House until 4 October 1996. Not seen. Review in *TLS* (20 September 1996) by Suzanne Wu: "Organized chronologically, the exhibition gives a clear overview of Dyson's career and of his struggle to maintain a moral focus in his work at the same time as it was making him a rich man. The most affecting image is an aquatint of George Bernard Shaw dressed as a clown and gazing sadly into a mirror. Dyson once wrote that Shaw was 'an honorable man but his value has been inhibited by his unending pursuit of the laugh.' This picture, and the exhibition as a whole, is haunted by the ghost of melancholy. The invisible face seen in the mirror could be Dyson's as much as Shaw's, full of the sadness, not of failure, but of the not-quite-good-enough" (p. 19).

Epstein, Jacob (Sir). "Shaw (George Bernard) Portrait in Bronze." *Sotheby's Catalogue LN6412 "NOAH"* (11 July 1996), p. 163. A bust of Shaw with a green patina on a composition base, 420 mm. high, excluding base, 1934. Other known casts are in

Canada's National Gallery, London's National Gallery, and New York's Metropolitan Museum. Shaw's reaction (positive) and Charlotte's reaction (negative) to the cast are represented in Holroyd's *Bernard Shaw*. Epstein wrote that "throughout my life in England, Shaw was an outspoken champion of my work. . . . I will not say that he understood what I have made. He seemed deficient in all sense of the plastic, but had a lively notion of how stupid the newspapers can be over new works. . . . He was generous to young talent." Asking price: £6,000–£8,000.

"Make a Date with George Bernard Shaw in 1997 with the *TLS*." *TLS* (27 December 1996), p. 7. Example of advertisement run for *TLS* over several weeks in December 1996 for the *TLS Calendar*, featuring cartoons by Peter Brookes of the "famous and infamous." These ads feature a caricature of a nude G.B.S. lying next to an opened copy of *You Never Can Tell*.

Patterson, Stuart. "G. B. Shaw," a line drawing, bust caricature of Shaw. *ELT* 39:4 (1996): front cover.

CONTRIBUTORS

John Barnes is Assistant Professor of Communication and Theatre at Western State College in Gunnison, Colorado, where he currently is serving as technical director for a production of *Angels in America*. He has been a finalist for the Nebula Award for best science fiction novel three times. His collaborative novel with astronaut Buzz Aldrin appeared in 1996.

Ray Bradbury has published more than 500 stories during the past fifty years. He is the author of *The Martian Chronicles, Dandelion Wine,* and *Fahrenheit 451*, the latter of which will have a new film version in 1997, directed by and starring Mel Gibson. He has written twelve books of poetry as well as thirty plays for the stage, including the musical *The Wonderful Ice Cream Suit* (filmed in 1996 by the Disney studio). In 1953 he wrote the screenplay of *Moby Dick* for the director John Huston. He has recently published a new book of stories, *Quicker Than the Eye.*

Fred D. Crawford, general editor of *SHAW*, has written several books and articles on modern British literature, most recently *Richard Aldington and Lawrence of Arabia: A Cautionary Tale*. He is completing a biography of the American news broadcaster Lowell Thomas and editing a volume of Thomas's letters.

R. F. Dietrich, Professor of English at the University of South Florida and member of the University Press of Florida Editorial Board, is a member of the *SHAW* editorial board and the author of *Portrait of the Artist as a Young Superman* (extensively revised as *Bernard Shaw's Novels: Portraits of the Artist as Man and Superman*), *British Drama 1890 to 1950,* and *The Art of Fiction*, as well as many articles on Shaw, Ibsen, and other modern writers.

Peter Gahan, a philosophy graduate of Trinity College, Dublin, is a filmmaker, broadcaster, and writer. His short film *Da Capo* (1990) was shown at the Edinburgh and Cairo film festivals. He has directed *Fanny's First Play* (1992) and *Candida* (1994) in Dublin. He also lectures on psychoanalysis and cinema.

Elwira M. Grossman is Stepek Lecturer in Polish Language and Literature, with a continuing interest in comparative drama, at the Department of Slavonic Languages and Literatures at the University of Glasgow, U. K.

Leon H. Hugo is Professor Emeritus of English at the University of South Africa and a member of the *SHAW* editorial board. He has contributed several articles and reviews to the *SHAW*, is the author of *Bernard Shaw: Playwright and Preacher*, and has recently completed a study of Shaw's Edwardian years.

Elizabeth Anne Hull is Professor of English at William Rainey Harper College in Palatine, Illinois, where she teaches literature and coordinates the Honors Program. Her doctoral dissertation (Loyola of Chicago, 1975) was titled "A Transactional Analysis of the Plays of Edward Albee." Among her publications are articles on Asimov, Biggle, Clarke, Harrison, Heinlein, and Merril, as well as on drama in science fiction, and she occasionally writes science fiction herself. She was also the 1996 Democratic nominee for the U. S. House of Representatives in Illinois's Eighth Congressional District.

Ben P. Indick has written two books of commentary on science fiction writers (Ray Bradbury and George Alec Effinger) as well as essays, fiction, and plays. He is a member of Dramatists Guild and Horror Writers Association.

Frederick P. W. McDowell is Professor Emeritus of English at the University of Iowa and a member of the *SHAW* editorial board. He has written many articles, essay-reviews, and reviews on Shaw and his works. He has also written two books on E. M. Forster.

Margot Peters, a member of the *SHAW* editorial board, is the author of *Bernard Shaw and the Actresses* and *Mrs. Pat: The Life of Mrs. Patrick Campbell*. She edited the facsimile edition of *Mrs Warren's Profession* and has written numerous articles on Shaw and Shavian theater. She co-edited, with Dan H. Laurence, *SHAW 16: Unpublished Shaw*.

Sally Peters, vice president of the Bernard Shaw Society and a member of the *SHAW* editorial board, teaches literature at Wesleyan University. She has published extensively on Shaw, modern drama, and dance and is the author of *Bernard Shaw: The Ascent of the Superman*.

John R. Pfeiffer, Professor of English at Central Michigan University, is the bibliographer of *SHAW*. His most recent articles are on Richard Francis Burton, Octavia Butler, John Christopher, and nineteenth-century science fiction.

Tom Shippey is Walter J. Ong Chair of Humanities at Saint Louis University and has recently edited both the *Oxford Book of Science Fiction Stories* and the *Oxford Book of Fantasy Stories*.

George Slusser is Professor of Comparative Literature at the University of California, Riverside and Curator of the Eaton Collection. His most recent books are *Immortal Engines* and *Science Fictions and Market Realities*, both from University of Georgia Press.

Julie A. Sparks is a doctoral student at the Pennsylvania State University specializing in Shaw and utopian studies.

Susan Stone-Blackburn is Professor of English and Associate Dean of Graduate Studies at the University of Calgary. She is the author of articles on science fiction, Shaw, and Canadian drama, and of *Robertson Davies: Playwright*.

Jeffrey M. Wallmann is an instructor in the English Department at the University of Nevada, Reno. He has more than 200 novels to his 22 pseudonyms in several genres—mystery, science fiction, western, and historical romance. He also has sales of more than 100 short stories, novelettes, and articles, with his work appearing in numerous anthologies in six languages, as well as television adaptations, movies, and television scripts.

Rodelle Weintraub includes among her books on Shaw *Fabian Feminist*, *Shaw Abroad*, and the Garland *Captain Brassbound's Conversion*. She has also co-edited, with Stanley Weintraub, two Bantam volumes of Shaw's plays: *Arms and the Man & John Bull's Other Island* and *Heartbreak House & Misalliance*.

J. L. Wisenthal, a member of the *SHAW* editorial board, teaches English literature at the University of British Columbia. His work on Shaw includes *The Marriage of Contraries: Bernard Shaw's Middle Plays*; *Shaw and Ibsen*; and *Shaw's Sense of History*.

Milton T. Wolf is a professor at the University of Nevada, Reno, where he is the Director of Library Collection Development and science fiction teacher/scholar with more than 70 publications. He was founding editor of *Technicalities*, co-editor of *Thinking Robots, an Aware Internet, and Cyberpunk Librarians*, co-editor of a special issue on "The Information Future" for *Information Technology and Libraries*, co-editor of the 1996 TOR science fiction anthology *Visions of Wonder*, and the author of "Cyberpunk: Information as God" in *Cybrarian's Manual* (ALA, 1997).